D1388139

Waiting for Sunshine

www.penguin.co.uk

Waiting for Sunshine

Jane Sanderson

BANTAM PRESS

TRANSWORLD PUBLISHERS
Penguin Random House, One Embassy Gardens,
8 Viaduct Gardens, London SW11 7BW
www.penguin.co.uk

Transworld is part of the Penguin Random House group of companies
whose addresses can be found at global.penguinrandomhouse.com

Penguin
Random House
UK

First published in Great Britain in 2022 by Bantam Press
an imprint of Transworld Publishers

A CIP catalogue record for this book
is available from the British Library.

ISBNs 9781787631946 (hb)
9781787631953 (tpb)

Typeset in 11.25/15.25pt Sabon MT Std by Jouve (UK), Milton Keynes.
Printed and bound in Great Britain by Clays Ltd, Elcograf S.p.A.

The authorized representative in the EEA is Penguin Random House Ireland,
Morrison Chambers, 32 Nassau Street, Dublin D02 YH68.

Penguin Random House is committed to a sustainable
future for our business, our readers and our planet. This book
is made from Forest Stewardship Council® certified paper.

MIX
Paper from
responsible sources
FSC
www.fsc.org   FSC® C018179

For Pip Rau

I

MARCH 1997

When the call came, they were at the cinema, watching a Week-end Classics screening of *Rear Window*, which they'd both seen before, but so had everyone else, that was the whole point. Not that Chrissie and Stuart were Hitchcock scholars; they were only there because it was something to do while they waited for the call, but everyone else in the audience looked studiously reverential, as if there'd be a test afterwards, or a Q&A with Hitch himself. Then Stuart's phone began to buzz and bounce in his jacket pocket, and the silent, unanimous censure spread like a cloud of dry ice through the auditorium, especially when not only did he fail to switch it off, but also took it from his pocket and lifted it higher so that Chrissie could see too. *Angela Holt*. They looked at each other across the phantom glow, and the name on the screen seemed to pulse like an artery. Their immediate neighbours tutted now, and darted pointed looks, but Stuart answered the call, right there in the middle of row G; he answered the call, stood up, and started making a path none too gently down through the legs to the central aisle, saying, 'Angela, hi, hang on, I'm just . . . sorry? No, it's fine, one moment, just bear with me . . .' while Chrissie followed, apologising in frantic whispers to their fellow cinemagoers, who stared at her, and refused to forgive. It was, after all, unforgivable.

Out in the foyer, Chrissie hung back while Stuart did that thing he always did on the phone, stalking about like a caged tiger, the handset pressed hard to his right ear. He always looked cross when he took a call; he always looked as though he was locked in verbal combat. She leaned against a wall and stared at the film posters without seeing them, hugging herself, wondering what news Angela had, bracing herself against over-optimism, and then he was in front of her, his face bright and alive with news.

'A girl,' he said. 'She's three. A very good match, Angela says.'

'A girl,' Chrissie said, on an outward breath. A girl, aged three. Older than they'd originally wanted, but they'd let go of all their own criteria months ago. So, a girl of three. A very good match. Such a strange term. Like an arranged marriage. She felt light-headed and let herself slide down the wall and sit cross-legged on the floor.

'She's in foster care, been there best part of a year,' Stuart said.

'A year? Wow.'

'Yeah.' He paused, considered the twelve months they hadn't known about her, then carried on. He was aware of an usher and a girl at the pick 'n' mix staring at them, doubtful looks on their faces.

'Angela says she could be ideal, although it'll have to go to panel obviously, but she says we could meet her soon, just a brief visit. She's in Whitstable of all places.'

'Nancy hasn't mentioned her. Does she know her?'

'I expect so. We didn't talk about that.'

'What's her name?'

Stuart halted. 'Ah, I didn't ask.'

Chrissie laughed. 'Stu! Here, let me call her back,' she said, and reached up for his phone. 'Remember what Nancy said?'

'I know!'

'If you can't live with the name . . .'

'You can't live with the kid, I know.'

She looked up at him while the phone rang out, said, 'God, what if she's called Angela?' then swiftly adjusted her tone when the other woman picked up.

'Oh, hi – hi, Angela! Hi, hello, yeah, it's Chrissie . . .' she said, and then tailed off when Angela immediately interrupted and began to speak. Stu couldn't tell what she was saying, but he heard the familiar cadence of her voice and pattern of her speech, her pedantic, circuitous way of communicating the simplest of messages. Of the two adoption officers currently invested in their future, this one – Angela – was senior to the other one – Nancy – yet her relationship skills were, by comparison, completely unevolved. Arm's-length and no closer, was Angela's philosophy, so that, eighteen months after they first met, they still felt they barely knew her. And yet they did know this: she always had something to say, and she liked to take her time saying it. Now Chrissie, who hadn't even managed to ask her question yet, suddenly saw and seized an opportunity.

'No, yes, I see, no, it wasn't that, it's just, we wondered what her name is?'

Pause. Stuart heard Angela's pedantic drone, circumnavigating the answer. What the fuck? he thought. Just say the name, lady. Then Chrissie's face seemed to soften and her eyes met his, shining.

'Oh, really?' she said. 'Ah, wow. No, no, sure. Thanks so much, yes, aha, yes, thanks again, bye.'

She hung up.

'Well?' Stuart asked.

'Sunshine,' Chrissie said. 'She's called Sunshine.'

Outside, they walked in the rain without noticing it, and told each other the things they knew they should remember; how far there was still to go, how they should pace themselves, hold this new breakthrough close, not tell a soul until there was something more certain to say. Then Chrissie caved in and rang Nina, and Stuart rang Carly in New Jersey. They stood facing each other in the street, a few feet apart so their conversations didn't collide, but looking directly at each other as they talked, then, afterwards, he opened his arms wide, and she stepped into them.

'Sunshine,' Chrissie said, into the warmth of his neck. 'Can you believe that? Wouldn't we have chosen it, for a daughter? She's Sunny for short.'

'Beautiful,' Stuart said, and pressed his lips on her hair. He held them there for a moment, then said, 'What did Nina say? Bet she was happy?'

Chrissie nodded. 'Cautiously happy. I ought to tell Mum, now Nina knows.'

'She's right to be cautious,' Stuart said. 'We mustn't run away with this.'

'How to help it, though? I have this strange feeling.'

'What, that she's ours?'

'No, no, yeah, sort of, yeah – a feeling that she's who we've been waiting for, which is crazy. I want her, I just really want her.'

'Nancy's Law,' Stu said, smiling. 'Maybe she makes a good point, after all.'

Nancy Maitland; loopy, lovely, with a kind of robust zest for the task of finding Chrissie and Stuart's child. Early on she'd told them – confidingly, as if sharing a secret – that she believed adoption placements were driven by fate, and when Chrissie and Stu had swapped sceptical glances, Nancy had only nodded and said, 'I know you think that's claptrap, but there's a child out there who already belongs to you. You just don't know each other yet.'

Chrissie hadn't bought the theory at the time, not at all; but now she wondered if she'd absorbed by osmosis some of Nancy's blind faith, because suddenly the world contained a little girl called Sunshine, and Chrissie had a sensation quite new to her, and very powerful, that this child's path and her own were about to converge. It wasn't merely a tug on the heart. She knew what that felt like; she'd had that before: Billy, a four-month-old baby boy, offered as a possibility by Angela, then placed elsewhere by Nancy; Rosie, the two-year-old girl they'd never met in the end; Celeste, another name, another baby, who had drifted into the frame, then out again, and now Chrissie couldn't even remember why. But Sunshine. Sunshine. Something did feel different. Something did feel right. Something connected to instinct; those feelings that reside in the gut and require neither thought nor learning, but that you somehow know should be trusted.

She said, 'So, what did Carly say?'

'She knew I was about to call,' Stu said. 'She sensed I had news about a child.'

They both laughed. You could never really tell Stu's mother anything she hadn't already gleaned through her famous sixth sense, but she wore her white witchery well. It manifested in a kind of bottomless positivity.

'Ah, but she was sweet,' Stuart went on. 'Six in the morning at Cape May, and I'd clearly woken her, but she was like, "Darling boy, a child named Sunshine has infinite potential for joy."'

A child named Sunshine. Chrissie let the words drift in her

mind for a few moments. There had been no one, and now there was Sunshine. A small girl, untethered in the world, whose destiny was now tilting towards Chrissie and Stuart. Extraordinary, she thought. Extraordinary.

Later, she did her duty and rang Diana, her mother, in Barnsley, and they talked about the weather and her dad's new car – a Bentley, of all things – and the new colourist at her hair salon in Sheffield who'd trained in London with Trevor Sorbie, before Chrissie at last broached the subject of Sunshine and caused a heavy silence to descend, a hundred and eighty miles away in South Yorkshire.

'I see,' Diana said, at last. 'Well, you've come this far before, Christine, and still been thwarted.'

'I know, Mum, but the system owes us, and Stu and I both have a good feeling about this one.'

'That's all very well, but it's not about a feeling, is it? It's about whether it goes your way.'

Chrissie rested her forehead against the kitchen wall and listened to her mother warning against false hope. She spoke from experience, because they'd been extremely unlucky so far, they'd been disappointed and demoralised, and had discovered that, in the parallel world of adoption, a child could be offered with one hand, then taken away with the other; available, then unavailable, as if, like a covetable couture handbag, they came in and out of stock, and bad luck, you'd missed out again. So yes, her mother knew well enough how Chrissie had suffered, because so had they all; but Diana's concern, as ever, came out as a kind of thistly impatience, as if all the brutal iniquities of the system they'd experienced were only to be expected, so why the fuss? Sadness was weakness, in Diana's opinion; she could barely tolerate it, and she possessed only this brand of mothering; steely, unbending, a cold, fierce love.

They'd got off on the wrong foot from the start, of course, when the day before their first adoption workshop, Diana had phoned to say it was all a waste of time, since they weren't husband and wife, and Chrissie had said, 'Ah, well, about that . . .' and then had had to confess the thing she'd been putting off, and putting off – that she and Stuart had got married three weeks ago, very quickly and quietly, at the Old Marylebone Town Hall; just Sol, Julia, Rocco and Kim in attendance, and coffee and cake afterwards at a cafe in York Street.

'We'll have a big wedding celebration when the time's right,' Chrissie had said, into the arctic silence. 'And that day, the day of the party, will be our real wedding, because the other was just for the paperwork, right? A formality. We didn't dress up, even.'

And this, finally, had forced Diana into a response. 'Please tell me you didn't wear jeans, Christine,' she'd said.

That was a year and a half ago, and now here they were still, wearily engaged in the attack and parry of a telephone chat about whether or not they should allow themselves to hope.

'Well, look,' Chrissie said, doodling on a notepad by the telephone and listening with only half her mind on Diana's doomy pragmatism, 'we've been given every reason to feel encouraged this time.' She'd written *Sunshine Stevenson* and *Sunshine Woodall*, and now she stared at the names, and adorned them with tiny flowers on snaking stems that twisted and curled through the letters.

'Your dad'll be worried sick when I tell him.'

'About what?'

'About another one not working out, obviously.'

'Well,' Chrissie said in a measured tone, 'I suppose that's understandable.'

'Anyway, who'll look after the child when you're playing concerts till all hours?'

'Well, that's a hypothetical problem if we don't get her, right?'

'I didn't say you wouldn't get her; I said it was a worry that you might not.'

'Agreed, it's a worry, but Stu and I are trying to stay positive.'

'So, tell me again then, how you'll manage this small child, with your lifestyle.'

'Mum! My lifestyle? I'm home more than most working mothers! And we've both given up cocaine until the adoption papers are signed.'

'Christine!'

'Joke. Obviously. Come on, Mum, please, we've been through this so many times.'

'Yes, we have, but I still don't know how you'll cope, or why you want to complicate an already very complicated life. It's not unmarried girls giving away their perfect babies these days, it's children from drug addicts, children who've been neglected.'

'Mmm,' Chrissie said, absently, 'you've mentioned that before, once or twice.' On the page of the notepad she'd written, *A child named Sunshine has infinite potential for joy*, and now she thought, thank you, Carly.

'Now you're being facetious.'

'Mum, I know you're anxious about this, but I'm sure you'll feel better when there's a living, breathing child instead of all this constant speculation.'

Diana snorted. 'Don't psychoanalyse me, Christine.'

Psychoanalyse Diana, thought Chrissie; where would she possibly begin? She sighed into the phone. Her mother was exhausting. How much of her adult life had she spent talking Diana down from the ledge of her furious indignation?

'I just want you to be happy for me, Mum,' she said.

'If it all works out, I'll be very happy for you, Christine,' Diana said. She sounded hurt now, and Chrissie took her cue and softened her tone.

'It'll work out, Mum. We'll make it work out.'

'A little girl, you said?'

'Sunshine, three and a bit.'

'Sunshine? As in, sunshine?'

'Yeah, Sunny for short.'

There was a protracted sigh. 'Well,' Diana said, 'there'll only be one of those on the school register,' and this was her, giving a little ground, and on these terms they were both content to say goodbye. Chrissie put the phone down, and, with the notepad in hand, she went to find Stuart.

'Sunny Stevenson,' she said, showing him her artwork. 'Or Sunny Woodall?'

'Sunny Stevenson-Woodall?'

'If it worked double-barrelled, we'd both be using it. I think it's one or the other.'

'Sunny Stevenson, then,' Stuart said. 'Alliterative and lyrical.' It was Chrissie's surname, and she smiled, and kissed him.

'I knew I liked you, for some reason,' she said.

'We're totally doing what we're not supposed to do,' Stuart said, suddenly serious.

'Yeah. But this is happening,' Chrissie said. 'Your mother's seen it in the tea leaves.'

There was going to be a child of their own; two of them, maybe three – vocals, drums, guitar – and everyone who knew them knew they'd make beautiful babies. They'd met in 1982 on a music course in Liverpool, first year, first week, first day. Chrissie had opened the door into her boxy room in the hall of residence and almost immediately tried to shoo away her parents, desperate that her glamorous mother didn't speak to anyone in the embarrassing Queen's English she tended to use on strangers, or that Doug didn't start mending a dripping kitchen tap or bleeding the radiators. He was proud as punch of Christine, he kept saying, while Diana wondered things out loud; which shelf of this horrible fridge might be Christine's? Who would put brown carpet and curtains in a girl's room? She maintained her usual elegant hauteur until the time came to say goodbye, when she surprised herself and her daughter by finding it hard to let go. Her hug was too tight, too lengthy, as if she was trying to communicate something very important, for which she didn't have the words.

'Right,' Doug had said, when the embrace lengthened into awkwardness. 'Let's be off, let's leave the lass to it,' and Diana had released Chrissie all in a rush and stepped away, a look of confusion on her face, like a sleepwalker who'd woken up in a strange place. Other students and their parents had stared covertly, in the way people always did at Diana. She was dauntingly lovely, possessed of a level of beauty that was almost inappropriate, and certainly disapproved of in everyday life. She looked a lot like Anne Bancroft – perfectly coiffed dark hair, smoky, smouldering eyes, the same exquisite symmetry to the face – and sometimes she got stopped in the street for an autograph, but only when she went beyond Barnsley, because there, everyone knew she was just Diana Stevenson, Doug Stevenson's stuck-up wife, Christine Stevenson's mother. Oh, how Chrissie had wished she had a plain, plump mum, in her growing-up years. How she'd longed for a homely storybook mother, with flour on her hands and flowers on her pinny. Diana had worn tailored tweed suits and silk blouses for her job as PA to the local head of the National Coal Board. She wore a single strand of pearls, and a sable collar on her winter coat. She wore red lipstick, and darkened her Anne Bancroft eyebrows with a special pencil, and nobody else quite like her existed in Barnsley. Doug had his own extremely profitable chain of plumbers' merchants, and was a tall, good-looking fellow who knew how to dress, but Diana was a knock-out, and she knew it.

'Yes,' she'd said, to Doug, outside the hall of residence. 'Let's leave her to it.' She'd pulled a powder compact from her handbag, opened it and assessed her immaculate face in the tiny mirror, dabbed at her small, straight nose with the sponge, then replaced it and snapped the compact shut. Then she'd drawn a long, controlled breath and said, 'There's a payphone in the foyer, Christine, so I'd like to hear from you once a week, beginning tonight.' She'd turned away, and sashayed over to Doug's silver Ford Granada, while Doug had given Chrissie a squeeze and said, 'I love you, cherub,' then hurried off to open the passenger door for his wife and settle her in the seat. He'd tooted the horn as they'd swept away, and Chrissie had known what her mother would be saying. *For God's sake, Doug, show some decorum.*

And when they'd gone, and Chrissie had turned to go back into the hall, there was Stuart, walking in too, and smiling at her.

Now, the two of them sat in their living room with glasses of wine, trying to talk and think of other things, but really only wanting to speak again to Angela Holt. They knew there was no good reason to bother her, other than to be sure they hadn't only imagined a girl named Sunshine, but eventually Stuart said, what the hell, he'd call her, and think of something relevant to say when she answered. But her phone rang out without being picked up, so they sat for a short while feeling thwarted and obscurely anxious, and then were disproportionately delighted when his phone rang and it was Angela. Stuart answered with an over-ecstatic 'Hi!', which made Chrissie start to laugh, and clearly gave Angela pause, because she said, 'Stuart? Is that you?'

'Yes,' he said, moderating his tone. 'Hello, Angela. Sorry, I was just—'

'I seem to have a missed call from you.'

'Yes, I'm sorry.'

'It is Sunday.'

'I know, sorry.' He mimed the slitting of his throat with one finger: death by Angela. Chrissie smiled encouragement.

'What is it, Stuart?' Angela asked, all snip and snap.

'We wondered how soon we could meet Sunshine,' he said, and Chrissie gave him a thumbs-up for his creative thinking, but from Angela there was a short silence followed by a deep professional sigh.

'Look,' she said, 'I fully appreciate your feelings of urgency, but while I do think you could be perfect for Sunshine, it still needs to be green-lighted by the panel, as you know. We can't simply rush forwards; the protocol is in place for good reason, tried and tested checks and balances we're all obliged to abide by.'

Stuart crossed his eyes at Chrissie and she grinned.

'Oh, sure, we know the ropes. But when do you think we *might* meet her?' he asked. 'Just, y'know, an estimate?'

'A couple of weeks' time,' Angela said. 'Maybe three. I'll need to speak again to Sunshine's caseworker about timings. You haven't met him, he's fairly new to the team, he's called Brendan Cassidy, and he's met Sunshine and the foster family, he can tell you much more about the child. He'll call you tomorrow to arrange to see you, so if you can make yourselves available at a time to suit him, that would expedite the process.'

'Sure,' Stuart said. *Expedite the process.* She talked like the logistics manager of a haulage company. 'Has Nancy met Sunshine?' he asked, and Angela might or might not have tutted, it wasn't quite clear. She said, 'I don't see what bearing that has on anything, but no, she hasn't.'

'But she knows about her, right?'

'Of course she does, Stuart, and, while you're on, I might as well tell you we'll need a recent photograph of the two of you. The foster parents and Brendan will introduce the idea of you to Sunshine before she meets you, and a visual image is the start of that process.'

'Yes, sure, we'll dig one out and get it to you pronto.'

'Good,' Angela said. 'I'll look forward to that, then, and we can proceed accordingly. But please do wait to hear from me, Stuart. I know you ring Nancy whenever you like, but I gave you this mobile number only for essential calls; it wasn't intended as a hotline.'

'Of course,' Stuart said. 'Of course, I'm sorry, I totally understand, I'll bike a photo over to you, and then you let me know when you need us.'

Chrissie mouthed, 'And thank you,' at him, so he said, 'And thank you, Angela.'

'My pleasure, Stuart,' Angela said, and the line clicked into silence.

Stuart let out a long breath and said, 'Jeez, she's a ball-breaker,' and Chrissie said, 'But she has our Sunshine.'

'Brendan Somebody has our Sunshine, in fact,' Stu said. 'He has to give us the once-over, although God knows what else there is to discover, because they already know everything from how often we argue, to where you buy your knickers.'

Stuart bent down to where Chrissie sat on the sofa, her legs curled beneath her, a glass of red wine in her hand, her unruly fair hair loose about her shoulders. She looked barely older than the day they met. He kissed her on top of her head, then on the cheek, then on the mouth.

'I'll get the photo box out,' he said.

'A recent one, though? And not a publicity shot, obviously. But can you think when we last had our picture taken together?'

'Last July,' he said, and grinned. 'Dancing on the table of that absinthe bar in Antibes,' and she laughed so much he had to take the glass from her hand.

They found a respectable picture of the two of them on that same trip, sitting side-by-side on the wide medieval city walls of Antibes, with the Mediterranean glittering in the background, and each of them looking what they considered acceptably normal. Stone-cold sober, eyes open, nice smiles; the sort of people who might make suitable parents for a child named Sunshine. Then Stuart wandered off to read the music reviews, and Chrissie lost the rest of the evening going through the box, all the way to the bottom, to where she knew their youngest selves were waiting. Two-year-old Chrissie standing between Diana and Doug in an attitude of complete ownership; seven years old and posing on the doorstep in her first Brownie uniform. Skinny little Stuart, five years old in the ocean at Cape May; nine years old and at his first summer camp in the Catskills, hanging upside down from the accommodating bough of a maple. Seaside pictures, picnic pictures, gap-toothed school pictures. A snapshot of Stuart on his way to the high school prom – young rebel, no tux, no bow tie, just a vintage dress shirt, and a scowl – and a picture of Chrissie screaming with laughter on a log flume at her school leavers' outing to Blackpool. No siblings, either of them; no rivalry for their parents' attention. Always, just Chrissie and Stuart in their separate existences, captured by the loving gaze of the eye in the lens.

She spread the photographs out on the carpet, absorbed and transported by the familiar images. On their opposite sides of the Atlantic, they had lived their young lives, and surely there'd been another fate in store for each of them then; another future? But the cards had fallen in their favour. Chrissie had travelled ninety miles to university, Stuart had travelled three thousand, and for the first couple of terms they were only friends, but that was never going to last, everyone knew it, they seemed a matching pair. When the box of photographs came to the part in the story where their stars aligned, Chrissie held her breath for a few moments and unconsciously placed a hand over her heart, at the glow in their faces, their casual, youthful beauty, their unconcern, their insolent confidence that together, now, they were invincible.

Stuart had turned up in Liverpool not with accompanying parents, but on his own, by plane and train, and to Chrissie this had been most alluring, added to which he carried a guitar on his back like the freewheelin' Bob Dylan, and he'd said, 'Hey, am I glad to see *you*,' in his New Jersey drawl. They'd both enrolled for the same degree – music performance and technology; a fantasy course, Chrissie had thought when she'd found it, a course she might have invented – she'd had to read the prospectus two or three times before she'd believed in it, this launch pad into the industry, taught by musicians and sound technicians, who were looking for passion and performing experience over exam results. There was a recording studio and a small stage for live performances and, at once, Chrissie had felt she'd found her people. Everyone there had lived and breathed music. Within days, her new friend Stuart had formed a band he called The Lineman, with two edgy London boys: Sol Cooper on bass guitar; and a guy who only called himself Rocco on drums. All three of them had wanted Chrissie on board – her voice, her keyboard skills, her look – and for a while she'd made them beg while she'd considered her options. But she'd already known in her heart where she belonged, and soon she was their lead singer, keyboard player, and songwriter too, her delicate, confessional lyrics a gift for Stu's shimmering chords.

They'd tried hard to remain platonic, protecting the fledgling band from a messy romance, spending many a long night resisting each other while working on words and melodies. And it wasn't until one of their earliest professional gigs that Stu had finally understood what she meant to him. They were in a room above a pub in Glasgow, a hubbub of people drinking, talking, disregarding the young band at the back of the room. Chrissie, waiting to begin, affronted by their inattention, spoke into the mic, and said, 'Good evening, everyone, please can we have some hush? We're about to play our songs for you.' There was a short, startled hiatus in the activity, but then all the faces in the small crowd slowly, miraculously, turned to the stage, and The Lineman played their set. From the start to the end, it was golden, and no one shone brighter than Chrissie, and Stu had known there could be no other woman in the world he wanted more. Their romance wouldn't be messy, it would be epic, and it would be lifelong; that's what he told her, and she was inclined to agree. So they became the couple they were meant to be, and she went on the pill and didn't come off it until ten years later, when she was twenty-eight, he twenty-nine, and they'd decided to start their own family of freewheelin' kids.

And even now, with all that had passed, and all she trusted that was to come, she found she still hadn't entirely forgotten those babies, those imaginary children of their own making, and remembering was like pressing down on a bruise. Pressing down, feeling the pain, but never speaking of it because they'd agreed that acceptance was a positive state, not merely a hopeless one, and they were already lucky; lucky far beyond their teen-aged dreams. But she hadn't known what success meant, when she was younger; she'd thought success was an album going platinum or a sold-out tour of the States, until there'd been this one precious and vital thing she'd had to accept seemed indis-putably beyond her reach.

For a while, Chrissie sat very still in her pool of memories. Then she stood up sharply, leaving the photographs spilled across the floor, and went to look for Stuart. She needed his reli-able shoulder, and his certainties.

2

The day before they were to meet Sunshine, Stuart had the welcome distraction of a meeting with Lila from the management company, so Chrissie called Nancy, who said she absolutely understood her restlessness and would happily meet her for a chat, in a cafe in Muswell Hill.

Her large black bicycle was chained up outside and she was already seated at a table with a coffee for each of them, by the time Chrissie arrived. She leapt up to greet her, and enveloped Chrissie in the sort of flamboyantly committed hug that made the people around them wonder what they were to each other.

'It was so good of you to come,' Chrissie said when Nancy released her, and then she took her seat, listening to Nancy tell her, oh no, it was fine, it was no trouble, she didn't have long but she would always make time, it was her job, that's why she'd given them her number. She'd become more friend than adoption officer as the months had passed, but she lived south of the river, somewhere beyond Peckham, and now Chrissie felt her own neediness had almost certainly put Nancy out, and she felt selfish for making the phone call, although Nancy's expression was a study in empathy as she reached across the table and rested a hand lightly on Chrissie's arm.

'You look . . . overwound,' she said. 'Try to relax, Chrissie, I promise you, all will be well.'

Chrissie held Nancy's gaze, hoping – as usual – for some kind of mysterious succour from this young woman, whose somewhat hectic, home-knitted appearance – wild and wiry hair, a permanently ruddy complexion, lumpy jumpers in rainbow colours – belied an uncanny talent for stillness, as if the turbulence of the world couldn't touch her. Now, she kept her placid, pale-grey eyes on Chrissie and said, 'This is going to happen. Sunshine is your child,' and of course it was precisely what Chrissie wanted to hear, yet now it had been said, Nancy's statement felt fanciful and unsafe, plucked from thin air with no basis in fact.

'Oh, I do hope so,' Chrissie said, on a deep outward sigh. 'But, well, I think about the past, and what happened before, and I know how it can all slip away, and now this little girl, well, she's far more than an idea, she's a living, breathing, beautiful reality, and I feel—'

'I know how you feel,' Nancy said, cutting in. She smiled and took hold of Chrissie's hands across the table. 'But I want you to believe in this match, because I do, very fervently.'

'And yet, you haven't met her,' Chrissie said.

'Oh, but I know her, through Brendan,' Nancy said. 'She's his responsibility, so there's been no reason for me to meet her, but I know all about her, from him.'

'Right. Are any other couples meeting her?'

Again, a pause; then, 'Chrissie, try not to think of this as a competition.'

'But it sort of is, isn't it?'

'No, it isn't, it's a search, and yours has ended. Keep the faith, Chrissie. You and Stuart are a perfect match for Sunshine, and I wouldn't say that if I didn't wholeheartedly believe in it.'

The Truth According to Nancy; it was irresistible. 'You can feel it in your water, right?' Chrissie said, with a smile.

Nancy laughed. 'In my water, my bones, my heart and my soul. I'll be thinking of you tomorrow, sending waves of love. I'd send waves of luck too, but you won't need it.'

'Thank you, Nancy,' Chrissie said, and they drank their coffee and chatted about other things, and when finally they parted and hugged tightly again, Chrissie thought she might actually be able to physically feel the warm waves of the young woman's conviction. Still, though, as she watched Nancy weave away along the Broadway on her bicycle, Chrissie knew she wasn't quite ready to go home to the empty flat. Nina, she thought; I need to talk to Nina.

~

Nina ran a small art gallery in Highgate, and had a tiny flat and a large studio for her own use, above it. If a customer entered downstairs, a bell rang upstairs, and Nina would down tools and descend the winding wooden staircase. But today was Monday, when the gallery didn't open, so Chrissie sat and watched Nina paint, knowing she had her entirely to herself. Nina had her back to Chrissie, and was pushing cadmium and cobalt greens about on a canvas with a palette knife, but she was paying perfect attention, Chrissie could tell that from the angle of her head, and the quality of her silence.

'Stu and I know too much about the system to be able to relax,' Chrissie said. 'That's the problem. We know things now we didn't know before.'

'Mmm,' Nina said.

'We won't be the only couple meeting Sunshine.'

'You might be, love.'

'We won't, there'll be others, I'm certain. There'll be other couples, with steady jobs and big houses and a nice car they don't have to share with their friends.'

Nina put her palette knife down and turned from the canvas. She was almost as blonde as Chrissie, no traces of grey yet, and today she had her hair scraped back with the help of a fat brown elastic band. Her face had its usual scrubbed-clean look, bare of make-up. She said, 'Hasn't Nancy spent all these months telling you those things don't matter?'

Chrissie said, 'I know, but—'

'And wouldn't Nancy have told you if there were other couples meeting Sunshine?'

'She swerved the question; I don't think she's entirely sure,' Chrissie said. 'But I bet there are, and I bet Angela Holt and Brendan Cassidy and probably even Nancy Maitland are going to end up choosing them.'

Nina looked round at her and smiled. 'You sound like you did when you were ten, and didn't get picked by Sharon Machin for her skipping games.'

'Well, yes,' Chrissie said. 'Now you mention it, that's exactly how I feel.'

Nina laughed, and looked at Chrissie with indulgent fondness. 'She was a nasty piece of work, wasn't she?'

Chrissie nodded. 'God, yeah. She rubbed mashed potato on Terry Butler's glasses at school dinner.'

'Blimey, that's dark. What became of her?'

'Dunno,' Chrissie said. 'Prison warden, maybe.'

Now they both laughed, and Nina wiped her hands on her jeans then came over, and sat down opposite Chrissie. She pulled a cigarette out of her top pocket, and popped it into her mouth.

'Don't lose heart,' she said. The cigarette wagged when she

spoke. Her matches were just out of reach, and Chrissie tossed them to her. Nina struck one, lit the cigarette, and took a long drag. She only ever smoked in her studio, said it helped her to work. It was one of the reasons Chrissie liked being here, the smell of tobacco smoke. Also, the smell of turps, which she found equally soothing. She wondered, sometimes, if the hours she'd spent up here with Nina counted as substance abuse.

'Did I tell you, there are no birth parents on the scene?' Chrissie asked.

Nina raised her brows. 'Yeah? Wow, how come?'

'She was dropped off at a housing office in South East London, Brendan said. Left there, by a young woman who scarpered.'

'Did they catch her on CCTV?'

Chrissie shook her head. 'Apparently not; she'd barely stepped inside the building when she managed to hand her over. Imagine doing that?'

'Desperation,' said Nina, 'can make people do the strangest things.'

'Yeah, I guess. Anyway, it simplifies the process, in a way.'

'Does it?'

'Brendan said so.'

'Well, good,' Nina said. She tipped her head and blew a column of smoke at the ceiling. 'And it sounds to me as though Brendan liked you a lot, otherwise you wouldn't be where you are now. They're not looking for big houses, Chrissie, they're looking for lovely people, and you and Stu are the dictionary definition of lovely. See what happens tomorrow, enjoy the experience, be yourself, and everything will be all right.'

Chrissie felt tears pool in her eyes. This happened a lot, these days; she felt nervy and restless and as vulnerable to acts of kindness as she was to misfortune. But Nina was right about Brendan – he *had* seemed to like them. He'd been friendly and unthreatening and a bit shambolic. He'd arrived by bicycle and forgotten to take the clips off his trousers, and then a kind of nervous energy had seized him and made him garrulous, and he'd spent the first ten minutes marvelling at their wall of music – all the CDs and LPs on purpose-built shelves the length and height of their living room. He said, 'I don't know much about music, me,' and then proved it by pulling out random sleeves and saying things such as, 'Velvet Underground? Funny name for a band,' then putting them back in slightly the wrong place, and Stuart had done a supremely good job of pretending not to care. Then, finally, Brendan talked to them about Sunshine, showed them her notes – scant details, really, and nothing at all about her infancy. He told them she was a lovely child, affectionate and sociable, and how well she'd settled with her foster parents, then asked them questions about their professional set-up, and how they'd fit their life as performers around a child, and Chrissie said – as she'd said before, to a poker-faced panel intent on winkling out a sex and drugs confession – that, apart from some studio work, they had no commitments until a European tour early summer next year, no gigs for months. So, she repeated, in the immediate future, just studio work, and song-writing at home, and anyway, if she had to give it all up for Sunshine, she would. She felt Stu looking at her, and kept her eyes resolutely on Brendan.

'Coo-ool,' Brendan had said, looking right back at her and seeming a little awed, although if he hadn't heard of The Velvet Underground, then he certainly hadn't heard of The Lineman. He'd been nice though, once he calmed down. He'd been with the agency a little under three months, he told them, and he seemed a good addition; more ordinary than Nancy, more relatable than Angela. When Chrissie had asked why Sunshine had been twelve months in foster care, he'd said, 'Good question, and I don't know,' which had been unhelpful, but endearing. Also, he'd kept the best till last and produced with a flourish an unexpected bonus, a short video of Sunshine playing in the back garden of her foster home; an amazing, surprising glimpse into her life, and her image was imprinted on Chrissie's mind's eye now: a little girl with a perfectly round face, a mass of dark, rich, brown curls, and a bold, humorous, defiant expression. She didn't look cowed by circumstance. Smaller, perhaps, than Chrissie imagined a three-year-old would look, but also very doughty and determined in dungarees and little blue boots. Years ago, when she, Chrissie, had idly and complacently thought about the family she and Stuart would have, she'd always pictured three fair-haired children; but here had been this girl with hair the colour of mahogany and dark, sparkling eyes, and Chrissie had thought, *Oh, my daughter!* She'd glanced at Stu, wondering if he'd had the same visceral flash of recognition, but he'd only smiled at her, then looked back at the screen, where a man off camera was saying, 'Say hello, Sunshine,' in a coaxing voice. The child had taken a deep breath and yelled, 'Hello!' and waved in a wild, outlandish arc, then dropped her arm, turned, and run off down the small garden and out of shot.

'I just won't be able to bear it, Auntie Nina, if we don't get picked,' Chrissie said, now, and Nina said, 'I know you think that, but you will.'

'Get picked?'

'No, bear it. But there's a strong chance you will be chosen, I'm sure they're being just as careful about your feelings, as they are about the child's. They don't want the same thing to happen again, any more than you do.'

'Remember Billy though?' Chrissie said. 'Swooshed off to a couple in the home counties.'

'Well, sure, of course I remember, and it was tough, but that child was not your child.'

'Now you sound like Nancy.'

'No, I don't mean it's all written in the stars, I just mean, they went elsewhere for solid reasons to do with their needs and their own best interests, not because the Fates had other ideas – and not, by the way, because you and Stu fell short.'

No, thought Chrissie. But she'd held Billy, the baby, in her arms for an hour. He'd smiled up at her; he'd clutched her thumb in his fist; he'd reached up and pulled her hair; he'd fallen asleep.

Nina looked at Chrissie's expression and sighed.

'Cup of tea?' she asked. 'Or glass of wine?'

At first, Nina Baker had been friends with Diana. Well, not friends exactly, but friendly acquaintances, exchanging pleasantries at the Barnsley Market veg stall where Diana found Nina working, one February morning in 1972. Nina had an open expression and a ready smile, and on that first encounter she gave little Christine an orange wrapped in tissue paper, fastened with a sticker that said *Produce of Israel*. She was younger than Diana – twenty-five to her thirty-one – but clearly she'd already lived a life, spoke of London, and Paris, and a failed attempt at selling her own paintings. Diana had said, 'What on earth are you doing in Barnsley?' and Nina had laughed and said she liked it, it was the friendliest place she'd ever lived. From the outset, Diana took an interest; she told Doug about Nina later that same day, said she'd seen something in her, and clearly she was wasted on a fruit and veg stall. So Nina became Diana's discovery, and was gradually absorbed into their family life, encouraged all the while by Diana, to fulfil her potential. She paid her to look after seven-year-old Chrissie so that Nina, in turn, could rent a better flat and fund a foundation course, and, eventually, a fine art degree, in Sheffield. When Diana decided to take a job in the offices of the coal board, it'd been Nina – by then Auntie Nina – who stepped in to help at home so that Doug could run his plumbing empire and Diana was relieved of domesticity. She became essential to all three of them, but especially to Chrissie to whom she was part of the fabric of her upbringing. And when Chrissie and Stuart finally gave up their itinerant life and bought a flat in Muswell Hill, Nina had already moved back to London to run the art gallery, a couple of miles away.

She was perhaps the most self-contained person Chrissie knew. The gallery was only sparsely visited by customers, leaving Nina with acres of time to paint, cook, walk, read, and listen to music. She had a handful of very good friends scattered across the world, she lived alone, she was serenely content, and it had ever been thus, Chrissie thought now, as she walked back home after two hours in her company, feeling not exactly peaceful, but certainly much restored. You knew what you were going to get from Nina, she thought; she was completely reliable. Once, when Chrissie was young, she'd asked, 'Why aren't you married, Auntie Nina?' and Nina had smiled and kissed the top of Chrissie's head and said, 'Because, my kitten, I have you,' and after that, Chrissie asked the same question often, just to hear the answer.

~

Sunshine's foster parents lived in a quiet Whitstable street, not far back from the sea. It was long and narrow and allowed no visitor parking, so Stuart and Chrissie had to prowl around in the car in tense silence until they found a place they could pay to park, then feed the meter with coins, until the time they'd paid for matched the time they knew they had. Just an hour, today. An hour, to meet the child who might be their daughter. Stuart dropped the money all over the pavement, and his hands shook as he retrieved the coins then slotted them into the machine, and Chrissie shivered in the April sunshine as she watched, although around them there were people heading for an afternoon on the beach, in shorts and summer dresses.

They'd had a dreadful journey; the longer they were on the road, the further away Whitstable had seemed. They shared this elderly vehicle with their drummer Rocco and his girlfriend Kim – dear friends, indispensable friends, but, on this occasion, unreliable friends, because, when Chrissie and Stu picked it up from them in Kentish Town, the tank was all but empty, and they'd driven to the nearest petrol station with dry mouths and pounding hearts, convinced they were going to run out. Then they'd crawled through the Dartford Tunnel in a line of cars that had moved slow as molasses for no evident reason, and then again on the M2 as they'd inched their way towards, and past, an accident. They'd allowed an extra hour for what should have been a ninety-minute journey, and had needed every second of it, and now they were here, on time, but strung out tight, too tense to talk, so they held hands and walked up the street to number twenty-three, and knocked on the door. It was so hard to arrange their faces into relaxed and friendly smiles in readiness for it opening, but they did their best, and suddenly, there they were, being shown by Barbara and John into their small front room where Brendan Cassidy had already taken a seat on the sofa. There were two other foster children, narrow-eyed, wily-looking twin boys of about six years old, with bright-orange hair, and names that Chrissie and Stuart were told, but immediately forgot. Sunshine wasn't there. She'd gone down for a nap, Barbara said brightly, as if this was a good thing.

'She'll be awake soon enough,' she said. She looked them up and down rather boldly, evidently judging their appearance: lean and blonde, good-looking in a way that Barbara probably recognised but almost certainly didn't admire. Scruffy, her eyes said. Jeans and T-shirts. Dirty canvas pumps.

'Brendan says you're pop stars,' she said, and he immediately reddened and Stuart laughed.

'We don't play pop and we're not stars, but otherwise, spot on.'

'I said musicians in a band, actually,' Brendan said.

'Well, you look like pop stars,' Barbara said. 'Don't they, John? Look like pop stars?'

John said, mildly, 'I've no idea what a pop star looks like on their day off.'

Chrissie, feeling brittle, said, 'Any chance you could wake up Sunshine?'

Barbara looked at her as if she'd just suggested they blow up the house.

'Not a good idea,' she said. 'I'd never wake a child from a nap; they do their growing when they sleep. She'll not be long; would you like a cup of coffee while we wait?'

Chrissie and Stuart did not want a cup of coffee, they only wanted to meet Sunshine, but they said yes please. John said, 'Please, make yourselves comfortable,' and they thanked him, though neither of them remembered to sit down. Chrissie smiled at the twin boys and they stared at her insolently, like a pair of urban foxes. Stuart chatted awkwardly to Brendan about their drive down from North London, which he said had been fine, because he didn't wish to talk about its awfulness. The twins suddenly began to wrestle on the floor and roar at each other, grabbing each other in lethal-looking chokeholds. John said, 'Lads, take it outside,' but they either didn't hear or they ignored him, rolling around, thrashing about, their white faces turning puce with the effort of trying to throttle each other. Then Barbara pushed the door open with her hip and came in with two mugs of coffee, but, as she passed them over to Chrissie and Stuart, she tipped her head and said, 'Ah, I can hear her now,' and she turned on her heel, so they stood there, clutching their unwanted coffee, watching the door, feeling, each of them, that this over-populated little room was not the place to meet Sunshine. Even Brendan seemed different, watching them in this new habitat with a kind of detached, anthropological interest.

'Look, here, let me take those mugs, they'll only be in your way,' John said, suddenly, and it was the kindest thing he could've done. He took the coffees off them, and then nudged the nearest twin with the toe of his slipper, and said, 'I bet you two can't get to the fence at the bottom of the back garden before I count to ten,' and the pair of them immediately leapt apart from their strangleholds and raced out, pushing and shoving and laughing as John winked at Chrissie, and said, 'They fall for that every time. Do sit down, you two,' and now, they did.

And then Barbara came back in, holding Sunshine in her arms, and the two of them seemed to Chrissie to be part of the same whole. The child clung on tight, and buried her face in the soft flesh of Barbara's neck, and when Barbara said, 'Here we are, then, who'd like a cuddle?' Sunshine seemed to cling harder, pressing herself further into Barbara's ample body. Barbara ran an expert hand up and down the child's back, patting and soothing and making her so extremely comfortable that it was hardly likely she'd want to leap into the unpractised arms of a stranger.

Chrissie said, 'Oh, no, give her a minute,' and Barbara said, 'She'll come around, she's a confident little thing usually.' Still welded together, they sat down next to Brendan, and Barbara prised Sunshine away just enough to swivel her round, so that she was facing out. Chrissie, without meaning to, said, 'Oh,' with a kind of gasp, because she was the child Chrissie had known she would be, the child that belonged to her. Her cheeks were pink from sleep, and one side of her face was plastered with curls. Her mouth was turned down, as if ready to cry. Her eyes, thickly lashed, were dark and watchful. Barbara jigged her knees and Sunshine bobbed up and down and almost smiled. Chrissie felt useless, helpless, but Stuart spoke up and said, 'Hello, Sunshine, I'm Stuart and this is Chrissie, it's so lovely to meet you,' and Chrissie, emboldened, said, 'It is, and we brought you a present, to say hello.'

At this, Sunshine perked up. She swivelled her head and said, 'A present,' to Barbara in a voice that was sweetly low and husky. Chrissie wanted to hear it again.

'Here,' she said. 'It's in my bag. Will you come over and find it?'

At once Sunshine slid from Barbara's lap – was it Chrissie's imagination, or did the woman hold her back, just for a fraction of a moment? – and crossed the room. Chrissie had dropped to the floor, and was kneeling now, although she still felt enormous alongside the child, who was very slight, a tousle-haired pixie. Sunshine bent at the hips and placed her hands on her thighs and peered down into Chrissie's bag. 'This?' she said, plunging her hand in and retrieving a box wrapped in orange paper, with 'Sunshine' written across it in silver pen. How they'd agonised in the toy shop over this purchase. Dolls and teddies and Play-Doh and fairy wands and plastic tubes filled with tiny dinosaurs had all in the end been rejected in favour of a jungle jigsaw puzzle, which now seemed the dullest gift possible.

'That's it!' Chrissie said, and Sunshine clutched the parcel to her chest and stepped away from Chrissie, as if the trophy might be snatched back. She was dressed in thin white leggings and a khaki T-shirt that said *little terror* beneath an image of a wild-eyed troll, and Chrissie tried not to think how much they looked like clothes she would never buy.

'Well, we weren't expecting that,' Barbara said, smiling. 'We weren't expecting a present, were we?'

She seemed to be addressing everyone, although she turned, now, to look at Brendan, who didn't reply and kept his face almost, but not quite, neutral, just allowing himself a small smile that could, quite frankly, mean anything. Chrissie immediately started to panic; had they crashed some secret protocol by offering a bribe to a child they still didn't know?

'What do you say to Chrissie, Sunny?'

This was Barbara again, brightly authoritative.

'Nothing,' Sunshine said. She squeezed shut her eyes and bunched up her mouth into a soft little knot.

'Oh, now,' Barbara said, 'that's not what we say when somebody gives us a present!' She glanced at Brendan, then back at Sunshine. 'What do we say, Sunny?'

Chrissie looked at Brendan, who was writing something rapidly on a form. Perhaps all this was a test. Or perhaps it was simply that Barbara always needed to parade her own understanding of social niceties.

'Tell you what, Sunny,' Stuart said, 'save it for later. Open it after we've gone.'

He knew how to speak to children. He used his own voice, but softened it slightly, whereas Chrissie knew she sounded inordinately bright and cheerful, like a children's television presenter. The little girl opened her eyes and looked at him shyly.

'Will you show us the garden?' he asked.

She nodded, and, tucking the present under one arm, she held out the other so that he could take her hand. That small moment, that first contact between Stuart and Sunshine – how significant it seemed, how moving, and how badly Chrissie longed to experience it. She could see that he'd been right to change the conversation, seize the initiative, and get them out of the room; but how had he understood that when Sunshine was no longer being scrutinised by five adults she'd be released from the pickle she'd got herself into? Chrissie followed them down the small hallway, through a long, galley kitchen, and out through a back door.

'Shall I take that?' she said to Sunshine, and pointed at the present.

'It mine,' Sunny said, and Chrissie smiled and said, 'Yes, it is, but I can keep it safe for you while you play,' and when the child relinquished the box, it felt momentous again, a first act of trust between them, and Chrissie thought, good grief, every tiny thing is imbued with significance; every small gesture magnified, every kind word amplified.

Sunny, looking cheerful now, announced that she could do a roly-poly and Stuart said, 'Me too!' so they performed a few together, on the grass, and the twins joined in, and Chrissie watched them, transfixed by Sunshine's throaty laughter, until Barbara appeared in the door and said, 'Time to say bye-bye, Sunny.'

On the drive home, Chrissie said, 'You're more fun than I am,' and Stuart laughed and said, 'Nah, just more childish.'

'No, you are,' she said. 'You're fun, and relaxed, and you know how to play with a child, but I don't, I don't know what to say, or how to be, I don't even like the way I sound when I do pluck up the courage to speak,' and then she burst into a flood of tears.

He slowed the car, indicated, pulled over.

'Hey,' he said, and he pulled her towards him, and wiped the tears with his sleeve. 'It's been a tough day.'

'I'm sorry. I'm pathetic.'

'You're fantastic. You've driven this campaign so far, Chrissie Stevenson, we wouldn't be here if it wasn't for you, and you're going to be an amazing mother.'

Through her tears she said, 'Am I, though? I felt stiff and awkward back there. I might turn out just like my mother, isn't that what happens?'

He laughed. 'No,' he said. 'It's not what happens.'

She sniffed deeply, sat back, looked at him. 'I want that child,' she said.

'I know. Me too.'

'But didn't you get the feeling Barbara wants her too?'

He shrugged. 'No, not really, she was just flexing her fostering muscles a bit, that's all.'

'Were you surprised she'd put Sunshine down for a nap?'

'Oh, well, not really. I don't know, I guess she knows what the kid needs.'

'You didn't find it passive-aggressive?'

Stuart laughed. 'I did not.'

Chrissie said, 'You're funnier than me, and you're nicer than me too.'

'Two very good reasons to stick with me, then.'

'Did you see how much Sunshine loved her?'

'I saw how attached she is. But that's a good thing, right? Attachment?'

'Did you hear her when she woke up? When Barbara said she'd heard her, did you? I didn't hear a thing.'

'I guess you get an ear for it.'

'D'you think? Will we learn how to hear her, when she wakes?'

'Yeah, of course. It's quieter at our flat anyway.'

'But Barbara is basically her mother, isn't she? As good as?'

'Well, she calls her Barbara, not Mommy.'

'Why would she ever want to leave Barbara and John, though? Twelve months is a long time, at that age. A third of her life.'

'Chrissie, if it was down to Sunshine, right now in this moment, she wouldn't want to leave, would she? But she's up for adoption, she can't stay in a foster home, and so we're going to do the best job we can of making up for that, and loving her, and raising her.'

'If we're given the chance.'

'Yeah,' he said. 'If we're given the chance.'

She fell silent, then. She couldn't talk about it any more. It all meant far too much, and nothing they said to each other privately, nothing they thought or felt or wanted, would make any difference to the outcome. Drown it all out, she thought; drown out all the unanswerable questions. She turned on the radio, and as if the station had only been waiting for her, The Pretenders came on with 'Stop Your Sobbing', bang on the opening lyric.

'Ahhhhh, impeccable,' Stu said. 'My second favourite Chrissie in the world.'

3

Some days, everyone – *everyone* – in Muswell Hill seemed to have children, and while she waited to hear once more from Angela Holt, Chrissie felt haunted and taunted by couples who callously paraded their fecundity through North London. They stalked the pavements, with their toddlers in buggies, their babies in slings, their school-age children in bottle-green sweatshirts and grey skirts or shorts, swinging their book bags and talking and talking and talking, barely pausing for breath. In a queue at the post office, Chrissie found herself gazing into the face of a baby who gazed back from her pram; a baby whose eyes seemed too large for her face, whose lips were like an unfurled flower, whose whole body and being were such a perfectly simple miracle, such a warm and vital work of art, that Chrissie became lost in her longing and had to be called twice to the counter. And when she got home, she'd cried, because her own faith was failing now, her own faith was turning to ashes, and the idea of Sunshine was becoming hard to bear under the weight of the increasing possibility of failure.

And then, glory be, Angela rang. She said she had good news, said she could now confirm they were the only couple considered suitable for Sunshine, said there was still a long road ahead, but they'd do their very best to avoid delays, and said a shortage of adoptive parents in the system right now had been very much in Chrissie and Stuart's favour. Put like that, it sounded rather as though they were a last resort, but still, Chrissie's head spun with unfettered joy and she sat down hard on the kitchen chair while she listened to Angela unpacking another series of complicated sentences about the formalities, the matching panel, the dotting of i's and the crossing of t's.

'Ah,' Chrissie said, when her turn came to talk, 'Angela, that's . . . that's . . .' and she started to cry, messily and noisily, gulping and gasping, drowning in her own relief.

'Can you put Stuart on?' Angela asked. But Stuart wasn't at home, so Angela had to wait as Chrissie tried to gather her wits, and said, 'Sorry' and 'Thank you' and 'Sorry,' again, and hoped Angela knew she wasn't unstable, but simply consumed by a kind of exhausted and inexhaustible gratitude.

'Look,' Angela said, 'I'll give you some space to gather your thoughts. Call me back when you're . . . when you've collected yourself,' and she'd scarpered, hanging up the phone – Chrissie imagined – to roll her eyes at her colleagues and get on with something tidy and manageable and bureaucratic, while Chrissie laid her head on her arms and waited for the shuddering emotions to subside.

She realised now that she'd been absolutely braced for failure, and she realised, too, that, for her, that would have been the end of the journey. To be introduced to Sunshine only to have been shown another child that could never be hers – well, she would have borne it, with Stuart's help, but she would never have risked her heart in such a way again.

She concentrated on steadying her breathing. She needed to call Stu, and she'd like to speak to Nancy, and she had to call Angela back. But first, she must govern her racing heart and mind, and she did this by focusing on the image in her mind's eye of Sunshine; Sunshine holding her hand, turning her face up to Chrissie's and calling her Mummy. Picture this, Chrissie told herself, for it shall come to pass. Trust the process, for nothing now will stand in your way. The past year and a half had often felt like a complex strategy game, the rules of which they didn't know; the early days, especially. Adoption workshops, where wary couples sat in semi-circles on plastic chairs in drab local authority meeting rooms, eyeing up the competition, performing tasks, recalling memories, being challenged, again and again, about their own expectations, so that every answer, however honestly given, felt like the wrong one. Boy or girl? Baby, toddler, or a child of school age? Single child or siblings? Could they cope with a history of sustained sexual abuse? Could they cope with mental or physical disability? And to what level? Could they cope with a child who had only ever known violence, hunger, loss? They were told it was OK to say no, but every time they admitted that they didn't think they could provide a home for two or more siblings or they didn't feel able to meet the needs of a severely autistic child, there always seemed to follow a short but intense silence, as if they were being given thinking time, to consider how shallow they were.

Now, Chrissie thought about Angela, who'd merely called with good news, and had received in reply hot tears and gasping incoherence. Poor Angela, so unbending, so formal; what must she have made of it, she who'd never betrayed a trace of emotion, never asked Chrissie or Stu a question that wasn't required by a form? She'd probably be as relieved to be free of them as they would to be free of her, and yet, thought Chrissie, there'd been a quiet kind of merit in Angela's detachment today, a quiet kind of weight to her words; *the only couple considered suitable for Sunshine.* And what else, but this, had they wished for?

Nothing at all. Angela was no fairy godmother, but still, she'd granted them their wish.

At last, Chrissie dialled Stu's mobile number to share the glad tidings, and on picking up he asked, 'Hey, hi, is it just us?'

'Just us,' she said, and his unalloyed joy made her cry again, but quietly this time; reasonable tears that didn't stop her talking.

'It feels so momentous,' she said. 'Like, y'know, like a breakthrough, like a beginning.'

'Yeah, right?' Stu said. 'The previous stuff, everything we've been through – it makes sense of it all.'

'It does, it really does.' She sniffed deeply, and he laughed.

'Ah Chrissie, we're going to have a blast, we three,' he said. She smiled into the phone.

'I mean, who would choose the easy route to parenthood?' he said. 'Who wouldn't want this feeling, the feeling we have now?'

Chrissie closed her eyes, and considered how much she loved this man, for saying that. She felt weak with love, she was fit for nothing, she was ready to sink to the floor.

'I love you,' she said, hearing the inadequacy of those words for the first time.

'Love you back,' he said. 'See you later.'

Fully equipped for conversation now, she called Nancy, but her phone rang out without being answered or switching to voicemail. Then, she rang Angela, who answered immediately, and launched into a list of what Chrissie and Stuart should now expect. She said that soon they'd get a date to visit Sunshine again, during which they could spend some quality time on their own with her. The photograph that they'd provided would have pride of place on the wall by the child's bed, and Barbara and John would begin to refer to Chrissie and Stuart as 'your new mummy and daddy'. They'd be invited back on another occasion, to put Sunshine to bed. Sunshine would visit them at their own home too, with Barbara and John. Back and forth they'd go, until by the time Sunshine came to live in their home, Angela said, she'd be completely familiar with them, and ready to make a happy transition.

'Oh, let's hope so,' Chrissie said, meaning nothing by this, except to convey her desperate wish that it came to pass.

'Well, if you're not convinced, or we're not convinced, then it won't happen,' Angela said, and Chrissie thought, me and my big mouth.

~

They took Sunshine to play on the beach. Barbara gave them a packed lunch of things Sunny liked to eat, so they 'didn't have to worry', and, as well, as she saw them out of the house, she told them the tide times and said Tankerton was better for paddling.

'Straight down to the seafront, then turn right and keep walking for ten minutes or so. You'll have to go around the harbour. Sunshine knows where we go, and she loves the beach huts, don't you, sweetheart? And it's a lovely clean stretch of beach there. There's a towel in the bag, and some dry clothes just in case, but I know you'll not take your eyes off her when she's in the water, will you?'

'Is you coming, Barbara?' the child said. The way she said Barbara was delightful, Chrissie thought. Two syllables. Barb-wa.

'Ooh, no, not this time. It's your new mummy and daddy's turn to take you.'

Sunshine regarded Chrissie and Stuart solemnly. 'But I don't like them,' she said, and Chrissie felt a thud of dread that already this was going wrong, but Stuart just smiled down at the little girl and said, 'I'm not surprised, Sunshine, but will you give us a try out? Now, which way is the sea?' He pointed in entirely the wrong direction, and said, 'Is it that way?'

'No!' Sunshine said, shaking her head vehemently. 'No, it not.'

'Will you show us?' Stuart said.

'Yes, I will,' she said, and she took his hand and said, 'Bye-bye, Barbara' – almost sung it – and set off down the pavement with Stuart. Barbara gave Chrissie a smile she couldn't quite interpret, and handed her the cool bag. 'He's got a good way with kiddies,' Barbara said. 'Have a lovely time,' and she stepped backwards into the house and shut the door.

Chrissie hurried along to catch them up, and Sunshine was saying, '. . . yes, I do, but they is silly and sometimes naughty,' and Stuart looked at Chrissie over his shoulder and said, 'Carl and Kevin, the twins,' so that Sunshine realised Chrissie was behind them, and she looked around too, and said, 'That is my food?'

'All in here,' Chrissie said, patting the bag.

'Is there my cheese string?'

'I don't know,' Chrissie said. 'Barbara packed this for us, so I don't know what's in it.'

'I want a cheese string.'

'Look,' Stuart said. 'I can see the water, can you?' He was still holding Sunshine's hand, and Chrissie longed to take the other, but the pavement was narrow as they processed towards the beach and she knew it would be only for herself and not at all for Sunshine, if she were to muscle in on Stuart's obvious success.

'It is sea,' Sunshine said. 'Not water.'

They stood for a while, the three of them, and looked out at the flat expanse; the wind turbines, a tanker, the Isle of Sheppey and, way across the estuary, the blur of the Essex coastline. The day was warm but cloudy, so the sea had no help from the sun and was a dull, uniform grey. But the tide was up just the right amount, and there were people walking along the beach and sitting in small groups against the wooden groynes. A small dog was digging furiously in the shingle.

Sunshine took a step backwards. 'I don't like it,' she said. They all looked at the terrier, which was making rapid downward progress amid a hail of small stones.

Dogs, Chrissie thought; is she afraid of dogs?

'Then we'll sit over there,' Stuart said, pointing to the empty expanse of beach beyond the busy terrier.

'Don't you like dogs, Sunshine?' Chrissie asked. All the things they didn't know, she thought. All the things they had to learn. Sunshine shook her head vigorously.

'I don't like that dog,' she said, pointing a small and delicate index finger at the foe.

Stuart said, 'She doesn't dig digging dogs.'

'If you hold mine hand, I can paddle,' she said.

Oh, she's adorable, thought Chrissie. She glanced at Stuart and he read her mind and said, 'I know, right?'

'Barbara said we need to walk to Tankerton,' Chrissie said. 'We're supposed to walk ten minutes that way.'

Sunshine plonked herself onto her bottom and started to pull at her sandals.

'Hang on there, Sunny,' Stu said. 'The stones are going to hurt your feet.' He turned his gaze right, but couldn't see beyond the harbour and an incongruous, pale-green factory.

'It's seems a bit far, don't you think? We don't have that long together. Let's do our own thing,' he said.

'Okaaay,' Chrissie said. And why not, she thought? This was their time, with Sunshine; it didn't have to be stage-managed by Barbara. She hoisted the cool bag off her shoulder and said,

'Here, your turn,' to Stuart, who took it saying, 'Oh, sure, yeah,' and Chrissie said, 'C'mon, Sunny, I'll race you to the sea. Who's going to get there first?'

It felt reckless; it felt like the most enormous risk she'd ever taken. If Sunshine had refused and clung on to Stuart, Chrissie didn't know if she would ever have recovered from the rejection, but instead the little girl grinned and jumped up, bouncing on her toes, and shouting, 'Me will win, me!' and she tore off onto the beach after Chrissie, laughing and squealing and nimble as a little sandpiper on the shifting stones.

They were leaping ahead, they knew. But as they held Sunshine by the hands and swung her out over every incoming wave, and basked in her peals of husky laughter, Chrissie and Stuart felt certain of their place in her future. Then they sat down on the stones and unzipped Barbara's cool bag, and there was no cheese string, and, from that point on, Sunshine's world turned dark. The child stormed, stood up, kicked Stuart, threw herself backwards in an alarming arc, landing flat on the stones with a crunch, then screamed and screamed. There were ham sandwiches in the cool bag, cut into tiny triangles, and triangles too of Dairylea processed cheese, and apples in a Tupperware container, cut into crescents, and three boxes of tropical fruit juice with straws attached, but no cheese string. They looked at each other across the rigid, howling, red-faced form of their little charge, and saw panic in each other's eyes. They didn't even know what a cheese string was.

'Sunny,' Chrissie said, placing her mouth very close to the little girl's ear, 'Sunny Sunshine, let's find a shop that sells cheese strings, shall we?'

Sunshine opened her eyes, and for a few seconds thought about what Chrissie had said, then she roared, 'I want Barbwa!' at full throttle, and then repeated it over and over again, and

they felt like child abductors, they felt utterly wicked, and irre-
sponsible. They scrambled to their feet, pulling Sunshine up
with them, and the shingle was such a dreadful obstacle to their
progress, so deep and slack that they waded up the slight incline
like drunkards, staggering and lurching in a bid for solid
ground. Stuart was holding Sunshine, but she squirmed and
thrashed so that people stared, and Chrissie wondered if it was
completely apparent to all that they didn't have a clue what they
were doing, and, anyway, barely knew the child.

On the promenade he put her down but she wouldn't hold
his hand or Chrissie's, and she continued to refuse all the way
back to Barbara's street, and kept trotting ahead with a desperate urgency, so they had to jog too, to keep some semblance of
control. When they reached the point where a road had to be
crossed, Chrissie said, 'Sunshine, please, hold my hand now,' but
the girl immediately tucked her left hand under her right armpit
so Chrissie had nothing to hang on to but the strap of her
vest. This is how they arrived at the front door, which flew open
before they knocked – had Barbara been watching for them,
from the bay window? – and when Chrissie released Sunshine,
she rushed at Barbara as if they'd been separated for weeks.

'Oh dear,' Barbara said. 'Oh, my.' She scooped up the hot
and furious little body and peppered the side of her face with
tiny kisses. Sunshine pushed her thumb into her mouth and
closed her eyes, and Stuart and Chrissie stood on the doorstep
feeling redundant – worse: feeling utterly useless.

'There was no cheese string in the picnic,' Chrissie said, and
although she knew this sounded banal, pathetic, certainly not
an explanation for returning a child so thoroughly wrung out
by distress, nevertheless she also knew it was key to this disaster. Chrissie heard her voice shake a little, and felt her eyes sting
with tears, but she was determined not to shed them here, in

43

front of Barbara, whose placid, passive enmity seemed to fill the hallway. She felt Stuart's hand rest in the hollow of her lower back, a gesture of old, a gesture of love and partnership and support. We two stand before you as one, it said.

'Barbara, can we come in?' Stuart asked, for they were still just outside the house, looking in.

'Oh!' she said. 'My manners! I was quite taken up with this little mite.'

She moved back, and to the side, so that they could come in and close the door.

'We need a chat,' Stuart said, with special emphasis. 'Why don't you get Sunshine a cheese string, whatever that is, and then come back and talk to us?'

Barbara's face turned from pliable dough to something like brick, red and stolid.

'Please,' Chrissie said, and at that, the other woman took off through the house to the kitchen, and returned a couple of minutes later without Sunshine. She stood before them, defiant enough, but perhaps a little less sure of herself than she had been, a little less certain of her ground.

'We won't stay much longer,' Stuart said, speaking pleasantly and evenly, 'but what could and should have been an important outing just now, with Sunshine, was traumatic for us, and I'm including the child in that. You saw the state she was in?'

'Well,' Barbara began, 'this is a confusing situation for—'

'It needn't be any such thing,' Chrissie said, picking up the baton. 'It needn't be confusing, or difficult and certainly it needn't be distressing.'

'You see,' Stuart said, 'Sunshine seemed sure you'd pack her favourite snack, and I wonder why you didn't, given the importance to all of us that our first short outing be a happy occasion?'

Barbara stared. 'I hope you don't think I deliberately didn't give her a cheese string? I hope you don't think that.'

'If you tell us it wasn't deliberate, then of course we won't think it was,' Chrissie said. 'It's just, it was such a small and easy way of ensuring Sunshine would enjoy her time with us.'

'Oh, there's all sorts of things can set her off. You don't know the half of it.'

'No, but we hope to, in time, and we'll need your help with that,' Stuart said.

There was a short silence, into which the sound of children's laughter came tumbling from the garden.

Chrissie said, 'Sounds like all's well again, now.'

'Do you want to go and say goodbye?' Barbara asked.

They did. They went, just the two of them, through the kitchen and out the back. The cool bag was open on the patio, the remains of the beach picnic spread about it. Carl was pushing Kevin in a wheelbarrow, charging in a loopy figure of eight around the lawn. Sunshine, now clutching a bright-orange stick of cheese, was squealing with merriment, and when Chrissie and Stuart emerged, she turned her glowing face upon them and said, 'I do has a cheese string!', and held it up for them to admire.

'Lucky you!' Stuart said. 'Hey, we're going now, we'll see you again soon, but can we have a hug, to say goodbye?' and Sunshine dipped her head in gracious acquiescence, so Stuart first, and then Chrissie, stooped down to encircle the child in their arms, and each of them felt her lean in, a compact, resilient, and – for the time being – self-possessed small girl. She smelled sweet and salty, fresh as the breeze. She was perfect.

4

On a blessedly warm afternoon in May, Chrissie and Kim sat together in the small patch of garden behind Stu and Chrissie's flat, where the scent of lilac and the heavy buzz of a drunken bee lent a bucolic air to the scene, although they were surrounded on all sides by Edwardian red-brick dwellings, exactly like their own. Stu was occupied in the kitchen, preparing a celebratory Sunday lunch, because there were three good things to toast: the Labour landslide ten days ago; Chrissie being thirty-three today; and a firm date for Sunshine to come and live with them, permanently, if not quite yet officially, one month from now to the very day. This last fact, in truth, eclipsed the significance of either the fatal wounding of the Tory government or the dawning of Chrissie's birthday. Sunshine was coming, and in the heavenly calm of the sunny little garden, Kim clinked her glass of cold rosé against Chrissie's and said, 'Cheers, my darling, here's to two becoming three,' then leaned in and wiped away the imprint of scarlet lipstick she'd left on Chrissie's cheek. Rocco was coming along soon, with Julia and Sol, but Kim's early arrival had been a treat, because these two women were rarely together alone; their friendship was long-lived and solid, but it seemed bound by the rules of the pack – or possibly, thought Chrissie now, the rules of Julia.

Chrissie had met Kim when Rocco did, at an early Lineman gig years ago, in the Union Chapel in Islington. Kim was writing it up for the *Guardian* in a piece about emergent bands, and she and Rocco had had a kind of epiphany when their eyes met, which was weird they all said, because although Rocco was a great drummer, he was such a runty little bloke, skinny in an undernourished way, with the pale skin of a nocturnal stoner. But there it was, love at first sight, and Kim let him continue to be himself, but somehow made him better at the same time. She'd reined in his worst excesses and encouraged his best ones. Rocco adored her, and so he should, they all thought. She was a clever, kind and funny friend, phenomenally well-connected in the industry, and also raven-haired and red-lipped, wore velvet coats and leopard-print trousers, and ankle boots with stiletto heels in which she walked with remarkable ease, as if she'd been born wearing them. Chrissie was longing for Sunshine to meet her, and she said this now, and Kim said, 'Oh, me too her; she sounds so much like my kind of kid.'

Chrissie smiled. 'Yeah,' she said, thinking of Sunshine with a small pulse of anxiety, wishing she could press a fast-forward button to a time when she knew precisely what kind of kid she was.

'I never wanted babies,' Kim said. 'Well, you know that, right? Me and Rocco, I dunno, there's already so many people on the planet, and anyway we just got really quickly into a way of only pleasing ourselves.'

'I know, you do it in fine style,' Chrissie said, and they both laughed, and then Kim looked serious and said, 'But adopting this little girl – it's the coolest thing you could do, Chrissie, it's completely right.'

'Thanks,' Chrissie said, lightly.

'No, seriously—' Kim leaned forwards, and slid her shades down the bridge of her nose to see Chrissie more clearly '—it's an astounding thing, I keep thinking about it, about her, and what her life could have been, and what it *will* be, with you and Stu. It's a generous, humane, incredibly cool thing to do.'

Chrissie nodded, but said, 'Y'know, don't you, that I desperately wanted to get pregnant? I'd have certainly had my own baby, if I could have done. Makes me feel awkward, accepting all your praise.'

Kim sat back again, pushed her sunglasses into place, took another deep drink of wine. 'Could've, would've, should've,' she said, waving a manicured hand, dismissing Chrissie's protest from the space between them. 'Don't underrate your motives, sweetheart. I'm so looking forward to watching this girl grow up with you as her mum.'

And then the others arrived. Chrissie and Kim heard the doorbell ring, heard Stu call to them – unnecessarily, because they weren't moving from their sunny idyll – 'I've got it, girls.' They heard laughter and chat and then Kim said, 'I give her twenty seconds,' but it was slightly less than that before they heard the unmistakable sound of Julia's heels moving smartly through the flat to the garden. The glass doors were propped wide open, and they framed her as she stood and surveyed the scene, wide-eyed, as if it beggared belief that they'd dared start without her.

Julia, Chrissie's oldest, though not always best, friend from their Liverpool days, was possessive of their friendship, yet sometimes careless of it. Now, for example. Annoyed by Kim's early arrival, certain she'd missed something important, Julia directed her ice-blue gaze at Chrissie and said, '*There* you are,' as if she'd been looking for an hour, then, 'We need to talk, I think. Happy birthday, by the way.'

Chrissie and Kim exchanged a quick look, which further maddened Julia, then Chrissie said, 'Talk about what? Come and sit down, Jules, there's a glass for you here,' and Julia trip-trapped in her lovely silver sandals across the small area of decking and down towards the sunny spot under the lilac tree, where Chrissie stood to receive two glancing Gallic kisses – the hallmark of her Frenchness for as long as Chrissie had known her, along with the shrug and the occasional, usually strategic, lapse into French.

Kim remained seated, but she raised her glass and said, 'Hey,' and the two women looked at each other through the dark amber lenses of their sunglasses, and smiled. Kim liked Julia, but didn't love her. Chrissie loved her, but didn't always like her. This was the difference. She pulled the wine from the ice bucket on the floor and poured a glass for Julia, who lifted it, and held it up for the others to reach forwards and clink.

'*Santé*,' Julia said.

'*Santé*,' said Chrissie.

'Cheers,' said Kim. 'So, Jules, just hazarding a guess, but do you need Chrissie to yourself for this chat?'

'Oh, I'm sure not . . .' Chrissie began, but Julia said, 'Well, it *is* about Sunshine, and it *might* be confidential,' which was only her way of asserting pre-eminence over Kim, as First Friend, but alarmed Chrissie enough for her to say, 'Oh God, what?'

'*Chérie*,' Julia said, patting Chrissie's arm, 'what I mean is, I have a question, and your answer might be confidential.' She looked regretfully at Kim, who said, 'Sure, whatever, I'll go join the boys,' and she gave Chrissie a friendly wink, and said, 'See you soon, darling,' and left them at the table.

Chrissie said, 'Jules, for God's sake, was that necessary?' and Julia gave that small, pretty shrug of the shoulders and said, 'You made me and Sol referees, not Kim and Rocco.'

And of course this was true, because Julia and Sol were parents themselves, and as such had seemed better qualified to answer the myriad questions that had to be asked by Nancy

Maitland and Angela Holt; rigorous, probing questions about their friends' habits and histories and their likely ability – or otherwise – to cope with the pressing needs of a displaced child. Chrissie had never asked Julia about the specifics. It would have been intrusive, not to say paranoid. And anyway, she'd trusted her friends to give a good account, and clearly had been right to, for here they were, on the brink of parenthood. 'So?' Chrissie said now. 'Shoot.'

'Well, it's a phrase Angela once used on us,' Julia said. ' "Sunshine and her little suitcase full of problems".' She drew speech marks in the air and pulled an ironic expression.

'Oh, right,' Chrissie said. 'Yeah, she can be really patronising, but Stu always tells me she means well.'

'Well anyway,' Julia said, 'I find it goes through my mind, that phrase, and Angela asked us things such as how we thought you'd cope, and whether you'd turn to your friends for support, y'know, and I presume she meant when the suitcase gets opened and the problems spill out.'

'Huh,' Chrissie said. She blew a strand of damp hair from her hot face, then pushed it all back, a tousle of blonde, and stuck her Ray-Bans on her head to hold it in place. 'It's so warm! I feel like having all my hair cut off.'

'Do not do that,' Julia said, very gravely.

Chrissie laughed. 'So, yeah,' she said. 'I think Angela uses the suitcase analogy on everyone, to be honest. It's only her way of saying we might be in for a rocky ride.'

'So-o,' said Julia, 'now that Sunshine is actually coming, I think you and I can talk about the problems in the suitcase, *oui*?'

Chrissie looked at her. 'No,' she said, and then more firmly, 'Julia, no.'

Julia pouted like a spoilt child, then said, 'I don't see why. I've always told you everything.'

'Oh, come on! This is totally different.'

'How is it different? You know something that I don't. If the shoe was on the other foot, I'd tell you.'

'Julia, listen,' Chrissie said. 'I'll never tell you what Sunny's file says. Never. It's her story to tell, if ever she wants to.'

'Pah,' Julia said. She downed her wine and held the empty glass out for more.

'Pah?' Chrissie reached for the dwindling supply of rosé and topped her up. 'What's that supposed to mean?'

'It means, what new-age twaddle! "It's her story to tell" – give me strength! Whose line is that? Because it's not yours.'

Chrissie smiled. 'Well, yeah, OK, I'm only quoting Angela. But, look, it's true – it *is* Sunny's story, and it's private.'

'I just think,' Julia said, swirling her wine, gazing into the whirlpool, 'that sharing Sunny's story with your closest friend would be a help, to me, as well as to you and Stu.'

'How would it help you?'

'I mean, help me understand Sunshine.'

'That's the thing though, we don't want her defined by a list of issues outlined in a Manilla file.'

'But aren't there things we *should* know?'

Chrissie stared. The penny dropped. 'For your own safety, you mean?' she said, flatly.

Julia returned the stare. 'Maybe. I'm thinking about Juno, she'll be her new playmate, and if we knew Sunshine's history, maybe we could avoid, y'know, flashpoints.'

Chrissie was silent. Julia, who for all their friendship had never known when she'd gone too far, said, 'I mean, has she witnessed violence, and will that make *her* violent? Has she witnessed abuse? Cruelty?'

Chrissie took a long breath. 'Sunny is a little girl who's had a difficult start, but for the past year she's been in a loving foster home, with John and Barbara. They might not be my cup of tea, but I can see they love Sunshine, they really do.'

'Ah, but they don't want to adopt her, do they?'

'Enough, Julia.'

'No, seriously though, why don't they want to keep her?'

'Jesus, Jules! They've fostered for ten years now; it's an income stream for them, it's a way of life. And anyway, you can't just decide to keep a foster child; that's not how the system works. I'm just saying, John told me they haven't been able to love all the children who've passed through, but they do love Sunshine. Anyone would, is what he said. No one who knows her can fail to love her.'

She'd enjoyed her talk with John. They'd met in Highgate Wood, Barbara and John having driven up from Whitstable with Sunshine to spend a Sunday afternoon with them. On their own turf, Chrissie had discovered she felt less self-conscious of how little she knew about being a mother. Also, she'd found, in John, some wise and patient counsel. They'd sat on a bench and watched Barbara and Stuart coach Sunshine as she navigated the wooden jungle gym in the playground, and Chrissie had said, 'How long did it take them to love each other?'

'Ah, now,' John had said, 'I don't think that's a useful line of questioning, my dear.'

'You did say, ask anything.'

He'd smiled. 'I did, and what I can say is that Sunny is completely lovable, and so are you, and any early difficulties will be ironed out quickly enough.'

Chrissie had said, 'I want her to love me like she loves Barbara.'

'She'll love you more. You'll be her mummy.'

'Is it going to be tough, saying goodbye?'

'Oh, well, you always hold a bit of yourself back, I suppose.

We're doing a job, caring for these kiddies. Barbara can be a bit possessive now and again, she finds it hard if a child stays with us a while, like Sunshine has. And you can't not love Sunshine, when you get to know her.'

'Does Barbara think I'm useless?'

John had turned his mild grey eyes upon her in surprise. 'Is that what you think?'

'Sometimes, yeah.'

'She thinks no such thing. And I think Sunshine is a very lucky girl.'

'Well,' Chrissie had said, 'I think we're luckier. Really, I do.'

Now, in the garden, Julia put down her glass and gave her friend a rueful smile. 'Sorry, *chérie*,' she said. 'Sorry, really I am. I don't want to cast a cloud over your lovely little Sunshine. I just can't help wondering what you know that you haven't told me, and it drives me slightly crazy. But I'll stop, OK? I really will.'

'Thanks,' Chrissie said. 'Appreciate it.'

'Friends?'

'Always.'

'Love you.'

'Love you too.'

'I'll go and fetch Kim,' Julia said. 'And the boys. And more wine.' Then she stood and walked back into the flat, leaving Chrissie to fume, quietly.

This is what Chrissie and Stuart knew, that Julia didn't, and it really wasn't much.

Sunshine was believed to have been born to the same young woman who'd left her at a housing office in South East London approximately two years later.

There were no records of the child's birth, and the father was unknown – that is, the mother hadn't disclosed his identity.

Wherever and however they had lived, mother and child seemed well, but when the young woman presented herself at the housing office, she said, 'This is Sunshine, please will you keep her safe?'

In the notes that were cobbled together from the testimony of a housing officer, someone had written that the mother was 'impassive and resigned', while the child was 'silent and somewhat anxious', which struck Chrissie as heartbreaking; this small girl, a little victim of circumstance, worrying quietly as her known world came to an end.

Without a paper trail, no one knew the child's date of birth, but judging by her size, her speech and the number of milk teeth she had, she was believed to be about two years old. She was given a birthday of 6 March, which was the date she was taken into care.

She showed no signs of physical abuse, and there was clear evidence of attachment between her and the mother, but when Sunshine was taken by the hand and led into an office, the young woman, who'd been asked to follow, turned on her heel and left the building. Outside, and on the busy street, she was immediately lost from view, swallowed by pedestrians and traffic.

All of this was in Sunny's notes, her Form E, the unemotional, official account of what little was known about her previous life. Brendan had brought it on one of his visits. There wasn't much there, it hadn't taken long to read and absorb, but one lovely late afternoon, not long after Chrissie's birthday gathering, Angela Holt dropped in on Chrissie and Stuart to lay this short history on the line once more. It was a sunlit Friday, and there was a chicken roasting in the oven, white wine chilling in the fridge, and Angela's visit was not exactly unwelcome, though certainly unexpected. But she wanted them to listen to what she had to say, she said, and, also, she'd brought them something to read. Sunshine's case was an unusual one, she wanted to stress. It was rare indeed to have such scant information about a child in care and her birth mother; their life together had been well below the radar. Everything they knew had been gleaned from that one and only opportunity in the local housing office, and then they'd taken charge of Sunshine, but lost track of the young woman.

'So, Sunshine was not quite, but almost, a foundling,' Angela said.

Foundling. Such an ancient term, and so incongruous, somehow, in the white-walled contemporary setting of their urban living room. Chrissie liked it, it gave her a shiver of hope, it meant that Sunshine was waiting to be discovered; that not every detail of her emotional and physical history was already written in indelible ink on the notes that travelled ahead of her. Form E, Form F, Matching Panels, Approval Panels, Care Orders. These new words were part of Chrissie and Stuart's vocabulary now; together, the two of them were knee-deep in a morass of unavoidable bureaucracy. Yet, there were gaps in the information on Sunshine's paperwork, and this seemed, to Chrissie, not a failure, but a triumph; it left some scope for uncomplicated happiness.

Angela said, 'So, I'm here – as you know – as your social worker, not Sunny's, because I want you to be completely informed about possible legacies.'

'Legacies?' Stuart said.

'Emotional,' Chrissie said to him, rolling her eyes. 'Not financial.'

Angela frowned and said, 'I do feel you occasionally make light of some very serious matters,' and it was like a bucket of cold water being chucked at them.

Chrissie said, 'Oh, no, Angela, we're absolutely not making light of anything,' and they'd sat there, solemn and chastened, listening to how children with a chaotic start in life could learn a kind of early – and very detrimental – self-sufficiency.

'Yes,' Chrissie said. 'They're liable to withdraw.' They were hearing nothing from Angela that they hadn't already heard at the pre-adoption workshops, but she thought about what she knew of Sunshine, with whom they'd now spent a significant amount of time; she seemed an uncomplicated, open-natured child – expressive, sociable, affectionate.

'To a degree,' Angela said. 'But also, hyper-vigilant, hyper-alert. They learn very early on that other people can't be trusted to meet their needs.'

Chrissie and Stuart remained completely silent. Angela waited, then said, 'It can take time to undo the damage of the past. A bright smile and willing spirit is all very well, but—'

'You think it won't be enough,' Chrissie said.

'I know it won't.'

'But you don't know what Sunshine's previous experiences have been,' Chrissie said.

Angela raised her eyebrows, as if a challenge, however mild, was the last thing she'd expected. 'It's a fair assumption that Sunshine led a chaotic life before she was fostered.'

'But we'll get there, right?' Stuart said.

'I hope so, I just want you to be fully aware of the challenges.'

'Oh,' Chrissie said, 'we're aware all right, copy that, message received, loud and clear.' She could feel Stuart looking at her, and she wouldn't look back, because he'd be giving her his 'pipe the hell down' face, and she didn't wish to pipe down; she wished to express some of what she was feeling.

Angela wore her usual unreadable expression. 'I'm not trying to undermine you,' she said.

Chrissie sighed. 'Look,' she said, 'Sunshine seems to me to have a great capacity for happiness.'

Angela nodded, but it was a non-committal gesture; acknowledgement of Chrissie's opinion, not agreement with it.

'And she appears to trust Barbara and John.'

'To a degree, yes.'

'What are you saying?'

'Only that you've had some experience of Sunshine's life in her foster home, but the bigger picture is probably more complex.'

Stuart said, 'We're not deluded, Angela.'

'No, I don't mean to imply that you are.'

'So, what are you saying?' Chrissie said. 'Please. Just be clear. What do we need to know?'

Angela said, 'You need to know that Sunshine may have had a very difficult start to her life, and as a result might have some of that negative self-sufficiency we've discussed. If she has difficulties with attachment, you might find that tougher than you realise.'

'She seems thoroughly attached to Barbara,' Chrissie said.

'Yes, she's done well, but it doesn't follow that you won't experience problems.' She was digging around in her leather briefcase while she spoke, and as she finished she produced a slim book, which she handed to Chrissie.

'I'd like you to read this,' she said. 'It might help you manage your expectations, further down the line.'

Chrissie read the title. *The Primal Wound: Understanding the Adopted Child.* She looked at Angela. 'Excuse me?' she said. 'Primal wound?'

'Yes, an important book,' Angela said, deaf to the dismay in Chrissie's tone. 'It's about the adoptee experience, not the adopter's. A lot of the problems I've seen come from adoptive parents who don't give enough credence to the child's earliest abandonment traumas,' Angela said. 'I'm simply trying to arm you with information.'

Chrissie flicked through the first few pages while Angela talked. Her eyes fell on the words, *What if the most abusive thing which can happen to a child is that he is taken from his mother?*

She looked up at Angela. 'Is this a counsel of despair?' she asked.

'Hey,' Stuart said, taking the book away from her. He placed it quietly on the coffee table, trying to convey 'thank you, we'll certainly read it later' in his expression and body language.

'Not at all,' Angela said, bristling now. 'It's research and advice founded in realism. I personally think it's extremely useful.'

'But you "personally" are not adopting a child, Angela,' Chrissie said. 'So, you "personally" can look at the process from a purely academic perspective.' Her voice was perfectly controlled; she felt entirely justified by the anger rising in her chest. There was a difficult silence. Then, 'I've only glanced at one page,' Chrissie said, 'and I already have the impression that there'll never be anything Stuart and I can do to fully make up for Sunshine's trauma.'

Angela nodded. 'Precisely,' she said. 'The primal wound of the title.'

'Angela,' Stuart said, 'is there anything else you think we need to know about Sunshine right now?'

She shifted in her seat, looked at her watch, gathered her papers. 'No,' she said, a little testily. 'I think that's all, for now.'

'Does Brendan know you're here?' Chrissie asked. 'Does Nancy?'

Angela bridled. 'Of course they do, Chrissie. This is a professional visit, but I might add, I don't need Brendan or Nancy's permission to visit you.'

'It's just, they both seem more positive than you about Sunshine, and our chances of success.'

Angela looked at Chrissie without speaking, then stood up.

'Manage your expectations,' she said, then. 'That's all I'm saying.'

Chrissie met her eyes. 'Noted,' she said.

After Angela left, Chrissie sat alone in a kind of churning solitary silence while Stuart poured them each a glass of wine, and the moment he came back in she launched into her grievance.

'It's as if she's willing us to fail! She doesn't know any more about Sunshine's early infancy than we do. And it's not as if she's ever been that supportive, right? I've always had the feeling she doesn't rate us; not the way Nancy does. Two musicians in charge of a small child? What a preposterous idea!'

'We're way past having to worry about Angela's preconceived prejudices,' Stuart said.

'Are we though? She could call it off whenever she likes, and she seems to be going all out to make me feel crap.'

Stuart sat down next to her. 'She's not.'

'Stu, you surely have to admit that this—' she indicated the book on the table in front of them '—beggars belief? And why's she waited until now? I just think she's taken against us.'

'Honestly, Chrissie?' he said. 'I know where you're coming from, but I do think she means well, and she's just trying to, I dunno, widen our understanding or something?'

'Oh, well, of course you do, Mr Nice Guy, always seeing the best motives in people. Take a glance at it, though. See how quickly it makes you feel worse than useless.'

He heaved a sigh and took a drink. 'Don't read it then. But there'll be some insight in there, or else she wouldn't have given it to us.'

Chrissie snorted.

'No, really,' Stuart said. 'And look, we probably *should* acknowledge all that stuff, the sense of loss, y'know, the—'

'Primal wound,' Chrissie said, savagely.

Stuart looked at her. Her misery was manifest, but really, what was there to be unhappy about?

'We're going to be fine, we three,' he said. 'And Angela Holt has nothing to gain by sabotaging our adoption of Sunshine. She wants this to work as much as we do.'

'Yeah,' Chrissie said, with a short laugh. 'I'm sure she does, just so long as she can suck every drop of joy out of it first.'

She was slouched on the low sofa, wearing the Chrissie Stevenson uniform of black T-shirt, cropped jeans, black Converse sneakers. When they'd first applied to adopt, she'd asked Nancy whether she should dress differently, more respectably. She was aware that being a singer in a band was hardly the stable, conventional profile that the adoption agency would be looking for. But Nancy had said, goodness, no, we want you just as you are. Stuart would always remember that, because it's what he'd thought too, the first time he saw her, and every time he'd looked at her since. *I want you just as you are.* She looked at him over the top of her wine glass.

'What?' she said.

'Give us a smile.'

She did, a little reluctantly.

'What are you thinking?' he said.

She laid her head on the back of the sofa and looked at the ceiling.

'I'm thinking, who would name a girl Sunshine, then give her away?'

～

Asha wasn't used to busy roads, or pavements crowded with people, but she had a way of containing herself, a kind of innate poise, that seemed to create a forcefield around herself and

Sunshine, so that they could move hand-in-hand through the street, unobstructed and largely unobserved. The child's hand in hers was soft, and warm, and full of trust, and why would it be anything else? Mistrust wasn't something she'd had to learn yet.

More than anything, Asha didn't want Sunshine to be afraid. This was a new beginning for them both, and Sunshine was so young, blessed with an open heart and a lovable nature; anyone would be lucky to call her their own. She was destined to live the happiest of lives. But they'd set out in moonlight, and walked for miles – Sunshine wound tight into a wrap of fabric, sleeping against Asha's chest – before being offered a ride in a lorry from a long-distance driver who'd been carrying sacks of dried chickpeas from Algiers to London. They'd climbed out in a place she called Peckham and he called Peck Ham. He hadn't wanted to leave them there. It wasn't nice, he'd said. He'd wanted to take them to Buckingham Palace, for that was a place fit for a beautiful girl and her beautiful child, he said. But Asha was working to a plan, so she'd thanked him, and stood respect-fully, with her head bowed in gratitude, as he'd driven away. Then she'd screwed up all her courage, and walked into the housing office, and said to the first sympathetic face, 'This is Sunshine, please will you keep her safe?'

She hadn't looked back, because she was determined to let her go.

This was the best thing for them both, and she knew Sunny would be cared for, because she had a friend whom Asha knew would never let her down.

5

Chrissie drove to Barnsley to show Diana and Doug the video of Sunshine, and when it finished, Doug said, 'She looks like a grand little lass,' and Diana stood up and rushed from the room. Chrissie followed and found her crying in the kitchen. Real crying, shuddering sobs, not a sniffle that could be excused as hay fever or the start of a cold.

'Mum,' Chrissie said. She was appalled, truly. Had she ever seen Diana cry? Witnessing this now, she believed she never had. Diana was a model of immaculate control, her emotions kept in permanent check like her twenty-six-inch waist and the incipient grey parting that would never, ever, be allowed to take hold. Now, she had her face in her hands, and made a keening sound like a wounded deer. Chrissie reached for her and Diana stepped to the side, out of range.

'I'm all right,' Diana said, irritated. 'I just need a minute. Go and talk to your dad,' so Chrissie went back to the front room, where Doug was rerunning the video.

'She looks a livewire,' he said, smiling, keeping his eyes on the screen.

Chrissie sat down next to him. 'What's up with Mum?'

'Oh, take no notice; she's all churned up.'

'But why?'

Doug looked away from the television and at his daughter. 'Now then, if I could answer that question, Christine, don't you think life would've been more straightforward this past forty years?'

Chrissie gave a small laugh. Her dad said, 'She's a complicated woman, your mother.'

'No, I know, it's just—'

'Yes,' Doug said. 'You thought this would make her happy. And I think it does, Christine, that's the bugger of it – I think she *is* happy.'

'Has she said so?'

'She hasn't said she's not,' Doug said. They heard her now, giving a couple of little coughs as she came back down the long hallway from the kitchen, letting them know she was coming in and they must stop talking about her. Doug played the video again, watched Sunshine shake her dark-brown curls and turn to the camera, and run towards it.

'She's very sweet,' Diana said. She was standing in the open doorway now, and the unspoken family rule was, always pretend she'd never left, always pretend she hadn't been angry or bleak or distant; never, ever pass a remark. Once, when Chrissie was only six, maybe seven, she couldn't quite recall, but anyway she was very young, and they'd been to the seaside for a week, and were driving home, and a long stretch of one of Diana's inexplicable black moods seemed to finally have shifted from shade to light, so that Chrissie, who had quietly suffered through this long bout of maternal withdrawal, had said in a voice full of hope, 'Oh! Are you happy again now, Mummy?' and the subsequent furious silence had lasted another whole day and a half. So, Doug and Chrissie, all these years later, were pitch perfect in their responses. Neither of them looked at Diana. Doug said,

'She is; she's a bobby-dazzler,' and Chrissie just nodded, and smiled at her little girl's unclouded face.

They had fish and chips from Pickerings, the same chip shop they'd always used, the one little Christine used to walk to every Friday night with Doug, for two haddock, one sausage, one chips and three pots of mushy peas, wrapped. It really wasn't Diana's scene – 'too Northern,' she said – but over the years she'd endorsed the ritual without exactly embracing it. She didn't eat much, on any day of the week; she'd had a difficult relationship with food since failing a screen test aged eighteen at Pinewood Studios because – she was told – the camera added half a stone and that made her about a stone too heavy, and although nothing had ever come of her big-screen ambitions, she'd never been able to let go of the possibility, so meeting and marrying Doug Stevenson and moving from Buckinghamshire to Barnsley didn't mean she was about to start eating chip butties and going to hell in a handcart. Therefore, on Friday evenings, she stayed at home and laid the table – a linen cloth, good china, a hock glass for herself and a tankard for Doug – and drank a quick, large vodka and lime to take the edge off her hunger before they got back. At the meal, she never had chips, but liked the white flesh of the haddock from inside the batter, and was a Southern convert to the special Northern qualities of a pot of mushy peas. But she would always stop when her plate was still more than half full, pushing it away moodily as if she already regretted her weakness, waiting for Doug to light a cigarette for her, so that through the soft focus of her own cloud of smoke, she could watch her husband and daughter wipe their plates clean with triangles of bread and butter.

Chrissie, walking now to the chippy with her dad, listened to him while he got a few things off his chest about Diana, her moods, the ups, the downs, the in-betweens. This was one of Chrissie's functions here, not to advise, just to listen, so that Doug had the catharsis of complaining bitterly to the one other person in the world who knew Diana almost as well as he did, and still loved her unreservedly. He'd suggested she join his golf club, he was saying now; he'd said the ladies' section would welcome her warmly, but she'd told him she'd rather drink bleach. He'd been hurt by this, but the story made Chrissie laugh and ask him why he'd want Diana along spoiling his fun anyway, so Doug saw it through Chrissie's eyes instead and laughed too, and agreed. She felt so glad to be with him, her arm tucked through his, letting his comfortable voice and the familiar streets take her spinning back through time to childhood. At school she'd been considered posh. She'd had piano lessons and elocution classes and they lived not in one of the warrens of sooty terraced council houses, but in a rather magnificent detached stone house off Keresforth Hall Road, and Diana – Mrs Stevenson, of course, to Christine's school friends – was glamorous and remote, and when she spoke it was like a voice from the BBC, *parst, clarss, barth, parth.* But there was nothing posh about Doug; he was pure Barnsley, and all his considerable success and trappings of wealth would never alter the way he sounded or the way his mind worked. He'd dodged the pits, trained as a plumber, called himself a 'plumbing engineer' and went on to grow a company and make a mint. He had good cars, camel coats and Cuban cigars, and Diana had whatever she wanted, not that it was ever enough. The town had wanted him for mayor, and Diana might have liked being First Lady, but he couldn't stand local politics, or the necessity of attending fêtes and factories, and shaking hands with folk he didn't know. Chrissie was proud of her dad, loved him in a restful, uncomplicated way, but she saw his limitations, and the yawning differences between him and her clever, dissatisfied, thwarted mother. Their marriage had been a useful blueprint, Chrissie always said, for how not to do it.

You never quite leave it behind, though, she thought now; Diana's unfathomable moods, Doug's helpless cheerfulness, the vegetal slowness of an empty afternoon, the unexpected claustrophobia of being only three people in a big house – these things would be with her until the end of her days. Good God, how happy she'd been to live in student squalor with her new American boyfriend, finding her way, writing and singing her songs, giving the finger to convention and respectability. Yet part of her would always not mind walking on eggshells in the childhood home. Part of her would always accept it was disappointing that her dad couldn't stand tall between her and her mum. Part of her would always be absurdly happy to breathe the salt and vinegar fumes of a hot newspaper parcel from the fish and chip shop.

Later, when they'd eaten and the plates were cleared away and Doug, at Diana's behest, had opened a second bottle of Mosel, she said, 'I want you to know I'm proud of you, Christine,' and this was astonishing. Chrissie and Doug looked at her, and Chrissie thought, that's the wine talking.

'Thanks, Mum,' she said, managing to contain her surprise, which was the Stevenson way.

'I hope it all goes well,' Diana said.

'Mmm, well, we've done everything we can. Nothing happens for months, then it all comes at you like a freight train.'

'You're ready for her, then?' Diana said.

'Think so.'

'And you finished her room?'

'It looks great, we've painted the floorboards and three walls white, and one wall blue, and Nina painted a huge yellow sun on the blue one, and Stu put some shelves up, for books, we've got a few already but we'll add more when we know what she likes. We don't want to make her conform to something we want her to be.'

'No,' Diana said. 'Don't be giving her a toy guitar, for God's sake.'

Chrissie smiled, and let that pass. 'We need to get to know each other properly.'

'Yes.'

'From Sunshine's point of view, this is all going to be pretty strange.'

'I suppose so.'

Chrissie hesitated. 'You OK, Mum?'

'Yes, why wouldn't I be?'

'I don't know. It's just, you seem . . .' She stopped.

Diana gave a small smile. 'I'll tell you what it is, Christine.'

Chrissie thought, here we go.

'If you'd given birth to this little girl, we wouldn't have been asked not to come, would we?'

Chrissie sighed. This again.

'I haven't asked you not to come, just not to come straight away.'

'Not to come for a fortnight. Isn't that right, Doug? We're baffled, I think it's fair to say.' This was classic Diana, claiming Doug for her team, without even asking. Doug, not knowing what to say, said nothing.

'Why are you baffled?' Chrissie said. 'I've told you what we've been told. I'm not making up some arbitrary rules that only apply to you.'

'I can't for the life of me see why we're on some sort of waiting list.'

'There's no waiting list, Mum, and if there was, you'd be top.' Chrissie chewed on her thumbnail and thought, *what's the rush*? Before she'd been told about the two-week rule, Diana had shown about as much interest in being a grandma as she had about joining the golf club.

'Then, if we're top of your list, why can't your father and I drive down when you've got her?'

'Because, as I've told you, it must just be me, Stu and Sunshine, for the first two weeks.'

Diana laughed grimly.

'What?' Chrissie said.

'You'll drive each other quite mad.'

Chrissie, who'd had precisely the same thought when Brendan had told them the drill, said, 'Well, I hope not, but we've been told it's necessary, to help Sunshine accept us as her parents.'

'Christine, she'll think you're her prison guards, not her parents.'

'Mum!' Chrissie laughed, reluctantly.

'Well, it's ridiculous.'

Chrissie said, 'I know, I mean, I know what you're saying, but we've been told it's best not to introduce her to too many people all at once, and for a while, it should just be the three of us.'

Diana said, 'It's up to you, though, Christine, isn't it?'

'You might think it should be, Mum,' Chrissie said, 'but it's not.'

Diana tutted at the madness of it all. 'You simply can't make us wait a fortnight,' she said.

'Can we see how we go? If the first week goes well, I'm sure it'll be fine to visit sooner.'

'And don't have Nina round before us, understood?'

Ah, Chrissie thought; there it was. Nina envy. Diana, waiting for confirmation, skewered her daughter with a steely gaze. Doug considered the contents of his beer glass.

'Right, no, of course not,' Chrissie said, taking the path of least resistance. The full force of her mother's will; always so much mightier than her own.

Diana nodded, satisfied. 'Right,' she said. If they'd been on the phone, she would have rung off at this point. Diana always rang off first. It was symbolic. It was an outward sign that she was living life on her own terms, and no one else's.

And then, before Sunshine came for good, Nancy stopped by to say she was leaving. Casually, as if it was no big deal, as if her imminent departure was already understood, she stood on the doorstep of Stu and Chrissie's flat, literally ready to go, her life packed up in a ninety-litre rucksack.

'What?' Chrissie asked, astonished, pained. 'Where? Why?' She felt like a teenager, being unexpectedly dumped when every-thing seemed to be going so well.

Nancy grinned. She wore walking boots and long shorts and her unruly hair was half-tamed into two Girl Guide plaits.

'India,' she said.

'What? God, Nancy. You never even mentioned this. Where in India?'

'Jaipur. I'm going to work with a charity for street children.' She let the lumpy rucksack slide from one shoulder and dropped it at her feet, but she'd already refused to come in; said she was off to Heathrow; said she was already late.

'Nancy,' Chrissie said. 'We'll miss you. We need you.'

She laughed. 'No, you don't,' she said. 'Angela's not going anywhere, and you have Brendan now too. They're a good team, Chrissie, they know you're perfect for Sunshine, and I know it's all coming together fast. It's a relatively simple process now, as long as you're happy and Sunshine's happy.'

'See, that's why I need you,' Chrissie said, in a kind of lament.

'You're so reassuring! Plus, I feel you're a friend, y'know? Or you could be a friend, now that we're not really clients any more. Can we stay in touch? How long will you be away?' She knew she was speaking too quickly, but Nancy just smiled and said, 'Yes, sure, and I don't know; it depends how it goes.'

She sounded so non-committal, thought Chrissie, and she wondered then if all Nancy's clients fell for her. She did have a very beguiling manner, all that faith in the fates, the power of predestination, and when those three other children were placed elsewhere, Nancy had comforted Chrissie and Stuart with the hundred-watt warmth of her remarkable, radiant positivity. Now, though, on Chrissie's doorstep, Nancy glanced at her watch as if she really shouldn't still be here, and Chrissie said, 'Oh, sorry, sorry, you need to go, well—' she broke off mid-sentence to give Nancy a quick, tight hug, then released her. 'Look after yourself, OK? We'll really miss you.'

Nancy delved into a capacious pocket on the side of her rucksack and pulled out an envelope. 'Sorry,' she said. 'Crushed it. It's only a card, just to say, oh, I don't know, well . . . anyway, you'll read it, I guess!'

They both laughed. Chrissie said, 'We would never have got this far without you. You've been . . . essential, Nancy – the positive to Angela's negative. I don't know what they'll do without you at that agency.'

'Didn't I tell you?' she said. 'Didn't I tell you your child was out there?'

'You did,' Chrissie said.

And then Nancy shouldered the rucksack, blew Chrissie a kiss, and strode away. Chrissie watched her until she turned the corner, towards the bus stop, then she went back indoors and opened the card. It showed a rising sun over a quiet sea, and inside Nancy had written, 'To Chrissie, Stuart and Sunshine, may bliss and blessings be heaped upon you. Be yourselves. Be happy.' She'd been a blessing herself, had Nancy Maitland; here for precisely the length of time they'd needed her, then gone, like Mary Poppins, to where she was needed more.

~

They were on the brink of a hectic week of planned activity, designed to blur the lines between life with Sunshine's foster family and her new life in North London, with Chrissie and Stuart, who were now officially known by Sunny as Mummy and Daddy, wonder of wonders, miracle of miracles. When Chrissie had first heard herself called 'Mummy', she'd wanted to turn cartwheels, string up the bunting, hire a brass band – or at the very least go away and write a song, but instead she'd managed to contain all the joy in a single glancing smile at Stuart. They'd driven to Whitstable to put Sunshine to bed, a contrived business, they thought, closely supervised as they were by Barbara and John, whose routines with Sunny were effective and established and – it seemed – unbending. 'Not like that,' Barbara said, when she looked in on Chrissie helping Sunshine put on her pyjamas, a task that surely had no wrong way, if the result was that she ended up wearing them. 'Two books, no more,' John said, when Stuart read the bedtime story. 'She'll have you there till midnight if you give her free rein.' And Sunshine, detecting the delicate tipping points of authority between the two sets of adults, darted sly, knowing looks, and pouted and fussed over whom she wanted to do what, and they all knew what she was up to, but even so, whenever she said, 'Mummy do it,' Chrissie's heart took flight.

Then there was the day Sunshine came for a sleepover. The Fosters – as Stuart and Chrissie had privately named Barbara and

John – had left the twins in the care of a favourite babysitter and booked a B&B off Muswell Hill Broadway, but they stayed a while with Sunshine in Chrissie and Stuart's flat, which comprised the ground and first floor of an Edwardian terraced house, in a long street lined with London plane trees. While Sunshine charged up and down the tiled hallway on a new scooter, Barbara went excessively quiet, and Chrissie felt sorry for her, assuming she was sad, until, sitting in the kitchen drinking tea, she finally said, 'It's like one of those places you see in magazines.'

'Oh,' Chrissie said, taken aback. 'Well, it's not usually this tidy.' They'd been running around polishing surfaces and plumping cushions before the visit, like teenagers cleaning up before their parents got home.

'I don't mean because it's tidy,' Barbara said. 'I mean, it's like a show home, this kitchen must've cost thousands?'

This was so brassy, so outrageous, that everyone laughed. Chrissie was confused. It was a standard North London two-bedroomed garden flat, bought – well, mortgaged – eight years ago on the proceeds of *Undying*, their third album. They'd done what they could with it, shopped thriftily in IKEA, like everyone else they knew, and felt lucky to live here, but it was only special because it was filled with their belongings, and the kitchen cabinets that Barbara so admired had been a holy terror to fit. They hadn't been able to afford a joiner, so they'd assembled them themselves at some cost to their sanity, and to this day the pan-cupboard door hung skew-whiff. Chrissie said, 'It's nothing special, Barbara, but we like it.'

'It's a lovely place,' John said. 'Modern. Not like our house. That's what Barbara means, isn't it, Barb?'

She nodded, but continued to eye up the fixtures and fittings, the knocked-through kitchen and dining room, the Swedish furniture, the double glass doors leading onto a small deck that dropped down two steps to a patch of grass and a brick patio just big enough for a table and four chairs. Nice enough, but nothing special, yet seeing it now through Barbara's eyes made Chrissie feel foolish, somehow; too preoccupied with style, as if a blond Scandi flat-pack dining table was proof that all her values were skewed.

Sunshine, though, was in a cheerful mood. She'd said, 'Hello, Mummy, hello, Daddy,' and submitted to a hug from each when they'd arrived. She loved her new scooter, and was pleased and amazed to be allowed to use it indoors.

'Your skirting boards,' John said, with vague distress, as he watched her go. She shouted, 'Whee!' and 'Beep-beep!' and John said, 'You can see how things are going to be; you'll not have a minute's peace,' but Chrissie and Stuart loved the racket; her voice was delightful to their ears, husky, with a sweet little break in it now and again. It belonged here, that voice; *she* belonged here.

'I's hungry,' she said, coming into the kitchen after exhausting the potential of the scooter, and eyeing the packet of biscuits on the table. Barbara said, 'You'll spoil your tea,' but Stuart offered Sunshine the packet, and she took one, very delicately, between her perfect little finger and thumb, then sat on John's knee to eat it, listening to the grown-ups talking, with her head tilted to one side like a blackbird. Chrissie and Stuart found it hard to look anywhere other than at her face, but she caught them at it once too often and cast her eyes down and shrank back deeper into John's comfortable old cardigan, pulling the two sides around her like a woolly cloak.

The Fosters were at last about to say their goodbyes, they were on the very threshold of the open front door, when Barbara said, 'Ooh, hang on, let's have a look at Sunshine's bedroom,' so they all trooped back in again and up the stairs to the room that until recently had been grandly called the music room, but only because Chrissie's keyboard and Stu's guitar collection were in there. They'd moved the guitars to their own bedroom, but the keyboard was still pushed against the wall, and somehow didn't look out of place. There was also a blue canvas bean bag and a hammock intended for toys, but currently hanging empty, between a bed post and a hook on the wall. There was a large round rug on the floor in rainbow stripes, and rainbow stripes on the bed linen too.

'Well, this is nice,' Barbara said, tightly. She picked up a cushion from the bed, and hugged it to her chest. 'And look,' she said, nodding at the painted sun. 'A sun, for Sunshine.' She looked as if she might cry, although this wasn't goodbye; they'd be back for Sunny tomorrow morning, to take her to Whitstable for a final two nights.

Sunshine looked around her, and went very still. They were all standing in the room, too many awkward adults with the silent child at the centre of them, and Chrissie was thinking, *please just go*, because until they did, there would remain this weird dynamic, this emotional volatility; Barbara and John's looming loss somehow heightened by the bright newness of the child's bedroom, and Sunshine herself, instinctively responding to the change in atmosphere, stepping now from one foot to the other like a highly strung pony.

Stuart said, 'What do you think, Sunny? Do you like it?'

She waggled her head from side to side, and pressed her lips into a hard line. 'No,' she said.

Barbara said, 'Now, Sunshine, this is going to be your room, just for you on your own. You won't have to put up with those silly boys any more,' which may or may not have been innocently meant, but without doubt it acted upon the child like the sudden release of a pin from a coiled spring, and she flew into startling, noisy action, shooting off towards the bed then throwing herself onto it, bouncing a couple of times, then jumping off again. She careered about the small room in a frantic circuit, bouncing like a billiard ball off the walls and shouting, 'This mine, and this mine and this is, and this is!', her little face red with exertion, her body shot through with a kind of uncontainable kinetic energy.

The adults watched her in uncertain silence, then Barbara said, 'Somebody's over-excited,' and John whispered to Stuart, 'She'll settle, just ignore her.' But Chrissie knew what it was, knew that the sunshine wall, the rainbow stripes, the bookshelves, the giant bean bag, the toy hammock waiting to be filled, meant nothing. The only thing of significance was this: Sunshine was a small girl, in an unknown home, with two sets of parents, one of the pairs all but strangers, and neither pair the originals. With a sudden searing wisdom, Chrissie understood this, and dropped to her knees to catch Sunny in her arms, just as she completed another feverish lap of the room. Chrissie held her still, and she let herself be held, breathing hard, keeping her body rigid, her arms by her sides. Barbara leaned in and said, 'Here, now,' but John tugged her away, and moved discreetly back towards the door.

'It's OK, Sunshine,' Chrissie said. 'It's OK.'

She felt the child's limbs slacken. Stuart mouthed at her that he'd see her downstairs, then gave her a thumbs-up: well done, nicely handled. Sunshine shifted her position, turning slightly to one side so she could fit her thumb in her mouth, and for a few moments, they stayed there in a precarious silence broken only by the damp chirrup of her sucking. Then she removed her thumb with a pop and asked, 'Where is mine sisters?'

*

Later, when Barbara and John were long gone to their B&B, and Sunshine was fed and bathed and fast asleep in their bed, and Chrissie and Stuart were at last alone, she finally told him. She was lying on the sofa with her head in his lap, Dusty Springfield soothing their souls through the speakers, and Stuart stared down at her, although her eyes were closed.

'Wow,' he said.

'Mmm.'

'Sunshine's missing past.'

'I know,' Chrissie said. 'It makes me sad to think there might be siblings out there.'

'Well, Brendan doesn't know about them, or Angela, or Nancy.'

'None of us know anything much. We should tell Brendan.'

'Sure, but look,' Stu said, searching for the bright side, 'it's not necessarily a bad thing, if she has a memory of her first family.'

'Isn't it?'

'No, not if her infancy was happy.'

'Why did she say "sisters", and not "mummy"?'

They were both silent for a while. Sisters. Who they were, where they were, what they meant to Sunshine . . . these unanswerable questions floated through their minds, as did the questions of who and where were her mother, her father, her grandparents. For Chrissie, there had been a kind of comfort to be found by the completeness of these absences. But that Sunshine should ask . . . well, had anyone known the child still thought of the significant people from her babyhood?

'What did you say?' Stuart said.

Chrissie opened her eyes. 'I said I didn't know where they were.'

It was only the truth, and it'd seemed the least she could do, answering Sunshine's direct question with a direct answer.

'Was she upset?'

Chrissie shook her head. 'Not at all. She just sighed.'

'Then what?'

'Then she said, "I's hungry," like she did before.'

Stuart smiled, remembering the gusto with which Sunshine had eaten the pizzas he'd made for dinner. The evening had gone smoothly, apart from her refusal to step back inside her bedroom, but that was fine, they said; she could snuggle down in their big bed and try her own bed another time. As for the rest, they'd been guided by her, because she, in turn, was guided by the habits laid down in her temporary Whitstable home. No messing about in the bath. Two books at bedtime. Bedside light off, hall light on, door wide open, and that was that. They'd hoped she'd come padding downstairs in her pyjamas, looking for them. It was almost disappointing not to have a disruptive first evening with her, Chrissie said. She was a bit institutionalised, Stu said; there was no fooling around at the Fosters'.

'Anyway, I decided not to make too much of it,' Chrissie said now. 'That's why I didn't say anything while Barbara and John were still here.'

'No, right.'

'Should I have mentioned it to them, though?' Chrissie said.

'No, it's none of their business, is it?' Stuart said. 'Not now, not really.'

'But perhaps she's said the same thing to Barbara and John, or to Brendan?'

'We'd know if she had,' Stuart said. 'It'd be in her notes.'

This was a good point, thought Chrissie. 'I'll talk to Brendan tomorrow. God, it was so strange, Stu.'

Stuart cupped a hand under her chin and tilted her face, connecting their eyes.

'Hey,' he said, 'maybe it was something about the way you held her.'

'What do you mean?'

'A memory, y'know, of a feeling she'd once had, when she was very young.'

Chrissie thought about Sunshine's tense body slackening against hers, the way she settled into the contours of Chrissie's body, as if she recognised the safety of it. It was natural enough to fill the gaps in the child's narrative with suppositions of neglect, hunger, loneliness . . . but perhaps there'd been comfort in her infancy too, and love, and trust. The person who'd named her Sunshine had good things in her heart, for certain.

'Maybe so,' Chrissie said now, to Stuart. He looked down at her, drew his fingers through her hair.

'And that's a good thing,' he said. 'I mean, good that Sunshine recognises a cuddle as comfort. Some kids don't. Some kids haven't been loved.'

'Mmm, sure, of course.'

'Right,' he said. 'And anyway, look, her past is less relevant than her future, and you're her mummy now; that kid has lucked out.'

On the turntable, Dusty in Memphis had faded to silence and the stylus was making its familiar muted protest as the record continued to spin.

'Mmm, I suppose so,' Chrissie said.

She got up off the sofa and lifted the arm of the record player, stopped the turntable, removed the LP and slid it into its sleeve. She looked at Stu, who was looking at her, waiting to hear what she had on her mind.

'Never mind,' she said. 'Let's go get some sleep.'

6

Sunshine came for good on the second Sunday in June. She was all packed and waiting when they arrived at the Whitstable house, sitting in the front room on a purple Adidas holdall, stuffed with her favourite clothes. Chrissie and Stuart were under strict instructions from Brendan to dress her in them, even if there was nothing there that they liked. She was very attached to her *little terror* T-shirt; she was wearing it now, and the same white leggings they'd seen her in before, which were so thin and worn you could see the pink flowers on her knickers, but Carl and Kevin were in their Sunday best, identical navy chinos and checked button-down shirts, and Brendan was there too, all smiles, although they were smiles of the social worker variety, a special breed of smile, more watchful than warm, Chrissie felt.

He helped load up the car with a few dog-eared books Sunny liked, and a small selection of her favourite playthings from the toy box, which couldn't be fully raided, because Sunshine's bed would soon be filled by another child, and after that, another, and the toys were needed for these new little children, whose names were still unknown. This is what Barbara said, yet it didn't stop her behaving as if she hadn't realised Sunshine was leaving; she was devastated, and she made sure everyone knew about it. John did the talking, trying valiantly to keep the tension from the room, but when Sunshine went to her foster mother for a goodbye hug, Barbara started to cry and had to be led out of the room by Brendan, leaving Sunshine – also now in floods – with John, who also looked very miserable indeed.

By the time they had her strapped into the car seat, clutching a flea-bitten stuffed monkey, everyone but Brendan was traumatised, and as they drove away, Chrissie and Stuart couldn't speak; if Barbara had phoned and said, bring her back, they would have done so at once, and with some relief. Sunshine's misery seemed bottomless; she cried and cried, and while Stuart drove grimly towards home, hoping never again to visit Whitstable, Chrissie reached back with an outstretched arm and tried ineffectually to comfort the sobbing child, until Sunshine found her own solution, stuck in her thumb, shoved the monkey up under her chin, and fell into a deep, deep sleep.

'Can we really do this?' Chrissie whispered, drawing back her arm and rubbing the stiffness out of it. 'I have to say, Stu, I'm terrified,' and she was, he could see that, her face was stricken, pale as ashes.

'Are you kidding me?' he said, digging deep. 'We were *made* to do this.'

Chrissie looked hopeless, helpless. 'She's lost two mothers now,' she said. 'And we're the people who've taken her away from a family she's grown to love.'

'Chrissie,' Stuart said, 'that, back there? It wasn't our fault, and it's over now, right? This is the start, this – me, you and Sunshine, in the car, driving home. We're all set now; it's cheese string central at our place, and Sunshine's going to be just fine.'

And it was, for a while. Sunshine woke up after an hour, and for the final part of the journey she answered their questions, made observations about the world outside her window – the pigeons, a man on a bike, and a red London bus. Then, unprompted, she sang 'The Wheels on the Bus' for them in her enchanting voice, and Chrissie turned to watch her, this sweet little stranger, their daughter. At home, they all stood on the pavement outside the house for a quiet moment, as if silently adjusting to their new circumstances. Then they went in and Sunshine stood passively while Chrissie unbuttoned her jacket and showed her the special low pegs, where all her coats would hang. She sat on a stool at the kitchen table and drank a small glass of milk, and solemnly ate half a banana, and agreed it was sensible to leave the rest for later. Then they all went up to her room to unpack her clothes, encouraging Sunny to help, to stack her T-shirts and shorts and skirts in the white chest of drawers, and hang her dresses and dungarees in the matching wardrobe, and for a while she helped, and then she said no, she wanted to show them her toys, which, apart from the monkey, comprised a skinny doll with changeable heads and hairstyles, and a small red plastic box filled with Lego pieces. So, they looked at her toys together, which for a short while seemed to please her, then her eyes took on that vacant, inward-turning look that Chrissie recognised from the time before and she stood up, looked wildly about her, then kicked the Lego box, scattering pieces under the bed, and started to cry fierce tears.

Stuart said, 'Hey, Sunny, sweetheart,' and reached for her, but she shrank from him and pressed her little palms into her eyes and stamped her feet, then simply flipped her lid. Everything that had been placed carefully in a drawer came out, in a blizzard of garments. She grabbed two fistfuls of socks and pants, and hurled them into Chrissie's face. She shouted, 'No, no, no!' when Stuart tried to contain the chaos and shove some of the clothes back again; she screamed piercingly and beat at him with her little hands, and shouted, 'Not there, no, not in that! In mine bag! In mine bag!'

In the end, they repacked her holdall, which calmed her. Then Chrissie picked her up and still she sobbed, but in a less committed way, and they went back down the stairs and into the living room. They sat on the sofa, stunned by events, Sunshine squashed close between Chrissie and Stuart. She plugged in her thumb and was perfectly quiet, apart from an occasional soft hiccup, which was all that remained, now, of the storm.

Brendan rang at four o'clock that afternoon, said he'd like to pop round, there was something he needed to talk to them about, nothing to worry them, but would tomorrow morning work? Chrissie, who took the call, walked away from the kitchen where Stuart was letting Sunny bash the keys of his laptop industriously with two rigid forefingers, because the sound it gave, and the effect of the strings of letters on the screen, was making her laugh.

'Things sound good there!' Brendan said, with bouncing good cheer.

'Yeah,' Chrissie said, amused and slightly rattled by his blithe cluelessness. 'Sunshine had a nuclear meltdown in her bedroom, kicked all her toys into touch, and now she won't go back in there, and she's insisted her clothes stay packed in her bag, but sure, otherwise, things are great.'

'Ah,' he said, 'OK, well look, she's a strong-minded little thing, and placement day's often challenging.'

Chrissie gave a small laugh. 'Made all the more challenging by that Shakespearean tragedy played out in Whitstable,' she said.

She heard him suck in his breath. 'Not the easiest handover,' he said.

'No.'

'It's impossible to judge how these things will go,' Brendan said. 'Try and see it as a positive thing, though, that Sunshine had a loving relationship with Barbara.'

'Yes, Brendan, we know the theories, but even so, you'll understand why I'm not Barbara's biggest fan right now.' Snippy. Sarcastic. Unyielding. She cursed herself even as she spoke, and was glad Stuart couldn't hear her, he'd hiss at her, 'Be nice!', because why would anyone risk antagonising the guy? But Brendan seemed disinclined to judge.

'Totally understand,' was all he said. 'And she's with you two now, not Barbara, and that's the very best outcome for her.'

That was kind, thought Chrissie.

'So, I'll call in tomorrow?' he said. 'About nine?'

'Oh, yeah, OK,' Chrissie said. 'What did you say it was about?'

'I didn't,' he said. 'I'll tell you tomorrow.'

'Right.'

'Don't worry.'

'No.'

'So, she won't go into her bedroom?'

Chrissie sighed. 'No, she seems appalled by the prospect, won't do it.'

'Can I make a suggestion?'

'Oh, God, feel free.'

'These early days, let her make some decisions, let her feel she has some control.'

'Right, yeah,' Chrissie said.

'It's not important whether her clothes are in a cupboard or in her holdall, right?'

'I suppose.'

'So, leave them in the bag, for as long as it takes.'

'It makes her presence here feel temporary, though.'

'Well, it's not temporary, is it? You're projecting your own insecurities there, Chrissie, and I'm not saying give her free rein. I'm just saying, well—'

'You're saying chill out.'

He laughed. 'More or less, yes.'

'See you tomorrow, then.'

'Great,' he said. 'And Chrissie?'

'Yeah?'

'You and Stuart are the best thing that's ever happened to Sunshine. Keep that in mind.'

She hung up, and when she did, she could hear Stu, playing his guitar, his old Martin acoustic, the one he'd been carrying when she first met him, the one that was always knocking around somewhere handy, somewhere within reach. She wandered back into the kitchen, and there they were, Stuart and Sunshine, each of them in a mellow mood, the poor, beleaguered laptop safe now on a shelf, and the child standing by Stuart, hypnotised by his fingers as they moved up and down the frets, playing something and nothing, a bluesy riff. He smiled at Chrissie, and paused his playing to hear what Brendan had had to say, but Sunshine looked at Chrissie and said, 'Look!' and pointed at the guitar. 'He can do this!'

'No way!' Chrissie said, and they all laughed. The child's face was bright and alight. She let Chrissie pick her up and place her on her lap, as she sat down, facing Stuart.

'Brendan said we're the best thing that ever happened to Sunshine,' she said.

Stu nodded. 'Cool. She's the next best thing that ever happened to me.'

Chrissie grinned. 'Schmoozer,' she said. 'Go on, play us a

tune, show us what you can do,' and Sunshine bounced herself up and down on Chrissie's knee.

'Yes!' she shouted. 'Make it again!'

That night they wilfully disregarded Barbara and John's bed-time routine and let Sunshine drift off to sleep on the sofa at what in Whitstable would've been teatime, and Chrissie and Stuart sat with her in the living room while she slept, played records, talked to their mothers, talked to each other, until she woke again at half past seven. Chrissie dreaded a scene, dreaded her panicking at the lack of Barbara or John, or the twin boys and their high jinks, but when Sunshine opened her eyes, she only smiled and rubbed her eyes with her small fists like a cartoon child then said, 'Hello, Mummy,' and Chrissie scooped her up for a cuddle then danced her around the room to 'Johnny B. Goode', and the child threw back her head and laughed then said, 'Daddy make it!' so they switched off Chuck Berry and Stuart played the song instead, and Chrissie sang the words. After that they had dinner together, and that was joy, pure joy. Not a cheese string in sight – although their fridge was stocked with emergency supplies – only Stu's spaghetti and meatballs, which Sunshine ate with a kind of wide-eyed wonder. She said, 'What it is?' and Chrissie said, 'It's spaghetti, and these are little balls of meat in tomato sauce.' She started to cut Sunshine's pasta into manageable strips, but the child went immediately bright red and shouted, 'No, Mummy!' so Chrissie stopped, and Sunshine's face returned to its normal creamy colour, and she smiled. Stu blew a long whistle.

'It's like watching the weather, looking at this kid,' he said. 'No wonder she's called Sunshine.'

'It's slippy,' Sunshine said, watching dolefully as each fork-ful of spaghetti ended in failure. 'What it is?' she asked again.

'Spaghetti,' Chrissie said.

'Pasghetti,' Sunshine said.

'Close enough,' Chrissie said. She reached across again with a knife and said, 'Look, let me cut it into little pieces, it's too long for you,' and again, the child looked stormy and said, 'Not little! Long!'

'OK,' Chrissie said. 'Watch me, see? Twirl a strand of it on your fork like this then get your face near the plate and suck it in.'

Dinner took over an hour, and she had tomato sauce in her hair, on her face, and all down her *little terror* T-shirt by the end, but she was happy, even though she'd asked for squash and found there was only water from the tap, or milk. She'd chosen milk, and had then taken the small tumbler handed to her by Stuart between her two hands, lending a kind of reverential air to proceedings. And this is what Chrissie knew she would never forget; Sunshine's eyes, as clear and complex as smoky quartz, watching them over the rim of the cup; her milky mouth, afterwards; her contented sigh when she swallowed her final mouthful of food and pushed away the plate.

There was a bottle of Valpolicella on the worktop that Chrissie and Stuart had been going to drink with dinner, but it remained unopened, because they couldn't bear to leave her out. Then they sang and danced to Stuart's guitar. He played 'Brown Eyed Girl', but she didn't want that; she wanted 'Johnny B. Goode' again and again and again. She squealed and clapped at Stu's Chuck Berry footwork, and by the time they packed up to go to bed, she was joining in with Chrissie at the chorus, in her enchanting honeyed-gravel voice, and Stuart said, 'Is it me, or does she sound like a baby Janis Joplin?'

And then she cried, at the threshold of her bedroom, so they all slept in the one big bed: Sunshine, out like a light; Chrissie and Stuart awake half the night, then deeply, profoundly asleep at 7 a.m., when Sunny sat up and announced, 'I's hungry.'

~

Brendan arrived on the dot of nine.

'Smells good,' he said, when Chrissie let him in.

'Pancakes,' she said.

She made as if to lead Brendan down the hall to the kitchen, but he said, 'Actually, Chrissie, if Sunshine's happily engaged in there, can we talk in another room?'

'Oh,' Chrissie said, stopping short. 'Sure.'

She was startled. His tone on the phone yesterday had been reassuring. She'd assumed he only wanted to see Sunshine in situ, or get their signatures on yet another document. She pointed, instead, to the open living-room door, and followed him in.

'What?' she said. 'Is there a problem?'

'Not really,' Brendan said, 'but something's happened that concerns you two and Sunshine.'

Chrissie sat down. She could feel her heart hammering, panic setting in. 'God, Brendan, what?' she said. The birth mother, she thought; the sisters. Sunshine hadn't mentioned them again since that moment in her bedroom, and when she'd told Brendan about it, he'd been emphatic, said there was absolutely no indication that Sunshine had siblings in the care system, said maybe Chrissie had misheard what Sunshine said and told her to disregard it. But still, she pictured them, regularly. Two little girls, she'd decided. Older than Sunny and lost in the world, wondering about their baby sister.

Brendan sat down next to her. 'Odd thing,' he said. 'Yesterday, a bag was left on a chair at the housing office in Peckham, the same place Sunshine was dropped off.'

'A bag?'

'This bag,' Brendan said. He opened his voluminous canvas satchel and pulled out a pretty drawstring bag in the palest of greens, decorated with exquisite white and yellow silk embroidery, depicting leaves and buds and branches and birds and, at their centre, the word Sunshine, stitched artfully in silver thread. Chrissie stared.

'Who brought this?'

'We have no idea.'

'What is it?'

'It seems to be a version of the memory box that we encourage birth parents to make for their children, before an adoption becomes final.'

'A memory box?'

He nodded. 'Bits and pieces from their early lives. Toys, cards, photos. They can help give adopted children a sense of themselves, and give the birth parents a feeling of connection with the child they're losing.'

'Right.' Chrissie's voice was tight. 'You guys and your theories.' The bag in Brendan's hand terrified her. 'Who found that?'

'One of the housing officers. It was left on a chair in the waiting area, and there was this too.'

He brought an envelope out of his satchel now, and from it withdrew a small piece of brown paper, a strip torn from the type of paper you might use for a parcel, tied up with string. In black ink, someone had written, *These items belong to a girl named Sunshine, please will you be sure she receives them?* The phrasing was elegant, the writing careful, beautiful, almost calligraphic. Brendan offered it for closer inspection, and Chrissie took it, read it, then said, 'What's in the bag?'

'I'll leave it with you; you and Stuart can have a look later.'

'Do you know what's in there?'

'I've had a quick look inside, but I didn't take anything out.'

'Tell me what you saw, then.'

'Chrissie, open it now if you like. I'm almost certain there's nothing in there to upset you. Just some things that obviously hold significance for someone, probably not significant now to Sunny, but, still, they're intended for her, and they're in your safekeeping, to show her when you think she's ready.'

He placed the bag on Chrissie's lap and she stared down at it, then said, 'It's very beautiful.'

'Yes,' he said, 'I've never seen anything like it.'

'But why now?'

'Yes.'

'Why on the very day she comes to live with us?'

'I know; we're asking ourselves the same thing.'

'And?' she snapped. 'What answers are you coming up with?' Christ, she thought, there's more Diana in me than I knew; nought-to-hostile in ten seconds.

'It looks like a security breach, I realise that. But it could just be coincidence.'

'A coincidence? That the day Sunshine starts her life with us, someone anonymously drops off a bag of memories?'

'I know.'

'Don't they have CCTV at the housing office?'

'They do, but it's of very limited scope; I doubt it'll shed a lot of light.'

No, thought Chrissie; and even if they found it, a grainy image of a figure leaving a bag on a chair wouldn't reveal to them who that person was, what they knew about Sunshine, why they had chosen her placement day to make this gesture.

'Do you think it was her birth mother?' she asked, and

Brendan opened his mouth to speak, but Chrissie said, 'It was, wasn't it? She left the bag in the same place she left Sunshine? Do you think?'

'Chrissie, we don't know. Try not to—'

Chrissie stood up. 'I need to talk to Stu,' she said, and Brendan hurriedly stood up, too.

'Call me, any time,' he said, but Chrissie didn't reply; she was walking out of the room, so he shouldered his satchel.

He was about to leave, but then, because he was unobserved, he lingered a little longer, drawn again to their mystifying wall of music, the stacked sound system, Stuart's glossy black guitar, a photograph of Chrissie onstage, standing at a microphone, a younger version of her present self but entirely recognisable: wild blonde hair; savage black eyeliner; a vivid smile.

He gazed at it all, quite lost for a few moments in their world, then he remembered himself, and tiptoed down the hall to quietly let himself out of the front door.

7

For a few hours, the memory bag sat unopened on a high shelf like a ticking bomb, until finally Stuart looked at Chrissie and she said, 'Yeah, OK,' meaning, let's defuse it. No point waiting for Sunny's bedtime before they had a look; sleep had been her response to stress today, and whenever the day had become fraught – and boy, had it ever – she'd just sucked her thumb and conked out, wherever she happened to be: the bottom step of the staircase; the coir mat by the front door; the terracotta tiles of the kitchen floor. Stu's pancakes first thing had been the day's great high point; her introduction to the species, which Stu – naturally – made the American way, thick and light and scattered inside with blueberries. He'd made mini ones for Sunshine, and stacked them in a pile of four, drizzled them with maple syrup, then sat back and watched while they blew her little mind. Chrissie had missed it, dealing with Brendan in the other room, but she'd arrived back in the kitchen in time for the first melt-down of the day, which was Sunshine's discovery that she couldn't wear her *little terror* T-shirt and white leggings, which were wet in the washing machine, after being plastered with last night's tomato sauce. Nothing else in the purple holdall would do, apparently, so she'd stayed in her pyjamas – a tiny replica

West Ham strip, in maroon and sky-blue nylon, with Dagen-ham Motors written on the front – until the other garments were dry, then screamed blue murder again when she finally got dressed, because they were wrong, wrong, wrong, but Chrissie and Stuart weren't sure what, in her furious distress, she was trying to communicate. Chrissie had taken them off her again, and she'd crawled under the kitchen table in only her pants, and glowered at them for a while through noisy tears, then knocked herself into oblivion by curling up and sucking her thumb.

This had kick-started a day of intermittent, unpredictable dramas, and by five o'clock, she was on her fourth shut-down of the day, fast asleep on the doormat, and in the blessed quiet of this hiatus, Chrissie and Stuart agreed to open the bag. Stu gingerly lifted the child and placed her on the seat of a big arm-chair in the living room, where she complained in her sleep but didn't surface, and Chrissie brought the bag, and the note that had come with it, down off the top shelf of the book case. She sat on the rug and looked up at him.

'I feel totally fucking terrified,' she said.

'Just open it, babe.' He dropped to his haunches next to her. 'Just tip everything out.'

The bag was beautiful, its embroidery faded with age, except for the silver lettering of *Sunshine*, which glittered in a newer, more contemporary thread. Even the drawstring was classy: a narrow black satin rope, which slipped readily from its loose bow, allowing her to pull the neck wide. She upended the bag, and shook it gently, so that three items dropped softly onto the rug before her.

A patchwork square of brilliantly coloured, embroidered silk, in the richest hues of red, purple, blue and cream.

A plain, flat, square, cardboard box with FOR SUNSHINE printed in capitals on the front and inside, a 7-inch Parlophone

Beatles single; 'Oh! Darling' on the A-side, 'Here Comes the Sun' on the B-side.

A black and white photograph, sealed into a heavy, ornate silver frame, of a young woman in a modest, knee-length, sleeveless dress, standing beside a big pram, the regal carriage type, in which a baby was sitting up and staring out of the picture with the same solemn eyes as the young woman, and an air of patient composure, as if her wisdom far exceeded her time on this planet. The baby in the pram and the young woman were posing for the photograph under the arching bough of an enormous oak, but neither of them smiled. The woman's arms hung by her sides. The baby's hands were folded demurely in front of her.

Chrissie moaned. Stuart reached out and touched her cheek. 'Hey,' he said, 'it's OK.'

She gripped the photograph at the edges of the frame and stared at it. 'Look at them though,' she said, but Stuart had picked up the single and was slipping it from its yellowing paper liner.

'This is extraordinary,' he said, and peered more closely at the printed label. 'Ah, pressed in Portugal, that explains it.'

'Explains what?' Chrissie said.

'This forty-five,' he said, not looking at her, but gazing at the record, holding it up to the light, examining it for scratches. 'I knew it wasn't released as a single in the UK.'

'God, Stu!'

He turned it in his hands with great care. 'Here Comes the Sun,' he said. 'Who knew it was ever a B-side?'

'Stu!'

He heard her properly now, heard the tension in her voice. 'What?' he said. 'What's up?'

She gesticulated all around, looked at him as if he was crazy. 'Doesn't this stuff freak you out?'

He looked genuinely perplexed. 'Not at all,' he said. 'It makes me hopeful that some of this immaculate good taste is in Sunshine's DNA. How many kids get a rare Beatles single in their bag of memories?'

He got up and started rummaging around in a drawer for a spindle adaptor so he could play it on the turntable. Chrissie, watching him, wondered which was the more normal response – his relaxed unconcern or her own fraught feelings of emergency. She picked up the note, just a curling strip of brown paper, and read again what she knew it said. *These belong to a girl named Sunshine, please will you be sure she receives them?* The letters in their quaint and artful cursive, the words that scanned like freeform poetry, yet written on a scrap of parcel paper like an afterthought. On the chair, Sunshine, still fast asleep, dramatically shifted position, so that she was bottom up, face down, with her legs folded beneath her. Her head was now turned towards them, and she looked as she had when they'd first had sight of her, fetched from her bed by Barbara; now, as then, sleep had flushed her cheeks with colour, and pressed her curls flat against the warmth of her forehead, so that they lay in delicate filigree patterns against her skin. She was a sleeping beauty and a tyrant and just a child.

The photograph lay in Chrissie's lap. She picked it up again and studied the faces, which gazed back at her with a kind of benign wisdom. The baby looked to be around six months old, the young woman about seventeen, perhaps eighteen. Her hair was tied back, off her face, and it was hard to tell its colour in this monochrome image. The baby's face was framed by short, soft curls. Sunshine, and her mother, thought Chrissie; where were they, when this was taken? Whenever Chrissie had imagined Sunshine's unknown beginnings, a high-rise squat would come to mind, or a dingy basement bedsit somewhere in the badlands of South East London, but there was no evidence of that here. So, was this a London park, perhaps? Yet if so, where were the other people, the dogs, the pigeons, the joggers? This photograph evoked a scene of bucolic comfort and peace; perhaps an expansive garden, a gracious home. And who was holding the camera? They didn't look unloved, this girl and her baby. They didn't look on the margins, or under the radar.

Stuart had found a middle for the record, and now George Harrison brought Chrissie back to the room with his comforting, familiar, opening acoustics. She felt Stu's hand on her hair, lifting it up from the nape of her neck, and she dipped her head to make it easier for him to stroke that part of her that always responded to his touch. With her eyes closed, and The Beatles on the turntable, and his fingers moving up her neck and through her hair, she could be anywhere; she could be in his room at university, or in a featureless hotel on the road, or backstage at any of the hundreds of gigs they'd performed together, or upstairs, in bed, about to sleep or about to make love. He dropped down behind her and pulled her to him, wrapping his arms around her, kissing her neck and shoulders.

'I love you,' he said.

'Oh, thank God,' she said, 'I was starting to wonder.'

He laughed and she leaned back, letting him take her weight, and listening to him whisper the words of the song into her ear. It altered them, somehow; filled them with a secret meaning, that only Chrissie and Stuart understood.

'Who is that young woman, though?' Chrissie murmured.

Stu stopped, sighed, and said, 'We'll probably never know, and that really doesn't matter, Chrissie.'

'Yes, it does,' she said. But she was calmer now, the sense of crisis subsiding as The Beatles' sweet music washed through the room.

'Well, no, what I mean is, don't let her worry you,' Stu said. 'She looks placid and kind. Look on her as someone who did us an almighty favour.'

The empty box was on the floor. Chrissie picked it up and saw there was something written on the underside. It said, 'Oh darling, here comes the sun,' in speech marks, as if the two song titles were a sentence, and together conveyed a meaning beyond the sum of their parts.

They contemplated this in silence, then, 'She's a lovely puzzle,' Stuart said. 'We have a lifetime to work her out.'

They both looked at Sunshine, cherubic in sleep. How she had filled their flat today, Chrissie thought; how she would fill their lives. She felt exhausted and exhilarated as if she'd spent the day on a roller coaster.

'This must be so weird for her,' Stuart said. 'Being told, this is your home now, these are your parents.'

'I know; except I don't find it weird thinking, this is our daughter.'

'True, although we'd never dress our daughter in a West Ham strip.'

Chrissie laughed. 'It's got to go,' she said, then she drew away from him, reaching forwards to pick up the silk square. 'But this – this can stay. This is beautiful. Those clever little silkworms.'

She pulled it through her fingers and felt it stream between them with the ease of water. The colours were rich, but muted, rare and ancient, and the stitches in the hem and the seams were tiny, immaculate, made by a painstaking, expert hand. Then Chrissie said, 'Hey, you.'

She was talking to Sunshine, who'd pushed herself upright and was rubbing her eyes in that way she did, with two synchronised fists. She yawned hugely, then lowered her hands and looked about her, as if trying to remember where she was. She cocked her head and looked at Chrissie, then at the scarf in her hands. Two small lines of acute concentration appeared between her eyes.

'That,' she said, pointing at the silk. She held out her hand.

'This?' Chrissie said.

Sunny nodded. She slid herself off the chair, landing with a small thud, and seized the patchwork silk from Chrissie's outstretched hand, then lifted it to her cheek, and gave a vast sigh. In her small hand, the silk square seemed bigger, almost the size of a flag. Sunshine pressed it to her face, closed her eyes and rubbed it between dimpled thumb and forefinger, and she seemed to have left them for another time, another place.

'Sunshine,' Chrissie said, then again, 'Sunny?'

Stu said, 'She's blissing out.'

Chrissie watched her for a moment, wishing she knew her daughter better, wondering where she'd gone, then she quickly picked up the photo, slipped it back into the bag, and stood up and lifted the record, now silent, from the turntable.

'Well, this made no impact,' she said, holding it up. 'She didn't even notice it.'

'Don't put that in the bag,' Stu said. 'Put its box in the bag, but not that.'

She looked at him, holding the bag in one hand, the record in the other.

Stuart said, 'It's just, I think it deserves to be here on the shelf, safely filed with its kith and kin.'

So, she nodded, and handed it over, then considered Sunny, who had somehow transcended the room. She was still holding the silk square against her face, but now she was very softly singing a strange little song, with words they didn't know, and a tune that had no beginning, no end, no noticeable shape. She glowed with contentment. They watched her for a while, slightly mesmerised, until she stopped singing, opened her eyes, and smiled at them. Now she had the silk, thought Chrissie, perhaps she'd be more open to suggestion. Perhaps the football pyjamas could come off at last. She said, 'Hey, Sunny, shall we go for a walk?' and the child beamed.

'To the sea?' she asked brightly.

'To the swings,' Stu said. 'Even better.'

~

Brendan rang two days later, for the low-down on the memory bag, and an update on progress.

Chrissie said, 'Oh, well, we've had highs and we've had lows. She absolutely loves that silk scarf thing; you saw it, right? We've named it Silky. It means a lot to her, she's very attached; it sent her into a sort of trance. We put the record away on the music wall, and its box, and the photo, and the note that came with it all are stowed in the bag upstairs. Did you look at the photograph?'

He said, slightly sheepishly, that he had.

'It's baby Sunny, obviously,' Chrissie said. 'With the mother?'

'The birth mother, yes, I'd say so. How did it make you feel?'

'Weird, and jealous.'

'Stu?'

'Oh, he's chilled-out about everything. He was raised differently to me.'

He laughed. 'How has she settled?'

'Well, she won't go into her bedroom, and she still won't wear anything other than her horrible West Ham pyjamas.'

'She won't get dressed?'

'No, she only wants to wear that T-shirt and leggings she came in, but she won't wear them now they've been washed.'

'You mustn't let her run rings round you. I know I said give her some control, but she needs to know a few boundaries.'

'Mmm, that's what my mother said. Sunshine's "taking liberties" and we're a pair of pushovers. But we can't force her into her clothes, can we? Coaxing doesn't work, being stern doesn't work; she just gets crazily upset.'

'And you're using the soap powder Barbara gave you?'

Chrissie hesitated. 'What?'

'Barbara gave you some of the detergent she uses, didn't she? It's a simple thing, but if their clothes smell the way they always have, that can really help children settle.'

'Barbara didn't give us anything.'

Now Brendan was quiet for a moment. 'That big carrier bag of stuff,' he said.

'Toys, and a few books.'

'Right, well, that's really odd.'

Not as odd as you might imagine, thought Chrissie. 'I'll give her a call,' she said. 'She must have forgotten.'

In bed that night, Chrissie whispered to Stu across Sunshine's starfish occupation of the centre ground of the bed. Chrissie had spoken to John when she rang, not Barbara, and he'd been as puzzled as Brendan, because he thought he'd put the box of soap powder in with the toys himself, but Chrissie's call had made him question his memory. It had been a fraught time, their last couple of days with Sunshine, he'd said. Barbara was grieving, in a way.

'She's never been this bad,' he'd said, speaking quietly, confidingly. 'She's cried on and off since you left, and it's hard

99

on Carl and Kevin. They're bringing us a baby tomorrow, only six months, a little boy, I'm hoping he'll take her mind off Sunny.'

Chrissie didn't much care about Barbara's emotional well-being. 'I don't trust her,' she whispered, now, to Stuart. 'She's trying to make this as difficult as it could possibly be.'

Stu, facing her, watching her, letting his mind wander in a carnal direction, said, 'Hey, shall we pop Sunny in her own bed?'

'I mean, did she actually take the sodding soap powder *out of the bag*?' Chrissie whispered. 'Like, deliberately remove the box that John had put in there?'

'She's fast asleep, after all,' Stuart said. He didn't want to talk about Barbara. 'We could lift her into her own bed, make sure she's got Silky to wake up with?'

It had gained a personality these past couple of days, the silken cloth. Whatever it had been in her past, it was now Sunshine's go-to ally in this new, uncertain world. She looked for it wherever they went, and if it wasn't immediately visible, then hell had no fury like this child's wrath; it consumed her, and anyone caught in its path. Stuart couldn't help retreating from it, as he might from an avalanche or a tsunami. He'd pick up a guitar and bound upstairs, or down, two steps at a time, to get wherever was furthest from the eye of the storm. Chrissie, though, she seemed to recognise the rage, and understand it. She said it was because she'd been raised by Diana, whose anger could fill their home like smoke in a burning building. So, when Sunshine threatened to combust, Chrissie was learning how to contain her, hold her, help her.

In the aftermath of one meltdown, she'd sat Sunny with her at the keyboard in her bedroom, settling the spent child in her lap and playing a few chords, a few notes, letting her see how simple it was to make music, and how soothing. That first time,

Sunshine had curled into Chrissie with her face turned away from the keys. She'd sucked her thumb and closed her eyes but then when the random chords became a song, and Chrissie's voice wove into the music, Sunshine had stirred and shivered with a kind of animal pleasure, and opened her eyes and turned her head to watch Chrissie's hands on the keys. And now, whenever they sat together at the keyboard, she would flatten her hands on top of Chrissie's, so that they played the music together, and it never failed to make Sunny smile. Stuart had watched this happen and had been humbled. He saw the mother in her, saw the mothering instinct that Chrissie had thought she might not have; she was magnificent, in Stu's eyes. But right now, he really didn't want her to talk about Barbara.

He propped himself up on one elbow, and looked at her, his beautiful wife, completely familiar and completely desirable, but too far away, over on the other side of their big bed. Sunshine had fidgeted and flung herself almost sidelong now; he had her feet, Chrissie had her head. She played, absently, with the child's curls, while she mused out loud on Barbara's suspected treachery.

'She couldn't possibly just buy regular detergent, of course, so now we're going to have to find a Spar,' she said. 'It's their own-brand, John said. Blue box, red writing.'

'Jesus, Chrissie.'

'What?'

'I mean, it's nuts, right?'

She propped herself up too, so their faces were level. 'What is?'

'Soap powder, all this Barbara stuff, finding a Spar, what the fuck? Why are we even having this conversation? Give it a day or so, and Sunny'll be used to the way we smell, which, by the way, is probably nicer than the goddam Fosters.'

Chrissie allowed herself a smile.

'Speaking of which,' Stu said, 'I wanna smell you, and I can't, because we're sharing our bed.'

'It's only her third night, Stu; let's see how we go.'

She flopped back down again, so he did too, and for a while they were both quiet, listening to Sunny, whose breath when she slept came in little puffs, as if she was gently blowing out a long row of candles.

'Anyway,' Stuart said, 'let's not go running off to find a Spar. She's got a bag full of clothes that all smell of Barbara's laundry, and she won't wear those either, so let's just wing it.'

'OK,' Chrissie said, 'agreed,' then she yawned, and said, 'Night, darling,' with unmistakable finality, from her place on the margins of the bed, just out of arm's reach.

∼

Chrissie hated to admit it, but Diana had been right; two weeks of a three-way confinement was at least one week too many. It was doing none of them any good, and it wasn't written on a tablet of stone, and would anyone know if Nina came over for a cup of tea? She was only in Highgate, after all. And although Chrissie had submitted to a kind of promise that Diana would meet Sunny before Nina, it'd been made under pressure and her mother had continued to badger and cajole and bully, and had sent a card saying, 'Welcome to the world,' as if Sunshine had just been born, while Nina had only waited respectfully and quietly. And now Chrissie longed for a dose of her wit and wisdom, longed to introduce her to Sunshine, and knew, also, that Stu really, badly needed to get out of the flat, alone. He never would have said, but Chrissie knew him like she knew herself; and, in truth, she needed to see the back of him for a short while – only, she said, for a semblance of normality between them, and so that he could come home and tell her something she didn't already know. So, on the fifth day of the first week, Rocco swung by in the Subaru and carried him away, and soon afterwards, when Nina tapped on the door, she opened it with Sunshine sitting on her hip.

'Look at you two!' Nina said. 'What a sight for sore eyes. Hello, kitten – you must be Sunshine.'

'This is Auntie Nina, Sunny,' Chrissie said.

Sunshine peeped at her from under her lashes, and didn't smile. Chrissie said, 'Kettle's on, let's go through,' and Sunshine clung to her; such a longed-for feeling, this tight embrace of a child.

'You mustn't tell Diana,' Chrissie said.

'I know, you said.'

'She'd go nuts; she's been really weird recently.'

'I've brought lemon cake,' Nina said. 'Is that allowed? Bribing the child with cake?'

'Anything goes, here,' Chrissie said. She moved around the kitchen and Sunshine clung on like a baby monkey.

'You look meant to be, you two,' Nina said.

'Apart from the West Ham strip,' Chrissie said. 'But it's all she'll wear, for the time being.'

She put Sunny down to make the tea, and the child whinged and complained and clung to her leg. Nina held up a gift-wrapped box. 'This is for you, Sunshine,' she said, and the child's demeanour, which had been so thoroughly clouded by displeasure, switched instantly to bright interest, making Nina laugh.

'What it is?' Sunshine asked.

'What it is, little kitten, is a present for you. Here, open the bag and see.' Nina held it out and Sunny darted over and took it. She held it up and said to Chrissie, 'Mummy, what it is?' and Chrissie said, 'Open it, sweetheart,' smiling at her, loving the supreme ordinariness of this scene, the blessed normality that Nina's visit had conferred on this new role, her new life.

The past few days had been difficult, surreal, a kind of suspended animation, a tripartite lockdown, family life being dinned into them by the unreasonable edicts of social services. They were supposed to keep Sunny close, go out as little as possible, no comings and goings, no goodbyes or introductions, no surprises, just their little threesome, bonding like billy-o, showing Sunshine that this was forever, making up for all the time they hadn't had together. Yet the longer they spent in cloistered domesticity, the stranger life had seemed; so intense, so claustrophobic, Chrissie said she felt they were a living experiment to give two musicians a feisty child, deny them all any form of social life, and see how soon they went crazy. Stuart said it was just that Chrissie couldn't stand being told what to do, and there was some truth in that, she'd often been the rule-breaker in their partnership. But he'd been happy enough to jump into the car with Rocco; happy enough to wave goodbye and blow a kiss, and drive away. And look, here was Sunny, happy as a lark, tearing at the wrapping paper on her gift, not remotely concerned that Daddy was gone. She held up the box and said, 'What it is?' again, and Nina kneeled next to her to show her it was a block puzzle, pictures on bricks that, when slotted together in the correct order, showed children on a grassy hill flying kites against a bright-blue sky, so Sunshine tipped the bricks out of the box with a tremendous racket and immediately got to work.

'Shall I help you?' Nina asked.

'No, me,' Sunny said. She pressed her lips together in concentration, and hummed as she worked. Nina made eyes at Chrissie, and Chrissie said, 'I know, right? Little dreamboat, some of the time.' She passed Nina a mug of tea and they both sat down at the table.

'Any more of the screaming abdabs?'

'Less, I'd say, yeah, she's doing fine, except for the getting dressed issue, which foxes us every day.'

'And you and Stu?'

Chrissie hesitated a fraction then, 'Fine, too,' she said.

Nina waited.

'No, really, we're fine. We weren't sleeping well, but Stu moved into Sunny's empty bed two nights ago, so that's good.'

'I bet Stu doesn't think so.'

'Well, no, and it's not for ever, just these early days. We all sleep better if he's in her room.'

She didn't say how much she loved to lie next to Sunshine and talk her to sleep with made-up stories about a field mouse called Bertie who went on his travels, and then to fall asleep herself to the sound of Sunshine's breathing. The two nights she'd spent alone with her had felt pure and priceless, and private too, tucked up together in infinite comfort. She could barely believe how quickly this small child had brought her to this, when, before, all she'd really needed was Stuart. He didn't seem to mind. Needs must, Chrissie had said, and he'd said, sure thing.

Nina said, 'What did you do with the memory bag?'

'Upstairs, in a cupboard in her room.'

'I'd love to see it.'

Chrissie opened her mouth to speak, then closed it, then opened it again and said, 'Oh, I . . .'

'Never mind,' Nina said. 'Shouldn't have asked, sorry.'

'No, I'm sorry. I just want to stop thinking about it, for now. I find it kind of difficult. The record's in the living room, though – Stu filed it with The Beatles. I do think it's weird, sending that. Makes me feel someone knows who we are.'

'Happy coincidence, I expect; that's all,' Nina said. 'Have you played it for Sunny?'

'Only once, when we first got it. Didn't seem to mean anything to her, although to be fair she slept through most of it. But she fell on Silky like a long-lost friend.'

'May I?' Nina said. She pointed at the silk square, which was draped over the back of a chair, its special qualities not presently in demand. Chrissie nodded and Nina held it up to study the design.

'Gorgeous,' she said. 'I saw fabrics very similar to this at the V&A, that Indian textiles exhibition.'

'Maybe she's the granddaughter of a maharaja,' Chrissie said gloomily and Nina laughed.

'It's hand spun,' she said. 'Lovely piece of work.'

Chrissie nodded. Nina shot her a knowing look.

'You're feeling threatened by her things, aren't you?' she said.

Chrissie shrugged.

'You shouldn't, Chrissie. Don't turn your back on her story.'

Chrissie felt a flash of irritation. 'It's the way they arrived that freaks me out,' she said. 'Dropped off in the same place that Sunny was left by her birth mother, on the very day she came here to us.'

'Yeah,' Nina said, conceding the point, 'that's kind of strange. But it was an act of kindness, after all.'

'Well, if you say so.'

'Chrissie, it was, if this piece of gorgeous silk is anything to go by, and a Beatles single, for heaven's sake! What's intimidating about "Here Comes the Sun"?'

'Nothing, obviously, at face value,' Chrissie said, and glanced down at the child, who was still absorbed. 'But rather a lot,' she went on, in a low voice, 'when it's a gift from her supposedly missing family.'

Now Sunshine announced, 'I's done,' in a tone of satisfied pride, beaming up at them from her place at the side of the puzzle; it was way off the mark, its kites upside down, its children in scattered and dislocated positions.

'That's great, Sunny!' Nina said. 'Clever girl!' and the child gave a shy smile and inched closer to Chrissie, who reached for her and pulled her up onto her lap. For a moment Nina scrutinised the two of them, as if she was sizing them up for a portrait.

'Beautiful,' she said. 'Just beautiful. I'm so happy for you, Chrissie. And look, I wasn't sure if I was going to say anything, but that West Ham strip is beyond the pale, so I'm going to risk it.'

'What?' Chrissie asked. 'Oh, please, tell me you have a solution.'

Nina dipped into her rucksack, and brought out a sleeveless tie-dye dress in indigo and white, which she held up for inspection. Sunshine looked quizzical.

'That is mine?' she asked.

'I don't know,' Nina said, looking at the dress as if it was just as new to her as to Sunshine. '*Is* it yours, Sunny?'

She nodded emphatically. She pushed herself off Chrissie's knees and started to tug off her shorts, and Chrissie said, 'Wow,' and left her to it, until the child looked at her and said, 'You can help me, Mummy?'

'You bet,' Chrissie said.

'I love the way she asks a question,' Nina said. 'It's very commanding.'

Sunshine raised her arms and Chrissie pulled the shirt off over her head. 'There goes Dagenham Motors,' she said. 'Now, where's Sunshine's dress?'

'There,' Sunny said. She pointed, so there could be no mistake, then raised her arms again in readiness. Her body was compact and perfectly formed, pale as cream, heart-wrenchingly slender but somehow strong too, like a tender sapling, with all that hidden vigour stored away for the task of growing.

Chrissie dropped the dress over the child's outstretched arms, and it fell into place, soft and fluid. It came to her knees. It was beautiful in its simplicity.

'There you are,' Chrissie said, and Sunshine nodded gravely and said, 'Yes, there I are.'

8

Diana and Doug came to visit, having booked three nights in a smart hotel near Regent's Park, a good half-hour's drive from the flat. Each day they arrived no earlier than ten o'clock, so that – as Diana put it – the turmoil of breakfast would be over, and if she said 'Put that child down' once, she said it a hundred times. Never had Chrissie felt so at odds with her mother; never had she seen, in such sharp relief, her father's compliance, his preference for an easy life. When Diana was elsewhere, he'd whisper urgently to Chrissie how difficult she was being, how unsettled she'd seemed, how he wished she could just relax and enjoy life instead of seeming all the time to fight it. But when Diana was in the room, telling Chrissie that she was a soft touch with no idea how to give a child parameters – well, Doug was a veritable clam.

'We don't like to tell Sunny that she's naughty,' Chrissie said, more than once. 'Instead, we ask her not to do what she's doing, and point out why,' and Diana would snort and say, 'Who's in charge here, then? There was no asking a three-year-old, back in our day. You *told* a three-year-old to behave, and in no uncertain terms.'

Stuart said, 'Let it pass, Chrissie. You'll not change her mind and she'll not change yours,' but it was easy for him to say: he wasn't the focus of Diana's judgemental remarks; he wasn't part of the prickly Stevenson dynamic. It seemed to Chrissie that Diana felt conflicted by the presence of Sunshine – who knew why? – and this then made Doug a little uncertain how to behave, although he couldn't help but be jolly, tickling her and blowing raspberries on her bellybutton at bath time. Diana hung back, watched from a distance, made remarks such as, 'Don't get her giddy, Doug, or she'll be up all hours,' and, 'That silk rag can't be hygienic.' She didn't know about its significance to Sunshine, because Chrissie simply couldn't trust Diana with the information when her mood was so combative. When Chrissie said, 'Mum, please, just be nice,' Diana gave her small, humourless laugh and said, 'You're very thin-skinned, Christine. Are you getting enough sleep with the child in your bed?'

Small distressing cameos from her own childhood began to come back to Chrissie in fragmented pieces. A taffeta party dress, furiously cut into ribbons with pinking shears by Diana because Chrissie complained it was scratchy. Her mother's red nails digging into her wrist as she pulled her from a game in the garden. And did Diana once slap the back of Chrissie's legs for showing her knickers in the street, in a handstand? Did Chrissie have red welts on the back of her thighs for a day or so, or was that a borrowed memory, someone else's story? She was convinced these things had happened until she shared them with Stuart who, never having heard the stories before, found them difficult to believe.

'She slapped the back of your legs?' Stu said, hesitantly, as if she was speaking a new language, and Chrissie said, 'Yeah, that was a thing, then, "I'll slap the back of your legs" or, "I'll flatten you." They were normal threats.'

'Flatten you? What the heck? You've never told me that before. So, she hit you?'

'Yes,' Chrissie said, then, 'No, well, sometimes, but hardly ever. Look, I'm not sure. It's just, seeing her, hearing her, in this context – it brings back odd memories.'

She stopped sharing them then; his doubt and her uncertainty made her feel she was doing Diana a disservice. And anyway, Stu didn't mind his mother-in-law; he found her amusing, and direct, and sometimes the things about her that made Chrissie bridle only made him laugh. So what if she didn't want Sunny's grubby fingers on her white silk blouse? Everyone was different, he argued, and the sooner Sunshine realised that the better. He could see Chrissie's point, he'd say, could see why she might feel under attack, but he liked to give people the benefit of the doubt, and nobody could ever suspect Diana of not loving her daughter. 'She's just tough, is all,' Stu would say. 'She's old school.'

Diana was charming to Stuart, though; all her adult life, she'd generally appreciated men more than women, and her manner towards him was lightly flirtatious, brightly attentive. 'Your mother does like an audience,' Doug said, not unkindly; almost proudly in fact. He and Chrissie were looking at Diana and Stuart in the back garden through the window of what had been the dining room and was now a playroom. Diana was regaling Stu with an anecdote, leaning forwards in her deck-chair to tap him on the knee, then tipping back her head and laughing at his response. She was aware of her powers, aware that she still turned heads. Slim, groomed, always well-dressed in her capsule collection of narrow linen trousers and silk shirts and cashmere cardigans. Today she wore a large-brimmed straw hat against the sun, and a chiffon scarf around her neck and décolletage, which she was determined to protect from the dreaded crêpe effect. She still exuded her trademark glamour, her sixties Hollywood style. Once, before he'd met her mother, Chrissie told Stuart that Diana was only ever truly happy in the moments after being mistaken for Anne Bancroft, so when he was finally officially introduced, he'd said, 'Ah, we meet at last, Barnsley's answer to Mrs Robinson,' and Diana had laughed delightedly and said, 'Well, don't get your hopes up, you're not my type,' which Stu and Doug found funny, and Chrissie found revolting.

'Neither of them are paying the least attention to Sunshine,' Chrissie said now, to Doug. They both looked at the child, who was filling a plastic bucket from a sandpit, and talking to herself.

'She's all right though,' he said. 'She doesn't need constant mollycoddling.'

Chrissie folded her arms. 'I didn't say she did.'

Doug put an arm round her shoulders and gave her a squeeze. Outside, Diana tipped her hat so that the brim cast greater shade across her eyes. Stuart said something to Sunshine, but she didn't answer, just kept up her industrious digging, and her private conversation, and Chrissie laughed and said, 'See that? She's giving him a taste of his own medicine.' She knocked on the window, and all three of them looked round at once. Sunny waved, Stuart grinned, and Diana gazed with detached interest at Doug and Chrissie as if she'd never seen them before in her life.

~

Nina came again while Diana and Doug were there, and pretended she was meeting Sunny for the first time, which was almost awkward because Sunny obviously remembered the kind lady who'd given her a new dress. She was wearing it when Nina arrived, and she said, 'Look!', and held it out at the hem, but all Nina said was, 'Very pretty, little kitten, don't you look lovely!' and the moment passed.

Chrissie called that garment The Dress That Changed

Everything, and she thought it could end up as a song title. From the moment she put it on, Sunny had forgotten her fixation with the West Ham pyjamas and the *little terror* T-shirt, which were now shunned in favour of brand-new clothes, of which there were very few, because Brendan Cassidy had instructed them not to buy lots of lovely garments before she arrived, and to dress her just the way Barbara had, for at least a couple of months. But Diana and Doug had come bearing a pale-pink dress with a full skirt and a smocked bodice, and a deeper pink cardigan with mother-of-pearl buttons, the kind of outfit that Chrissie herself might be seen in, in photographs from her own infancy and childhood. The only garments Chrissie and Stu had bought before Sunshine came to live with them were a pair of denim dungarees, a red and white striped T-shirt, and some white denim shorts. They'd expected to buy more after the Whitstable purdah came to an end, but then Nina had unwittingly ended it early, by tapping into Sunshine's delight in anything new. The purple holdall remained unpacked in the bedroom she still hadn't slept in and Brendan had said he'd leave it be for a while, in case she regressed, but then Barbara and John could have it all back.

'Brainwash some other kid into supporting the Hammers,' Chrissie said, and Brendan said, 'Damn, you've rumbled us,' and they'd both laughed. She liked him, he'd grown on her, but still, she hadn't told him they were having visitors. This seemed too great a flouting of the terms and conditions, even to Chrissie's rebellious spirit. She still saw absolutely no harm in it, still thought – most of the time – that she was a better judge of Sunshine's needs than the adoption team, and anyway, it was only Nina, and her own parents . . . and yet sometimes, at arbitrary points in the day or night, she was ambushed by the horror of being told they couldn't keep her. Stu said, 'I'd like to see anyone try and take her off you,' and when she confided her fear to Diana, she only laughed and said, 'Take her off you and give her to whom?' which was a valid point, but felt more undermining than supportive, as if the only reason they would keep Sunny was because there were simply no other feasible alternatives.

Everything improved when Nina came, because despite all the complaints she made about Nina's proximity to Chrissie and Stu and her involvement in their lives, Diana was more relaxed in her company, and when Diana relaxed, everyone did. Nina knew Diana very well, and had a special gift for dealing with her; she combined flattery with a kind of earthy humour, and on this occasion, she brought her Nikon and a tripod, and held a photo shoot in the open-plan back room, where the afternoon sun lit the walls and floor with a honey glow. Diana loved to be photographed. The camera was her friend; there was barely a bad shot of her in existence. Something about the symmetry of her features and her bone structure, and a certain knowingness from her long-ago shoots with modelling agencies and film scouts – how much to dip the chin, turn the head, place the feet; she never looked caught out.

'Is it boring, being so bloody gorgeous?' Nina asked her. 'I mean, don't you sometimes long to be just ordinary?' She was snapping away while Diana sat immaculate and glossy on a simple wooden chair, her slender legs crossed, with Sunshine sitting side-saddle in her lap, now wearing the new pink frock, patient, demure, as if some of Diana's poise had rubbed off on her. Diana laughed, and Nina captured it, a beautiful laugh, eyes flashing, her face alive for the lens, and Sunshine, as still and solemn as a baby owl. Nina took dozens of other photographs, but this was the one Diana chose, when the prints were ready. She didn't want any of the ones of Chrissie and Stu, with Sunny larking about in their arms. Diana was irritated that they hadn't changed out of their jeans and T-shirts, and that Chrissie hadn't brushed her hair.

'This is how my hair is supposed to look, Mum,' Chrissie said, dragging her fingers through it and pulling an ironic face in the mirror. 'The Chrissie Stevenson trademark.'

'Ridiculous,' said Diana. 'You're thirty-three, and now you're in charge of a child.'

'Have some decorum,' Stu said, grinning at Chrissie.

'Precisely,' Diana said, and she patted her chignon, as if she needed to check it was still there.

'Why don't you call Sunny's bedroom her playroom?' Nina suggested, over lunch. 'Leave the bed in there, obviously, and let her befriend it in her own time.' So later, she and Sunny looked together at the toys currently stowed downstairs, and together they carried up a basket of Duplo and another of plastic animals, and Nina said, 'We're building a zoo; we'll call you when it's finished, OK?' by which she meant, take a break, and it was surprisingly pleasant, thought Chrissie, to sit in the living room with Doug and Diana, talking about this and that, while Stuart picked at the strings of his guitar and the murmur of Sunshine and Nina's conversation drifted down to them: small, contented particles of sound. For forty-five minutes, Chrissie left them to it, then couldn't resist going up to Sunny's room, where she found the child busy squashing animals into their Duplo pens, and Nina beside her on the floor, examining the photograph from the memory bag.

There was a profound, distorted silence, as in a dream, or under water. Chrissie had the advantage, in that she had three seconds to stare at Nina before Nina realised she was there, but it didn't feel advantageous; it felt like the end of the world. Nina looked up and said, 'Chrissie, I—', but then Sunshine realised

Chrissie was there, and her face broke into a happy smile and she said, 'Look, Mummy, mine zoo,' and there was nothing to be done, but admire it. Nina stood up.

'I'm sorry,' she said, but Chrissie couldn't speak to her, not yet. She heard Stu bounding up the stairs two at a time, and she thought, oh, thank God, because his presence would be a line of defence between herself and the way she was feeling. He looked in the room and said, 'Wowee, check out that menagerie,' and Sunshine said, 'Zoo, Daddy.' She sat back from her labours with a satisfied sigh, and he dropped down onto his haunches to get a closer look and saw the photograph on the floor, the memory bag beside it, and immediately registered the strange energy between Chrissie and Nina, one kneeling, one standing, neither able to speak. He looked at Nina.

'Hey,' he said, amiably, 'what's the story?'

She shook her head; her expression was almost sullen. 'I just thought I could have a quick look, with no harm done,' she said.

'And there isn't, right?' He looked at Chrissie.

'Let's not do this,' Chrissie said.

'Do what?' Stu said. He smiled and winked at Sunny, who tilted her head and made a strenuous effort to close one eye, but could only close both.

'Let's not pretend that this is fine,' Chrissie said.

Obviously, it wasn't the end of the world. Just because Chrissie felt that way, it didn't make it true; certainly, nobody else thought so – even Stuart truly struggled to understand what was so controversial about Nina proving to be nosier than they'd realised.

Sunshine was oblivious to the ripples of tension between the grown-ups. She was tired after all the attention she'd received, and now she was drifting off on the sofa, her thumb plugged in,

Silky bunched up against her cheek in her free hand. Nobody raised their voice, for what was there to be angry about? But still, there were all these layers of hurt and unhappiness, the day felt ruined, and Chrissie longed for everyone to leave so she could try to explain to Stu the betrayal she'd felt, when she saw Nina studying that photograph. Nina couldn't adequately explain it. She said, 'I was fascinated to see the bag, to see what was in it, and I knew you weren't ready to share it, that's all,' and Chrissie said, 'Then you should have waited until I was,' and this was irrefutable.

Meanwhile, Diana was stirring her own whirlpool of drama by being deeply, theatrically wounded, because until this point, she'd known nothing about this bag of bits and bobs from Sunshine's past. Nothing at all! And it was surely no less a betrayal, she said, that Chrissie had told Nina about it but not her, Diana, the child's grandmother, for heaven's sake.

'Why must you be so secretive?' Diana asked Chrissie, sharply, but quietly, so as not to disturb the child. 'Why must you play Nina off against me in such a way?'

'Hey,' Stuart said, keeping it calm, keeping it friendly, 'Chrissie doesn't play those sort of games, Diana; she's done nothing wrong,' and he pulled Chrissie towards him and kissed her on the temple, which turned Diana to stone for a while. Doug was hopeless and helpless, and kept glancing miserably between his wife and daughter, his discomfort palpable, at a loss what to say or do, and Nina had her coat on and was packing up her camera lenses when Chrissie suddenly said, 'Oh, fuck it, let's just show everyone the bag. I don't care any more; it's just stuff,' and Diana, speaking for the first time in fifteen minutes, said, 'Christine! We did not raise you to use the F-word,' and this, at least, made Chrissie laugh.

Stuart fetched the bag and passed it over for inspection, then sat with Chrissie on the sofa, his arm round her shoulder. Sunny sat up, stared sleepily around the room, then swivelled herself around and lay down again, her head in Stu's lap. He combed her curls with his fingers, and she shivered and sighed and dropped back into sleep. Chrissie closed her eyes too, and listened to her parents and Nina, as they examined the bag, the little note with its pretty penmanship, the cardboard box the record had come in, and the photograph. Nina still looked sad, and when she said, 'I'm really sorry, Chrissie,' she received no reply, but she had the framed photo in her hand, now, and she didn't try to disguise her fascination. Her creative eye was drawn to the scene, although, really, you didn't need to be a professional to appreciate the artless beauty of the girl, the child, the sheltering oak.

'Black and white film is such an extraordinary medium,' she said.

'Mmm,' Stu said.

'This photo . . . it looks timeless.'

'Odd lot of stuff, though,' Doug said, handling the bag, fingering the embroidery, examining the black silk cord as if he was trying to price the item up for sale.

'There's a Beatles single as well, a rare foreign pressing,' Stu said.

'Is it worth something?' Diana asked.

'Priceless, Mum,' Chrissie said, flatly.

'That bag looks very old,' Nina said, to Doug. 'But her name's been added more recently.'

He sniffed doubtfully, and passed it to her, and she passed him the photograph.

'Now then,' he said. 'What a pretty lass. Look at that figure, and them eyes.'

Diana gave him a little clip round the back of the head, half in jest, half not. 'Don't ogle,' she said, 'and give that here,' and when she had the photograph in her hand, she said, 'My goodness, doesn't the baby look like her mother?'

There was a beat of silence, then Chrissie sighed. 'I'm her mother,' she said. 'That's the person who didn't want her.'

Diana drew in a breath, doubtless to deliver a sting, but Doug bravely placed a hand on her arm, and for once, his wife chose to concede the point. 'Of course,' she said. 'My mistake.'

~

Sunshine's beginnings are locked in her senses. There's a smell – sweet and musky and dense – and a taste – earthy, complex, and sometimes bitter. Of touch, she occasionally recalls the cool comfort of silk against her face, and the ineffable peace of being tightly swaddled next to someone's heartbeat. Certain kinds of music make her still and thoughtful too; a certain kind of song, the meandering kind, that rises and spirals upwards like smoke.

She remembers, also, a wooden place of many rooms, and many people. A man with two different eyes, who seems as tall as a tree, lifting her high in his arms and pointing at birds in the sky. The press of lips on her cheek, and on the top of her head. The comfortable crush of other children. Laughter and noise. Pebbles under her bare feet. The wash of the waves around her ankles. She doesn't have the words for these things, but they come to her as pictures, unbidden and surprising. If she closes her eyes she sometimes sees them, and they make her feel happy and cosy, just as Daddy does when he dances with her, and as Mummy does when she sings, and as Auntie Nina does, when she calls her kitten.

9

The best part of Diana and Doug's visit was saying goodbye; even Sunny, who tended to wave as if her life depended on it, seemed to wave with extra vigour as the big car pulled quietly away from the kerb. It was an ostentatious maroon Bentley these days – very embarrassing to have it in the street outside their flat, as if the Queen was calling. They were lucky to be leaving with all four hub caps, Stu said. When the trio went inside and closed the door, Chrissie felt so good, so released, and even the walls around them seemed to slump a little with relief, although traces of Diana's cologne still hung in the air and for a while Chrissie was careful what she said about her. Then Stu cracked open a couple of beers and they sat outside and watched Sunshine apparently digging to Australia in her sandpit while they took apart the past few days, the performances of Doug, Diana and Nina, and their own solidarity, their absolute preference for each other above anyone else in the world. Carly was coming over from the States next, but not for a while, and anyway that was different, that was like having an older sister turn up and hang out for a while. But for now, it was just themselves and their friends. Ordinary bliss.

'Is it awful that this one thing happens, and I feel like taking a break from Nina?' Chrissie said. They'd parted with a hug and a kiss, and Nina had said sorry, again, for overstepping the mark, but Chrissie, again, had allowed the apology to go unanswered, which was ungracious, but she hadn't been able to help herself. It was just so painful, remembering the sight of her poring over the photograph, as if she was trying to crack a coded message.

Stu said, 'It's your call, but don't let it fester, she didn't do much wrong.'

'Yeah,' Chrissie said. 'I'll ring her tomorrow. Make friends.'

In silence, they watched Sunshine dig tidy holes, working her way around the wooden square of the sandpit.

'She's very diligent, isn't she?' Chrissie said.

The tip of Sunny's tongue poked out from her mouth as she worked, and occasionally she sat back to survey the job, tilting her head and scowling slightly, like a demanding foreman.

'Great job, Sunny,' Stu said, and she glanced up at him and took the compliment with a complacent smile.

'We're going to go shopping for clothes and shoes,' Chrissie said. 'Aren't we, Sunshine? New shoes, and some new things to wear?'

The child beamed. Her teeth were perfectly pearly white, so small and straight, so exquisitely formed, and Chrissie found herself thinking, who cleaned them, when they first grew? Who looked after those pretty teeth? And from whom did she inherit her conscientious streak, her assiduous approach to playtime? Chrissie smiled back at this brand-new daughter, and wished these thoughts didn't form in her mind, wished she could remember those feelings of joy and release she'd had, when Angela Holt first uttered the word *foundling*. Back then it had seemed only positive, a beautiful, big blank canvas on which to paint the child's new life. Now, fragments of the past had been delivered to them in an embroidered bag, and Chrissie felt their presence all the time, and heard their whispers; *we know who she is, we knew her before.*

'All that stuff Angela told us,' she said now, to Stuart. 'It was kind of bogus, right?'

'What, the open wound session?'

'Yeah.'

'Well,' Stu said, 'I guess Angela was making assumptions based on past experience of other children.'

'But she knew Sunny, didn't she? At least, Brendan did, so she knew her through him. And yet she talked to us as if we were stepping into flames.'

He laughed. 'Is that what you took from that conversation?'

Chrissie pulled her pinch-mouthed Angela Holt face, and in a passable imitation of her pedantic delivery said, 'A lot of the problems we see come from adoptive parents who don't give enough credence to the child's early traumas,' and Stu laughed again. 'Uncanny,' he said. 'Please stop or I'll have to leave.'

Later, she left the photograph out of the bag, and put it on an empty bookshelf in Sunshine's room. She knew it was too high for the child to notice, really; but still, it felt like progress.

~

It was a Thursday in early August, week eight of life with Sunshine. Stuart was in the living room with Rocco and Sol, loafing about, playing riffs, putting melodies to new words. Chrissie had written some lyrics lately, worked on a few piano chords to get the guys started, and it was, she thought, the first decent stuff she'd done for a while. *The Dress That Changed Everything* had been a joke when she first mentioned it, but it had stayed and stayed, and now it was a song, and maybe the album title too, who knew? Anyway, she never could stand the process of listening to her words being chewed over by the boys, so she'd left them to it and by the time she and Sunshine came home, they'd all had a couple of beers and the empties were on the floor, and Rocco, the band's only remaining smoker, had the window open so he could hold his cigarette outside, as if that made any difference. Chrissie and Sunshine came in, and Stu shouted, 'Hey, happy days, my girls are home,' and Chrissie stood for a moment to inhale deeply and surreptitiously enjoy the residual smell of Rocco's latest smoke, then she stuck her head round the door.

'It smells of fags, Rocco,' she said. 'And Angela Holt's coming later.'

'Shit, sorry,' he said, but it was Stu she was looking at.

'No, that's tomorrow,' he said.

She shook her head. 'Stu, I told you she changed it, from five o'clock Friday to half four, today.' She cast a glance around the room. 'It's OK, it's a few hours away, but this isn't a good look. Anyway, how'd you get on?'

Sol said, 'Listen,' and he waited for Stu to pick up his guitar then they played a beautiful little chord progression that transcended Chrissie's irritation, and made her nod and smile. 'Yeah, that's great, love it.'

'We missed you, though,' Sol said. 'Our indie poet queen.'

Stu said, 'How'd it go for you two?'

'Eventful,' Chrissie said. 'I'll tell you later.'

They'd been out, up at the children's shoe shop on the Broadway, looking for new sandals and perhaps a pair of trainers, with Velcro straps that Sunny would be able to manage herself. It had not been a visit without incident. Sunshine had homed in on a pair of bright-red patent-leather sandals with a small heel, intended for older girls and not – thank God – available in her size, and then, when the assistant brought instead a tower of shoe boxes and said, 'Let's see if any of these fit the bill,' Sunshine had tucked her feet right under the chair and looked determinedly away, meeting no one's eyes, answering no one's questions. The assistant, busy, unimpressed, chilly, had said to Chrissie, 'Is she always like this?' and Chrissie had thought, how would I know? She was more of a novice at this than anyone in the shop, including Sunshine. She'd had to blushingly admit, when asked, that she had no idea what size shoes the child was currently wearing, then, when the sliding foot measure came out, Sunshine knew exactly what to do, while Chrissie watched, feeling like a fraud. Two months into probationary parenthood and she still didn't feel authentic, anywhere other than home. She passed other parents in the street who walked along with their offspring as if, together, they owned the pavements. Same here, in the shoe shop; the other mothers – there were no men shopping for their children's shoes, Chrissie noted – were completely in control of their small charges, who obediently let themselves be shod, then marched proudly up and down the shop floor, while assistants watched for slippage and felt for pinching. Meanwhile, Sunshine, disgusted that the red sandals were out of bounds, looked away, and her expression was dark and her mouth was compressed into her special, displeased, thin line.

'She's a handful,' the assistant said, not kindly.

'Come on then,' Chrissie had said to Sunny. 'Let's not bother.' She'd stood up, and held out a hand, at which Sunshine had roared, 'I do want shoes,' making every face in the shop turn towards her. Then a woman said, 'Forgive me, but are you Chrissie Stevenson?' Chrissie had admitted that yes, she was, and she'd signed her autograph on a scrap of paper and answered a few intense questions about the next tour and the sleeve notes on their last album. The shop assistant had stared, evidently puzzled, and the woman had said to her, 'Chrissie Stevenson, sings with The Lineman, don't tell me you didn't recognise her?' and Chrissie had said, 'Ah, no, look, it hardly ever happens,' which was true, thank God. The shop assistant, none the wiser, had said, 'Right, well, anyway . . .' and had turned back to Sunshine to try and tempt her with second-best shoes, but, quick as a flash the child clambered up onto her chair and started growling her version of 'Johnny B. Goode' in a grunge style Chrissie had never heard from her before. The intense woman, the fan, said, 'Oh my, is she yours? She's amazing!'

Chrissie had smiled, rolled her eyes, said, 'That's one word for her,' but what she thought was, she *is* amazing; this bold, badly behaved, beautiful child, and, yes, she's mine, almost. Some of the other customers looked askance, others laughed and one or two applauded, but anyway, the distracting moment of fandom had altered the vibe in their favour, and now the shop assistant willingly opened the lids of all the boxes she'd fetched from the stockroom, and asked Sunshine to pick her favourite. So now, she was wearing a pair of pale-blue Converse – 'like mine mummy's but more nice' – and carrying some sandals that looked as if they were made out of silver, sparkly jelly. She pushed her way into the living room and made a beeline for Stuart.

'Daddy, see,' she said and raised one foot.

'No way! Baby Converse!' He put his guitar down and reached for her, and she curled into him.

Sol said, 'Uh-oh, Juno's going to want some.'

'Zuno is here?' Sunny asked.

'No, honeybunch,' Sol said. 'Juno is not here.'

Juno was in France, with Julia, and Julia's parents, in their elegant home in Versailles, the town, not the palace. Juno, having a half-French mother, was bilingual, but her confusion over when and where to use English or French was no barrier to her friendship with Sunshine, which was firmly established on the strength of only two meetings, and Julia's fears for her daughter's safety with a delinquent child from the care system had not been realised; if anything, Juno was more prone to small acts of violence than Sunny, not that Julia had acknowledged this, being possessed of a composed insouciance towards her own misjudgements. Now, Sunny cast herself off Stuart's knee and shouted, 'Where Mummy is?' then charged out of the room without waiting for an answer.

'That's wild, the way she says that,' Rocco said. 'Where Chrissie is, is where she wants to be.' He tapped out a beat on his teeth with the rim of his bottle of Peroni.

'OK, guys,' Stu said, 'if you'd kindly fuck off, we have to remove all traces of you before Angela Holt gets here.'

They lit a scented candle in the living room and left the window open too, and binned the bottles.

'Sorry,' Stu said. 'I really thought it was tomorrow.'

'No, it was tomorrow, and now it's not, and I told you, but hey, whatever.'

'Sorry,' Stu said, again.

Chrissie said. 'It's fine, it's just, y'know.'

'Yeah, I know. So, go on, how was the shoe shopping?'

Chrissie gave a laugh. 'She was a pain in the arse, then she was awesome. She sang "Johnny B. Goode", standing on a chair. I got recognised by a super-fan, who'd read the liner notes on *Never Say Ever*, and had a few queries.'

Stu said, 'In the shoe shop?'

'It all happens there, apparently. Oh, and you can now tell anyone who asks you that Sunny takes a size twenty-four in shoes.'

'Twenty-four? Sounds huge.'

Sunshine was on her scooter, and every few seconds she swooshed past the open door of the kitchen then was gone, like an apparition. Stuart started making coffee to help the place smell good for Angela, but Chrissie just stood and stared at the doorway, waiting to see the essence of Sunshine rush by again, then again. Diana, her mother, had said to her on the day they left, 'You're besotted with that child,' in an accusatory tone, as if being besotted was a terrible thing, yet she expected to hear from Chrissie every other day with Sunshine updates, so she was evidently nurturing her own little obsession, and there was something addictive about Sunny, for sure. Chrissie would call Diana later with the shoe shop news, though she'd have to deliver a tightly edited version, with no mention of 'Johnny B. Goode' or the autograph for an over-excited Lineman fan. Those were the sort of anecdotes that pitched Diana into silence. If Doug answered – and this was so rare as to be almost miraculous – it was different; he'd take anything Chrissie had to give him, and her status in the music industry was a matter of great pride and interest to him, although he always said it was a mystery why she could sing, when he and her mother couldn't hit a note if their lives depended on it. At her Buckinghamshire girls' grammar school, back in her teenaged years, Diana had been given a place in the cantabile choir because of her ravishing looks, but was asked only to mime the words, not to sing. The retelling of this family legend was one of the few occasions Diana permitted laughter at her own expense, and even then, it always ended with her saying to Chrissie, 'Anyway, what you do wouldn't have passed for singing, not in nineteen fifty-four.'

Angela Holt reminded Chrissie a little of Diana, now she thought about it. The default setting of general disapproval. The line of her mouth as she jotted down unseen notes. Just as with Diana, so it was with Angela; you could never tell what they were thinking, but if you hazarded a guess, it would probably be something peevish.

'I hate these visits,' Chrissie said now, to Stu.

'I know you do,' he said. 'Me too.'

'They should make it official, and quit checking up on us.'

Stu said, 'It's a process, though, right? They're not just breaking our balls, they're ticking boxes.'

'It's such bullshit, kowtowing to Angela. Cleaning the flat whenever she comes.'

'She doesn't ask us to do that, to be fair.'

'Arranging our faces into pleasant smiles, for her.'

'You do a terrible job at that,' he said, and she laughed grudgingly. He was grinding coffee beans, and they both had to raise their voices to be heard over the appalling clatter. Stu made coffee like an artisan craftsman; there had to be something beautiful at the end of it, every time. When they'd first got together, he'd had no interest in good food, or fine coffee, only music and sex. That's what Chrissie remembered anyway. She sometimes felt nostalgic for the days when a smoke and a bottle of Woodpecker cider would take the place of a meal. Not that she didn't appreciate the food he placed before her these days, but she did – in her secret self, never to be admitted to Stuart – think it was sexier to forget to eat, than to think about Saturday's dinner on Thursday.

The scooter skidded to a dramatic halt in the doorway, and Chrissie said, 'You's hungry?' Sunshine nodded, and her dark curls bobbed around her face. 'I's hungry,' she said.

'Come on then,' Stu said. 'Take a seat in my cafe.'

Bang on time, Angela rang the doorbell. Sunshine behaved like a society hostess; showed off her new sneakers, then – encouraged by Angela's reaction – fetched the bag containing her silver-flecked jelly shoes, and offered those, too, for her delectation.

'*So* confident!' Angela said, eyebrows raised, as if confidence was the very last thing she'd expected.

'I think she might even be happy,' Chrissie said, and Stu nudged her gently with an elbow, but it was all right, Angela only nodded and said, 'I can see that.'

'So,' Stu said, 'does this mean we can apply yet, for full adoption?'

Angela looked at him over the top of her reading glasses.

'No,' she said, and shook her head, as if she thought her meaning might not be clear.

Chrissie said, 'We thought, I don't know . . .' She glanced at Stu. 'I suppose we hoped it might be quicker than usual. Nancy once said something to that effect . . .'

'Oh, doubtless she did,' Angela said, a little waspishly, 'but this hasn't been slow, you know.'

'No,' Stu said. 'We're just really keen.'

Angela sighed and looked down at her notes, then, when she spoke, she did so wearily, as if reciting some oft-repeated and perfectly obvious truth. 'Everyone is really keen, Stuart. But a child must have lived with the adoptive parents for ten weeks before they can submit an application to the family court.'

'Right,' said Stu. 'Of course, yeah.'

'There'll be another official review before your ten weeks is up, then assuming all's well, you can apply. But you'll more than likely have a wait for the hearing. I can't say how long that might be, it's out of our hands.'

She stopped speaking. Sunshine squinted at her for a moment, then said, 'You is cross?' which made Chrissie and Stu laugh. Angela waited for them to stop.

'In any case,' she said, 'there's a person at the housing office who thinks he noticed a woman of Indian descent, carrying what might have been the memory bag.'

There was a heavy silence, like the one that might follow a landslide.

'What?' Stu asked, flatly.

Sunshine, bored, ignored, stuck out both her arms and began to spin in the centre of the room, eager for the attention to fall upon her once more. Chrissie said, 'Sunny, careful, you'll get dizzy,' then, to Angela, 'What did you just tell us?'

Angela said, 'Yes, a female, possibly of Indian descent, around the time the memory bag was found. Given the ethnic nature of the bag itself, there's some speculation that she might have left it.'

'Indian descent?' Chrissie said.

Angela nodded. 'That's correct.'

'What does that mean?'

This was Stuart, whose voice had an edge that Chrissie noticed and Angela didn't.

'She seemed to be wearing a sari,' Angela said. 'That's what I mean.'

'You have an anecdotal report of a woman in a sari, and on that basis, you can delay our adoption of Sunny?'

His voice was extraordinarily steely. He rarely lost his rag, he rarely even raised his voice, but sometimes, when pushed, he seemed to become another man altogether. Angela, who barely knew him at all, said, 'No one mentioned delaying the adoption.'

'It was implied,' Stu said.

Sunshine spun and spun, and started to hum.

'Anyway,' Chrissie said, 'what are you gonna do? Interview every sari-clad woman in South East London?'

Angela said, 'All I meant to convey was that you can't make the assumption that matters will be entirely straightforward.'

'Not if you have anything to do with it anyhow,' Stu said. He stood up, partly because he was too angry to stay seated, and partly to stop Sunshine's crazy dance. She was almost blurred at the edges when he reached for her, and then she stepped out of range, stumbled, fell, and hit her head on the edge of the fireplace.

Chrissie leapt up and dropped to her knees beside Sunny, whose face was splintering into tears. Stu said, 'Oh, thank God she's crying,' and Angela gave him a sidelong look.

'I mean, thank God she's not unconscious,' Stu said. 'Obviously.'

'You'll still need to have that looked at,' Angela said. 'A blow to the—'

'We know! We're not fucking morons,' Stuart said.

Chrissie lifted Sunny, cradled her in her arms, and said, 'We need a lift to the Whittington, Angela.' There was a small cut on Sunshine's head, not easy to see through her hair; about an inch long, just above her left ear. A fine streak of blood ran down along the line of her jaw. The child sobbed and turned her face into Chrissie's T-shirt, and she felt such a tremendous swell of love for her that she almost smiled.

'But I thought you had a car?' Angela said. 'I have other clients to see.' She was on her feet, preparing to leave, looking between Stu and Chrissie with an expression of professional calm. Stu opened his mouth to speak, then thought better of it.

'Call a cab, Stu,' Chrissie said.

'Well, I—' Angela began.

'Bye, Angela,' Stu said. 'Thanks for everything.' He sounded so savage that even Chrissie stared.

10

Julia and Juno were back from Versailles. Two weeks with the elegant French mother and suave English father, who, when their daughter visited, paid a local girl to come and play with the child, so that Julia could have wine at lunchtime and snooze in the afternoon. They had a cocktail hour, the Bouvier-Smiths, and they dressed for dinner. Their life was characterised by ease and glamour, and when Chrissie went there with Julia, in the summer after their first year of university, she felt obscurely angry with her friend for failing to prepare her sufficiently for the casual splendour. At dinner, she was given artichoke vinaigrette and had to cast covert glances at the Bouvier-Smiths to see how they tackled the prickly, ugly object on the plates before them. Then she'd torn off the leaves and sucked at the scant flesh, and wondered if it was all an elaborate practical joke, but no, Julia and her older brother Marc, and her little sister Remi, and her two immaculate parents, had torn and dipped and sucked and chatted – in English, for the benefit of their guest – so Chrissie had followed suit and striven to exhibit the same indifference as everyone else when staff appeared to clear their plates away.

'You look exhausted,' Julia said now, to Chrissie.

'Why, thank you,' Chrissie said, as if she couldn't be more flattered, and Julia laughed and said, 'Sorry, *chérie*,' but Chrissie said, 'No, you're right, I do look exhausted.' And she was. Sitting here on a picnic rug in Julia and Sol's verdant garden, beside Julia's groomed and biscuity perfection, she felt like a lower form of human. She wasn't sleeping well, she was anxious, and watchful, and she snapped at Stu, unfairly and too often. Since Sunshine's fall she'd felt less qualified to care for her, less capable in general, even while she fully understood that this was irrational. Angela Holt had made a note of the incident – she made a note of everything; she was hardly likely to let this pass – but still, there it was, in their file, a fall, a cut to the head, the car they shared with their friends all the way over in Kentish Town when they needed it. And Brendan had been on the doorstep the next day – so studiously kind and concerned that he somehow undermined his own efforts to reassure.

'You should have come with us; it would've been much more fun for Juno and me, and a total break for you,' Julia said.

Chrissie stared at her, but her friend's eyes were hidden behind a pair of large, very dark, sunglasses.

'I can't take her out of the country,' Chrissie said. 'Obviously.'

'Oh, well yes, I know.' Julia yawned, and lowered herself down so that she was fully stretched out on the rug. 'Next time though, for sure. Get her on your passport. Oh, by the way, Remi's coming over; she'll be here all September.' Julia's little sister, a prodigiously talented singer, the baby of the family, but the least indulged or, rather, the most independent, of the three siblings. She scraped a living singing in clubs and cabarets and had ditched the Bouvier to be plain Remi Smith on stage, her personal two fingers to the dynasty. Chrissie said, 'Cool. Shame we don't have any gigs, she could guest appear.'

'Highlight of her life, that time she sang with you guys.'

'One of the highlights of ours too,' Chrissie said. 'What a voice.'

'Redolent of the street corners of Montmartre,' Julia said, and it was true that her baby sister had done a little busking, now and again, because if a girl wouldn't touch her trust fund, then naturally, she had to hustle for her daily bread.

'What's she going to be doing here?'

'Small gigs, not sure where, and she's seeing an A & R woman from Decca, they heard her sing, want a chat.'

'God, they ought to snap her up.' Remi had sung with The Lineman two years ago, at a three-night run in a venue in Paris. She was only nineteen at the time, no formal training, just natural talent and all the right musical instincts. She reminded Chrissie of her own young self – all that self-fulfilling confidence; I sing, therefore I am.

For a few minutes, Julia basked like a pampered cat in the afternoon sun, while Chrissie sat and watched the girls. Juno was older, just turned four, and this gave her most of the authority in this partnership. She was tall for her age, with skinny, tanned limbs, wide-set blue eyes, and very fine fair hair, which Julia kept extremely short, in the belief it would encourage it to thicken. Julia thought Sunshine was far more beautiful than her own daughter, and Chrissie demurred, of course, while nevertheless privately agreeing, but when Sunshine looked at Juno, it was with the adoring, respectful, grateful gaze of an acolyte. Now and again, Juno forgot where she was and spoke in French, and, when she did, Sunshine stood very still, with her head cocked and her brow furrowed, as if it was entirely her failing that she hadn't understood. Julia would say, 'English please, Juno,' and Juno would shake her head crossly, as if she had water in her ears, and flip back into English. Now, they were playing under the sweeping branches of a weeping willow, crawling like little bears on their hands and feet, one behind the other, in meandering circles, until one of them would abruptly change direction and they'd both roll about amid peals of laughter.

'I just can't shed the idea that we've blown it,' Chrissie said.

Julia, from her prone position, languidly flapped one hand. 'Nonsense, she didn't even need stitches. Juno broke her arm on that slide when she wasn't quite two, and nobody tried to take her away from me.'

Chrissie said, 'Jesus, Julia! That's because she's yours!' and Julia lifted her sunglasses up from her eyes and said, 'And Sunshine is yours, body and soul.'

Chrissie said, 'Not in law, not yet.' She spoke more quietly, trying to be patient. It shouldn't need spelling out, and yet, time and again, Julia made sweeping assumptions, and each new one felt to Chrissie like a jinx on the outcome. Stu said it was because Julia had been thoroughly spoiled since infancy – her path to fulfilment had always been so clear of obstacles, she tended to assume that everyone she loved would enjoy the same happy trajectory.

'It's what it says on the paperwork that counts,' Chrissie said. 'And now the paperwork has a black mark against us.'

'Chrissie, no one thinks you're abusing that child,' Julia said. 'That Holt woman was there when it happened – she knows it wasn't your fault. I mean, God, she's more at fault than you, quibbling about the car, letting you call a cab.'

'Angela looks at me as if she wouldn't trust me to look after her goldfish.'

'She has goldfish?' Julia said, with naked distaste.

Chrissie laughed. 'I've no idea; I didn't mean it literally.'

'No way does that woman have the power to stand between you and Sunny.'

'I just want it to be official. I *need* it to be.'

Chrissie plucked at the fibres of the rug they were sharing. She felt edgy, agitated, but this had nothing to do with the conversation, or her friend's blithe and uninformed confidence. It was because Stuart had accused Angela of unprofessional behaviour, and started some sort of internal process that Brendan said might – or might not – hold things up. But she *had* been unprofessional, Brendan had conceded, privately. He'd been shocked when he heard she'd raised the matter of the woman in the sari; this information was nothing new, he said; it was something someone had said on the day, and was inconclusive, and meaningless in the context of the adoption. 'I didn't share it with you at the time,' he'd said. 'You seemed stressed enough at the existence of the bag.'

'How much longer?' Julia asked.

Chrissie shrugged. 'I don't know. This business with Angela . . .'

'She's a goldfish-owning bitch,' Julia said. 'She should be sacked.' Then she smiled and said, 'Listen to those two, aren't they just the best, together?' She was still lying down, so she couldn't see them, only hear their bubbling laughter.

Chrissie, though, she hardly took her eyes off Sunshine these days, and now she smiled at the sight of them, two little compadres, whispering theatrically into each other's ears, then dissolving into giggles.

'What?' Chrissie said, looking at Sunshine. Sunshine smiled back at her, with mischief in her face, glee in her eyes.

'What?!' Chrissie said again, starting to laugh.

Juno said, 'It's a secret,' and Sunny, who always followed Juno's lead, said, 'A secret,' although Chrissie was almost certain the child didn't completely understand what a secret was.

Julia sat up. 'What've you done, Juno?'

'Not me,' Juno said. 'Sunshine did it.'

'What has Sunshine done?' Julia asked, and Sunshine's expression altered fractionally, as she prepared herself to be betrayed.

'A wee-wee on the flowers,' Juno said.

∾

And then, all of a sudden, she was theirs.

They went to the family court. Sunshine wore the pink frock and cardigan Diana had bought for her, and looked scrubbed clean and cherubic. Chrissie wore a sleeveless linen dress and put her hair up, out of the way, and Stuart wore a black suit and a white shirt, with a narrow black tie. Rocco and Kim drove them there, to spare them the hassle of parking, and as Kim watched the three of them arrange themselves in the back of the car, her eyes filled with tears and she pressed all her fingers against her mouth, and Rocco stared at Chrissie and said, 'It's Dusty Springfield!' and Chrissie had laughed and rolled her eyes and said, 'Just drive, Rocco.'

Angela had been side-lined from their case on the grounds of personal differences, but Brendan was there, looking slightly damaged and very flustered, having come off his bike on Waterloo Bridge, and the new Angela, a young woman called Grace, who had lived up to her name by behaving with courtesy and goodwill in every encounter they'd had with her.

There were many people milling about the building, but none of them seemed to Chrissie to have worried like she had about what to wear, and neither Brendan nor Grace were dressed any differently than usual because this was, after all, just another working day for them. Chrissie said, 'Oh God, we look like we're going to a garden party,' and Brendan, gazing directly at her, said, 'No, you look perfect,' then blushed, which made everyone laugh. They sat on pale wooden chairs, waiting for their names to be called. Chrissie and Stuart held hands, and Sunshine folded her own in her lap and swung her legs back and forth, and sang 'Go Johnny, go,' but very, very quietly.

The courtroom door opened and a smiling man, short and plump, with a shining bald pate, ushered them in. A judge in all her regalia stood up from where she'd been sitting at the bench and came to greet them, dipping down into a half-crouch so that she could take Sunshine's hand and say, 'I'm so pleased to meet you, Sunshine,' which seemed exceptionally kind and normal from a woman in an elaborate black gown and a tightly curled long grey wig. Sunshine was speechless. They all sat down at the same big table, which was a huge relief to Chrissie, who'd pictured the three of them in the dock, and the judge bringing down her gavel to pronounce sentence. Brendan and Grace sat at a slight distance from the family, and the judge was seated on the opposite side of the table, Sunny's file in front of her.

'Now,' she said, still addressing herself to Sunshine, 'today, you're being adopted, Sunshine, which means that your mummy and daddy here will be your mummy and daddy forever.'

Sunshine turned her head towards the door, as if she thought someone else must have walked into the room.

'Your mummy and daddy *here*,' the judge repeated, with greater emphasis, indicating Chrissie and Stuart with one hand, and Sunshine stared, then smiled when Stuart winked at her.

'And your name will be Sunshine Stevenson,' said the judge. 'Is that correct?' Now, she looked at Chrissie, who nodded yes, and then the judge made a flourishing signature on the front of the file and said, 'There, it's official. Congratulations, Sunshine, you've now been adopted by your mummy and daddy. Congratulations, Chrissie and Stuart, you've adopted Sunshine.'

'Is that it?' Chrissie asked. The work of seconds, after all these anxious months.

The judge smiled, and said, 'All it took was my name on the paperwork.'

Sunshine pointed at the judge's head. 'What that is?' she asked.

The judge lifted her hand to her wig. 'This?'

Sunny nodded.

'It's my special judge's wig. Look.' She lifted it from her head, and Sunshine's eyes were round with shock. Underneath the wig, her hair was perfectly ordinary, mid-brown, pinned up at the sides and at the nape of her neck. 'I hope I didn't look too scary in it,' the judge said. 'I wear it for special days, such as today.'

Sunshine, once again lost for words, leaned in towards Chrissie, who lifted her into a cuddle.

'Hello there, Sunny Stevenson,' she said, and Sunny said, 'Hello, Mummy.'

On the steps of the courthouse, under a hard, blue sky, Stu gave Grace his camera and she took photographs of the brand-new family, Chrissie and Stuart on either side of Sunshine, who held up her adoption certificate and beamed obligingly. Then Brendan asked if he could have one taken with them too, and he tacked himself on to the line-up beside Chrissie, and Grace took a couple more shots. After that, they all said goodbye to Grace, who had a client meeting in Camberwell, but Brendan hung about like a man at a loose end, and an awkwardness began to develop.

'Phone me, won't you, if there's anything you need?' he said, although Grace had only just told them they'd receive a call soon from a new support worker, someone from the team of volunteer post-adoption counsellors.

'Sure,' Chrissie said.

Stuart said, 'Where's your bike then, Brendan?' which was as overt a clue as he could possibly have given that he'd like him to get onto it and pedal away, but Brendan just smiled, then said, 'Hey, look, I was wondering if I could come to one of your gigs?'

There were a few beats of silence, then Brendan said, 'I mean, I've played a lot of your music since meeting you, and – I dunno – I just feel, like, connected, or no, that's not what I mean, not connected, more, erm, *invested*.'

'Right,' Chrissie said.

'We're doing a European tour next year,' Stu said, but he was talking over his shoulder, descending the steps, scanning the road for Rocco and Kim in the Subaru. 'Dates and places are on the website. Anyone can come, you included.'

'Oh, sure,' Brendan said. He sounded hurt. He picked up his rucksack and strapped on his helmet. There was a rip in the sleeve of his jacket from the tumble on the way over. Chrissie, sorry for him, smiled and said, 'Let Stu know what suits you and he'll make sure there's a couple of comps at the door.'

'Oh, that wasn't . . .'

'No, Brendan, I know you weren't on the cadge, but we're not going to let you pay, so sure, come along to a gig; we'd love to see you.' She looked down at Sunshine. 'Ready?' she asked her, and the child nodded and looked at Brendan with her head on one side, squinting up at him, and said, 'I's having cake.'

'You're having a party,' Chrissie said. 'At which there'll be a cake.'

'And Zuno.'

'And Juno, yes.'

'And cake.'

'Yep,' Chrissie confirmed, laughing. 'And cake.' She smiled again at Brendan. 'My Auntie Nina's at our place, preparing Sunshine's adoption tea party.'

'Sounds perfect,' Brendan said, and he sounded so doleful that Chrissie almost invited him to come along, but she held her tongue and the moment passed. Then Rocco and Kim razzed up, windows down, The Cure belting out at top volume for all of Peckham to enjoy. Kim was driving. She silenced the car, whistled through her fingers and shouted, 'Sunshine Stevenson, your carriage awaits,' and the child laughed and, holding Chrissie's hand, jumped on two feet down the steps then ran to the car to show Kim, and then Rocco, her certificate. Chrissie felt giddy, euphoric. A new life, she supposed; that must be it. A new life, unmonitored by Brendan Cassidy and Angela Holt. The Sunshine file was signed, and sealed, and closed. She strapped the child into her booster seat, then, as she straightened, felt Stuart behind her, and she turned to him. He held her face between his hands and placed a kiss on her forehead, her cheek, her mouth.

'Here comes the sun,' he said.

~

Nina had made a splendid cake, precision cut into a wavy sun, glossy with lemon-yellow icing. She'd made delicate sandwiches on soft white bread, and miniature quiches, and quail's egg Scotch eggs, cut in half to show the orange yolks. The garden was all set up for the party, with champagne waiting in silver ice buckets and jugs of cold homemade lemonade, swathes of gold and silver bunting strung along the larch lap fencing and, also, a surprise; her adoption-day gift to Chrissie. A large canvas, propped up at the back of the garden, facing them as they stepped outside, bearing an extraordinary portrait of Chrissie holding Sunny in her arms, their heads tilted towards each other, their foreheads just touching. You could see, from the fine creases by their eyes and the turned-up corners of their mouths, that they were smiling. It was an intimate, arresting sight. Chrissie's tousled blonde hair, Sunshine's brown curls. Chrissie's hands locked under Sunny's bottom, Sunny's arms locked behind Chrissie's neck. They looked integral, permanent. They looked in the grip of a fierce and joyful love.

Chrissie's hand flew to her mouth and Stu said, 'Nina, my God!'

Rocco and Kim stood staring at it too, stunned into silence, but Sunshine barely glanced at the painting, then said, 'Nina, where mine cake is?' and Kim, who felt she and Rocco were prying on a deeply private moment, said, 'Come on, Sunny, let's go on a cake hunt,' and she and Rocco took the child by the hands and skipped her along the garden path, back into the flat.

Nina said, 'You like it? I was afraid you might feel, I don't know, invaded somehow.'

Chrissie looked at her. 'Invaded?'

'You didn't know I was painting it. I've never done that before, painted a portrait in secret, and, well, it was a kind of theft, I suppose, given that this was done from a print I didn't show you.' There was uncertainty in her voice, an insecurity; Chrissie reached for her hand.

'It was just a photograph, Nina,' Stu said. 'And you've turned it into something magnificent.'

'Sorry, yeah,' Nina said. She looked at Chrissie. 'I'm so proud of you,' she said, 'and happy for you too, and your happiness means the world to me, you know that, don't you? You are the coolest, most creative, most wonderful mummy to Sunshine.'

Chrissie said, 'Don't make me cry, I'm wearing mascara,' and they laughed, and hugged, and Chrissie couldn't understand why she'd ever managed to be hard on Nina, when all her life Nina had only ever been kind to her, and loving.

Then Julia and Sol arrived with Juno and Julia's sister Remi, and Rocco emerged from indoors, galloping around the small lawn with Sunny on his back, followed by Kim who was bearing the cake on its white china stand. Nina opened some champagne, filled eight flutes, passed them around. Sunny and Juno had plastic flutes of lemonade. They raised their glasses in a toast to Sunshine, and then had to do it again, to Juno.

The food was perfect, the mood was mellow, the afternoon melted into evening, and although they gravitated indoors, no one made a move for home. They put 'Here Comes the Sun' on the turntable, and all the adults sang along, which Sunny and Juno found inexplicably hilarious. Then Stuart and Sol played some low-key guitar, and Chrissie sang a song she'd written, 'The Ballad of Sunny and Juno', and the two little girls quietened down and sat still for once, listening with rapt faces, smiling every time their names were mentioned, amazed that they were in a song. Then Remi made hot chocolate for them, with real chocolate pieces and warm, creamy milk. She gave them each an espresso cupful, and they sipped it in a state of bliss and stared sleepily at the grown-ups over the rim of their little cups.

Stu carried the painting in from the garden and leaned it against a wall in the living room where it drew the gaze whenever there was a lull in the conversation. Nina made her excuses and went home. The little girls fell asleep together on the sofa. Rocco rolled a mild joint for himself. Remi sang some Édith Piaf, her party piece since childhood. Kim put 'Into the Mystic' on the turntable, and the room slipped into a Van Morrison trance. Chrissie sat on the floor between Stuart's knees and he drew lines with his fingers on the back of her neck and up through her hair, and for the first time in weeks, she felt calm and centred and completely happy. She closed her eyes and listened to the music, and felt lucky, and loving, and loved.

That night, Juno stayed over, and slept with Sunshine in Sunshine's bed, the two of them curled under the duvet together like nuts in a shell, and Chrissie and Stuart lay together in the big bed, reunited, and made quiet love, so as not to disturb the little girls, then they all slept late the next day, in perfect peace until that peace was shattered by Sunshine, bowling into their room, hurling herself onto their bed, saying, 'Me and Zuno is hungry,' and her breath was so close to Chrissie's face that she came back to consciousness inhaling the sweet, hot, smell of her own beautiful child.

Then Brendan rang, not on the landline, but on Chrissie's mobile phone. It buzzed on the bedside table beside Stuart. He picked it up, glanced at the screen, and passed it across. 'Your biggest fan,' he said. 'Missing you already.'

'Chrissie?' Brendan said, after she'd answered but before she'd had time to speak.

'What is it?' she asked. Sunshine rolled off the bed, and went looking for Juno, and Chrissie watched her leave and thought, was there more paperwork, a discrepancy, another signature required, one more reference?

'Chrissie, I just had a call from Barbara in Whitstable.'

She relaxed. It was nothing, then. It was soap powder or cheese strings or the correct way to wash Sunny's hair.

'Right, and?'

'A woman turned up on her doorstep last night, asking about Sunshine.'

At once, the colour of the day darkened. Chrissie's heart pounded and her breath came fast and shallow. Her face was a pale mask.

'What?' Stu asked. 'Chrissie, what?'

Chrissie looked at him, but she couldn't speak.

'I'm so sorry,' Brendan said. 'We have no idea who she is, or how she knew Barbara's address.'

'What did she want?' Chrissie asked.

Brendan hesitated. His silence seemed to crackle like static down the line.

'Brendan?'

He said, 'Sorry, yes, she wanted to know where Sunshine is. She said she wanted to know who has her now.'

11

Brendan was coming straight over, so Stuart rang Julia, who drove across at once to whisk Sunshine and Juno away. Chrissie wasn't sure about the wisdom of this; she didn't want Sunny anywhere but here, with them, at home. But Stu talked her into it, and it was true that a crisis meeting with Brendan was no place for Sunshine.

'Do not let her out of your sight,' Chrissie said to Julia.

'Of course not.' The morning was overcast, but Julia still wore her dark glasses, which meant she was hungover.

'Seriously, I mean, not even for a second.'

Julia sighed. 'She'll be indoors, with Juno, OK? Can I come in?'

'God, sorry,' Chrissie said. She stepped aside to let Julia through the front door, just as the girls came down the stairs, still in their pyjamas.

'No, Mummeeeee,' Juno wailed, halting mid-flight. 'I don't want to go!'

'But Sunny's coming with us too,' Julia said. 'Did you know that, Sunny? Breakfast at our house today; Remi went out for croissants.'

Juno, very interested now, hopped down the remaining stairs, and Sunshine followed, but more slowly. She had Silky bunched up in her right hand, and clutched the bannister with her left. She looked a little uncertain, and Chrissie's heart lurched.

'I's hungry, Mummy,' she said.

'I know, darling, and Julia has a treat for you, at Juno's house.'

'And can we watch *The Lion King*?' Juno said.

Julia nodded. 'You can.'

'I want a nanana,' Sunny said.

'A banana, good thinking,' Chrissie said. 'You can eat it in the car.'

'Eat our croissants and watch *The Lion King*, *at the same time*,' Juno said, with non-negotiable emphasis.

Julia grinned and said, to Chrissie, 'She drives a hard bargain' and '*Oui, d'accord*,' to Juno, who started cheering and jumping about, so Sunshine did the same. Stuart came down the hall from the kitchen and blew a kiss at Julia. 'Oh, what a night,' he said.

Julia said, 'Who gave me Cointreau? It can't have been my idea, it gives me the most hideous headache.'

Chrissie said, 'You're not just going to go back to bed, Jules, are you?'

'No, I'm not,' she said.

'Oh God, you're going to go back to bed,' Chrissie said. 'I know that face.'

'OK, I was going to, but now I won't. I'll stand by the locked front door. And if I do happen to fall asleep, there's Sol and Remi available for sentry duty.'

'It might be better if she just stays here, though.'

Stu put an arm round Chrissie's shoulders. 'Two hours,' he said. 'Three max, then Sol's bringing her back. We can't be talking to Brendan interrupted, or in whispers.'

'You got me out of bed on a mercy dash,' Julia said. 'I'm not going home empty-handed.'

So, the little girls left with Julia, still in their pyjamas, Sunshine eating a banana and dragging Silky along behind her down the path. Stu fixed Sunshine's seat next to Juno's in the back of Julia's sexy, low-slung car, and strapped the children in. They held hands and laughed at each other. Chrissie leaned in for a kiss. 'Don't get banana on Julia's car seats, and don't lose Silky,' she said to Sunny, then, to Julia, 'On no account let her lose Silky, Jules.'

'Good grief,' Julia said, and she pressed the electric buttons that closed the windows, so Chrissie stepped back from the kerb, and watched the car until it was gone.

12

Brendan said the knock on the door had come at just after nine last night, and Barbara had answered expecting it to be John, who'd gone out for a pint, but there was this woman on the doorstep, who didn't say hello, only smiled and said, 'Thank you so much for looking after Sunshine. Can you tell me where she is now?'

'Total shock,' Brendan said. 'Unprecedented breach of security.'

'Do you believe her?' Chrissie asked.

'Who?'

'Barbara. Do you believe her story?'

Brendan said, 'What?'

Stu said, 'Chrissie's always had the impression that Barbara didn't have our best interests at heart.'

'And you,' Chrissie said. 'You thought that too.'

'Kind of, but more you. Anyway, do you believe Barbara's story, Brendan?'

'Hang on, we definitely both thought she'd deliberately left the soap powder out of the bag of stuff, Stuart.'

'Chrissie, whatever, OK?'

'No,' she said. 'Not OK, not if you're going to make out I'm paranoid.' She felt a surprising, rising fury and she had to look away from Stu, who was considering her with a maddeningly patient gaze. With difficulty, she swallowed and said, 'Go on, Brendan.'

He said, 'I've no reason to disbelieve Barbara, but I do acknowledge your concerns, Chrissie.'

Stuart gave a small laugh, and Chrissie said, 'What?' but Stu just shook his head and said, to Brendan, 'So, this woman, what did she look like?'

Brendan looked at his notes. 'Fresh-faced, pleasant, medium height, dark hair, red coat. She was friendly, not threatening. Barbara said her manner was formal.'

'Formal?'

'That's what she said.'

'How old was she?' Chrissie asked. 'I mean, young? Middle-aged? Old?'

Brendan looked at his notes again, as if this was a detail he might have overlooked. 'She didn't say,' he said.

'Did Barbara give this person any information?' Stu asked.

'Of course not,' Brendan said.

'Did she ask the woman any questions about herself?'

'She says she panicked and shut the door in her face, then rang me this morning.'

Chrissie said, 'Is it at all possible that Barbara told her what she wanted to know? Or even, that she contacted the woman herself, and then cobbled together this spurious scenario?'

Stu said, 'Chrissie, come on.'

She glared. 'Don't undermine me. This is a fucking nightmare, but I thought that at least we were in it together. Or do I have that wrong?'

Quietly, he said, 'You do not have that wrong.'

Brendan said, 'I know this is the last thing you need, but whoever she was, she's gone, and she knows nothing.'

'She knows who Barbara is, and where she lives,' Chrissie said. 'I mean, come on!'

'Sunshine is ours, Chrissie,' Stu said. 'She's legally our daughter now. Whoever that woman was, she has no power over us.'

Chrissie put her face in her hands.

Brendan said, 'Stuart's right, Chrissie.'

'No, he's not,' she said, looking up at him, then Stu. She felt profoundly uneasy; their gentle voices, their calm. 'He's not right. That woman has tremendous power over us, over me, in any case; I can't speak for Stuart, it seems.'

'Hey,' he said, but she ignored him.

'Someone's looking for Sunshine, and they're already closer than they should be.' She stood up. 'And I don't trust Barbara.'

'Where you going?' Stu said.

'Julia's.'

'Because you don't trust her either?'

She stared at him, and didn't answer, just grabbed her jacket and bag, and left the flat without shutting the door, and even as she charged off up the street, she knew how irrational her actions looked, how precipitous and desperate. But she hadn't wanted Sunshine to leave the house – it hadn't been her idea – and now she needed her back, simple as that. She wanted Sunshine's warm hand in hers and then, once she had hold of her, she wanted not to let go. With this sense of urgent purpose, she walked swiftly, head down, out of Muswell Hill, along the main road towards Highgate tube station, and she hadn't got far before she heard Stuart behind her, running, his unmistakable loping footfall, so she stopped and turned around, and he seized her with a kind of frustration, as if she'd been avoiding him for days, and pulled her into his arms where he held her tight for a while, and pressed his lips against her hair. Oh, how she loved that feeling, of being almost too precious to him, of his love for her being beyond words.

'I'm sorry,' she said. 'But I need you to feel exactly what I'm feeling.'

He said, 'Oh, Chrissie, I can't promise that – you're you, I'm me. But I promise you I'm going to keep Sunshine safe, and you happy.'

'How can you keep Sunshine safe from a threat we don't understand?'

He took a step back, but still held her within the frame of his arms.

'That woman, whoever she is – her search stops there, in Whitstable. She drew a blank.'

Chrissie said, 'How did she know where Barbara lived?'

'God knows. Who cares?'

'I care, and you should too. Why do you imagine she'll stop looking?'

He gave a sort of groan. 'Look,' he said. 'Sunshine's ours, Chrissie. She's safe, with us. You have to believe that.'

She was silent for a moment, then, 'I need my daughter back from Julia and Sol,' she said. 'I want her with me.' She shrugged away from his hold and began to walk, so he followed her, just a fraction behind, and in this way, they walked the rest of the way to the station, in silence.

Remi answered the door, because Sol and Julia had gone back to bed.

'He-eyyy,' she said, smiling warmly, letting them in, kissing their cheeks. Julia – fair-skinned, tall and athletic – took after her English father, and nobody ever guessed she was French. Remi, however, couldn't be anything else; dark hair, flashing brown eyes, sweetly petite.

'Sunny's been a darling,' she said, to Chrissie. 'I thought Sol was going to drive her home?'

'Change of plan,' Stu said.

'We thought we'd take her to the Heath,' Chrissie added, although this hadn't been discussed.

'Cool,' Remi said. 'Come through.'

They followed her down along the spacious hallway. She wore denim cut-off shorts and a white vest and her bare feet made no sound on the tiled floor. Her wavy black hair was cut very short, and her exposed neck was pale and slender. Chrissie had always found it difficult not to stare at Remi, even the child she'd been when they'd first met. She drew the eye, and held it. On stage, she was utterly magnetic, a kind of fallen angel, innocence and debauchery combined, a singing voice grown from cigarettes, coffee and wine.

'*The Lion King* isn't finished,' Remi said, opening the door to Juno's playroom, giving Chrissie and Stuart a back view of the two little girls, each sitting on her own beanbag, mesmerised by a duet between a warthog and a meerkat. Evidence of their croissant breakfast lay all around them. Neither of them turned around.

'No sweat, we'll wait,' Stu said, so they went through to the kitchen and Remi made them coffee, and they talked about her London gigs, where and when they were, and about Decca, and whether they'd sign her, and whether she wanted to be signed, and then Julia wandered into the room, saw them, and said, 'Ah, damn it, rumbled.'

Chrissie laughed. 'I know you too well,' she said.

'Tell me you weren't checking up on me?'

'I wasn't checking up on you.'

'Were you, though?' Julia took the mug of black coffee that her sister had intended for herself, knocked back an urgent mouthful, then grimaced. 'God, I don't remember the last time I felt this bad.'

'I wasn't checking up on you, I just needed to get my hands on Sunny again,' Chrissie said.

'You,' Julia said, pointing at Chrissie, 'should chill out,' and Remi said, 'And you, dear Julia, should show a little more understanding.'

Stuart smiled at Remi, who smiled back and rolled her eyes. Chrissie said, 'I am chilled out. Sort of. We're going to Parliament Hill Fields, if you want to come.'

'Christ, no,' Julia said. 'Can't think of anything I'd less like to do.'

'Sometimes,' Chrissie said, 'I find it hard to remember why we're friends.'

Julia blew her a kiss. 'You don't need to remember why; just accept it as fact.'

Then Sol sloped in, looking handsome and rakish with his dark stubble and his mussed-up hair and an old washed-out Lineman T-shirt celebrating The Wilderness Tour, 1989. He squeezed Julia's backside as he passed her, and winked at Chrissie, and said, 'Greetings, all.' If he thought it was surprising to see them here, he didn't say so. What he did say was, 'Hey, I've been thinking, suppose nobody had told you about this encounter Barbara had with that mystery woman?'

'Yeah,' Julia said, nodding. 'Suppose that.'

'Well, then we'd not have known there was a woman asking for Sunshine's new address,' Chrissie said. 'How would that help?'

'Because, she'll never find it,' Sol said. 'The system protects the adopted child. You didn't need to know she came calling; I don't know why that Brendan guy had to tell you.'

'He has a duty to, for a start,' Stuart said. 'Plus, we'd both rather know than be kept in the dark.'

'What do you know, then?' Julia said. 'What did Brendan divulge?'

Chrissie didn't like her tone, which was borderline sarcastic, as if she couldn't take them, or this subject, seriously. Because of this, Chrissie didn't respond, but Stu said, 'Fresh-faced, dark hair, medium height, red coat.'

Julia laughed.

'What?' Chrissie said.

'Fresh-faced? Is that a legit facial characteristic?'

Nobody replied.

'And the red coat – how will you ever find her if she takes it off?'

Remi said, 'It's not funny, Jules,' and Julia pulled a face and said, 'Oh, believe me, I know.'

Sol poured himself a tall glass of orange juice, and everyone watched him as he opened his throat and swallowed it. The fridge here was the size of a double wardrobe. Periodically, it refilled its own ice dispenser, releasing new cubes into a plastic box with a muted clatter. Sol swung open one of the huge doors, and put the jug of orange juice back on a shelf. The inside of the fridge was loaded with desirable food; French yoghurts in glass pots, an expensive-looking yellow-skinned chicken, long, pointed red peppers, carrots in a bunch with their green topknots intact, butter in printed waxed paper, a big jar of cornichons, a wheel of Brie, a strawberry tart under a glass dome. It looked as if they'd arranged it for a photoshoot, but the whole house was the same, achingly stylish, their wedding gift four years ago from Julia's parents, a kind of bribe to get them to marry before Juno was born. In this house, thought Chrissie now, their friends lost their grip on reality; the trip wires and time bombs that blew up other people's lives left them untouched, even Sol, who was a working-class lad from Walthamstow. There was a time, years ago, before

Sol realised it was lust he felt for Julia and not dislike, when he'd referred to her as Marie Antoinette and said things such as *vive la révolution* when she walked into a room. But he'd long ago stopped noticing the luxury in which he lived. Not that you should wear your past like a yoke, thought Chrissie, but God, you should never take for granted a fridge that knew when the ice was low, and got on with topping it up.

Remi lit a Gauloise and stepped outside, disappearing down the stone steps into the back garden. Julia yawned and stretched, and the loose silk tunic she was wearing rippled like a puddle in a breeze. Sol threw himself down among the cushions of the capacious sofa, and said, in a comedy Northern accent, 'Don't meet trouble halfway, Christine.' He grinned at Chrissie. 'Isn't that what your dad would say?'

Chrissie said, 'For God's sake, Sol, my daughter is being stalked by a stranger,' and Julia said, 'Oh, purr-lease, let's keep a sense of proportion.'

Stu stood up.

'We gotta split,' he said.

He left the kitchen, scooped up Sunshine and Silky from the beanbag without explanation or apology, and was out of the front door before anyone had quite realised what was happening.

Sol said, 'Whoa!' and Julia said, 'What's eating him?' but Chrissie just said a quick goodbye then raced off out of the house after him. She felt good, closing the door. She felt proud of Stu, and grateful; she felt he'd stood shoulder to shoulder with her against the flippancy of Julia and Sol. He was walking briskly away from the house with Sunshine on his shoulders and she had to jog to catch them up, but when she did, he spun round and his face was not the face she'd expected; it was taut and unsmiling, grey with anger.

'What?' she said, utterly taken aback.

'*Our* daughter,' he said, savagely. 'Twice this morning you've called her yours. She's *ours*.'

'Oh,' she said. 'Have I? OK, OK, yes, I know, I'm sorry; I didn't mean anything by it. I'm sorry.' Her shock was extreme, as if he'd slapped her. It made her voice shake, made her unsteady on her feet, and queasy, aware of the presence in her throat of the coffee she'd so recently drunk. Stu's anger against her was so rare that she hardly knew how to bear it.

'Right,' he said.

Sunshine reached out her arms and said, 'Mummeeeee,' which she'd learned today from Juno, but Chrissie stopped herself from lifting her down and said, 'No, Daddy has you. Come on, let's go and find a tree to climb.'

The child was still in her pyjamas, and shoeless, the way she'd been dispatched this morning. But it hardly mattered, Chrissie thought. The weather was fine and warm; she only had to salvage the mood.

'Stu, I'm sorry,' she said again as they walked on, just to make him speak to her.

'I know you are,' he said, which wasn't the same as 'That's OK,' but anyway, it was a start and by the time they got to Parliament Hill Fields, he was himself again; that is, he was level, and loving, and warm. They bought ice cream cones from a kiosk and sat on a broad, low bough of a tree to eat them. Passers-by smiled at them, this young mother and father and their beautiful child. Sunshine swung her legs and waved, and Stu made her laugh by bouncing the bough. Chrissie laughed too, and tried to relax; tried not to scan the Heath for a dark-haired woman in a red coat.

They shunned the tube and the buses and chose to walk all the way home, taking it in turns to carry barefoot Sunny on their shoulders, meandering along, up through the streets of London. The day had been clear and bright when they left the Heath, and it was still very warm, but now a low bank of grey cloud had moved in and there was a tropical quality to the heat that presaged a downpour. Sunshine was delightfully grubby; her fingers, currently knitted together under Chrissie's chin, were sticky and sweet-smelling from vanilla ice cream and raspberry sauce. Her face was sticky too, her pale-pink pyjamas were stained with grass, and the soles of her feet were dusty and damp. Chrissie held her round the ankles and occasionally lifted first one dirty little foot, then the other, to kiss the tiny, miraculous toes. She was so precious, so perfectly formed, such a life force, and here she was, this warm and welcome weight on Chrissie's shoulders, a gift to them, from strangers; *Oh, you want a child? Then, have this little girl.* Now that she was theirs, it had all seemed too easy. She wanted to say to Stu, aren't you terrified of losing her? Doesn't the thought of it turn your blood ice cold? But because she didn't want to cast a shadow over what had turned into a blessed afternoon together, she stayed quiet. Anyway, she had to accept that he didn't think like her; his imagination tended to stay in the sunlit uplands. She understood, too, that she had to learn to live with her own fear; live with it, but not let it ruin her happiness.

Stuart said, 'Here, I'll do the last leg,' and lifted Sunshine, a little floppy now, a little sleepy, up and off Chrissie's shoulders. The child yawned hugely, so he carried her in his arms for the last half-mile. Chrissie said, 'Look at her, no shoes, no nap, and an ice-cream cone for lunch.'

'Little feral cub,' he said, and kissed her on the nose. She gazed at him, completely relaxed, heavy-lidded. They were very nearly in their street when there was a crack of thunder, very distant, and in the same moment the rain came, a thrilling warm deluge, pouring from the heavy clouds so that water immediately began to run in rivulets down the kerbside and in seconds the three of them were soaked. Sunny struggled to be free, laughing as the raindrops bounced off her face. Stuart put her down on the pavement, just for a moment, just for the joy; she marched on the spot, seeing droplets of water spark up from the ground under her feet, and she held out her hands, palms upwards, and tried to catch the rain. They all grinned at each other, delighted to be witness to this wonder, then Chrissie said, 'Come on, time to go home,' and Stu swooshed Sunny up off the ground, said, 'Up, up and away,' then tucked her under his arm like a small, compact battering ram, charging forwards, making her squeal. They rounded the corner into their street, and Stu and Chrissie saw at once that outside their front door there was a couple, a man and a woman, squashed together under the narrow porch roof, trying to keep out of the rain. They stopped, and stared, and Chrissie clutched at the place where her heart was, to stop it leaping out of her chest. For a few seconds, she was consumed by fear – it flooded her blood and her bones – and then the woman turned her head, only a fraction, but enough for Chrissie to see her face in profile, and she said, 'Barbara. It's Barbara and John,' and the fear receded, as rapidly as it had come, and she felt light-headed with relief that this wasn't a predator from Sunshine's past.

Stu said, 'What the hell? Can they just turn up like this?' He switched Sunshine onto his hip, and she darted her eyes between him and Chrissie, startled by the change in atmosphere. Then Barbara noticed them and, at once, she stepped into the rain and onto the pavement and cried out, 'Sunshine!' in an emotional, carrying tone, and the child spun her head at the familiar voice and lit up with happy surprise, then stretched out her arms towards her, and waited to be rescued.

13

In the flat, Sunshine continued to cling to Barbara like a ship-wreck survivor, and she did look a little as though she'd been pulled from the sea. Barbara looked both tragic and ecstatic, a suffering soul who at last had been offered succour and comfort. She took considerable self-righteous pleasure in Sunshine's bedraggled appearance; kept uttering short declaratory sentences, heavy with reproach, such as, 'She's still in her pyjamas!' and, 'Well, she's soaked through!', while Chrissie and Stuart dripped on the hall floor and worked hard at regaining their composure. They left Sunshine in Barbara's arms, because to haul her away would have been upsetting for everyone. But it was hard to watch the child nuzzling into the folds of Barbara's fat, comfortable neck and, occasionally, leaning back, gazing at her face, then patting it gently all over, as if to reassure herself that this really was a miracle, not an illusion. Chrissie raced upstairs to run a bath and hide her distress, and Stu said, to John, 'This seems a bit irregular, dropping in unannounced?'

'Did you lose her shoes?' Barbara asked, and her eyes condemned him. She held Sunny's feet in one hand, and rubbed them softly, as if she was trying to warm a frozen chick. 'Why ever isn't she dressed?'

'We rang,' John said. He looked abashed, uncomfortable. 'We got no reply.'

'So, you came anyway? All the way from Whitstable?'

John slid his eyes in Barbara's direction. 'There was no stopping her,' he said.

They both looked at Barbara, who was intently communing with Sunshine, crooning at her, oozing maternal compassion. Stu decided enough was enough and he took a firm hold of Sunny from behind, and tickled her ribs slightly, which she never could resist. She started to squirm and laugh, and it was easy then to slide her away from Barbara's hungry embrace.

'Bath time, baby girl,' he said, and blew a raspberry on her neck. He bounded up the stairs with her, and Barbara, invigorated and encouraged by Sunshine's rapturous welcome, began to follow, but without turning Stu said, 'No, not you, Barbara. You go and sit down, we'll see you soon,' and Sunshine – flighty creature – just waved merrily at her foster mother's disconsolate face and said, 'See a soon.'

In the bathroom, Chrissie was waiting, sitting on the edge of the tub. She'd poured bubble bath into the warm water, and arranged her face into a calm and cheerful smile, and when they came in, she started to peel off Sunny's damp pyjamas and said, with a bright and positive air, 'Let's get you clean and lovely for John and Barbara.'

Stuart said, 'Hey, Chrissie, it's fine.'

She looked at him desperately. 'How they love each other, though,' she said, in a low voice. 'It seemed so visceral.'

He sat next to her. 'We shouldn't try to limit the number of people who love Sunshine,' he said. 'It can only do her good, surely?'

'But you saw her with Barbara just now. She loves her back!'

'Well, she's a kid with a big heart,' Stu said. 'She seems to love people liberally.'

They both looked at Sunny, who lifted her arms and said, 'Up and away?' and they all laughed. Stu picked her up and zoomed her up, down, then into the bath, and she shivered with pleasure. A soft cloud of bubbles rose and swelled all around her.

'Is that good?' Chrissie asked her, and she said, 'Mmmmmm,' with her eyes closed. Stu placed a kiss on Sunshine's head, and another on Chrissie's. 'Take your time,' he said, heading for the door. 'I'll go down and find out what the Fosters want.'

Chrissie said, 'Wait,' and she stood up, and went to him. 'You're amazing,' she said. 'You are my love.' She kissed him fiercely and for a few moments they stayed like that, breathing each other in, feeling the connection they'd always had and that sometimes, these days, eluded them.

Behind them, Sunshine clapped her hands in a heap of suds to see them fly.

Chrissie put her in Nina's tie-dye dress, and the silver jelly shoes, and tied her curls back from her face with a red bandana. Then they considered the effect in a full-length mirror.

'Very rock chick,' Chrissie said. 'You're one cool customer, Sunshine Stevenson.'

Sunny sniffed the air and said, 'Daddy is cooking?'

Chrissie laughed. 'Yeah, Daddy is cooking. What do you think it is?'

The child sniffed again, and had a think, then, 'Pasghetti,' she said, with a rising note of hope in her voice.

'Shall we go and see if you're right?'

She nodded, and lifted her hand so it could be held, and they went downstairs together. She'd forgotten Barbara and John were there, and was excited all over again when she saw them, but Chrissie didn't mind any more, she had a warm glow of joy in her heart, the imprint of Sunshine on her soul, and Stuart was probably right: the more people who loved her, the better. The little girl danced about the kitchen for the visitors, showing off and being indulged, then threw herself onto John's lap, and he enclosed her in his cardigan, just like the old days. She shut her eyes and sighed, and he pulled the wool tighter around her, so she seemed like part of him.

They'd had the conversation, Stuart, Barbara and John; they were sorry to barge in, sorry to break protocol and turn up unannounced, but Barbara hadn't slept last night after the encounter with the stranger, and she'd got the impression from Brendan that Chrissie didn't trust her story, thought she, Barbara, might know more than she was letting on. This, plus heartache following the absence of Sunshine, meant she'd cried most of the night, and the only thing that would comfort her was an audience with Chrissie and Stuart, and a cuddle with Sunshine. She said, 'Oh, don't you look a picture,' when the child skipped into the kitchen with Chrissie, then John took Sunny away to look at her sandpit, so that Barbara could spill the anxiety in her heart, all over again, to Chrissie. They sat opposite each other at the small kitchen table, while Stu got on with dinner behind them, and Barbara had to raise her voice a little, to be heard over the sound of water rushing into the big pasta pan, and the sizzling of sausage meat in a skillet.

'I would never do anything to jeopardise that child's happiness,' she said, to Chrissie. Barbara's eyes were dull and red-rimmed, and she looked strained, as if her head ached.

Stu said, 'We know that, Barbara,' because at the table, Chrissie stayed silent and looked sceptical, thinking about the missing cheese string, and the missing soap powder. Oh, these small but critical details.

'I told her nothing,' Barbara said. 'I shut the door on her . . . well, I was petrified, I don't mind telling you.'

'But she was pleasant, Brendan said?' Chrissie asked.

Barbara nodded. 'Pleasant, yes, that's a good word for her. Polite and pleasant.'

'How old?'

'Well, how could I possibly say?'

Chrissie sighed. 'I mean, your best guess? Young enough to be Sunny's mother? Old enough to be her grandmother?'

Barbara said, 'I wouldn't like to say. I wouldn't like to mislead you.'

Chrissie gave her a long look, then said, 'OK, can you tell us again what she said to you?'

Barbara seemed to be considering this. 'I just don't want to get it wrong,' she said.

'Well, you won't, I'm sure,' Stu said. 'This isn't a test, Barbara; we just want to hear it from you, instead of second-hand from Brendan.'

'She said, "Thank you for looking after Sunshine so well, where is she now?" Or words along those lines. Anyway, she was very polite.'

'And she wasn't dressed in a sari?' Stu asked.

Barbara looked perturbed, as if she didn't understand the question, and it struck Chrissie that the Fosters wouldn't have been told about the memory bag, or the spurious connection to Sunshine of a woman in a sari.

She said, 'Don't worry, Barbara. It's just, Sunshine seems to have had more people in her life than we realised, and apparently one of them might be a woman in a sari.'

Now the older woman shook her head and looked mildly panicked, as if all of this was beyond her.

'Barbara,' Chrissie said. 'Please think.'

'I don't know,' Barbara said.

'You don't know what?'

'Anything,' Barbara said. 'I don't know anything, apart from what I've told you. She was wearing a red jacket. I didn't see what she had on under it.'

'Jacket?' Stu said, and Barbara nodded.

'Brendan said coat,' Chrissie said.

'Pardon?'

'He said you told him she was wearing a coat, not a jacket.'

Barbara had a think. 'Well, yes,' she said. 'It was a longish jacket or shortish coat, and it was pillar-box red.'

Chrissie and Stu shared a look. Barbara seemed to be studying the grain of the wooden table.

'Do you think,' Chrissie asked, trying a different tack, 'that Sunshine might be related to her?'

Barbara looked up. Her mouth hung slightly open, but she didn't speak.

'Barbara?' Stu said. 'She was dark-haired like Sunshine, right?'

'Well,' she said, 'yes, she was, but I can't say I was struck by a resemblance. I can tell you she was very nicely spoken, though, and she wasn't persistent, she didn't knock again after I shut the door.'

'But Barbara, she can't just have been some polite but random stranger,' Stu said. 'She had to be someone from Sunshine's past, right?'

'I suppose so, yes.'

'So can you remember anything at all about her that might distinguish her from the hundreds of thousands of other dark-haired women in the population?'

His tone was becoming interrogatory, and Barbara twisted round to look at him, as if she wanted to check it was still

Stuart. Her tired eyes and soft, downturned mouth made him feel like a brute.

'I'm sorry,' he said, more gently. 'I just mean, did anything else jump out at you?'

In the spirit of someone who wanted to show they truly wished to please, Barbara screwed up her face in concentration, and made inarticulate thinking noises for a short while, then said, 'We-ell, now that I think about it, she wore bangles on her right arm. They jingled when she held out her hand.' She darted a look at each of them now, and added, 'I shook her hand before I knew what she wanted, you see. I wouldn't have shaken it otherwise.'

Chrissie had her elbows on the table, and her chin and cheeks were cupped in her palms. She was sick of this now. Barbara's drooping features. Barbara's useless observations. 'Bangles,' she said. 'Right. I mean, that's not really a distinguishing feature, Barbara, but never mind.'

Barbara leaned in a little towards Chrissie and said, 'I don't think you're being very nice.'

'Sorry,' Chrissie said, without feeling. Stu waved an open bottle of red wine at her, and she nodded. He poured three glasses and put two on the table, one in front of each woman.

'Ooh, that's kind,' Barbara said, brightening. She picked up the glass and was about to take a sip, but then, as if she felt compelled to reward them for this olive branch, drew back from the glass and said, 'The main thing is, she got nothing at all from me. I mean, as if I'd tell her where to find Sunshine! I love that child like my own.'

'Well, thank you for that,' Stu said. He turned back to the large pan of now fiercely boiling water, and upended a packet of linguine into it, pushing its length down into the turbulent depths. Barbara had swivelled on her stool and now she observed him with kinked eyebrows, like a cinema-goer who finds themselves watching a foreign-language film by mistake.

Chrissie chewed on her thumbnail. Christ almighty, she thought; what the hell is going on?

Because Sunshine was so happy with their company, Barbara and John were invited to stay to dinner, before embarking on their tedious drive home. They accepted, and Sunshine danced in giddy circles when she heard they were eating with her, and then sat between them, bouncing a little with glee, as Stuart placed pasta bowls on the table, containing linguine with Italian pork and fennel sausage. Barbara and John stared down at their meal.

'Goodness, what's this?' Barbara asked, and Sunshine said, 'Pasghetti and sausage.' She began digging in with a fork, hamfistedly twirling it in the pasta, then getting it up to her mouth as best she could.

'Well, I never,' Barbara said. 'Does she eat this sort of thing, then?' She'd already finished her glass of red wine, and that, plus the emotional drama of her reunion with Sunshine, had left her feeling peaceful, but wrung-out. A piece of cheese with Branston pickle is what she fancied. Or a baked potato, with butter. She'd seen plates of food like this in television dramas, yet to serve it to a child seemed wilfully, and unnecessarily, controversial. But no one answered her question, because it was evident that, yes, Sunshine ate this sort of thing, and what she lacked in efficiency, she made up for in gusto.

'Oh, well,' John said, 'in for a penny,' and he tucked in, much like Sunny, hanging his head over the plate and slurping. Barbara dithered, then asked for a knife, as well as her fork, and proceeded to chop her linguine into small pieces.

'I don't cook pasta,' she said.

'Right,' Chrissie said. 'It's practically all we eat, but I guess it's not for everyone. My parents never cook it either.'

'We stick with potatoes, don't we, John?' Barbara said. 'I know where I am with a potato.'

John laughed. 'A potato is a damn sight easier to spear on a fork,' he said. 'This is like wrestling with live eels.'

'You're getting there,' Stu said. 'Take a leaf out of Sunny's book, and abandon your dignity.' They looked at her, applying herself with single-minded diligence to the task of carrying strands of pasta to her mouth. She focused entirely on her meal; she had no idea that all eyes were upon her.

'It takes her a while to finish,' Chrissie said. 'But you've got to admire her staying power.'

Barbara, unable to resist, blurted, 'You should chop hers up like I have mine.'

Chrissie smiled, and said, 'Go ahead, Barbara. Cut it up for her.'

Pleased and a little smug, Barbara leaned in with her knife and fork, and hovered them over Sunny's plate, then leapt in her seat when the child yelled, 'No!', her face an instant thunderstorm. 'Keep my pasghetti long!'

John started to laugh, hiding his mouth behind his hand, his shoulders shaking. 'That told you, Barb,' he said. She was flustered, and Chrissie felt a tiny bit sorry for her, but not regretful.

'Keep my spaghetti long, *please*,' Chrissie said to Sunny.

'Keep my pasghetti long, *PLEASE,*' Sunshine shouted.

'Well,' Barbara said, withdrawing, her mouth a tight purse of disapproval.

Sunny, her countenance cheerful again now her linguine was out of danger, cocked her head at Barbara and said, 'You is cross?'

Stu said, 'Nobody likes being shouted at, Sunny,' then he winked at her, and she closed both her eyes and beamed.

John said, 'Moral of the story, Barb, is mind your own bees-wax,' which Barbara took remarkably well, managing a nod of agreement.

She accepted a second glass of red wine, and after a few mouthfuls became quite voluble and – unasked – began a list of foster children she and John had cared for, by name, age and circumstances. John cut her off at number five, and changed the conversation by saying that Carl and Kevin were going now, too. Adopted together, by a couple in Seasalter, just down the coast. He said they'd always be able to spot them on the sea-front, those two little carrot tops. They'd been a handful, Barbara said, and John said, not really, they were just little lads.

'It was like having red setter puppies in the house,' he said. 'Sunshine was a proper little lady by comparison.'

'Are they happy?' Chrissie asked.

Barbara shrugged. 'Happy enough, I'd say.'

'Happy enough,' Chrissie said, musingly. 'Happy enough – isn't enough. I want Sunshine to be entirely happy.'

'Hundred per cent,' Stu said. The child had finished eating and he lifted her down and began swabbing her face with a damp cloth. She chatted to him about Juno, and the bits of *The Lion King* that had stayed with her. The funny bird. The naughty lion cub. Then she trotted off to find a book for John to read to her before they left. He said, 'She's such a smashing kid.'

Chrissie nodded.

'No problems, then?' Barbara asked.

Stu said, 'She blew her top a few times, the first couple of days.'

'Like, ballistic,' Chrissie said. 'She took against her own bedroom.'

'She settled with us straight away,' Barbara said.

'Well, the other kids helped, I expect,' John said. 'She seemed to like company, and we had another one, when she first came. There were four of them in that room.'

'It was tough, the day we picked her up, all that crying,' Stu said, and John said, 'I know; we didn't do you any favours, I'm afraid.'

'Did you mean to leave out that soap powder, Barbara?'

Chrissie asked the question in a neutral voice, but there was no hiding the sting. She wouldn't meet Stu's gaze, because she knew he'd be giving her the look. But Barbara considered the contents of her wine glass for a moment then said, 'I did, yes.'

'The soap powder when she came here?' John said. 'I put that in the bag myself.'

'And then I took it out again.'

He stared at his wife, and she nodded.

'I'm sorry,' she said. 'I couldn't bear it, letting her go. I think it sent me a bit round the bend.'

'Good heavens,' John said.

Barbara swallowed, as if she was preparing to make a speech, but then she said nothing.

'Can we talk?' Chrissie asked her. 'In private, I mean?' She looked at Stu, and at John. 'Do you mind?'

Chrissie let Barbara sit in apprehensive silence while she made herself a coffee and poured Barbara a third glass of wine. If the older woman had denied her culpability, she wouldn't have seen her or spoken to her again, let alone shared their good Chianti with her. As it was, she'd confessed, and seemed ashamed, so Chrissie had decided to trust her, but still, she let her sweat for a few minutes, let her feel the weight of the wrong she'd done them, for the time it took for the coffee machine to run its course. Then, 'Look, I get it,' Chrissie said, returning to the table. 'I don't think I'd want to let Sunshine go either, if I were in your shoes.' Barbara looked at her with doe-eyed gratitude, which Chrissie found irritating. She slid the glass of wine across the tabletop, and Barbara took it, and said, 'Lovely, thank you.'

Chrissie said, 'How many children have you fostered, Barbara?'

Barbara, a little startled, said, 'Oh,' and had a drink. 'We totted this up not long ago,' she said. 'Thirty-three, I'm proud to say.' She took another sip, but kept her eyes on Chrissie over the rim of the glass.

'And have you ever done this before?'

'Done what?'

'Tried to sabotage the settling-in?'

Barbara winced at this bald statement of fact. 'No,' she said.

'So, what is it about Sunshine in particular?'

'Pardon?'

'I mean, why have you never felt this way about any of the other thirty-two?'

'Oh, I see,' Barbara said. She had to think again, now. Chrissie could see her features working, almost hear the cogs grinding, as she considered the question.

'Thing is,' Chrissie said, 'I only have experience of adopting one little girl, and I was braced for a tough ride. Angela Holt told me and Stuart all about the separation wound that never heals, and the hyper-vigilant child who's been raised in chaos and never known love, and all the other miseries we should prepare to face. And I know for a fact that other adoptive parents disappear into a vortex of hopeless exhaustion with kids who've been abused, neglected, coerced, whatever. But Sunshine – give or take a few tantrums, she's pure delight, right?'

Barbara nodded, but she looked as though she was finding it hard to keep up. Her eyes were damp, her mouth looked soft, and sad. The combination of a guilty conscience and a sleepless night had taken its toll, made her look older than her sixty-one years.

'Tell me,' Chrissie said. 'Please, Barbara. Tell me how Sunshine is different to the others.'

Barbara took another big gulp of wine, and bowed her head, as if she was gathering herself, or praying.

'Sunshine,' she said. 'Sunshine, Sunshine, Sunshine.'

Chrissie shifted on the chair; thought, perhaps, that Barbara was drunk, or losing her mind; that John might have been the better choice for a one-on-one. But then Barbara began to speak, and the words tumbled out, faster and faster as she found her stride.

'Oh, she was such a lot of fun,' she said. 'Even the day she arrived, she knew how to laugh, and how to make other people laugh, and she could sing little songs that none of us understood, and lark about, and she knew how to play with other children, and, like John said, she liked the other kiddies, liked being in a gang, the more the merrier. If anything, I was worried that she trusted us too quickly, sometimes that's a sign of a lack of attachment, you know, a sign of not being able to rely on anyone. But she knew what a cuddle was, she didn't shrink back in fear if me or John went to lift her up, and if we ticked her off about something, she didn't cover her head with her arms as if she was about to get a beating. Oh, we've had so many children who expect to be hit, or who lie flat on their backs in a cot, silent as the grave, because they don't expect anyone to fetch them, or who've gone without food so often they don't know when to stop eating. We've had children who've been afraid of their own shadows, or cruel to their siblings, or cruel to us, or just angry, all the time. But Sunshine came, and well, she lit up the house, that's all I can say. And she didn't have night terrors, or use bad language, she didn't know words a child shouldn't know, and some of them do, you know, some of them have learned terrible words.'

Barbara paused, and took a few long, steadying breaths, another mouthful of wine, then another. Chrissie waited.

'I've always felt,' Barbara said, hesitatingly, 'that me and John gave the children we've cared for a better life. But with Sunny, it was the other way around.'

'You mean, she improved your life?'

Barbara thought for a moment, then said, 'No, although she did, but that's not what I meant. It was more that I got the impression she'd come to us from somewhere better.'

Chrissie felt a stab of recognition, and a kind of relief. Barbara, of all people, had articulated precisely what Chrissie had felt from the start. She thought about the black and white photograph upstairs; a lovely girl, a composed, confident baby, a benign, sheltering oak.

'Better how?' she said.

'I don't exactly know. I just think she must have been loved.'

Chrissie nodded. 'Once, the first time she stayed here with us, she asked me if I knew where her sisters were.'

Barbara looked blank.

'She never said anything like that to you?' Chrissie asked.

'Well, she may have done, but if she did it didn't register.'

'It would have registered, Barbara, surely?'

'Well,' Barbara said, and shook her head. It was as if she'd expended every drop of energy with her previous speech. Her face turned doughy and unresponsive. She sipped at her wine, and Chrissie had to sit on her hands to stop herself snatching the glass away, and demanding she concentrate.

'And this woman, at your door, can you think of any details you might not have told me?'

Barbara shook her head slowly.

'Was she black-haired, or brunette? Or do you think her hair might have been dyed?'

The woman was taking on a strangely bovine appearance, heavy lidded, swaying slightly in her seat. Chrissie said, 'Barbara, are you OK?'

With some apparent effort, Barbara lifted her eyes to Chrissie.

'Barbara? Could you tell if she'd dyed her hair?'

'Stop asking me questions,' she said, petulantly. 'I want to go home.'

Later, Stu told Chrissie she was like a stuck record, going on and on about what they did and didn't know, and, even though she knew he was right, she stormed off and sat on the floor of Sunshine's bedroom, to listen to her sweet breathing and examine the only tangible evidence she had of the little girl's past. Sunny was fast asleep, her face rosy with comfort and bliss. One night of sharing with Juno and she'd declared this her 'best' bed, and had tonight climbed in unbidden, on entirely her own terms, Silky in one hand, Monkey in the other. 'Sorry, Mummy,' she'd said, 'I like mine best bed best now,' which is when Chrissie had realised she must've been looking sad at this new development, so she'd grinned and said, 'And I like my best girl best,' and Sunny had shouted, 'Sunshine!' and Chrissie had kissed the end of her nose and said, 'Yes, the one and only.'

Now, she held the photograph and wondered yet again what secrets it held. Familiarity had worked its magic, and its presence in the house caused her less anxiety as the weeks had passed. Once, she'd even lifted it down from the shelf to show Sunny, but the child had been distracted at the time, and the light streaming in through the window had bounced onto the glass in the frame. Sunny had only glanced at it before saying, 'No, come to mine shop, Mummy' – an establishment that comprised a collection of toys arranged on an upturned box, available for Chrissie to 'buy' – a game with no end, Sunny's absolute favourite – and if Chrissie was completely truthful, she might admit she'd deliberately chosen her moment to show the child a glimpse of her past. For while Chrissie's anxiety had lessened, it had by no means entirely abated, and this would always be more than just a photograph; it would always be a photograph that someone unknown, someone much closer than they should be, wished Sunshine to have.

So, for the umpteenth time, Chrissie stared into the eyes of the young woman and traced the lines of her face with her finger, then scrutinised the baby, surely little Sunshine? Everyone who'd seen it assumed so, although the pram she sat in belonged to another time, and while it wasn't impossible that this first elusive family of hers might have owned an old carriage pram, it did suggest to Chrissie that perhaps they were all wrong, and that the infant might be Sunny's mother, and the young woman her grandmother. Or was the child in the pram one of the sisters she'd mentioned?

Now, Chrissie remembered a picture in her own box of family photographs, one in which the subjects were similarly arranged, although it was fizzed up by Diana in a full-skirted dress and heels, holding the handle of Chrissie's pram so lightly that it seemed as if the pram, and the baby within, were merely props in a magazine photoshoot. On the back, Doug had written *Diana and Christine, April 1965*. He'd always labelled his snapshots in this rather pedestrian way, a ritual which used to seem utterly pointless to young Chrissie, because didn't the three of them already know exactly who they were?

'Posterity, Christine,' he'd said, when she quizzed him. 'I do it for posterity, for the people who come, when we're long gone.'

Abruptly she stood up, and left Sunny's room, still holding the photograph. As she descended the stairs, she called Stuart's name, but he was playing The Clash, which he sometimes did when he wanted to temporarily forget his responsibilities. He would put on one of their albums and whack up the volume, and Chrissie would know he was blue. She went down.

'Stu?' she said, but even though she was now in the living room, he still couldn't hear her; he was lost in the swagger of 'London Calling'. His own music — *their* music, the music made by The Lineman — it was nothing like this, but if Stu could change places with anyone, it'd be Joe Strummer, in 1976.

'Stu,' she said, and put a hand on his shoulder, making him start. 'I'm sorry,' she said, meaning for going on and on, for dragging him down, and she leaned in and kissed him on the mouth, then sat beside him and pulled his arm up and around to make him hold her, then she waited for the record to play out.

He tipped his head on the back of the sofa, closed his eyes, sang along, then when the last track ended he said, 'OK then, what's up?' He was smiling, looking at her as if he liked her again. She loved the way he dealt with ill-humour, never letting it fester. She waggled the picture at him.

'I want to get this photo out of the frame,' she said. 'I want to see what it says on the back.'

∽

The past flickers behind Sunshine's eyelids as she sleeps. Faces rise and fall, smiling at her. They have kind eyes and shining dark hair and clothing as colourful as a box of paints. The room smells of fresh green leaves, and there is the low lullaby of women's voices, and the cushion she's lying on is rough against her skin, but also deep and generous, and completely familiar.

In the dream, someone she loves wakes her, very gently, by blowing softly on her eyelids, and then she lifts her up, and presses a finger on her mouth, which Sunshine knows means hush. Soon the room with the beds is far away and they are together, in the dark, holding hands.

'It's a moon walk,' she says. 'Look, Sunshine. The trees are silver.'

In the dream, Sunshine doesn't care about the silver trees; she just wants to sleep.

And then daylight comes through the curtains, and she's waking up in this home, to the smell of toast, and her mummy singing in the shower.

14

In September, Stuart's mother came to stay at last, occupying the flat like a breath of Cape May fresh air. As there was no spare room, and as she flatly refused to usurp Sunshine in her newly accepted bed, she was sleeping at night on the living-room sofa, which she did with great enthusiasm and good grace. Chrissie tried to imagine Diana in the same situation – and couldn't. Even jet lag didn't disrupt the harmonious flow of energy through Carly's seven beautifully balanced chakras, and everything about Sunshine fascinated and delighted her. On the morning of day two of Carly's visit, Nina stopped by to say hello, and to take Sunny out to the park, so Chrissie took the opportunity to bring out the memory bag and its component parts for Carly to examine. Predictably enough, she was captivated, but it wasn't the note or the record's box or the photograph that she seized upon first, but the embroidered muslin bag, because she knew precisely what she was looking at.

'This,' she said, running her fingers lightly over the meticulous needlework, 'is called chikankari.'

Chrissie leaned in, to look more closely at the object she'd pored over so often, she could probably replicate the design from memory. 'What is?' she asked. 'You mean, the bag?'

'The embroidery,' Carly said. 'This bag's been made out of a piece of muslin that was already embroidered in the chikan style,' Carly said. 'Probably it was made from an old sari or a kurta, and by old I mean a fair few decades ago, judging by the fade of the thread. It's gorgeous.'

'Does it tell you anything about Sunshine?' Chrissie asked, and Carly looked up, gave her slow, loving smile, and with the pad of her thumb, smoothed the anxious furrow that lay between Chrissie's eyebrows as if she was anointing her with holy oil.

'I'd say, she came from people who had taste,' she said, carefully. 'People whose life put them in the orbit of artistry and craftsmanship.' She turned the bag so that the design on the front faced Chrissie. 'This would've been block printed,' she added, tracing the outline of the leaves with an index finger, 'then the stitches were applied to that pattern, which later would have been washed away. It's probably from Lucknow, that's where this style originated. The silver thread looks very new, and perhaps not quite so accomplished, but I think the original fabric is nineteenth century.'

'That's very clever of you,' Chrissie said, looking with new respect at the stitching. 'There's Silky as well, also incredibly lovely; you've seen it, right? Sunny carts it around as if it were an old hankie, but Nina said it looks like something from the V&A.'

Carly nodded. 'Yes, another clue, I suppose, if clues are what you're looking for.'

'It's hard *not* to look for them,' Chrissie said. 'I mean, who wouldn't?' She was chewing on the corner of her thumbnail, and Carly gently reached out and touched her other hand and said, 'Hey, don't be anxious,' so Chrissie stopped gnawing at her nail and tried a bright smile, but she could see Carly wasn't taken in. She knew that what she saw was a much edgier, quieter, more reflective version of the Chrissie she was used to, the Chrissie she'd last seen two years ago, when she and Stuart went to stay with her for two carefree, idyllic weeks by the sea in Cape May.

She said, 'At times, I can't stop thinking about her, Carly.'

'Who, darling?'

'The mother.'

'Oh, honey.'

Carly put the bag down, and took one of Chrissie's hands in hers, and gave it a squeeze. 'First of all, *you're* Sunshine's mother now, nothing can change that. Second of all, motherhood alters everyone, and motherhood through adoption, well . . . it must bring a whole new layer of challenges, but your little girl is a pure delight, cute as a button, and it makes my heart swell to see how amazing you and Stuart are with her.'

True though this doubtless was, none of it seemed to address the point, Chrissie thought. She looked at Carly's beatific expression, and wondered if she quite understood the issues. 'But there was that woman who knocked on Barbara's door on the day we adopted her,' she said. 'And there's this stuff, which came on the day Sunny moved in . . .'

'Chrissie, try to dwell on the positives, and when the negatives intrude, breathe them away.' She demonstrated a healing breath, a long, long inhale through the nose, and a long, long exhale from the mouth. Chrissie said, 'Thanks, Carly, that's sure to help,' and Carly, being Carly, missed her tone and only said, 'My pleasure, honey. And look, whoever gave Sunny this—' she lifted the bag '—must be a decent, thoughtful person.'

Chrissie said, 'Mmm, actually that isn't a comfort, really, but never mind. Look,' she said, passing Carly the photograph, which was now out of its frame. 'Tell me something else. How come this gorgeous child got left at a random council office? That doesn't seem decent, or thoughtful.'

Carly stared at the image. 'Oh my,' she murmured. 'Oh my,' and for a short while Chrissie let her simply lose herself in the picture, because everyone who saw it for the first time always did. It had special powers; it drew the viewer in. Then Chrissie said, 'Now flip it over,' and Carly did as she was asked.

'See?' Chrissie said.

Carly peered at the handwriting. 'Asha and Athena, Perfect Happiness,' she read, aloud. 'Wow.' She looked at Chrissie, and said, 'Beautiful names, but this baby *is* our Sunshine, right?'

Chrissie smiled. She loved the way Carly said that, *our Sunshine*, laying claim, sharing ownership. But then, she loved everything about Carly, even her blind faith in the healing powers of the universe. In particular, she loved having her about the flat. She'd only been here for a day and a night, and already Chrissie was hoping she'd never leave, because unlike the snow queen Diana, who cast shards of ice into people's hearts to make them cross and dissatisfied, Carly was love and colour and understanding.

'And this is the frame,' Chrissie said, passing it across. 'We had a hell of a job getting into it, it was papered shut, at the back.'

'Wow, again,' Carly said, feeling its weight. 'It's like an heirloom.'

'I know,' Chrissie said. 'It really belongs on a mantelpiece in a Victorian drawing room.'

Carly, cross-legged in her harem pants on the big sofa, turned the photo over again, to consider the two faces. 'They look very solemn,' she said. 'I wonder who took it?'

'I wonder that too, whenever I look at it. Who was the third person there that day?'

'And why aren't they smiling?' Carly said. 'I mean, babies

are often serious when they gaze at a camera, but this young woman . . .'

'Looks sad,' Chrissie supplied. 'I know. She looks very far from feeling perfect happiness.'

'I wonder which is which? Asha and Athena, which one is the baby? And then, if it's really Sunshine, who renamed her?'

'See?' Chrissie said, and she laughed. 'It's infectious. You've caught the bug, you'll be asking yourself these questions all the time now.'

The front door opened then, and they heard Nina say, 'Hang on, wellies off,' and then Sunshine sang out, 'Hello, Mummy, where you is?'

'Oh my, I hope she never stops saying that,' Carly said.

'In here,' Chrissie called. The living-room door burst open and Sunny barrelled in, green duffel coat, pink mittens, rosy cheeks. They could hear Nina putting boots on the rack and shedding her own coat, and Carly called out, 'Hey, Nina,' but Nina just said, 'Hi, be right there, I'll just put the kettle on,' and didn't come in, or even stick her head round the door. They heard her footsteps heading down the hall and Carly said, 'Is she OK?' and Chrissie just shrugged, then put the silver frame down to ready herself for one of Sunny's exuberant hugs. 'Hello, lovely girl,' she said. 'Did you have fun?'

'A lot of fun, and Mummy?'

'Yeah?'

'I did make a friend.'

'Cool, a boy or a girl?'

'A boy. He was funny.' She climbed off Chrissie and onto Carly, whom she barely knew, but seemed very much inclined to like.

'What a very democratic child you are, sharing your hugs,'

Carly said. 'Mmm, you smell of wood smoke and leaves. You're delicious. Let's get these toggles undone.'

Sunshine stood obediently while Carly freed her from her coat and mittens, and, while standing, noticed the photograph lying on the sofa. She tilted her head and looked at it. Chrissie picked it up, so the child could see more clearly, then she turned it over and pointed at the writing on the back.

'This says *Asha and Athena*,' she said, carefully, watching Sunny's face for signs of recognition, the dawning of some new truth. 'And this says *Perfect Happiness*.'

Sunshine stared, but didn't say anything.

'Perfect Happiness,' said Carly. 'We're not convinced by that at all.'

'Mummy?' Sunshine said.

Chrissie looked at her, and saw how very much she looked, in that moment, like the baby in the pram; those round, serious eyes, her solemn poise.

'What is it, sweetheart?' Chrissie asked.

'Do you know where is mine sisters?'

The child kept her gaze on the photograph as she spoke, and Chrissie, hearing these words for the second time, caught a breath in her throat, but only smiled, and said calmly, 'No, Sunshine, I don't know.' She held out the photograph for her, and she took it at once.

'Hold it gently,' Chrissie said. 'It's very precious.'

Carly said, 'Is that your sister, honey? Or that?' and pointed first at the young woman in the picture, and then at the baby. But Sunshine just said, 'I don't know,' with a kind of regretful sadness. She did as she'd been asked, held the photograph with scrupulous care, and she stared at it as if she was seeing it for the first time, which in a way, she was. It seemed different, out of the heavy frame; it seemed more intimate. That young woman and her baby were closer to them now.

Chrissie left Sunshine with Carly and went to find Nina.

'How was the park?' she asked. 'Did you have a good time?'

'Great!' Nina said, and there was something about her tone – a fraction too bright, a fraction too high – that immediately told Chrissie something was wrong.

'What?' she said.

Nina said, 'Chrissie.'

'What?' Chrissie paled and said, 'You're scaring me.' She dropped down into a chair.

Nina said, 'I'm sorry, I don't mean to, but something just happened.' She turned back to spooning leaves into the teapot, as if all was as it should be, and the kitchen wasn't beginning to spin out of control.

'You mean, in the playground?'

Nina nodded. 'Sunny started playing with a little boy. He ran up to her with a big smile on his face and said hello, and for a while they ran around in circles together, laughing and larking about.'

'She said she'd made a friend.'

'Yeah, well, he was a sweet kid, but I couldn't see an adult, so I was looking around for one—'

'You were still with Sunshine though, right?

Nina shot her a reproachful look. 'Yes, I was. I was watching her, and at the same time, looking for an adult, I thought someone might be frantic, I thought he might be lost. Anyway, when I looked back at Sunny, she'd stopped playing, and I saw she was looking at someone, not someone in the playground, but a woman over the other side of the fence, by that huge lime tree.'

'Nina, oh my God.' Chrissie put her face in her hands.

'She was fine!'

'But how could you take your eyes off her?'

'Chrissie, darling, can I ask you to stop judging me, and listen?'

Chrissie looked at her hands, which she saw were shaking. She placed them carefully on top of the table, and said, 'Yes.'

'Thank you,' Nina said. She took a long breath. 'I walked over at once. It was a young woman, but she'd stayed in the dappled shade of that lime, so it was difficult to see her features. I said, "Can I help you?" and she smiled and said, "Oh, no, not at all, I'm just saying hello to your charming granddaughter," and then she said maybe she was being presumptuous, maybe the child wasn't my granddaughter, and I said that no, she wasn't.'

Chrissie moaned, and laid her head on the table. 'For God's sake,' she said on an outward breath. 'I can't believe you're telling me this.'

Nina said, 'Chrissie, Sunshine is in the front room, right as rain, so sit up and look at me, and stop catastrophising.'

It must have been twenty-five years since Nina had used that tone on Chrissie, and she lifted her head at once, ready to listen, just as she had as a little girl, when she'd cried over a playground spat or panicked over her long multiplication, and Nina had straightened out the world with her own brand of loving authority. For a few moments they stared at each other, then Nina said, 'Look, OK, I briefly let Sunny out of my sight, and yes, my first feeling when I saw the woman speaking to her was alarm. But here we are, safe and sound, and all I can say is that there was absolutely nothing menacing about the encounter in the park.'

'Was it the same woman? The one in the photograph? The one who went to Barbara's?'

'Well, we don't know much about the one who went to Barbara's, do we? As for the young woman in the photo . . . it's so hard to say, possibly a similar build but she had a much more . . . well, a more contemporary appearance, I suppose. Jeans and boots and a pink quilted jacket, and a woolly hat pulled down over her ears.'

'Never mind her clothes. Tell me exactly what she looked like.'

'I can't say exactly, Chrissie, all I got was an impression, she stepped further back when I approached the fence, and the leaves cast a lot of shade. But let me see, well, she was slight, and very pale-skinned. She was attractive. Large eyes, in a smallish face. Her hair – what I could see of it, below the hat – was a darkish shade of auburn, I'd say; quite long, too, and wavy. She was composed – calm, and polite. Spoke very slowly, or, rather, spoke deliberately, as if she didn't want to waste her words, and when I—'

'Did you ask her who she was?'

'I was just about to tell you. Yes, when I asked her who she was, she said, a well-wisher. I said that was an odd thing to say, and a well-wisher would hardly engage a child she didn't know in conversation, and she said, "But I do know her."'

Chrissie stood up. Her face was white, and she felt cold sweat in the creases of her palms. Air. She needed air. And she needed Stuart. Blood pounded in her ears and the kitchen seemed to be caving in, as if the room was a collapsible box and someone was pressing on the sides. Down came the ceiling, in came the walls. She edged away from the table. Nina said, 'Don't look at me like that.'

'We'll have to leave,' Chrissie said. 'We can't stay here.'

'No, darling, look, I'm sorry. Maybe I've told this story too bluntly, I know it all sounds weird, but I honestly came away feeling no fear for Sunshine.'

'Well, and that worries me, too, frankly,' Chrissie said. 'Did Sunny recognise her?'

'I thought she may have done, at first,' Nina said. 'She was looking across at her with that little questioning frown she has when she's doing a puzzle, but when I asked her afterwards if she knew the lady, she didn't answer. It was all over very quickly.'

'What did she want?'

Nina said, 'Nothing. I mean, I don't know, but she was very undemanding. She said, "She looks very happy," and then Sunshine's new little friend shouted something to us from the top of the slide, and the woman just somehow melted away, and Sunny and I were standing there looking at where she'd been, as if we'd both had the same dream.'

Chrissie said, 'Nina, God, who was she?'

'I don't know, and yes, it's alarming on one level, but also, she was rather lovely. She said she hoped she hadn't scared me, and she asked me to, now how did she put it . . .? She asked me to send you her blessings, I think.'

'Me? Christ, Nina, does she know me too?'

Nina said, 'Not sure. She didn't use your name.'

Chrissie looked into Nina's eyes, and in that moment, even while she silently acknowledged this was grossly unfair, she hated her.

'Who the fuck was she?'

Nina stood up, feeling a flare of indignant anger. 'Do not shoot the messenger,' she said. 'I wish I knew who she was, but I don't, not yet.'

'You let Sunny out of your sight. You let this happen.'

'Chrissie! What harm was done? So, Sunshine has a past? What did you think? That she hatched from an egg, fully formed?'

Chrissie spun round and left the kitchen. She needed Stuart. She grabbed her mobile phone and stalked out into the back garden, but the call went straight to voicemail and she didn't have the words to express what she was feeling, so she hung up, and just stood for a while on the grass, contemplating the jeopardy in this new world she inhabited, and simply willing him to look at his phone. She knew he'd ring the moment he saw the missed call. He was in a bar near Euston, having a conversation with a man from the Roundhouse who wanted The Lineman on the bill for an Aids benefit gig he was putting together, late October. They hadn't been going to perform until next year, they'd cleared their diary for an extremely good reason, but the booker was a friend from way back, a good guy that Stu wouldn't want to say no to. She thought about Stu, in a bar on Warren Street, and knew he'd be thinking, 'Why not?' but he didn't yet know that they had to leave London; that's what he needed to know.

Her phone rang, and she picked up and just launched into the story, said, 'Stu, a person in the park knew Sunny, spoke to her, not a random encounter. I think they were waiting there for her, they're closing in, Stu, they're coming for her.'

'Chrissie, slow down,' he said. 'Where are you?'

'At home.'

'And Sunny's there?'

'Yeah. I need you. We both do.'

'On my way,' he said.

She felt calmer as soon as he walked in, and his hug made her feel planted more firmly on the earth, but still, she'd made up her mind, and wouldn't be dissuaded. She wanted them both to leave with Sunshine, take her away to a different part of the country; she wanted to outrun Sunshine's past, leave no trace, outwit whoever it was who currently knew where they should look. But the band, Stu kept saying. The band. It was unthinkable, to remove themselves from Rocco and Sol, not to mention Julia and Kim, and Nina, and this lovely flat in a part of

London that made them both feel lucky. Chrissie said she didn't feel lucky any more; she felt hunted. Nina said running from Sunny's past seemed counter-intuitive to her, because wouldn't it be better to stand firm, and face this together, and find out exactly what they were dealing with?

'This is where all your allies are, Chrissie,' Nina said. 'All the people with a passionate interest in your happiness.'

'You're forgetting my parents,' Chrissie said coldly, and Nina fell quiet.

Stuart couldn't sit down; he paced the room, filled with a kind of primeval frustration at his powerlessness. Carly said, 'Stuart, darling, be still,' but he didn't hear, his mind was too crowded with thoughts, and Chrissie was killing him, her wild-eyed determination to cut and run, as if the three of them could go live in a cave, go live on a rock in the ocean. And Sunshine zipped about on her scooter, up and down the hallway, happy as a skylark after a lovely trip to the park with Auntie Nina and a special dinner made by Grandma Carly of grilled cheese sand-wiches and a big glass of milk.

It was decided that Chrissie, Sunshine and Carly would, for now, go to Barnsley, and stay for a while with Doug and Diana. Stuart would stay at home and keep The Lineman ticking over. Remi would sing at the benefit concert, because Chrissie couldn't, or wouldn't. Stu would come and stay with them when he could. And, unlikely as this was as a solution, Chrissie seemed released by it; positive and surefooted. She'd suggested Remi as the obvious solution, and it was a good call, everyone realised that. They'd all met at the studios for a run-through of the benefit set, and the sound guy's jaw had dropped when Remi had started singing. She wasn't better than Chrissie, she was just different – Gallic, gamine, ultra-cool in an unscripted way.

She sang with her hands locked together behind her back, her mouth close to the mic, her eyes flashing this way and that, at Stu on one side, Sol on the other. Afterwards Rocco said to Chrissie, 'Weird playing your songs, without you,' and she said, 'Yeah, well, she made them her own, right?' and Rocco laughed. 'I wouldn't say that,' he said. 'There's only one Chrissie Stevenson.'

~

They went by train. Euston station to Sheffield, then Sheffield to Barnsley, and there was Doug, waiting in the Bentley, when the three travellers emerged from the station. Carly blinked and looked around and breathed her first lungful of northern English air. She stood out like an exotic bird before the red-brick backdrop of Barnsley Interchange, in her turquoise silk harem pants, a huge yellow coat and flat leather sandals, because she hated the feeling of her feet being enclosed in shoes or boots.

Doug leapt out of the car and, uncertain whether a hug was in order, instead held her at arm's-length by the shoulders and said, 'Now then, must be ten years,' which it was, at least.

Sunshine was excited and garrulous. She'd been allowed a KitKat from the refreshment trolley, and this is what she told Doug, as he squeezed her in a bear hug, although she called it a KatKit. Doug laughed, released her, then held open the rear passenger door, and welcomed her into the car with a chauffeur-like flourish.

'A KatKit!' he said. 'What a treat. I hope your mummy washed your hands.' He winked as he said this, as if nothing mattered less to him than the cream leather seats of the Bentley. There was no booster seat, so Chrissie sat the child on her lap and strapped them both in together. Carly went up front. She stroked the buttery upholstery and said, 'Oh, my, this is very fine indeed,' and Doug took this remark as interest in the vehicle specifications, which he detailed in full, then asked her what she drove at home.

'Oh,' Carly said, 'well, I only have a bicycle,' then, when she saw his crestfallen expression, added, 'but my neighbour has an Oldsmobile station wagon, and sometimes I borrow that.'

'Oldsmobile,' Doug said, rolling the word round his mouth like a humbug. 'Oldsmobile.'

'Dad's obsessed by cars,' Chrissie said. 'Especially this one, because the Queen has one like it.' She could see him glancing in the rear-view mirror now and again, and she knew he'd be worrying about whether any of that KitKat was still on Sunshine's fingers.

'Well, it's beautiful,' Carly said. *Bee-yoo-diful*. She gazed at the drab town centre through her rain-streaked window, and Doug said, 'I'm sorry I couldn't organise some better weather for you,' and Carly smiled and said, 'Just as well we brought our own Sunshine, I guess,' which made Doug roar.

Sunny plugged her ears with her fingers. 'Grandad's LOUD,' she said, vehemently, which only set him off again.

'How's Mum?' Chrissie asked. Again, she saw his eyes in the mirror, there, and gone.

'Not bad,' he said. 'Not bad at all,' which they both knew was the best either of them expected.

And she was fine, as it turned out. She didn't mind women such as Carly Woodall who wore baggy clothing and shunned make-up, because Diana felt it only made her own beauty shine more brightly. That was one of the reasons she relaxed around Nina; same deal. It was – as Doug had guessed – a decade since Diana and Carly had been in the same room, and, in her mind, Diana had her pinned as a rival, a kind of flower-power beauty, with flowing locks and a crown of daisies. The reality reassured her enormously. She herself had been to the hairdresser's that morning for a cut and colour, and she could see now that she needn't have bothered.

'Diana!' Carly said, when Doug shouldered the front door open and Chrissie's mother appeared in her narrow black capri pants, cream satin blouse and pearls. She had a Martini glass in her hand, as if she'd stepped out of a cocktail party to say hello to newcomers. 'My, oh my,' Carly said. 'You look a million dollars!'

Chrissie held Sunshine's hand. Here they were, in her childhood home for the first time since she'd gained a daughter, and Diana was too busy cherishing her own glamour to say hello. Instead of ignominiously waiting to be greeted, Chrissie walked upstairs with Sunshine, and took her to the room she still thought of as hers, and soon there was the genteel trip-trap of Diana's footfall coming after them.

'Don't be surly,' Diana said. 'I didn't forget you two, I just got distracted by Carly's dreadful trousers.'

'Mum, be nice,' Chrissie said. 'Carly's been a godsend,' but Diana was having none of that and instead simply turned to Sunshine, who was regarding her grandmother with placid interest.

'Hello, Sunny,' Diana said. 'Hello, my little fugitive granddaughter.'

'Hello,' Sunny said, then she pointed at Diana's pearls. 'They is pretty.'

'Well, thank you!' Diana said. 'Would you like to see my jewellery box? It's like a treasure chest. Come, let's leave Mummy to sulk,' and she held out her hand, pale, slender, the nails gleaming pastel pink, and Sunshine took it eagerly, more eagerly than Chrissie wished her to, in truth. Diana trilled the fingers on her free hand and said, 'Toodle-oo.'

Chrissie moved to the window and gazed out at the rain, which fell fine and steady. For the first time since adolescence, she felt very glad to be here. She'd rung Brendan Cassidy and told him what had happened, and his silence had told her how shocked he was. He'd said he had no idea how that could have happened, but he'd try and find out. He'd said sorry, very sadly, as if he'd let her down. He'd said, call me any time you need to. Stuart often laughed at Brendan, said he was love-struck, a guy with a hopeless crush, but Chrissie liked his commitment. It was validating. It comforted her.

She could hear Doug and Carly downstairs, not what they were saying, but the timbre of their conversation and the intermittent rise and fall of laughter. Doug could chat to anyone and was never anything but himself. Carly too. She had an interest in the human condition, and it manifested as warmth and a kind of flattering concentration on whoever she was with. Diana had said, 'Why does Stuart's mother need to come?' when Chrissie had first mooted this plan. 'Surely she'll be surplus to requirements?' And Nina, when she'd heard the arrangement, had looked hurt and a little lost. But Chrissie was firm, she was resolved, and – rightly or wrongly – Nina had become part of the problem, while Carly had flown to England to get to know Sunshine, and it made no sense to separate them. Anyway, Carly made all the difference, to Chrissie, here in Barnsley. She would be the filter, through which every word and deed of Diana's would pass and be rendered innocuous.

Chrissie knew she ought to go downstairs and join them, but instead she put Joe Jackson into her old tape deck, and lay on the bed to listen to one of the cherished albums of her youth. *What the hell is wrong with you tonight? I can't seem to say or do the right thing.* She'd always thought that lyric could've been written for the Stevensons. The Lineman had covered 'Different for Girls' in the early months after the band was formed, and at a gig Chrissie would always sing that opening couplet looking directly at Stu, with a hint of a snarl, and he'd smile right back at her, basking in the irony, because there never was a girl and a boy more in synch with each other than they were. But here, in this imposing house built two hundred years ago from solid Barnsley stone, saying and doing the right thing remained as much of a mystery and a minefield as it had ever been. Chrissie didn't care, though; she didn't care at all. She was in the familiar landscape of her childhood, where the details of life that once had maddened her now brought a feeling of immense calm, as if her mother's moods, intractable and opaque, were all necessary elements in the chemistry of a safe and simple life.

15

It struck Chrissie that maybe the woman in the park was the same person as the woman in the shoe shop, the one who'd asked for her autograph, and admired Sunshine's shameless exhibitionism. Same sort of age – mid-twenties – and she'd had auburn hair too, Chrissie thought; wavy, kind of reddish anyway, maybe, or was it? Yes, wavy, she decided, but other than that, she remembered no distinguishing features. She hadn't paid much attention to the woman's appearance; she'd been keen to corral Sunshine, get her off the chair, get some new shoes on her feet. Now she thought about it, though, she could swear there'd been no child with her. A woman in a children's shoe shop, without a child? Every other adult customer in there had been very obviously attached to at least one small person, but this super-fan had given all her attention to Chrissie, without ever once looking about her for an errant child. Instead, she'd asked about European tour dates and then queried why a session musician was credited on the sleeve notes on two of the tracks, a detail so fanatically geeky that Chrissie hadn't had any inclination to spin out their conversation. How she wished now, though, that she'd logged her height, her weight, the colour of her eyes. She rang Nina with her theory, and Nina said, 'Well, perhaps you're right, but what can we do? She's not still going to be in the shoe shop, is she?' which was only the truth, but Chrissie felt thwarted and discouraged.

'Do you think she followed us there?' she asked.

Nina was silent for a few moments, then said, 'I couldn't possibly say, Chrissie. She may have done, I suppose. But also, she could have been a perfect stranger, and a fan of The Lineman.'

'Would you recognise her again if you saw her?' Chrissie asked.

'I'd recognise the woman I saw, but I wouldn't recognise the woman *you* saw.'

'Don't use that tone on me,' Chrissie said.

'What tone?'

'Careful, and patronising, as if I'm feeble-minded.'

Nina laughed.

'No, I mean it,' Chrissie said. 'You sound just like Stu did, when I asked him if he's constantly watchful for a red coat in a crowd – "Oh, Chrissie, sweetheart, no, not really" – as if he pities me.'

'Well, look,' Nina said, 'you each have different ways of dealing with the situation you find yourself in. Stuart can only be himself.'

Not good enough, thought Chrissie. Not good enough. She felt increasingly isolated. Even Carly, when Chrissie had tried to explain how she felt, had said, 'Well, Stuart has always thrived on his positive energy,' and this was true, Chrissie knew, because it was a trait she'd always loved about him – his irrepressible optimism, his rock-solid belief in a golden future, and to date, he would say, nothing had ever happened to disprove his theory. These mysterious women who materialised on the fringes of Sunshine's existence – they would be vanquished by the passing of time and the power of the Stevenson-Woodall good fortune;

this is what Stuart believed. Chrissie was on red alert, while Stuart was neither cowed nor particularly concerned, and he'd said this to her, before she left with Sunshine and Carly for South Yorkshire. He'd said, 'Don't stay too long from where you belong.' He'd said, 'I get it, I know you need to do this. But we're going to be fine. We're going to be absolutely fine.'

She'd said, 'But that's *why* I'm going, Stu – so that we'll be absolutely fine,' and he'd done the thing Nina kept doing, the understanding nod, the sympathetic smile, the soft light of loving concern in his eyes for her mental well-being. Nina and Stuart thought she was over-reacting and that the threat, such as it was, should be met head-on. Carly, the soul sister, the fence-sitter, tried to be sympathetic to all points of view. But Chrissie – she knew there was a net around Sunshine, and by increments, it was closing.

~

Diana, in a low voice, said, 'Change her name to Susan, why don't you?'

They were having dinner, and Diana had finished her habitual two large vodkas and lime and was now enjoying what she called 'Doug's Claret' with their Saturday-night steak. Sunshine was seated with them, eating the soft insides of a jacket potato with a teaspoon. She was wearing a long, thick rope of cultured pearls that pooled in her lap as she sat, and a pair of huge clip-on earrings. On each of her tiny lobes sat a ruby, set into a wide circle of diamonds. ('They're only paste, Doug,' Diana had said. 'Don't have a heart attack.') It was a miracle, thought Chrissie, that their weight didn't land Sunshine face-first in her potato, but she seemed to have developed a regal bearing for the occasion, a kind of quiet, queenly stoicism.

'Susan?' Chrissie replied, also quietly. 'What?'

'Oh, well, Suzanne, then.'

Diana's theory was that if someone was looking for a child named Sunshine, they would always be easy to find, and it was true that, even in the fashionable bohemia that was London N10, where organic and free-range names such as Apple and Honey and Leaf might regularly be heard being called in the playground, Chrissie had yet to encounter another Sunshine. But it was her name, and it was a beautiful one; she had precious little else that was hers alone.

Chrissie watched her now, carrying delicate quantities of buttery potato to her mouth, as if it were caviar on a silver spoon. She was seated next to Carly, who also had only a jacket potato on her plate, because she didn't eat meat – a fact that Diana knew perfectly well, but had ignored, because she considered vegetarianism an inconvenient fad, and anyway Diana and Doug had steak every Saturday night, and they were not in the habit of bending to anyone else's preferences. The steak was never less than excellent, however; sirloin for him, fillet for her. Doug's sirloin always hung over the edges of his plate, while Diana always had a small medallion, which she would eat in wafer-thin slivers, until it was not quite half gone, and then she would stop and eat no more, laying her knife and fork a little regretfully on her plate. Chrissie had been given a fillet too, because Doug considered them ladylike. It was delicious, as was the claret. They were now on the second bottle, and the edges of the evening were becoming pleasantly blurred. Diana wasn't as nasty when she was drunk; she was far nastier sober.

Now, Chrissie, addressing the Susan suggestion, said to Diana, 'Out of the question,' very quietly, because even though Sunny wasn't paying attention, she didn't wish the child to overhear her grandmother's plans to reinvent her.

'You were going to be Susan,' Diana said, at a normal volume.

'Was I?' Chrissie thought she knew everything about her beginnings, but no one had ever mentioned Susan before.

'Your dad favoured it.'

'Did you, Dad?'

Doug looked up from his steak. 'Yes,' he said, 'if your mother says I did, then I did.'

Chrissie laughed. The claret must be making him bold.

'But I preferred Christine,' Diana said. 'So.'

'And if I'd been a boy? Did you have something lined up?'

'You were never going to be a boy,' Diana said.

'I might have been!'

'You would've been Douglas,' Doug said.

'No, you wouldn't,' Diana said. 'But it never came up, because I knew you were a girl.'

Carly, her chin cupped in her hand, swivelled her gaze from Doug and rested it on Diana and said, 'You mean, sensed it? I know what you mean. I sensed Stuart was a boy; isn't it amazing, how that happens?'

There was a pause, and Diana, realising she was meant to fill it, said, 'Astonishing.'

'Well,' Chrissie said, 'there was a fifty-fifty chance, to be fair.'

'Yes, indeed – you wouldn't have got good odds at the bookies',' Doug said.

Carly, dreamy with recollections of the past, oblivious to the light rain of scepticism, said, 'Of course, I didn't mind, either way, boy or girl, but there was Stuart all along, entirely himself, and Col, his father, had Cilla lined up for his baby daughter—'

'Cilla?' Chrissie said, exploding into laughter. 'Stu would've been Cilla?'

Carly said, 'A girl would have been Cilla. Col was very set on that. I do not know why, something to do with Liverpool, but I let it go, because I knew I was carrying a boy. I just knew . . .' She stopped, and lifted her hands, palms flat. Her smile was beatific.

Chrissie and Diana exchanged a rare private glance. Discreet. Amused. Cilla, oh my God, thought Chrissie. She worked very hard to control her features.

Diana said, 'Horses for courses,' which no one understood. She looked at their baffled faces, then said, 'I wanted a girl, therefore I got one.'

'Oh, but boys are just wonderful,' Carly said. 'I mean, girls are wonderful too, obviously—' she nodded, here, at Sunshine, who all this time had been quietly eating her potato and concentrating on wearing her jewellery '—but I would never have wished for a girl over a boy.'

Diana sniffed. She found Carly's spiritual enlightenment aggravating, and her general air of contentment inexplicable.

'I didn't say I wished for a girl over a boy. I said I knew Christine would be a girl.'

'Just as well, because it's a damn silly name for a boy,' Doug said, and looked pleased with himself when Carly and Chrissie laughed.

'Pipe down, Doug,' Diana said.

'Stuart was his father's choice of name,' Carly said.

'Named him for Stu Sutcliffe,' Chrissie said, to Doug, whom she had some hope might have heard of him. He looked blank.

'The lost Beatle,' Chrissie said. 'Left the band in sixty-one.'

Doug said, 'Bad business decision, leaving The Beatles.'

'Well, and then he died,' Chrissie said.

Carly said, 'And so did Colin,' as if this was a remarkable coincidence. She was tipsy, and her New Jersey accent seemed broader the more she drank. 'The Beatles,' she said, 'Stuart's father was *crazy* about that band. That's why Stuart went to Liverpool to study, you know. It was a sort of pilgrimage, wasn't it, Chrissie?'

'It was,' she said. 'A Colin pilgrimage, not a Beatles pilgrimage, although The Beatles connection didn't hurt.'

'Stuart and Chrissie played "I'm Only Sleeping" at his dad's funeral,' Carly said, and doe-eyed, she reached for Chrissie's hand, so Diana tutted and Doug occupied himself with refills, while Chrissie took a moment to oblige Carly, and hold Colin in her thoughts. Chrissie had very few memories of Stu's father, but they were all fond ones. She'd met him only once, the first time they went together to the States, in 1986. Colin was a Scouser through and through, although he'd lived in New York by then for two-thirds of his life. He loved his Stu Sutcliffe story, and how he'd seen The Beatles play before they were famous, the fab five, not four. His son used to mildly berate him for picking the name of the only guitarist in the line-up who couldn't really play guitar.

'Ah, ey, he did all right,' Col would say. 'Picked it up fast, like. An' I'll tell you wha', Chrissie girl, he was better looking than Lennon or McCartney.' Stuart, her Stuart, was better looking than Lennon or McCartney too; this was what Chrissie thought now, her memories of Colin returning her to the present; to lovely Stu Woodall, who hadn't wanted her to run away to Barnsley, but was doing his best to understand. When she looked up, Carly was watching her, and in that unnerving way she had of seeming to see what others couldn't, she said, 'You've done the right thing coming here, darling, and Stuart knows that.'

Diana looked up and said sharply, 'What? Of course she's done the right thing, surely that goes without saying?'

Doug said, 'Stay as long as you want, love.'

'That goes without saying too, Doug,' Diana snapped. 'But I will say, again, that the child would blend in so much better in Barnsley as Susan. For a thing, if they come looking, they won't be looking for a girl called Susan, and for another thing, if they do, she'd be very hard to find.'

Sunshine placed her spoon carefully on the side of her plate and said, 'What is Susan?' which, although it wasn't quite the right question, was definitely the first time she'd put the words of such a question in the correct order. Carly gave a wistful little pout, and it did feel a little sad that, unassisted, Sunny had recalibrated her grammar, but Chrissie smiled, and said, 'Susan is what Grandma and Grandpa were going to call me, but then they chose Chrissie instead.'

'You,' Diana said, pointing at her daughter, 'are Chris*tine*.'

'No,' Sunny said, emphatically. 'Her is Mummy.'

Later, lying on her bed together, they called Stuart and he spoke to them both in turn, Sunny first, then Chrissie. Sunshine had the small child's inability to recall the events of her day without constant prompting, and she kept whispering to Chrissie, 'Mummy, what else happened exciting?' and Chrissie reminded her of the KitKat, Grandad's car with soft, white seats, the pearls and earrings that Grandma had let her wear at dinner, the baked potato and the tiny spoon, then the game of Pairs that she'd played with Mummy and Grandad, the same game Mummy used to play when she was a little girl, fetched out of the loft after dinner, by Grandad. None of Sunny's retelling was particularly lucid, but Stuart got the gist. Finally, she passed the phone to Chrissie, and Stu said, 'Hey, you,' and Chrissie smiled and said, 'Hey.'

'Did you win at Pairs?'

'Nah, she thrashed us both. I swear she didn't forget a single image after seeing it once.'

'She sounds great. What a time she's having – pearls, potato and Pairs . . . doesn't get much better than that.'

Chrissie said, 'She's had a lovely day, marred only by the fact she had to take her jewels off in the bath.' Sunny, listening in, knew she was at the centre of the conversation and she smiled sleepily at Chrissie, and popped in her thumb. Chrissie pulled her closer, and Sunshine closed her eyes.

'Diana OK?'

'She's OK, yeah. She *loves* having Sunny here on her own turf – she's much less narky with her than she was at ours. Also, she's all relaxed about Carly now, she's not threatened by her because she doesn't wear lippy, and her clothes are baggy. We talked about your dad, earlier, and Stu Sutcliffe.'

'Did you, now? My namesake. Ah, jeez, my old man would've loved our little girl.'

'I know, he really would.' She glanced down at the child, whose thumb had already fallen slackly from her mouth. She'd dropped into sleep like a stone into water, and was puffing softly through her sweet, damp lips. 'Diana wants to change Sunny's name to Susan,' Chrissie said, and Stuart laughed. 'Suzanne, if we can't cope with Susan,' she added.

'She's priceless.'

'That's what I thought, then later I thought, does she make a good point?'

'She does not. What we gonna do, dye her hair yellow while we're at it?'

'No, I know, I just think about the years ahead, when anyone can ask at a school, say, if there's a girl called Sunshine? That note, the one that came with the memory bag – it said, "These items belong to a girl named Sunshine," and that was all they needed to identify her.'

'Chrissie, we're not changing her name. It's the first thing we loved about her.'

'I know. I know.'

'So, Sunny she remains.'

'It'll make her stand out, that's all.'

'She's a stand-out kid, for all sorts of reasons.'

Chrissie chewed the edge of her thumb. She wanted to ask, what's *wrong* with you, that you can be this relaxed? She wanted to ask, how did that woman know where Barbara lived? How did the other one know which playground Sunny would be at? She wanted to ask, who, in our extended circle of trust, is feeding them information? But she said none of this, because none of it was new, and none of it got them anywhere. He could tell though, from her silence, where her thoughts were taking her, so he said, 'We had a good session today. Remi's done her homework, slotted right in.'

'At Sol's?'

'Yeah. Oh, and Kim and Rocco suggested a trip north, to see you and Sunny. All of us, Sol and Jules too, and Juno obviously.'

'What, here?'

He laughed and said, 'Don't sound so horrified.'

'No, I mean—'

'I know what you mean, and no, not at your folks' house. Kim knows a guy with a house in Castleton, a big place he rents out for writers' retreats and yoga weekends, that kind of thing. She and Rocco are going, and she thought we could all tag along and hang there for a long weekend. We'd have it to ourselves, there'd be no retreats going on.'

'Right,' Chrissie said.

'Not keen?'

'No, I mean, yes . . . it's just, we've only just got here.' She shifted position slightly, so that Sunshine's head rested on a pillow and not on her arm. She looked down at the child's dark lashes; sooty fringes against her creamy skin. Her ear lobes still bore the faint, red imprint of Diana's heavy earrings.

'Oh, well, no, I didn't mean right away, I mean when this gig's behind us. You'll likely be ready for a change of scene by then anyway.'

Chrissie thought about it. 'Castleton's nice,' she said. 'I went for a picnic there once, and on a school trip to the caves.' She remembered standing in a cavern with a huddle of classmates, being dripped on by mighty stalactites. Sunshine and Juno were a bit young for all that but, yeah, Castleton, the Peak District; drystone walls, sheep in the road, beer and crisps in pub gardens.

'So, it's a plan?' Stu said.

'It's a plan. You'll come up here on your own, before that though, right?'

There was the smallest hesitation. 'Sure,' he said. 'If I can.'

'You mean, you might not?'

'Ah, look, there's a lot to get on with here, and I'm back-to-back meetings and rehearsals for the next two weeks, but I'll be there if I can, OK?'

'OK,' Chrissie said, but thought, no, not OK, not really. She wanted him to come and, more than that, she wanted him to want to come. They were rarely apart, their lives were entwined, and yes, it was she who'd disrupted their world with her bolt to Barnsley; but it was for Sunshine, and for her own peace of mind, and for Stuart too. She was protecting him from a threat that, at the moment, she saw more clearly than he did.

After they'd said goodbye, she carefully lifted Sunshine and slid her sleeping form under the covers, tucked her in, peppered her face with soft kisses that landed weightless, like butterflies, then she went downstairs, to be sociable.

~

It was as if Carly viewed the world through the lens of a kaleidoscope, turning the drabbest of surroundings into a tumult of ecstatic colour. She said Barnsley had a way of embracing her that made every day pass pleasantly. She said the people here were earthy and kind and without pretention or judgement. This made Chrissie smile; she'd seen how people in the town centre eyed Carly's flapping lemon-yellow coat and multicoloured, layered silks; they'd never seen anyone like her, and even toddlers in pushchairs, who hadn't yet been taught to judge, stared and swivelled their heads as they passed, trying to keep this exotic creature in their range of vision a little while longer.

In Locke Park one day, she outdid herself by turning up to meet Chrissie and Sunshine without her sandals, treading with strong, tanned feet along the paths and across the grass, not wincing once, not even if she trod on a stone. Jaws dropped, all around her. It was early October and the autumn sun wasn't fooling anyone else into even shedding coats, let alone footwear, but Carly said a barefoot walk was Mother Nature's reflexology; a free and natural opportunity to reset the balance of the body's natural rhythms. This was the kind of remark she made, without any sense of the solid Northern roll of the eye with which it was almost always met. She was smashing, Doug said, but slightly crackers, and Chrissie couldn't disagree. But Carly had a remarkable ability to take the very best from every situation, and because Barnsley was nothing like Cape May, she felt privileged to be getting to know it. She would set out most days with

Chrissie and Sunshine, and one way or another, she would be bowled over by something.

Today, it'd been mushy peas. 'Like a vivid green daal,' she was saying, to Diana, when they got home. 'So good!'

Diana said, 'You don't need to tell me about mushy peas, Carly – they're very ordinary.'

'You could sell them from a food cart, in Mumbai,' Carly said, her passion quite undiminished by Diana's lack of it. 'Call it Barnsley daal.'

Chrissie laughed, but Diana simply couldn't see a funny side to Carly's apparently bottomless enthusiasm for every small aspect of Northern life.

'Barnsley daal, my eye,' she said. 'They're just plain old marrowfat peas.' She busied herself at the cutlery drawer, re-arranging the knives so that they all pointed in the same direction. 'Whoever unloaded the dishwasher did it any old how,' she said. 'This drawer looks like a bomb went off in it.'

'That was Sunshine,' Chrissie said. 'She was helping Dad this morning.'

'Oh,' Diana said. 'Well, in that case.'

She couldn't be cross with her granddaughter, they'd dis-covered. Sunny had pierced Diana's heart in a way that no one else had ever quite managed. The child was outside in the gar-den with Doug, chasing bubbles the size of footballs. They could hear her squeal with laughter each time one popped, and now and again Doug shouted something such as, 'Here's a big 'un,' or 'Bullseye!' He'd told Chrissie that the little girl was a gift, a treasure. They'd been up early, Doug, Chrissie and Sun-shine, making a brew, pottering together in the kitchen. Chrissie had said, 'That means the world, Dad, thank you,' and he'd stood still, teapot in hand, and fixed his daughter with a gaze.

'Now, give over, Christine,' he'd said, and tapped her on the end of the nose with one finger. 'Thank *you*.'

'So,' Diana said now. 'Am I to understand you had a pie, Christine, or did you all just have a bowl of peas?'

'I shared a pie with Sunshine,' Chrissie said. 'Not that I should have to account for myself. It was lunchtime, after all.'

Diana shook her head, mystified. 'A pie, for lunch.'

'Mum doesn't eat pies. Or lunch,' Chrissie said to Carly.

'All that pastry,' Diana said. 'Who would?'

'Well, I can't speak for the quality of the pie, but I don't mind saying again that my bowl of mushy peas was wonderful,' Carly said. 'They gave me a dear little jug of mint sauce, too. I do see why you love it here, Chrissie.'

Diana gave a small snort of derision, which Chrissie understood very well to mean, 'Oh, please! Christine comes when it suits her, which is only rarely.' But out and about in Barnsley market, Chrissie had felt more happy and relaxed than she had for weeks. She felt less vulnerable in this community of no-nonsense people, whose countenances seemed familiar, even when she didn't know them. Did faces have a regional topography, just as the landscape did? Here, there was a certain set to the mouth, especially, that seemed to say, 'Pleased to meet you, but don't expect me to say so.' An old man, a pal of Doug's, seeing her for the first time in fifteen years, gave her a minimal nod, an economical 'Ey up,' and no smile at all, yet his eyes shone beneath the crags of his brows, and she felt a warmth spreading through her as he patted her arm and moved on. They'd wandered around the stalls, bought a bobble hat and a giant bubble wand for Sunny, and a commemorative bunch of bananas from the place that *might* have been the stall where Nina used to work, then settled into a hot, bustling, pie and pea cafe where they ate their food from a bowl, with spoons.

Between mouthfuls, Sunny drew squiggles and smiles in the steam on the window by their table and smiled at people walking by, while Carly and Chrissie drank mugs of strong Yorkshire tea, and chatted.

Only once had Chrissie felt fear flood her veins, when a man stopped at their table and said, 'Christine Stevenson?' She'd started, and instinctively reached for Sunshine's arm, but then had recognised the features of a boy she used to know, half-disguised now by extreme baldness and a large belly, which strained at the buttons of his plaid shirt. Andy Clark; half a lifetime ago he'd been the drummer in a local band called On A Thursday, so named because that's when they'd rehearsed. Because he fancied her, and because they used to be in the same class for A-level Music, he brought her in as lead singer. They were famous for five minutes in Barnsley, and then she went to university. Back then he'd had a headful of tousled blond hair and a chiselled face, and looked enough like Roger Daltrey for her to submit to a snog once or twice.

'Andy!' she'd said, collecting herself, feeling her heart settle. She'd introduced Carly and Sunshine, but all he'd wanted to do was stare at Chrissie. They'd had a chat, and he'd kept his gaze on her all the while. He knew all about The Lineman, all about Stuart Woodall, Sol Cooper, Rocco. Andy worked in a music shop in Sheffield, he'd said, and taught drums to kids whose parents seemed to want them to play more than they did.

'You've not changed a bit,' he'd said, just before he left. 'You look just the same. I knew you'd make summat of yourself,' and when he'd gone, Carly had grinned and said, 'You're the local celebrity.'

'You know that's rubbish, right?' Chrissie had replied, a little sharply. She'd looked around her, at all the people intent on their food, heads down, elbows on the tabletops. They were here to eat, and in Barnsley, eating was a serious business, to be accomplished as efficiently as possible.

'See?' Chrissie had said. 'Not a single other soul is interested in me.'

'Well, he seemed star-struck.'

'Not really. It's just life, isn't it? You see somebody you used to know, and it's arresting, and a bit confronting – seeing your own past, and wondering where the time went.'

Carly had looked sceptical. 'That guy was looking at you ve-ry significantly,' she'd said.

'Well, OK, I confess he had a thing for me, when I was seventeen. I let him kiss me. I mean, I kissed him back, too. He had an earring and was really intense. Skinny as a beanpole back then, with a mop of gorgeous hair.'

Carly had laughed, and said, 'Right, well, I think it's fair to say he's not over you, Chrissie Stevenson.'

Chrissie, irritated, had looked away again from Carly's sparkling eyes, and settled her gaze instead on the restful sight of Sunshine. She'd been eating what was left of their shared pie with her fingers, but delicately, fastidiously, tearing off tiny pieces of the suet crust pastry and letting them melt on her tongue. Feeling Chrissie watching her, she'd glanced up and given a little wave. She was an uncommonly precious and wonderful child, Chrissie had thought. She'd wondered if someone, somewhere, had realised that the adoption was all a mistake, and that Sunshine still belonged to another woman. She'd heard such a story, on the adoption grapevine; a couple who'd been given a baby boy, and grown to love him unreservedly, then been forced to return him after six months, because a dreadful error had been made, and he should never have been offered for adoption in the first place. The pain, Chrissie thought: the oceans of grief.

'I don't want to be known as anyone other than Sunshine's mummy,' Chrissie had said, then, to Carly.

'Oh, darling.' Carly had taken one of Chrissie's hands in hers and squeezed it. 'Did I upset you?'

'No, I'm fine, but I do mean what I say, Carly. I'm choosing to be Sunshine's mother, over everything.'

Carly had said, 'Well, honey, that's beautiful, but you can be Sunny's mom and still be yourself. You're a singer, you're a success, you have talent and charisma and a band of boys who all adore you.'

'I want to be anonymous, and I want to find a place to live where no one will ever find her.'

'I just think Sunny would be so proud, to see you perform.'

'Well, I'm happy for her to think me boring as hell, if it means she stays safe.'

'Chrissie, you do know that everything is going to be just fine, right?'

'You sound just like Stuart.'

'No,' Carly had said. 'Stuart sounds just like me.'

They'd smiled at each other. 'I'm so glad you're here,' Chrissie had said. It was almost impossible to imagine anything bad happening in Carly Woodall's orbit. Like a fairy godmother, she seemed to come with an aura of goodness that enclosed and enveloped everyone she cared about.

Sunshine had heaved a great, contented sigh. 'I like that pie,' she'd said.

'Good,' Chrissie had said. 'Now, let's go back, and blow giant bubbles,' and Sunny, who'd forgotten all about the bubble wand, had clapped her hands and bounced on her bottom in the chair, and the waitress who'd come to their table to clear the dishes nodded in Sunshine's general direction and said, 'Well, at least somebody's happy.'

'Oh!' Carly had said, a little puzzled. 'But we all are.'

Now, back home and in the kitchen with Diana, Chrissie said, 'We saw Andy Clark in the cafe, Mum,' and Diana said, 'Marjorie's boy?'

'Yeah,' Chrissie said. 'He used to be good-looking; I used to quite fancy him. But all that lovely hair's gone and he's got a right belly on him.'

'Yes!' Diana said earnestly, spinning round from her task, with a handful of knives. 'Too many pies, you see,' and when Carly and Chrissie burst into laughter, she looked very pink and pleased, even though she'd been making a serious point about the calorific value of the Barnsley pie, and the danger it posed to the waistline.

16

Carly made plans, booked herself onto a coach tour of North Yorkshire, so that 'the young' wouldn't have to accommodate her on their weekend together in Castleton, and Doug drove Chrissie and Sunshine cross country through the wild weather into the Peak District. The others were there already, their cars parked to one side of what turned out to be an extraordinary house, a small stately home, glowing with two hundred years of history. The old Subaru looked shabby and shame-faced alongside Sol and Julia's smug silver Porsche, but in fact both vehicles seemed out of place here; the sweeping circular approach called for a coach and four, at the very least. Still, Doug's Bentley looked the part, and he remarked on this as the three of them gazed out at the elaborate topiary, the stone fountain, the porticoed entrance. He drew to a halt by the wide stone steps and gave a long, low whistle. 'Who did you say lives here?' he asked.

Chrissie peered out of the rain-lashed window. 'I didn't,' she said. 'It's all hush-hush. Some millionaire in the music world.'

'Not a singer then,' Doug said, and from her back seat, Sunshine shouted, 'Look! Mine daddy!'

Stuart had come out of the vast double doors and was battling with an umbrella, which was clearly unequal to the task.

The rain came sideways in the gale, small darts across a blighted land. Doug unbuckled his seat belt but Chrissie said, 'Dad, stay put, stay dry.' She pushed the door open against the wind and it pushed back, quite as forcefully as her. Stu gave up on the brolly and ran down the steps to help Chrissie, as she hauled first a bag and then Sunshine out of the car and let the wind slam the door shut, then he pulled them both into a fierce embrace, a three-way squeeze that only ended when Sunny braced her little arms against his chest and shouted, 'Daddy, let go!' The wind swallowed her voice and swept it away, but he placed her carefully down, shouldered the bag, then they all held hands and ran for cover, while Doug blew a kiss, shouted cheerio, and rolled majestically away.

They hurled themselves into the house, wet through, blown about, laughing at the battering they'd taken, then Sunny stopped short, and stared about her. They were in a baronial hallway, wood-panelled walls, and shining floorboards, the smell of beeswax, and the crackle of blazing logs in the stone fireplace.

'Mummy?' she said. 'Is this mine house?'

Stuart laughed and said, 'Only for two nights, kiddo, don't get used to it,' but Chrissie saw Sunny's absolute stillness and the fleeting confusion in her eyes, then there was the clatter of feet on the staircase and Rocco's voice shouting, 'Let the revelries begin,' like a town crier, then a squeal from Juno when she realised her playmate was here, and all at once Chrissie and Sunshine were surrounded, being hugged and kissed and fussed over, then the little girls took off at a canter, careening around the entrance hall like a pair of foals in a paddock.

Eventually they all gathered below stairs in the kitchen, a vast and inviting space with flagstone floors and gleaming copper cookware and a mighty seven-door Aga to warm the bones. The others had been at the house for a couple of hours already and they immediately settled back to what they'd been doing; the preparation of brunch, which turned out to be a double act featuring Stuart and Remi, chef and sous-chef, with much lively debate about which of them was which. Remi was breaking what looked like dozens of eggs into a bowl for scrambling, Stu halved tomatoes, chopped parsley, cut slices from a huge farm-house loaf. The room smelled of grilled bacon and coffee. Rocco and Sol scattered plates and cutlery and condiments across the long wooden table as if they were dealing cards, and Kim and Julia sloshed vodka and tomato juice into two big glass jugs, for Bloody Marys. They were all so busy, so hell-bent on entertaining each other with banter, and Chrissie had a peculiar sensation of interrupting something, of being the odd one out, the seventh adult in an established group of six, so she took refuge in her phone, on which she saw she'd had a missed call from Brendan Cassidy.

'Oh,' she said. 'Brendan rang,' and she stood up, but no one had heard her. 'Stu?' she said, and when he turned to look at her, she said, 'Brendan rang.'

'He's probably lost and can't find the house,' Stu said, and the others laughed.

'We've been hearing all about him,' Remi said, turning around, holding a wooden spoon in the air like a conductor would hold a baton. 'Devoted, Stu says.'

'Well, who can blame the guy?' Rocco said.

Julia said, 'Ah well, it's nothing new. Chrissie's gone through life being fallen in love with by men she barely notices,' and Chrissie thought, what utter bullshit. She didn't smile – there was no reason to – and Kim saw Chrissie's eyes and said, 'Are you OK, darling?'

Chrissie smiled, but only at Kim. 'I'm fine,' she said, and waggled her phone. 'I just need a signal.'

'Right,' Kim said, 'so, stand in the entrance hall, directly under the chandelier.'

'And,' Sol said, 'once you're there, plant your feet, and do not move an inch. Literally. There's about a square foot of signal in the whole house, and it's there.'

Their voices continued on, fading gradually as she went up the pretty, wainscoted staircase that led back to the ground floor. Halfway up, Sunshine and Juno sat with a posse of cuddly toys, Sunshine's monkey, Juno's armful of Beanie Babies.

'Story time, children,' Juno was saying. 'Sunsine, don't let Monkey be naughty.'

Chrissie said, 'Hey girls,' as she squeezed past, and Sunshine said, 'Mummy, I come too,' and stood up.

'Stay here, sweetie, I'll be back in a minute,' Chrissie said, but Sunshine said, 'No, Mummy, I come too,' and she picked up Monkey by the ears and followed her.

Juno watched her leave, without comment, but with a pout of disappointment that made her look just like Julia. Chrissie said, 'Won't be long, Juno,' and Sunshine climbed the stairs effortfully, planting two feet on each step before scaling the next, and chatting brightly to Chrissie about where they were going. My little shadow, Chrissie thought, with a pulse of undiluted happiness. Brendan had said it was a great sign of deep attachment, when a child became clingy. Give them what they need at that stage in their life, he'd said, and they'll fly straight and true as an arrow in adulthood. Well, Sunshine wasn't exactly clingy, thought Chrissie now, but it was nice being followed about occasionally, like a mummy duck with a favourite duckling. She said, 'So, listen, Sunny, I have to call Brendan, and you need to stay quiet as a little mouse,' and Sunshine arranged her face into a serious expression, and nodded.

In the entrance hall, Chrissie did as she'd been advised, and it was true that the moment she stood beneath the myriad crystal drops of the chandelier, four steady signal bars appeared on her phone. There was no danger of accidentally wandering out of range, because Sunshine immediately plonked herself down on Chrissie's feet and leaned back against her shins, staring around at the burnished oak walls. Chrissie wiggled her toes in her sneakers, which made Sunshine laugh, then she called Brendan's number and he answered on the second ring. He was outdoors, and there was traffic noise. 'Are you on your bike?' she asked.

'Yes, but stationary,' he said. 'I'm perfectly safe to talk. How's things? Are you in Castleton now? I've been thinking about you and Sunshine, and your weekend away.'

This was, Chrissie conceded to herself, a little weird. 'We're fine, Brendan,' she said. 'You rang.'

'Ah, yeah,' he said, clearing his throat, adjusting his tone. 'I had a call at the office from Nancy Maitland.'

'Nancy!' Chrissie said, and her tone made Sunshine twist and look up. Chrissie smiled at her, and Sunny grinned and turned back.

'Yes, Nancy, and of course you know her well, far better than I do, in fact.'

'She's in India though,' Chrissie said. 'Isn't she?'

'Not any more, she rang on a UK landline.'

'Oh? She hasn't been gone long. Is she all right?'

'From what I could tell, yes, but like I said, I don't know her as well as you do.'

Chrissie said, 'She was our guardian angel, that woman. I wonder why she didn't just phone me?'

'She said her mobile phone's on the blink, and all her numbers are in it.'

Chrissie said, 'Ah damn, I'd love to see her. Where was she, when she called you?'

'No idea, but it was a phone box. I heard the pips before the money went in.'

'A phone box?' That seemed a little desperate, somehow. 'What did she say?'

Brendan said, 'Well, that's the thing: she said she needed to know if you and Sunshine were well, and happy, and I thought that a little strange, her *needing* to know, rather than just wanting to know.'

Chrissie thought about this, for a moment. 'It might just be the way she speaks,' she said. 'She's the sort of person who blesses you when she says goodbye. What did you tell her?'

'That you were thriving. I didn't mention the security breaches,' he said. 'That's not her business any more, unless you want to talk to her about them, of course.'

'Right,' Chrissie said, thinking she'd love to talk to Nancy about the security breaches, but not quite wishing to say that out loud to Brendan.

'I said you were doing brilliantly, that Sunshine had found the sort of mother that any child would be lucky to have.'

'And father,' Chrissie prompted.

'Yes, and Stu, yes.'

'So . . .?'

'What?'

'Can I get in touch with Nancy? Does she know where I am? Like I said, if she's around, I'd love to see her.'

'The money ran out,' Brendan said. 'We got cut off.'

'Right. Well. That's a shame.'

'I'm sorry.'

'Well, Brendan, it's hardly your fault. If she calls you back, will you be sure to give her my number?'

'Sure, sure.'

There was a pause.

'Anything else?' Chrissie asked.

'Nothing,' Brendan said, 'I'll let you go.'

'Thanks, Brendan.'

She hung up, and for a moment stayed where she was, her feet pinned to the rug by Sunshine's bottom. She thought about Nancy Maitland, wondered what she'd make of everything: the memory bag, the woman in Whitstable, the woman in the park. Certainly, she wouldn't be dismissive or complacent, and now that Brendan had invoked her name, Nancy was the one person with whom Chrissie longed to speak. Nancy had a big heart; she'd made Chrissie and Stu feel . . . what was it, exactly? She'd offered something more than support, that's for sure; something more than encouragement too. They'd felt *held* by Nancy, that was it, thought Chrissie. She'd held their hopes and dreams so respectfully. She'd talked about fate, and love, as if they were scientific facts on which they could and should depend. She'd promised them their perfect fit, and here they were now, with Sunshine.

'Chrissie?'

This was Stu, who was suddenly right there, right behind them, and both Chrissie and Sunshine jumped at the sound of his voice. He laughed, then said, 'Food's ready. It's on the table and those eggs won't wait.' Sunshine sprang up and ran at him, and he swept her up into a cuddle. She had a way of holding on that made anyone who held her feel especially beloved.

'My girl,' he said. 'Are you hungry?'

Sunny nodded into his neck, then threw back her head and said, 'Mummy, you is hungry?'

Chrissie wasn't, but she smiled at their daughter, which passed as a yes, and together they walked back across the hall, towards the stairs.

'So, what did Brendan have to say?' Stu asked, his voice

lightly laced with scepticism, because it was his firm belief that the guy was becoming a pest, clinging on to Chrissie way beyond the call of professional concern. So much for the post-adoption team taking over – Brendan had continued to stay in touch, said they were short of volunteers for the support roles, but Stuart's theory was that the guy just couldn't let Chrissie go. Brendan, Stu believed, had a vested interest in keeping her anxiety alive, added to which, he thought, Chrissie made him feel fascinating. He was sure Brendan continued to ring when he had nothing new to report, just so that he could casually say to his sad little circle of friends, 'Chrissie Stevenson? Yeah, I know her really well.' All of this remained unsaid now, but passed between them anyway, condensed and contained in a single look.

'Nancy's back,' Chrissie said, and her voice was defensive, because she knew precisely what Stuart thought about Brendan, and knew, too, that he was probably right. 'That's why he rang.'

'Nancy?' Stu said, interested now. 'What about her Indian street children?'

'Yeah,' Chrissie said. 'I know. I wonder if things went awry?'

'Does she want her old job back, then?'

Chrissie shrugged. 'She just wanted to know how we were doing, he said. But then they got cut off, so . . .'

They'd stepped into the kitchen now, and their conversation was lost in the party atmosphere. Sunshine immediately loosened her hold on Stu's neck and let him plunge her down to the floor. Juno called out her name and Sunny ran to sit beside her. The room now smelled of toast, the table was laden with good things to eat and Remi stood at one end, doling out her softly scrambled eggs, then passing the plates down the line. Kim waved a jug of Bloody Mary and said, 'Chrissie, hon, let me pour you a sharpener,' and Chrissie thought, yes, absolutely; vodka was precisely what she needed to catch up with this crowd.

The benefit gig had gone thunderingly well, The Lineman's short set the focus of waves of love, and Remi still seemed to be shining, high on the buzz, so young, so grateful, so earnest. Chrissie had always felt such affection for Julia's little sister, but here she was, everyone's favourite since she'd apparently stolen the show at the Roundhouse. Julia, usually so sparing with praise where anyone – but particularly her siblings – was concerned, said, 'Honestly, Chrissie . . . oh my God, it was electric.'

It was evening now, and they were all arranged in a dove-grey drawing room: Kim, Rocco and Sol at a green-baize card table playing poker; Remi and Stuart messing about at the Steinway; Chrissie and Julia on a wide armchair, built for two. The little girls were on a window seat, with the yellow silk curtains drawn, to create a den.

'What was electric?' Chrissie asked, hating the edge in her voice, helpless to desist.

'The energy, the way Remi seemed to have the guys in thrall.'

'Oh,' Chrissie said. 'Right, great.' She was silent for a moment, then decided to say what she really meant. 'No, actually, Julia, what the fuck?'

'Oh!' Julia said. 'No! I can see how that sounded, but I mean, it was just their stage thing, she kept glancing at Sol and Stu like she couldn't choose between them.'

'We're not about that, though, are we?' Chrissie said. 'The Lineman doesn't do that three-guys-and-a-sex-symbol thing. I mean, who does, these days?'

Jules gave her a look, brows raised, head tilted. 'I probably put it badly,' she said. 'I wasn't trying to wind you up, darling, and anyway, Sol's her brother-in-law, and Stu, well, Stu's yours, until the end of time.'

'I think you *were* trying to wind me up,' Chrissie said. 'It's what you do, when the fancy takes you.'

Julia laughed, as if no harm was done, and they both glanced across the room, where Stuart and Remi were squashed onto the piano stool, trying between them to recall the chords for 'Imagine', finding them, losing them, laughing together when they went wrong. So annoying, thought Chrissie, when she herself could have sat on that stool and played the song note perfect, wearing a blindfold.

Julia said, 'Friends, that's all.'

Chrissie ignored her. She looked at Remi's tender, slender neck, the blunt, cropped dark hair; her allure. Was Stuart drawn to her, she wondered? Well, what man wouldn't be drawn to Remi? She found to her surprise that she remained quite dispassionate as these thoughts formed, and she couldn't have said if this was because she didn't care, or because she knew she had no reason on earth to doubt him.

'It was only one gig,' Julia said.

Except, thought Chrissie, perhaps it wouldn't be. Later, in bed, she asked Stuart what he thought about Remi doing the tour next June, so that she could concentrate on Sunshine.

'But the tour is to promote the new album, with your voice on it.'

'We need to think about nursery schools,' she said. 'We need to give a structure to her life.'

'We do? I thought we just needed to love her.'

He'd been lying on his back, staring up at the ceiling, but now he rolled onto his side and propped himself up on one elbow so he could see her properly. 'Are you telling me you want out? Because that's a big deal for all concerned, including the nice people who own us.'

'Don't you think, Stu, that it'd be better for Sunny?'

'No, I don't. Do you think you're the first woman in the industry to have a child?'

'Don't be like that.'

'But Remi's no replacement for you, for God's sake! Are you telling me you want to permanently leave the band?'

'I suppose I'm telling you that it's a possibility,' she said, and then she closed her eyes, because his gaze was making her sad. She knew what he was thinking, as clearly as if he was speaking aloud. The Lineman was the passion of his life, and part of the reason for that was that they'd created it together; he considered it quite as much hers as his. From the outset, he would say, she'd used her way with words to write songs of singular beauty, and they'd fast become the hallmark of the band, track after track in which the vocals rather than the beat led their songs. In the late eighties, they were a bright new sound; but it was Chrissie's lyrics that raised them above the pack, Chrissie's voice that wove the magic.

'Chrissie?' Stu said now.

She opened her eyes. He looked into them, very directly, then said, 'Please come back to me.'

'We will,' she said. 'Another week or so.'

'That's not what I meant,' Stu said. 'That's not what I meant at all.'

~

As well as the house, there was a Land Rover Defender at their disposal, complete with its own inscrutable driver in a Belstaff jacket and aviator shades. Crazy, especially as no one was allowed to ask him who he worked for. Kim was the only one who knew whose place this was, and she said they were only here on condition that she didn't breathe a word. Even Rocco wasn't allowed to know. Well, Kim said, *especially* Rocco, who'd never kept a secret in his life. She said, 'They're not that interesting, it's not Bowie or anyone, so just stop asking me, and soak it all up.' But there was something both intriguing and absurd about clambering into the immaculate black Defender and speaking to each other in hushed voices because the guy at the wheel with the buzz cut and shades – on this rainy day – inspired an intimidated silence. Only Juno and Sunshine felt no inhibitions. They sat side by side on their mothers' knees and sang a terrible song they'd named 'Bumpety Bump', more of a chant than a song, really, bumpety bump rhyming noisily and pointlessly with thumpity thump and lumpity lump, and after two minutes of it, Julia clapped a hand over Juno's mouth, and said, 'Cease, girls!' and the peace that followed was heavenly. Jules leaned her head towards Chrissie's.

'I miss you,' she said, very quietly. 'I haven't always been a good friend to you lately, and I'm so sorry, and I miss you.'

Julia's chin was resting on Chrissie's shoulder, and her lips touched Chrissie's ear when she spoke. Chrissie smiled, remembering all the times in their friendship that Julia had used intimacy as currency, buying her way back into Chrissie's good books with a brush of her lips upon Chrissie's cheek, a seductive murmur against her ear, a hand trailed through her hair with a lover's touch.

'I miss you too,' she said, although it wasn't quite true.

'Then come home,' Julia said, more loudly now, so that the others heard her too.

'Oh, Chrissie,' Kim said. 'Yeah, come home, darling.'

Chrissie smiled and nodded, and gave nothing away. She felt

an odd sense of separation from her friends, their lives, this dynamic, but it wasn't unpleasant; it only made her feel more resolute. She kissed the top of Sunshine's head. When she looked up, Stuart was watching her. They locked eyes, and stayed that way for a few moments, as if they each were trying to read the other's mind, and then Stu gave in and said, 'Penny for your thoughts.'

'I was thinking,' Chrissie said, in a light, casual voice, 'of a little terraced house with a long garden and views of the hills; a solid northern house, sturdy and anonymous – a little fortress.'

The car fell silent. All eyes were upon her now, and of course it was always going to be Julia who spoke up first.

'You mean, you want to leave London?'

'Yes,' Chrissie said. 'Maybe.'

'Are you mad?'

Chrissie looked at Jules. 'No,' she said. 'I'm not.'

Rocco said, 'Chrissie, we need you.'

Chrissie said, 'I can write songs wherever I live. Remi can sing them.'

Sol said, 'Sure, so could any number of talented singers adrift in the industry, but you're Chrissie Stevenson.'

Remi said, 'Adrift? I hadn't realised I was adrift.'

There was another short silence, then Stu said, 'Look, let's talk about this later,' and Chrissie nodded.

'Sorry,' she said. 'I'm bringing the mood down, but I think it's weird that nobody ever talks about what's happening to us.'

'It would be pretty weird if that's all we talked about, too,' Julia said.

'Yeah, but there's a middle ground, Jules, where you show a concerned interest in my mental well-being, without it dominating the weekend.'

Flatly, Remi said, 'You should know by now to expect no

empathy from Julia or Sol,' then looked away from everyone, at the rain-streaked world outside the vehicle.

'Guys,' Stu said, 'let's talk about it later.'

Chrissie leaned back against the seat, and closed her eyes, and felt Sunshine lean back against her, in turn. She laced her hands across the child's tummy, and relished the warm weight of her, and that newly baked smell she had, sweet and buttery, as if, being a little girl, she really was made of sugar and spice.

～

Juno started to cry in Speedwell Cavern, her sobs bouncing off ancient rock as they travelled in a small wooden boat along a narrow tunnel hewn out of the Derbyshire hills. They couldn't go back because there were other paying customers in the vessel, so instead everyone endured her amplified wails as the guide talked stoically, and at length, about eighteenth-century lead mining. It was almost intolerable, until Sunshine passed Juno her Silky, and Juno, recognising the enormity of this gift, covered her head and face with it and sat like this, veiled and sad, until the ordeal was over. Claustrophobia, the guide said. He was a man of indeterminate age, with a lugubrious voice, in which he explained that over the years he'd seen the low roofs and close walls have a dramatic effect on people far older, far more worldly-wise, than Little Miss there. They should try Treak Cliff, he said. 'Stalactites and stalagmites,' he said, 'and right high roofs.' But none of them had the appetite for being underground now, and instead they wandered aimlessly through the wet streets of Castleton, past coffee shops and gift shops and jewellers selling Blue John, until Rocco asked if anyone fancied a pint, and how about the Nag's Head, and the mood of the group immediately lifted. They colonised a big old table by a roaring log fire, and ordered chips, and cheese toasties and Guinness. Sunshine and Juno sat under the table with a packet of crisps each, and a bottle of orange Fanta, with straws in the neck.

'God,' Sol said, clinking his pint glass against Chrissie's half, 'Castleton just improved a hundred per cent.' He was sitting next to her, with one arm draped around the back of her chair, and he drank Guinness like he drank everything: simply tipped up the glass and half its contents disappeared down his throat.

'It's nice, though, in decent weather,' Chrissie said, feeling a little protective of her memories. There'd been the school trip to the caves with her classmates when she was nine, a crocodile line of children, awed into silence by the drip, drip, drip of stalactites and the witchy faces that seemed to loom from the rock in the glow of the lamps. But also, she'd been here with her parents on a day when the clear blue sky made the Hope Valley look like the Garden of Eden. She remembered a wicker picnic basket, and a tartan wool rug, and a grassy plateau on top of a hill. Tinned salmon sandwiches, hard-boiled eggs, and an individual pork pie each for Doug and Chrissie. Diana had taken off her shoes and lain down on the rug with her eyes closed and a small, contented smile on her face, while Doug and Chrissie ate their lunch then played catch with a tennis ball. Diana unpinned her bun that day. When they walked back down the hill to the car, her hair fell in lustrous waves below her shoulders, and Chrissie thought there'd never been anyone more beautiful than her mother. Diana had slipped off her shoes and carried them, walking barefoot down the cool grassy slope, and when they got to the rutted track where the car was parked, Doug had scooped her up into his arms and carried her the rest of the way. Chrissie, trudging behind with the hamper – awkward to hold, heavy even with most of the picnic eaten – had nevertheless trembled with happiness, because Diana laughed so gaily at something Doug was murmuring to her, and in the car she'd placed a hand on Doug's thigh, and kept it there all the way home.

Sol said, 'Look, Chrissie, I'm sorry you think we don't care.' He spoke quietly, so that only she could hear.

She said, 'I know you care, but even so, you don't know how I feel, and nobody ever seems to ask.' She stared down into the creamy head of her Guinness. There was a perfect shamrock, drawn by the barman with the last drops of foam from the pump.

'So, how do you feel?'

She sighed. 'A lot of the time, I'm happier than I've ever been. I thought I'd have to learn to love Sunshine, but she made it easy, she shot into my heart like a little beam of light.'

'And the rest of the time?'

Chrissie turned her head to look at Sol. 'Well, obviously, there are people looking for her, and it terrifies me.'

He nodded. 'I know, but we all feel we can protect you and Sunshine. We all feel that the last thing you need is to be isolated in a part of the country where you don't have friends who love you.'

'Sol, the only people who can protect Sunshine are me and Stuart.'

'That's not true. You need your people, Chrissie. We are your people.'

'Well, and you always will be,' Chrissie said.

She was quiet for a few moments, as she wondered whether she could tell Sol that The Lineman felt almost disposable now. Or, at least, it felt secondary. A secondary concern, and a distant second at that, to Sunshine.

'You can't leave the band,' Sol said. 'The management want you on the album tour, for a start, and I wouldn't want to be the guy to tell them you've legged it. And Remi's terrific, but nobody wants to see her at all our live gigs, standing where you should be.'

'Jules said she was—'

'Oh, Jules . . . she likes to stir up the pond, you know that. Don't leave the band, Chrissie.'

She didn't answer, but leaned her head against his shoulder and he brought his arm closer around her, and they sat like that for a while, comfortable in their affection for each other, listening to the chat around the table, and to the children underneath it. Then she felt her phone buzzing in her coat pocket, took it out and saw it was her dad, who never rang. Stuart looked at her from across the table.

'It's Doug,' she said, and stood up. Stu did too.

'Dad?' she said, making for the door.

She heard a kind of noisy silence, her father's efforts to collect himself, heaving air into his lungs to steady his breathing. Stuart, right by her side, watched her face intently for clues. Her heart hammered in her chest.

'Dad,' Chrissie said. 'Please, what's wrong?'

'It's your mum,' he said. 'Can you come back, Christine? She's . . . it's . . .' Then he seemed to drop the telephone, and all she could hear was the alien sound of her father, weeping.

17

Diana reclined in her hospital bed, a tender hothouse flower, crushed and spoiled. The left side of her face was slack, and hung a fraction lower than the right. Her left arm and hand lay useless on the bed. If she tried to speak, her tongue seemed to clog her mouth and the words were unintelligible, so she'd given up trying, and now she just stared silently at nothing. A blocked artery in the brain, Doug told Chrissie. 'A cerebral infarction,' he said carefully, repeating the term the consultant had used, his voice shaking, wringing his hands. When he wasn't speaking, he was crying, and often he did both, and this version of him was unrecognisable to Chrissie: her handsome, strapping father, his emotions always so firmly in check. But the shock seemed to have reduced him, and in some ways this made him more of a problem than Diana. He was morose and helpless, and while Chrissie understood his grief, she wished he could . . . well, she was loath to say it, but she wished he could pull himself together. She'd never seen her father cry, and now he couldn't stop.

Diana had a private room in the hospital, and when they arrived in Barnsley, Chrissie had gone there immediately, while Stu and Sunshine drove back to the house. She and Doug had a long hug, from which she was forced to untangle herself, pushing him gently away. She was sorry for him, and embarrassed for him; he whimpered and slumped in a chair, the very image of frailty, while Diana, the stroke victim, maintained an attitude of controlled indifference. She was propped against two fat pillows, and was wearing a dreadful green hospital gown. Her hair was unkempt, slightly matted and neither up nor down – what Diana would have called a bird's nest on any other woman. Thus far she'd been spared a look in the mirror, but Chrissie could tell at once from the determined dullness in her mother's eyes that she knew precisely what she would see. Here was a woman who believed she was entirely defined by her great beauty, a gift of nature which she had strived always to enhance and protect, and without it, her existence lost its meaning, her presence lost its power. Chrissie's heart went out to her, this vain, difficult, demanding woman, whose face now mocked her own high standards.

'OK, Dad,' Chrissie said. 'Pass me a pen. I'll make a list of things Mum needs,' and Doug dithered damply and ineffectually, while Chrissie itemised Diana's battery of grooming products and wrote down where in the bathroom or bedroom he would find them, these essentials of her daily routine. She also listed two chiffon nightgowns, a long silk scarf, which always hung on the inside of the cloakroom door in the entrance hall, and the diamond earrings he'd bought for her on their first wedding anniversary.

'Go,' she said, 'there's no better thing you could do for her than this, Dad,' and he bumbled off, casting one last, long tragic look from the open door before he left. He'd slept by her bedside last night, on a low folding bed like a big, sad dog, although Diana had given no indication that this was a comfort. Now, Chrissie sat on the bed beside her, kissed her good cheek, took her good hand, and said, 'Hey, Mum, it's me,' but Diana remained impassive, as if she neither saw nor heard anything, so Chrissie just held her hand, and told her that Doug was bringing all the things that were going to make her feel like herself again. Diana's slender hand, protected over the decades by rubber gloves at the sink, intensive cream every night, was immaculately pale, and her nails looked recently varnished in her favourite shade of blood red; but still, it sat limp in Chrissie's palm, with no loving, appreciative, reciprocal squeeze. This was purely her choice, the consultant said, when she entered the room on her ward round, ten minutes later. She was an imposing woman – tall, stern, brusque – and she told Chrissie that Diana's unresponsiveness wasn't neurological, but simply an expression of her state of mind.

'Well, good,' Chrissie said. 'That's good, isn't it?'

The consultant continued as if Chrissie hadn't spoken. 'Your mother is capable of making a full recovery. She knows this, although she won't acknowledge it.'

'Yet,' Chrissie said. 'Won't acknowledge it yet.'

'She'll regain the use of her left arm and hand, and the facial palsy should gradually lessen until hopefully it's altogether gone, but we're going to need some cooperation from Mrs Stevenson if we're going to see these improvements.'

Every word she said made sense, but even so, Chrissie was glad when she left, taking her steely authority with her. She gave her mother a complicit, sympathetic smile, but Diana maintained a non-seeing gaze, so Chrissie just sat with her and talked about the house in Castleton, and about Sunshine, the funny things she'd done and said since Diana had last seen her, until Doug came rushing back after three quarters of an hour, crashing into the room with an endearing sense of urgency and a small suitcase containing everything he'd been asked to bring.

Then Chrissie asked him to leave the room, and said, 'Mum? Pretend you don't know me, I'm just a new girl at the salon and you're having the full works, OK?' and the merest shift in Diana's expression seemed, at least, to indicate some sort of acquiescence.

Tenderly, she performed services for Diana that yesterday, before any of this had happened, would have been unthinkable, outrageous, impossible. She breached the privacy that had always existed between herself and her mother's body, but she did it with Diana's unspoken consent, and with no sense of embarrassment or shame. She pulled away the sheets that covered her, then untied the hospital gown and removed it. Next she slipped an ivory silk nightgown over her mother's head, and gently threaded her thin arms through the sleeves, then helped her raise her hips so the fabric could be tugged down and smoothed out over her elegant knees, down to her ankles. Then she brushed and brushed her hair until it could be contained and wound into a shining whorl at the nape of her neck. Chrissie performed this task as well as she could, although in all her life she had never done it, only watched, heaven knew how many hundreds of times, as her mother's deft hands accomplished perfection. She wound the silk scarf around the chignon, and draped its ends over one shoulder, a dazzle of burnt orange on the vanilla cream of Diana's gown. Then she took up the pot of shockingly expensive moisturiser, Diana's totem, the elixir of youth that she stockpiled for fear of ever being without, and smoothed it onto the fragile skin around her mother's mouth and eyes, then over her cheeks, and her throat. Chrissie's fingers were cool and she kept her expression neutral, because now, Diana was watching her closely and Chrissie knew she was being used as a mirror, scrutinised for signs of revulsion. The corner of Diana's mouth was drawn down on the left side, as if she was half-disapproving. Her left eye followed the same line, a distinct downturn at its outer edge. These imperfections were small, Chrissie knew, in the broad scheme of facial disfigurement, but on Diana, they seemed shattering, a desecration of a work of fine art. Her mother's gaze remained upon her throughout, but Chrissie only smiled and said, 'There you go,' and replaced the lid onto the jar of cream then set to work with a light foundation, a peachy blusher, a lick of mascara – non-smudge, brown not black, because black was for evenings – and a few strokes of colour on her Bancroft eyebrows.

'Lippy?' she asked. Diana gave an ungracious, peremptory nod, and Chrissie thought, we none of us need worry that it's not Diana Stevenson in there. She applied soft pink to her mother's lips, then reached for the box containing the earrings, which was when Diana drew a determined breath and, as if she was speaking through a wad of wet cotton wool, forced out 'No!' and waved her good hand, index finger raised in warning, to emphasise her point. Chrissie was confused. Here were the diamonds that legend had it had almost broken the bank; the diamonds that Diana had always turned to if she needed to lift her mood or complete her look, and elevate her glamour and beauty further beyond the reach of ordinary mortals. But, 'No!' she said again, and she pushed the box away with unexpected vigour so that it fell out of Chrissie's hand and onto the floor. Then she slumped back against her pillows and closed her eyes, apparently defeated by the effort of speech.

Back at the house, Chrissie rang Nina. She could hear Stuart and Sunshine, their voices faint but animated, drifting down from somewhere upstairs, and she was glad they had the place to themselves for now, glad that Doug was refusing to leave Diana's side, his devotion apparently increasing in direct proportion to the chilliness of her supreme indifference. Nina answered, and Chrissie told her what had happened, then found that Nina had already heard, from Doug.

'Oh, right,' Chrissie said. She'd been all set to tell the story, and felt oddly thwarted. 'I must say, I know it was an awful shock but he's all over the place. How did he sound when you spoke?'

'Well, it had only just happened, so he wasn't making much sense,' Nina said.

'Literally only just happened?'

'Yes,' Nina said. 'I think so. How's Diana now?'

'So, Dad rang you at three a.m.?' Chrissie had struggled to piece together the complete chronology of events from her father's tearful account; but Diana had got out of bed at just before three o'clock this morning, then collapsed on the bedroom floor. Of that, Chrissie was certain.

'Oh, well,' Nina said. 'I wasn't looking at the time, but yes, I think so. Does it matter?'

Chrissie didn't know. Certainly, it *seemed* to matter. Her own phone call from Doug hadn't come until half two in the afternoon, hours after the initial drama. Wouldn't his only thoughts have been first, to call an ambulance and next, to call their only child? And also, given that he *had* called Nina, wouldn't she, on learning the news, respond to the crisis by dashing up to Barnsley immediately? These thoughts ran through Chrissie's mind, but there was nothing urgent or agitated in Nina's tone. Instead, she was only calm and grave and respectful.

'How's Diana now?' she asked, again.

Chrissie took a steadying breath. 'I mean, she's recovering, I think,' she said. 'Physically, it'll depend on whether she co-operates with the rehabilitation process. Emotionally, she's struggling.'

'Of course,' Nina said. 'And you? Are you doing OK?'

'Oh, well, I guess so,' Chrissie said. 'Such a horrible shock, and Dad's lost the plot, and Mum's catatonic with despair, but Stu's here, thank God, and Sunshine too, so yeah, I'm OK.'

'Good, that's good.'

Now, she heard Nina pull up a chair. The only telephone she used was a seventies circular-dial model, mounted on the wall, and Chrissie listened to the sound of the chair legs scraping on the floorboards of her studio, and she felt a wave of relief, and realised that she hadn't been sure Nina even wanted to speak to her, but here was a sign of her commitment. She knew that sound so well, and she knew the chair too; wooden, with three small heart shapes in a row cut out of the back and a painted garland of blue cornflowers winding around them. Little Christine, holding Nina's hand on an outing to Sheffield, had spotted it in the window of a junk shop and stopped in her tracks to tell Nina it looked just like something Heidi's grandfather might own, in his little house at the top of a mountain in the Swiss Alps, and Nina had said, 'In that case, I must have it.' How comforting it was, thought Chrissie, to know Nina was now seated on that chair, listening. She had a sudden powerful longing to be there with her, in the studio.

'So,' Chrissie said, 'did Dad tell you what happened?'

There was the fizz of a match being struck, the sharp inhale of a first drag on a new cigarette. Oh, to be a smoker again, Chrissie thought.

'Well, he was very upset,' Nina said. 'He was so garbled, I had a job to make sense of it.'

'I know, same. I gather that Friday evening she couldn't walk in a straight line, though. She was heading for the living-room door but she walked diagonally across the room instead.'

Nina said, 'Right.'

'But that could just have been the vodka,' Chrissie said. 'If she started too early, on an empty stomach?'

'Mmm,' Nina said. 'Maybe.'

'I think they might have had a fight about something,' Chrissie said. 'I mean, I know it only happens once in a blue moon, when Dad stands up for himself, and I've no idea what sparked it, but she's treating him to a special stony disregard at the moment, I mean, more so than usual. You'd think she might need him. He'd love it, if she needed him.'

Nina said, 'She does need him.'

'He said she'd had a searing headache when they went to bed. They hardly slept, he said. Then she got out of bed in the dark, and immediately fell over. He thought she'd tripped, but when he put the light on she was lying there staring at him, unable to move. At least, I think that's what he told me, is that what he told you? He can't seem to stop crying.'

'I know, poor Doug,' Nina said. 'Have you ever seen him cry?'

'No, never!' Chrissie said. 'I think he thinks he could have prevented it happening, though God knows why, he could hardly have predicted this.'

'Guilt can be so debilitating,' Nina said.

'Auntie Nina?'

'Yes, darling?'

'Why haven't you come?'

Nina pulled on her cigarette. Chrissie closed her eyes and could see her tipping her head, blowing smoke at the ceiling, tapping the ash into a plant pot.

'Auntie Nina,' Chrissie said, into the silence, 'surely you're not waiting to be invited? Please don't think you need permission, Nina.'

She rested her forehead against the wall and waited, and one tear, then another, rolled down her cheek, because this hesitation, this sense of words unspoken, and of the distance between them, was in danger of breaking her heart. Chrissie knew she was the cause of it, knew she'd hurt Nina, lashed out in anger over the woman in the park, then maintained a cold indifference, which she hadn't dropped before fleeing to Barnsley.

'Please come, Auntie Nina,' she said quietly.

Nina said, 'I do need to be in London, just now, I really can't leave just yet. But thank you, sweetheart. Thank you. I promise I'll be there very soon.'

When they hung up, Chrissie felt dazed and unanchored. She wandered about looking for Stuart and Sunshine and found them in the loft, Sunshine's favourite part of the house, due to the piratical drop-down ladder and the thrill of ascending it through a hatch in the ceiling. This was where Chrissie's childhood was stored, and Sunshine already knew which boxes contained the toys, which the books, which the clothes. Stu, though, had never been up here, never seen the trove, and for a few moments Chrissie watched him unobserved from the top of the ladder. The light up here had a gentle, filtered quality, as if you were looking through exceptionally fine muslin. It made Stu look younger – he could have been twenty – and she stared at him and thought about a moment in the past, on a bench seat in a Liverpool pub. She'd written a song in her spiral-bound pad and he was staring down at it, hearing chords in his head, unaware that she was watching him, and her heart was so full of their new love, she could hardly bear the happiness. It had seemed too much, too soon, and yet here they still were, and she was watching again, and this time he had a faded green school exercise book open in his lap and was reading aloud a story about pit ponies, penned by Christine Stevenson in 1974.

Sunshine had extended her own reconnoitre of the loft, and was now making inroads into Diana's impressive stash of hats; currently, she sported a little green pill-box with a net over her eyes. She half-listened to the pit pony story while examining her reflection in the mottled glass of a cheval mirror. She peered through the criss-cross of black netting as if she was looking at a stranger.

'In springtime,' Stu read, 'the ponies were allowed one week in the fresh air and sunshine, and when they were led out of the pit and into a nearby field, they went mad with joy, and leapt and pranced about on the fresh green grass. The miners watched them and felt happy and sad, because they knew what the ponies did not. In seven days, they would be back down the crow-black, coal-black mine for another year of struggle and toil.'

Chrissie said, 'Ten out of ten, excellent work, Christine. Well researched and beautifully written,' and Stu looked up, and laughed.

'You were a prodigious talent,' he said. 'Crow-black, coal-black? You were a child laureate.'

She climbed the rest of the way in, and was immediately assailed by the smell of age and dust and mothballs. 'I nicked it,' she said. '"Slow black, crow black, fishing boat bobbing sea."'

'What?'

'Dylan Thomas, *Under Milk Wood*. But my teacher in Top Juniors hadn't read it.'

'Phenomenal,' he said. 'What a kid. No wonder your folks kept it all. I mean, it's like the Chrissie Stevenson Museum of Childhood up here.'

She looked about her and was startled by the unusual mess. A few upturned crates, some spilled paperwork from decades past. She said, 'Did Sunshine do this?'

'Do what?'

'Tip up those boxes? Everything's usually immaculately squared away.'

He shrugged. It all looked pretty organised to him. 'This is how we found it, I think,' he said, then he held out the exercise book, and she dropped down onto her knees next to him to look at it. Her heart lurched as she plunged into the past. Those careful italics, the controlled handwriting somehow at odds with all the fervent emotion packed into that little essay. She remembered writing it, now she was looking at it; remembered sitting at a square table with Sharon Machin, David Wickes and Dean Fox; remembered she'd been put on their table by the teacher in the hope that her diligence and desire to please would be a good influence on the three most disruptive children in the class; remembered telling her mum at teatime, and Diana storming in the following day, an Amazon among mothers, terrifying in her determination to have Christine placed back where she belonged, with the hard-working children, the clever ones, the achievers. Stuart had pulled this book from a crate containing . . . what? Perhaps thirty such books, maybe more? And every one contained a raft of memories of her growing-up years. And that was just one crate of many, because there they all were, stacked in pairs, pushed in the space under the eaves, bearing the archive from infant school to A levels.

The ponies were small and strong, and very brave. Some of them saved lives by leading miners out of the pit after an explosion because they knew the tunnels better than the men did. They were heroes, and the miners loved them.

'I was very ardent,' Chrissie said, looking up at Stu, 'about pit ponies. I interviewed Grandad, Dad's dad, and taped it.' She glanced around the loft. 'It's probably up here somewhere, that cassette. It'd be nice to hear his voice again.' She was pale, and there were bluish smudges under her eyes from lack of sleep. Stuart had never thought of her as fragile, but she seemed it now. 'God,' she said. 'All these memories.'

'Well, but you knew they were up here?'

'Yeah, but I've never thought about them before as anything other than stuff stored by Doug and Diana just because they have the space, y'know? Push things up in the loft, shut the hatch, forget they're there. They seem different now, though. More significant.'

'Because?'

Chrissie hesitated, searching for the right words. 'Oh, well, because we have Sunny, I suppose, with her little bag of objects from the past that none of us can interpret for her, and I used to think, clean slate, blank page, but now that seems achingly sad, like part of her got lost forever. And I've always thought Mum was unsentimental, but this loft is full of sentiment, right? My preserved childhood. And now she's so terribly sick, and she hasn't looked in a mirror yet, she hasn't seen her face. Oh God, I know I'm not making sense.'

Her eyes welled, and he reached for her. She leaned into him and sniffed. 'I took all this for granted, all this—' She waved an arm, taking in the whole of the loft space. 'All this dogged and faithful interest in me. I mean, I've always known it, but I treated it with such disdain.'

'We all do that,' Stu said. 'That's what kids are meant to do.'

'And I think I've pushed Nina away. All my doubts and accusations. She was sort of distant, just now. Keeping me at arm's-length.'

'Never,' Stu said. 'No way.'

'And I feel as if life's suddenly all on a slant, and I can't be sure of my footing, I can't be sure of anything any more.'

The last few words came through tears, and she gave herself

up to them, swamped by an obscure sense of imminent loss, and Stuart said, 'Hey, you can be sure of lots of things; you can be completely sure of me, and you can be completely sure of Sunshine, right, Sunshine?'

The little girl had turned from the mirror, and was regarding Chrissie gravely. She'd swapped hats. Now she wore a jaunty boater, with a red grosgrain ribbon; far too big for her head, it wobbled when she moved, and when she walked towards Chrissie, she did so very steadily, her arms outstretched, as if she was a glass of milk, full to the brim.

'Mummy,' she said, 'why is you sad?'

Chrissie couldn't speak, but she opened her arms, and Sunshine threw herself into them, letting the hat spin off like a frisbee and land upside down on the wooden floor. Chrissie held onto her, this sweet, giving child; and off it went, her ungovernable mind, forcing her to wonder yet again who had done all the groundwork, who'd shown Sunshine the meaning of love, who'd taught her to sympathise and to empathise and to open her heart so readily whenever the moment was right. The bliss, she thought, of having your own baby, and being able to take all the credit; then she thought, as she always did, good grief, just enjoy this moment, just be grateful for this gift of a child. But she couldn't, not fully, not ever, because the tortuous tracks of her mind only ran on and on, as they always did; they would never oblige.

She telephoned the hospital and spoke to Doug, asked him if he'd like to come home for something to eat. Stu was making risotto and there was enough to sink a boat, but no, Doug said in his sad, flat voice, he'd get something from the hospital cafe and stay with Diana. Then Chrissie's mobile phone rang, *Nancy Maitland*, the screen told her, and she snatched it up, cried out,

'It's Nancy!' to Stu, then said, 'Nancy, are you all right? Where are you?!'

Nancy said, 'I'm fine, I'm in London, where are you?'

'You found your phone.'

'Where are you?'

'At my parents' house, but listen, how come you're back? I thought we'd lost you for a couple of years at least?'

'Long story, but I go where I'm needed, and I was needed back here,' Nancy said.

'Oh, ah, right,' Chrissie said. She felt a quick flash of shame at how little she knew of Nancy's personal life; the months during which she'd been part of their life had been so intense, so significant and fruitful, but almost entirely one-way. She had no idea what Nancy's personal circumstances were, or where exactly in London she lived, or where she'd grown up. Absorbed by their own needs, their own objectives, and encouraged by Nancy to always speak only about themselves, she now realised they knew next to nothing about her.

'So, where do your parents live?' Nancy asked. 'And how's Sunshine?'

Chrissie looked at her daughter. She was standing on a chair at the stove, attending to the risotto while Stuart held her tight with a fistful of T-shirt. Sunny stirred and stirred with a wooden spoon, which she held with two hands, and it seemed quite an effort, but nevertheless she was forging on with considerable élan, while Stu added an occasional spoonful of grated parmesan, like a lowly kitchen hand.

'She's a joy,' Chrissie said. 'She's right here in the kitchen, with Stuart.'

'And where's the kitchen?' Nancy said.

'What?'

'Where in the United Kingdom is your parents' kitchen?'

'Oh, yeah, I'm sorry, we're in Barnsley. Mum had a stroke and—'

'So, you're staying in Barnsley for the time being?'

Chrissie halted. She couldn't ever remember Nancy cutting into a sentence in such a way. Listening was always Nancy's great skill.

'Nancy?' Chrissie said. 'Are you all right?'

'Me? Of course! I hardly have any battery left, that's all.'

'Oh no! I wanted a long chat. Did you know about the security breaches? Is that why you're calling? Weird things keep happening, Nancy.'

There was a brief pause, when Chrissie thought she'd already lost her, then, 'Yeah, I know, I'm aware of that, look – I'm coming up.'

Chrissie felt a rush of shining relief. She said, 'Oh, God, Nancy, I'd love that, we both would. It's all been so strange, so unsettling. How did you know? Did Brendan tell you?'

'Can you let me have the address, Chrissie?'

'Sure, yes. Do you have a pen?'

'Yes!' Nancy said, sounding almost vexed. 'Of course I have a pen, but I'm almost out of—'

'Battery, I know,' Chrissie said, then she told Nancy the address, and Nancy read it back to her.

'Yep, that's it, so Nancy, who did you speak to, about the breaches? It's just, Brendan said you'd called him, but that he hadn't told you.'

'Oh, Angela Holt filled me in,' Nancy said.

'Angela,' Chrissie said. She'd almost forgotten about Angela. 'Are you back with the adoption team, then? Where are you living?'

'Tell all when I see you, I'll be there very soon.'

'Any idea when?'

'Not exactly, but as soon as possible,' Nancy said. 'You sit tight, I'll be—' and then she was gone, leaving Chrissie with the uniquely bottomless silence of a dead mobile phone.

'That was weird,' Chrissie said.

Stuart lifted Sunshine from the chair, and she pedalled her feet furiously in the air and shouted a protest, but down she went, onto the floor, away from the heat of the hob and the bubbling risotto. She plonked herself onto her bottom and fumed, while Stu wiped his hands on the back of his jeans and looked at Chrissie.

'In what way?'

'She just sounded strung out. And she didn't say why she came back from India. And she told me to sit tight.'

Stuart said, 'I suppose she means, don't scarper again until she's seen you.'

'Oh, she needn't worry on that score, I'm not going any-where any time soon,' Chrissie said, and Stuart, who didn't like that answer, said nothing in reply.

There were a few beats of quiet in which they both perfectly understood the other and had no idea what to say, then Chrissie sighed and rubbed her face with both hands. 'God, I'm dead beat. What a day,' she said, and she looked down at Sunshine, who was still sitting on the floor in the middle of the kitchen with an expression of black mutiny on her sweet face, and her stirring spoon in one hand.

'Ohhhh, I'm so sorry, chef,' Chrissie said. She tucked her hands under Sunny's arms and swept her up onto her hip, then kissed her cheek, soft and yielding as a ripe peach. 'I'll tell you something for nothing, Sunny Stevenson,' Chrissie told her. 'We could not have made a child more wonderful than you, however hard we'd tried,' and Sunshine nodded sternly, as if she under-stood her mother perfectly, and entirely agreed.

~

Sunshine sometimes had the sensation of going backwards in time.

In the big house, where she played with Juno, the wooden walls had felt like home, but not for long, only for a moment, like a light flashing on, then off again.

The lady in the park with Auntie Nina, the lady whose smile had made her remember a feeling, but then that feeling slipped away, it always did, and it made her feel dizzy. She had to stand very still when it happened, and remember where she was now, not where she was then.

18

On Sunday morning there was a hammering on the door with the heavy brass knocker that entered Stu's dream before it fully woke him, so that he bounded out of bed, pulled on his jeans then rushed downstairs to face the Feds, who were here to question him about his drugs racket. Julia was standing there on the steps, with Juno.

'Surprise!' they chorused together, a nice little rehearsed moment, perfectly executed.

Stu scratched his head and squinted in a befuddled way, then held open the door for them. 'What time is it?' he said. 'Man, that was weird, I thought it was a drugs bust.'

'Those were the days, my friend,' Jules said. She offered him her cheeks, first one, and then the other, and he dutifully planted a peck of a kiss on each. '*Merci*,' she said, '*et bonjour.* It's seven o'clock, which I grant you is too early, but I've had Juno in my ear since five, and the only way of finding peace was to first find Sunshine. Apparently it's horrid and stupid in that big house without her.' She looked about her and said, 'Ah, Stevenson Towers; good to be back. How's poor Diana?'

'Better, I think, more serene since Chrissie made her up like

Gloria Swanson,' Stu said. 'She can't speak, but it'll come back, apparently, and her face has slipped a bit.'

Julia gasped, said, 'Oh, Diana, how she'll hate that,' then called up the stairs in a ringing, imperative tone, 'Sunshine? Juno's here.' Juno hopped about, holding Julia's hand and gazing expectantly up the stairs. Julia said, 'I suppose Sunshine's sleeping in my room?' and he laughed, because it had to be twelve years since Julia had been in this house, and anyway, she'd only ever come a couple of times, travelling over from Liverpool with Chrissie, making a visit home infinitely smoother, infinitely more fun. Diana had made a snap judgement, based on the double-barrelled surname and her vintage Hermès weekend bag, that Julia was a good influence on her daughter, which wasn't true at all; quite the reverse if anything. But to Diana, Julia's cross-cultural upbringing, her connections, her stories of the Versailles townhouse, and a sunflower farm in the Tarn Valley, and a penthouse apartment in Cannes, which they only used during the film festival . . . well, this all had an aura of wealth and style and the sort of deep-rooted classiness that she felt her own destiny had once promised, but never delivered. Julia had brought Chanel No 5 as a gift for her, and a beribboned box of pastel-coloured *macarons* that, of course, Diana wouldn't eat, but, oh, how she'd loved the way they looked, piled into a pyramid on a glass platter. Doug had said, 'Very fancy, but give me a fruit scone any day of the week,' and this had made Julia howl with laughter, which meant Diana had had to press her lips together and tightly smile, to hold back the verbal slap that was on the tip of her tongue.

On the coach back to Liverpool, Chrissie had said, 'She'd swap us, if she could. She'd swap us in a heartbeat, and call you her own,' and Julia had said, 'Well, I'm fabulous, she's fabulous, and actually, I look a lot more like her than you do,' and

Chrissie had cheerfully conceded that yes, this was true. She had never actively set out to be the kind of wayward daughter she'd become; never actively set out to antagonise Diana, with the way she dressed, the way she wore her hair, the way she patiently reiterated that the new band, The Lineman, was a worthwhile pursuit; but nevertheless, antagonised Diana most decidedly was. Doug would say, don't worry, cherub, it's not you. Your mother's a conundrum, lovely to look at, impossible to please. But Jules pleased her. Jules was always welcome in this house.

Now, Stuart said, 'Your room's a kind of office now, big desk where that bed was,' and it gave him some satisfaction to see Julia purse her mouth in disapproval. He laughed. 'You're priceless, you are. Sunny's still sleeping, tucked up with Chrissie, who's also out for the count. It was a hell of a day for her yesterday.'

'Oh, but . . .'

'Nope,' Stu said. He scooped up Juno before Julia could dispatch her upstairs, lifted her up onto his shoulders and set off for the kitchen. 'Coffee for the grown-ups, banana toast for you,' he said, and she said, 'I like banana toast, but don't smush the banana.'

'Don't smush the banana, *please*,' said Julia, and she followed them down into the kitchen, knowing when she was beat.

But of course it was thrilling for Sunshine to wake up and find Juno had magically appeared overnight. They hugged each other in a contained and quaintly mature manner, like a pair of tiny grown-ups reunited after too long an absence. Chrissie watched them from the door, enchanted, then grinned at Julia, who said, 'Hey honey, you look tousled.'

'Hey you,' Chrissie said. 'It's a long time since you were at that table.' She stooped to kiss her friend on top of her head. Julia's hair smelled of flowers.

'I know, right? Feels good.'

Chrissie kissed Stu, accepted a mug of coffee, and sat down beside Jules. 'So, were you missing me?' she asked.

'Not exactly, but sort of,' Julia said. 'Juno was a pain in the *derrière* without her partner in crime, so I caved in and drove her over here. I thought I'd take Sunny back with us.'

Chrissie shook her head, said, 'Well, you thought wrong,' and the smile fell instantly from Julia's face.

'Oh, come on! Don't be a spoilsport!' she said.

'You can leave Juno here if you want, though?' Chrissie said. 'Go back without her, pick her up tomorrow?'

And Julia's countenance brightened again, at an outcome that was even better than the one she'd proposed. Stuart laughed and Julia said, 'What?' She glanced at her watch, and said, 'I might as well split after I've drunk this. Shall I swing by the hospital? Is Diana receiving visitors?'

'Give me time to get dressed and I'll come with you,' Chrissie said. 'I feel you might need me as a kind of floodgate between you and Dad's tears.'

'Poor Doug,' Julia said. 'His goddess is struck down.'

'Yeah,' Chrissie said, but she didn't really know if that was what was at the root of her dad's distress. After she'd finished making up Diana yesterday, Doug had returned to the room only to be once more assailed by despair, as if the fact that the vision of his wife looking a little more like herself was just another reason to grieve. And still, Diana had no time for him. She *could* smile – her face was not frozen – but she wouldn't. Chrissie knew that before the stroke befell her, something must have been said, or something must have been done, that had angered Diana and cast Doug into the wilderness. Her displeasure could be like a

Siberian winter. Even a crisis such as this one would not shake Diana from a bad mood. Rather, it would exacerbate it. She probably blamed Doug, for everything.

~

Diana's face registered sheer delight when Julia walked into the room, and Julia swept over to her, kissed her twice, then looked very directly into her eyes and said, 'I'm sorry I've stayed away so long, dear Diana,' which sounded like a line from *Brief Encounter*, but was just classic Jules, using her wiles to freshly secure her place in Diana Stevenson's heart. But she did, very genuinely, admire Diana. Yes, she'd heard all Chrissie's tales of emotional woe, and she'd witnessed first-hand how impossible she could be, how disparaging, how remote, how theatrically bored. However, Diana had never used these weapons on Julia; she had only ever been completely lovely. Now, she was scribbling words onto a little ring-bound notebook, and then she turned it for Jules to read.

'You look wonderful in black,' she'd written. 'Beautifully thin.'

'Oh, Mum,' Chrissie said, tapping the notebook. 'That's a good idea, writing stuff down,' but Diana didn't answer, she was still looking expectantly at Julia, who said, 'Well, thank you, Diana, and you look wonderful in ivory silk.'

Diana took up the pen again. 'What's your secret?'

'Oh,' Jules said. 'You mean, to the thinness?'

Diana nodded.

'Nothing special,' Jules said. 'I just try not to eat, even when I'm hungry,' and Diana wrote, 'Oh, good girl!', which made Julia tip back her head and laugh, while Diana looked pleased, and her eyes glittered with an old light. Chrissie decided to leave them to it so she took her dad downstairs three floors to the hospital cafe, bought two cups of grey coffee, then sat him down and asked him straight out, what was the cause of his despair?

'You're annoying her,' she said. 'You're not yourself, weeping and lamenting like an old Greek widow.'

Doug said, 'I'm sorry, Christine.'

'Don't be sorry, just buck up.'

'Yes,' he said, but continued to look so doleful that she said, 'Oh, Dad,' and took up his hands in her own.

'This is what I want you to do,' she said. 'Go home. You know Sunshine's there, and now Julia's little girl, Juno. They'll cheer you up no end, and you can take a bath and change your clothes while Stuart makes you some bacon and eggs. The world hasn't ended, Mum's on the mend.'

He looked at her. Oh, she thought; my darling dad. He looked so much older, suddenly; hadn't slept well for two nights now, and anyway seemed weighed down by his inordinate sadness, dragging it around like a bag of wet sand.

'In a way,' he said finally, 'it has ended,' but then he wouldn't be pressed further, said he couldn't explain, said he knew he was crying too much, but he thought it might be because he hadn't cried since he broke his arm in 1946, and this made Chrissie laugh, while Doug gave a watery smile, which was something.

'It's true,' he said. 'I fell out of a tree, and the bone snapped and part of it was poking out of the skin like a broken twig, but when I started crying, your grandad gave me hell, and clipped me round the back of the head.'

'Grandad did that?' she said. She'd never heard this story, and found it hard to believe. The Grandad Stevenson Chrissie knew had been a mild and patient old man who grew tomatoes

in a greenhouse, and cabbages and chrysanthemums in his bor-
ders. He'd had all the time in the world for his granddaughter.

'I never saw him cross,' she said now, 'apart from when
snails got at his cabbages. Once, I helped him pick every snail
out of his garden and put them in a carrier bag, which he tied at
the top. Then he took me and the snails on the Cawthorne bus
and, when we got off, we tipped them all into a field.'

Doug said, 'You never did!'

Chrissie nodded. 'We did. It was really hard to shake them
all off the plastic, and then when the last one fell, he said, "There
you go, you little buggers," and then winked at me and said,
"Don't tell your mam I swore."'

'You never told me that,' Doug said.

'Well, you never told me about your broken arm.'

'He was hard as nails, my dad,' Doug said, 'until you came
along, and then he was a changed man, you lit him up like candles on a cake.'

Chrissie smiled. 'I think Julia's doing the same for Mum,'
she said.

'Aye,' he said. 'She always liked that lass.'

Then they held hands and sat there peacefully for a while
longer, not drinking their unspeakable coffee. He was feeling a
bit better, he said. He wouldn't go home though. He wanted
Chrissie to come back again this afternoon with some clean
clothes, but he wasn't leaving Diana, he said, not yet.

They should probably never have married. Their meeting, in a
hotel bar in Slough, had had all the appearances of love at first
sight, but that wasn't it at all; it was just a confluence of objectives. Doug wanted a beautiful wife he could parade on his
arm; Diana wanted security and an escape route from the per-
ceived humiliation of passing Pinewood Studios every weekday

morning on her way to the secretarial college. All of Bucking-hamshire was tainted for her since the rejection, and she'd had no idea how else to remove herself, respectably, from the county. But beyond the satisfaction of each achieving their immediate goals, they were woefully ill-matched in every other important regard. He was a simple man, she was a complicated woman. Their minds worked in entirely different ways, and anyway, Diana had come to the marriage with thwarted dreams, so Doug didn't really stand a chance, starting as they did with a deficit of hope and a surplus of disappointment. Oh, they had their moments, early on. Doug had plenty of money; Diana had plenty of ambition. They went to the French Riviera when their neighbours went to Llandudno or Skegness. They threw Christmas parties in their lovely home and sent the ladies away with a party favour – a little net bag of sugared almonds, a gold-plated hat pin – and a stiff, white, pre-printed card saying *Happy Christmas! With our very best wishes, Diana and Doug.* They held dinner parties, during a phase when Diana subscribed to a Cordon Bleu cookery course, delivered weekly through the letterbox in seventy-two parts. Sole *Bonne Femme*, Rum Baba, Beef Wellington, Lobster Thermidor. Unheard-of dishes, untold expense, and every woman who sat at their dining table noticed how very little of her own flashy food Diana Stevenson actually ate. Little Christine noticed this too, but she simply accepted, as children do, the version of normality laid before her, which was that everyone's mummy preferred to watch her family eat, than to eat herself. She was shocked, the first time she went for tea with a friend. 'Do you know, Mummy,' she'd said, wide-eyed, the moment she got home, 'and this is *true*, Mrs Pickering ate all her food then had a second helping.'

She was telling Stuart this now, and he laughed, although he felt a pang for that little girl three decades ago, who'd yet to work out that her mother was the odd one out, the dysfunctional eater, the film star manqué, the judge and jury, and a whole lot more. They were sitting on the echoing wooden floor of the loft – yet again – while Sunshine and Juno dressed up in Diana's satin and lace. The children were being gracious, taking it in turns to decide what the other should wear. Juno preened and twirled in a coral silk slip that fell almost to her ankles and Sunshine clapped her little hands in appreciation then placed her fingers flat against her mouth like a *couturier*, who, seeing their creation brought to life, was simply lost for words.

Stu said, 'How old were you when you realised your mom was your biggest headache?'

Chrissie thought for a while. 'About eight, I think,' she said. 'It dawned on me over a series of events, I suppose. I think Mum was very unhappy, for a while.' She let her mind range over the past. A week, one long, hot summer, when Diana wouldn't speak to anyone. A whole poached salmon thrown at Doug when he said it still looked a bit raw. The terrible day she cut Christine's party frock to ribbons. The occasional hard slap, nothing unusual in Barnsley in the early seventies, but Doug never did it, only Diana. And in between these episodes were acts of kindness, moments of tenderness, fierce acts of loyalty, bouts of gaiety, and even in the darkest of days, Chrissie had always known she was loved; but learning to navigate her mother's moods was a lifelong study, and neither she, nor Doug, had yet completed the course.

'I wasn't unhappy though,' she said, now, to Stuart. 'When I think about my childhood in broad strokes, it's in warm colours not cold ones. And Nina then became such a big part of our lives, too, and everyone was happier, when we met her, including Mum.'

They were both silent for a while, thinking about Nina.

Chrissie couldn't remember a single time she hadn't come when she'd needed her. She longed to see her, now. Longed to behold her calm countenance and hear her wise counsel. Nina's presence was normality and reassurance.

Stu put his arm around Chrissie's shoulders and kissed the side of her head. 'Do you want me to take those things up for Doug? I mean, if you've had enough of the hospital, for one day?'

She shook her head. 'I'll go. I'll not be long. I didn't see much of Mum earlier – well, she was mesmerised by Jules. But I'd like to see her, on my own, now she's writing things down. I don't know whose idea that was; wish I'd thought of it.'

Stu said, 'OK, well, I'm taking these two to the park.'

'Wait till I get back, maybe? I can come with you.'

'Or meet us there? I'd like to get them out of Diana's lingerie and into the fresh air.'

Chrissie felt the familiar chill in the pit of her stomach, the grip of anxiety around her heart. She wanted to plead; wanted to say, please wait until I'm back; wanted to say, but how can you keep Sunshine safe, if there's Juno to think about too? But Stuart was on his feet now, saying, 'Who'd like to go to the playground?' and the girls started chanting, 'We do, we do,' laughing in each other's faces, the way they did, whipped up by combined energy, jumping about without really remembering why.

So, OK, Chrissie thought; this was a test, a test of her faith in Stuart, to care for Sunshine in the same way that she did, which was with a kind of cleverly casual vigilance, never letting her out of her sight while appearing to be completely relaxed. It was a hard act, and it took extreme concentration, and Chrissie didn't know if Stuart understood that he must give Sunshine the freedom to be herself without ever dropping his guard, or placing any faith in the kindness of strangers. But to say that to him now, well, she knew what would happen; he'd look at her as if he was sorry for her, and he didn't know who she'd become. And truly, she had to trust him. Daily life was unfeasible if she didn't trust him.

'Great,' she said. 'I'll see you at the swings.'

~

Sunshine was gone, even before Chrissie arrived, but she didn't know that as she entered the park; instead, it dawned on her, by terrible degrees. She took a diagonal path across the grass towards the playground. She remembered thinking how busy it looked over there, remembered trying to identify Sunshine's green duffel and red wool beret among the small figures in hats and coats and mittens, remembered thinking, as she got closer, how odd it was that none of the children were on the swings, or the slide or the climbing frame. All of them seemed to be standing dully, holding hands with their grown-ups, and when she was closer still, she could see that the faces of those adults were grave and alert, and there was something linking them all, some common interest, or joint concern.

She felt a weakening of her limbs, and then almost immediately, a powerful resolve. She broke into a run, and heard Stuart before she saw him, heard him bellowing Sunshine's name, heard it again and again, and then heard his voice shatter and collapse. She saw him, bent double, gasping for air, and she could see that his fear had filled the playground, and strangers with their own children safe by their sides were talking now in low, important voices, using Sunshine's name, taking ownership of this drama. Chrissie pushed through them, to get to Stuart; heard a woman say, 'It's her name, they call her Sunshine,' and another voice, a man's, say, 'Is she lost, what's she wearing?' She heard other voices chiming in, keen to be involved; 'Green duffel coat,' and 'Red hat,' and 'She's only three,' and 'She can't have got far,' and all these voices were hollow and distant and distorted, like words in a television drama that you might hear from the sofa, through a fog of sleep.

'Stuart,' she said, quietly. Abruptly, he lifted himself at the sound of her voice, and she'd never seen such agony as she saw in his face.

'I'll find her,' he said. 'Chrissie, I'll find her.'

She shook her head, because she knew he wouldn't. He was at such a disadvantage, she thought. He'd never believed in the reality of this nightmare, and now she pitied him the trauma of realising he'd been wrong. She wanted to hold him, give him some comfort, but she couldn't bring herself to touch him. Instead she said, 'Tell me how it happened?' – because she'd known it *would* happen; she just hadn't known how or when – but Stuart couldn't speak. He couldn't even look at her; he shivered and his teeth were clenched, and his eyes darted left and right as if he saw Sunshine everywhere, a flash of green, of red, of shining brown hair, then he began to run again, away from the primary colours of the playground, towards the dense and silent trees. Sunshine wouldn't be among the shadows, thought Chrissie. If someone had meant to harm her, she might be there; but she'd been taken by someone who simply wanted her back. Chrissie knew this. Stuart . . . well, perhaps he didn't know, not with the same certainty. Again he was calling out their child's name, and it was with such terrible howling intensity that Chrissie thought, if Sunshine – wherever she was now – could hear him, she'd be afraid.

People moved over to her; a man said, 'Shall I ring the police?' and a woman said, 'She'll only have wandered off,' someone else said, 'Here, love, take my hankie, it's clean,' and it was only then that Chrissie realised her face was a sheet of tears. Then she heard yet another stranger say, 'This isn't her, is it?' and Chrissie spun around, to see Juno, white-faced and speechless, holding out both arms to be lifted up.

'Have they found her?' a person said, and 'Oh, thank God, look, she's back,' said another.

'No,' Chrissie said. 'This isn't Sunshine.' She'd forgotten about Juno; God, she'd forgotten about Juno, and clearly, so had Stuart, the child's existence eclipsed by Sunshine's vanishing. Chrissie looked at this child she'd known since birth, and felt only a terrible indifference, but she lifted her up, because she knew she must, and Juno gave a shuddering sigh of relief and burrowed her face into the crook of Chrissie's neck. Her body in Chrissie's arms felt compact and warm and she was perfectly safe; but Sunshine was gone.

Nobody knew what to do. The strangers milling about in the playground with their children looked grim and grey, as if they had suffered a comparable loss, and one or two tried to offer some reassurance to Chrissie but she stared at them vacantly, and turned away. While Stuart raced through the park, checking all exit points, Chrissie rang the police and heard herself quietly reporting that her daughter had been taken from Locke Park, then she rang Julia, and heard herself delivering the news once more. She stood very still, with Juno in her arms, and the phone pressed between her ear and her shoulder, and because Juno was complaining – she was cold, she was hungry, she wanted her mummy – Julia understood that her child was safe, without having to ask, and Chrissie was conscious of the infinitesimally small consolation of not having to shatter her friend's world. After that, Kim rang, and she cried and told Chrissie she loved her, and Chrissie listened to her friend and watched a small fleet of police squad cars draw up silently outside the park, and this event made her start to shake, and rendered her speechless. She ended the call, without being able to say goodbye.

Two police officers drove them home, and another was waiting at the house when they arrived. A whole host more stayed among the spectators in the park, taking statements. No one had seen anything unusual. Stuart hadn't either. Sunshine had been there, and then she had been gone. He had to supply answers to the questions, however; he had to paint the picture, explain how he could have presided over such a terrible occurrence. He spoke in broken sentences, as if he wasn't quite able to complete each thought.

'We hadn't been there long, I mean, maybe fifteen or . . . I had both girls by the hand and they were . . . they wanted to go on the little roundabout, so we did that first, but Sunshine was . . . then we had to wait our turn for two swings to . . .' He dropped his face into his hands and swallowed. Chrissie watched him.

'Sunshine was what?' she asked.

He looked up at her. 'She didn't like it,' he said. 'That particular roundabout. She wanted to get straight off.'

Chrissie nodded, thought, she's gone, before we had a chance to know everything she doesn't like. She realised Stuart was under suspicion. They'd each been interviewed when they got back to the house; interviewed separately, in different rooms, but they kept Stuart longer. Wasn't that what the police always thought? Didn't they always start by looking at the father? But Chrissie knew Stuart had lost Sunshine, not taken her, and his agony was palpable; no one could doubt his pain. Plus, the police officers now knew that Sunshine was their adopted child, and that Chrissie had been fearful – 'had *known*,' she corrected

Stuart – that someone from her past would reclaim her, if they weren't at all times vigilant. They understood that; it was all written down, and enquiries would now be made by detectives in London and Kent, of Barbara and John, of Brendan, Angela, and Nancy, if they could find her.

Now, however, they were gently but persistently trying to nail down the chronology, the sequence of events that had led Sunshine into harm's way. Stuart said the girls were on the swings, the ones for young children, the enclosed ones with a T-bar across the front. When they'd had enough, he drew the swings to a halt, then lifted Sunshine out first and her beret had fallen off, so he'd put her down, placed the hat back on her head, and bent down to kiss her on the cheek. He'd winked at her, she'd smiled back. She'd been there, he said. Right there. He pointed at a spot on the kitchen floor, to demonstrate how very close to him Sunshine had been. Then he'd turned to Juno, but her boot got stuck, sort of twisted against the bar, and she and he had laughed and he'd had to sit her back down and straighten her out, so that he could lift her up again, and out. It was the work of moments, yet when he turned, Sunshine was gone.

'It was moments,' he said again, and he was looking at Chrissie, not at the detective inspector. 'Just seconds. Five seconds, four.'

Chrissie accepted the information without comment. If she'd been there, she thought, she would have lifted Juno out of the swing first. The playground was only partially fenced in, it was close to one of the main exits, close to a road where a parked car might wait, and five seconds would be plenty of time to take Sunshine.

She noticed the officers exchanging a glance, and she thought she knew what it meant – *why is she so calm?* – but then the detective constable, a family liaison officer who'd introduced herself as Karen, said, 'Chrissie, can I get you a tissue, or a handkerchief?' and she realised it was happening again, tears coursing silently down her face like a wall of water; distress pouring out of her, silently, and with a will entirely of its own. Then Stuart gave a great, dry sob of suffering, and automatically she reached out her hands and he clutched at them as if he was falling. She felt alone, though. There was no comfort in his touch, and doubtless none in hers.

In meticulous, painful detail, the detective inspector read back the physical description of Sunshine, and what she'd been wearing. He was sympathetic without being reassuring. He listened patiently to Stuart's account of his disbelief, his – he admitted this – lack of concern when he first saw she was gone from the spot he'd placed her. He'd looked about him, and then looked further, and even then, when there was no immediate sign of her green coat and red hat, he'd known he would see her soon, jigging about impatiently, waiting for him to catch her up so that she could play on something else. But his heart had started to thud in his chest and when he began to call her name and there was no emphatic answering cry of, 'Daddy, I is *here*!' he'd known . . . he'd known that she was . . . and he hung his head and concentrated on fighting the impulse to smash something, to wreak dreadful havoc, to create noise and mayhem in place of what he wanted to do, but couldn't, which was find and kill the abductor then carry his darling home.

Daddy, I is here.

The words hung in the air, invoking the sweet idiosyncrasy of Sunshine, and Chrissie could hardly bear it. She whispered, 'Where is she?' and Stuart started to cry.

Julia and Sol arrived, and were discreet and careful, and their presence brought some unexpected relief: their dear faces, their love and quiet concern. Jules knew for once how to be, and what to say, and both seemed to understand what Chrissie knew for a fact; that Juno had never been in danger, because the person who'd taken Sunshine, had only wanted Sunshine. The police officers weren't so sure, but then, of course, how could they possibly express an opinion at this stage in the investigation? They had snapped shut their notebooks, taken their respectful leave, and left them with promises to provide whatever support the family needed. There'd be door-knocking throughout all the residential areas surrounding the park and beyond, Karen was available all the time, day or night, and they were to call her for whatever reason, whenever they wished. South Yorkshire Police were already on red alert; the news would be broadcast locally with a description of Sunshine, but at this stage, names would be withheld. The youngest of the three officers, a pink-cheeked detective constable, admitted he knew they were Stu Woodall and Chrissie Stevenson of The Lineman, so the detective inspector said they wouldn't get the full publicity circus out yet; they didn't want to attract the wrong kind of interest. They'd move swiftly to close the net, and do every single thing in their power to return Sunshine home. But when they closed the door after them, Chrissie said to Stu, 'They won't find her, unless whoever has her wants her to be found.'

Stuart said, 'Chrissie,' but could say no more, and then Jules, picking up Juno's coat from where it had been discarded on the hall floor, said, 'What's this?'

She'd found something in the pocket, a tightly folded square of paper, and the others watched as she quickly opened it, glanced at the contents, then passed it at once to Chrissie, who read the words, and stiffened, and when Stu took the paper from her, she didn't feel it leave her hand, and neither did she see him, or Julia, or Sol. She saw nothing but an image of Sunshine, being cast away from them as miraculously as she'd arrived. Chrissie truly suffered, then; suffered the first deluge of complete understanding of the magnitude of her – of their – loss. Stu's voice trembled and broke as he read the words aloud. *Forgive us, and take comfort from this; we cherish Sunshine as you do.*

'I don't forgive,' Chrissie said, 'I. Do. Not. Forgive.'

And then, finally, the torrent of noise she'd managed to contain until now burst forth, and all the house was filled with her grief.

19

Juno slept, of course, but no one else did, yet the night ended and the next day dawned and the *Daily Telegraph* dropped through the letterbox as if the world was just as it should be. Julia and Sol and Juno left to pick up Remi then head back to London, and no one knew what to say, so they said nothing, just hugged each other for longer than usual then parted.

Chrissie felt Sunshine's absence like a gaping wound. If Stuart had told her she was bleeding, she wouldn't have been surprised. Stuart had guilt as well as grief to deal with, but they found that neither one of them could help the other with their suffering. After Jules and Sol drove away, Chrissie became inert and uncommunicative, and Stuart paced the floor, expressing his pain in activity and anger. He was going back to the park, he said, to walk its perimeter, walk the streets, retrace his steps. He couldn't be still, he said; he couldn't just sit and wait. Then, when he put his coat on, he felt in a pocket for his gloves and there was Sunshine's Silky, given to him by her in the playground for safekeeping, and he had kept it safe; it was Sunshine he'd lost. They both stared at it in horror, each of them imagining how very much she'd need it now, then he placed it on the table, and left the house without a word.

Chrissie was glad he'd gone. In the empty house, she sat for a long while, twisting Sunny's silk scarf in her hands, listening to the seconds passing on the kitchen clock, thinking, this time yesterday, this time yesterday, this time yesterday. She knew she should ring her dad, but knew, too, that she couldn't. Nina then, she thought; she must call Nina. She looked at her hands and found they were gripping the edge of the kitchen table so tightly that the bone of her knuckles showed white. She didn't want to break the news to anyone, she realised. She didn't want to form the words, didn't want to turn the nightmare into someone else's reality, as well as her own. At best, and if Nina were right there in front of her, she might be able to write the words down and push the paper across the table. But to dial her number, hear her dear voice, then darken her day immeasurably . . . she couldn't do it.

She looked at the ticking clock. Nine fifteen. This time yesterday, she thought, again. This time yesterday Sunshine was here, playing with Juno. The crumbs from their banana toast were still on the worktop, the plates were still in the sink. She couldn't think why, now, she'd left Stuart in sole charge. She felt she'd taken a grotesque gamble, by feigning unconcern at his plan to take them to the park. And for what? For him? To show him she'd trusted him, even when she hadn't? She couldn't speak to him about these feelings, yet she knew he knew what she felt. The subject squatted between them, ugly and unmentionable. Yesterday, she'd felt an initial rush of sympathy for him, for the terrible shock he'd felt at discovering his fallibility. Now, she found she could only think of him in a detached way, observing his anguish, but knowing he'd caused it, and too preoccupied with her own visceral pain to be able to offer comfort. She believed he felt the same. They circled each other, watchful, alone with their agony; and their intimacy, their love, their golden union – it seemed, overnight, to count for nothing. Objectively, she knew she mustn't blame him for the loss of Sunshine. Subjectively, how could it be helped?

Her phone rang, a startling, brutal explosion of sound. An unknown number showed on the screen, and she seized it, her heart racing, but it was only a journalist, a colleague of Kim's from the *NME*, seeking an interview about . . . Chrissie didn't hear what, because she hung up almost at once. Then she thought about Nancy. Nancy needed to know, and Nancy was a person she could talk to. She found her number and called it, and it rang three times, then cut out. She tried again, and now it went straight to voicemail, and this felt so much like a slap, or a door slamming cruelly in her face, that she left no message, only glared balefully at the screen of her uncompliant phone. Now she had a desperate, critical need to find an alternative to Nancy, someone whose pain on hearing the news would only be a fraction of her own. Brendan, she thought. Brendan Cassidy. She dialled his number in absolute confidence that he would answer, so was surprised when a woman said, 'Adoption services,' in a voice at once crisp and brisk and uninviting.

Chrissie thought, Angela Holt; the foe. She said, 'Angela?'

There was a pause, then, 'Chrissie,' Angela said, her voice softening on a descending sigh. 'Oh, my dear, I'm so sorry, I'm so, so, sorry.'

It was Angela's voice, but not as she'd ever sounded before. So kind. So genuinely sad. Chrissie had to make a rapid mental adjustment.

'Angela? That's you, right?' she said.

'Yes, yes, sorry, Brendan's with a client.'

Another couple, thought Chrissie. Another child. She never thought of Brendan as anyone else's property, and it crossed her mind now that perhaps he was as devoted to everyone as he seemed to be to her and Sunshine.

'The police have been here,' Angela went on. 'We've all been questioned, doubtless we will be again; they're working fast on Sunshine's behalf. Everyone's so devastated for you and Stuart.'

Chrissie said, 'Thank you.' She was confused by this version of the woman they'd come to regard as a thorn in their side. Then she asked, 'Is Brendan there, though? I mean, is he in the building?'

'He's not, at the moment. There's a panel; he needed to be there. His mobile switches to the office when he knows he can't answer. He's terribly upset for you, Chrissie. He's very invested in your happiness. I did suggest he should call you, but he felt it better to wait until you—'

'Angela,' Chrissie said, interrupting, suddenly struck by a thought, 'do you have another number for Nancy?'

'Nancy?'

'Nancy Maitland?'

'Why, no,' Angela said. She sounded puzzled. 'Isn't she abroad?'

'No, she was, but she's not now, but look, you spoke to her a couple of days ago? Told her about the security breaches? The women looking for Sunshine?'

Silence. Then, 'Not me,' Angela said. 'I haven't spoken to anyone about it, apart from the team here, in the office. I wouldn't do that, and even if Nancy had called, she'd no longer be entitled to such privileged information.'

Chrissie said, 'She rang me, and said you'd told her all about it.'

'I have no idea why she'd say that, Chrissie.'

Chrissie's mind spun. She tried to recall what Nancy had said. She wanted to come and see them. She was back in the UK and she was looking for them, and now she wanted to come up to Barnsley, to talk things through.

'I gave her the address here, my parents' address,' Chrissie said.

'Did you tell the police that?'

'No, I . . . it never occurred to me. She's . . . she's a friend.'

Angela said, 'Well, even so, she lied to you about speaking to me, and I think, now you know that, you should mention it to the police.' Her voice was soft, much gentler than it ever had been before in their dealings with her.

'Angela?'

'Yes?'

'I'm so sorry that, y'know, we—'

Angela said, 'Oh, Chrissie, I'm sorry too. I was officious and unsympathetic and unprofessional and I . . . I can't quite explain why.'

'Oh,' Chrissie said, touched by her candour.

'I've thought a lot about it, and obviously I've had to account for myself here at work, and I believe I always felt that I came a poor second to your relationship with Nancy, and I found that difficult. But it's no excuse. I didn't behave with professional care or compassion, or at least, not always. All I can say is, it happens, sometimes, that case workers and clients don't hit it off. Not that any of that matters now.'

'No . . .'

'Keep in touch, and we'll keep in touch with you. Take care now, and stay strong.' There was a click, and she was gone.

For a moment, Chrissie sat very still, disorientated by this new version of Angela, and then she heard the front door open, and Stuart's footfall on the tiles of the hallway. She thought he might head straight upstairs, but he didn't, he continued on towards the kitchen, and pushed open the door. The colour and life seemed leached from him. He opened his mouth to say something, but Chrissie said, 'I think Nancy took Sunshine.'

He stared.

'I just spoke to Angela. She hasn't heard from Nancy, but Nancy told me that's how she knew about everything. She said Angela told her.'

Stuart walked into the kitchen and sat down at the table, opposite Chrissie. 'Right,' he said. 'And she asked for the address here.'

'Yeah, I told her where we were.'

'Nancy, though. Why would she take Sunshine?'

Chrissie shrugged. 'Maybe she's her mother?'

'But . . .'

'I know, I know, it doesn't make sense. But there it is. She's the only person who knew where we were.'

'Well, not the only person. Brendan knew.'

She looked at him, askance. 'Brendan hasn't got her,' she said.

Stu said, 'Well, he's someone Sunny knows.'

'So?'

'It's possible she'd go with him, I mean.'

'But Stuart, what are you accusing him of?' She was horrified. Brendan, mild, conscientious, devoted. 'You think he's abducted Sunshine?'

Stuart said, 'Well, you think Nancy has! And anyway, Brendan might do something like this, to keep you dependent on him.'

This was absurd, she thought; the logic of extreme helplessness.

'No, Stu, it's not Brendan.'

He dropped his head and said, 'Well, I don't suppose it is.'

'But it could well be Nancy. She was unlike herself, on the phone. Maybe she has a connection with Sunny that we just don't know about. Oh God, Stu, I told her where we are.'

'You had no reason not to,' Stu said, but she laid her head on the table, on top of her folded arms, and felt fear and sorrow tear through her, as it did periodically, when her belief that Sunshine was safe seemed less tangible than her belief that she might never see her again. She concentrated on breathing, slow and steady.

Stuart stood up. 'I'll let the police know.'

'I'm not dependent on Brendan,' she said, her head down, her voice muffled. 'I'm dependent on you. Or I was.'

He reached out and touched her shoulder. 'I know,' he said. 'I'm sorry.'

~

He spoke to one of the detectives, told them what they now suspected about Nancy and then came back to Chrissie. He said, 'I spoke to Carly too.'

'Oh, Stu,' Chrissie said, and even from her island of pain, she felt for him, alone on his, knowing how difficult that must have been, how much she dreaded having that conversation with Doug. 'How was she, I mean, how—'

'She's on her way back,' he said, with bleak practicality. 'She won't be long. It'll be good to have her here.'

'Yeah,' Chrissie said, and she knew that he meant it would be good to have Carly's support, Carly's unconditional love, because at the moment there was none available elsewhere.

'I rang Nina as well,' Stu said. 'I rang her to let her know, and because I know you need her, and because I think you're finding that call too hard to make.'

Chrissie stood up, and they stared at each other across the no man's land of their misery. 'How did she take it?' she asked. 'It's a terrible thing to hear.'

'Hard, yeah, she dropped the phone, she cried, she said she loves you.'

Chrissie gave a kind of sob. More than she wanted Stuart or Carly, she wanted Nina. Far, far more.

'I want to make everything right for you, but there's so little I can do,' Stuart said. 'Calling Nina was the only thing in my power.'

She felt a kind of shift in her vision, as if he'd come more clearly into view, and she could see that even now, amid all this hurt, he was still Stuart, her Stuart, but she didn't know how to return to him, or even whether she could. Yet he must have seen something change in her eyes, because he risked everything and held out his arms, and only a woman without a heart, she thought, would turn away. She hesitated, just for a second, then stepped towards him and let herself be held.

～

Stu walked up to the hospital for an early visit, because alarm bells would surely ring if neither of them went, and he somehow made it through, without either Doug or Diana learning that Sunshine was lost. Characteristically Diana, far more astute than her husband, far more forensic, studied Stuart's face closely when he sat down at her bedside, and immediately seized her notepad and wrote, 'What's wrong?'

He said, 'Ah, nothing that a good night's sleep won't cure.'

Diana had taken up the pen again and written, 'No. What's wrong, Stuart?' and Stu had managed a laugh and said, 'Nothing,' then Doug had come in, and provided enough of a distraction that the moment passed. Stu felt terrible, though; deceitful. But he'd spoken to the consultant, explained the situation and she'd agreed that, in their present state, neither Mrs nor Mr Stevenson could possibly deal with any more trauma.

'Of course, if Mr Stevenson takes a break from his unnecessary vigil and goes home . . .' she said.

'Yes,' Stuart said. 'In that case, we'll tell him. But he's . . . well, he's less robust than we thought, I guess, and we don't want to add to his sorrow, if it can be helped.'

'Less robust or more devoted, who knows,' she said airily, and then she remembered the context, and altered her tone. 'And I'll hold you and your little girl in my thoughts. I fervently hope she's found very soon.'

He said, 'Thank you,' but he'd wanted to bolt, or scream, or both, as she said this. It was irrelevant, he told his mother. It was gratuitous, and was more about the consultant than about Sunshine.

'So pious,' Stu said. 'So pleased with her own compassionate gravity.'

'Oh, honey, no,' Carly replied. 'No, it was well meant, I'm certain, and I'd say just the same to you, if I'd been her.'

He'd cried again when she arrived, not for long, only for moments really, and there was something almost more heart-breaking about his struggle for control than about his brief lack of it. But Carly possessed a healing hug, and just as she'd done when Stuart was a boy, she somehow made every good outcome seem possible. She didn't read the Tarot or make predictions from the lines on an upturned palm – Carly *felt* the future, and it was set fair, she said. Yes, this was a terrible ordeal, but the note placed in Juno's pocket, wasn't that, in its way, reassuring? It was with the police now, but the words were forever etched into Stu and Chrissie's memories, and Carly saw positivity in them, she really did. She saw Sunshine in her mind's eye, safe with someone she knew. She talked about when, not if, Sunshine came back to them. She talked about loving each other and not letting their sense of loss push them apart. She took each of them by the hand, said, 'Form a linked circle,' then asked them to close their eyes and visualise Sunshine, use the power of their loving imagination to connect them to her. Stuart complied, Chrissie was self-conscious and uncomfortable, and broke free after a few moments, but then found that she did inexplicably feel a fraction more peaceful, as if Sunshine had come closer to her through the power of Carly's positive thought. Later, when they were alone together, Carly held Chrissie's face in her hands and said, 'Try not to let blame take a hold in your heart, darling.'

Chrissie said, 'I'm trying, Carly. It's so difficult.'

'I know, but this isn't about whose fault it was; it's about supporting each other until Sunshine comes back. Blame is such a toxin; it gets in the way of conversation, and understanding, and every good thing that can make you stronger.'

She released Chrissie's face, but they stayed close enough that if they'd dipped their heads, their foreheads would have touched.

'I wouldn't have let her out of my sight,' Chrissie whispered.

'You think that, darling, but you don't know it, because you weren't there.'

'I asked him to wait for me, so that he didn't have both girls to look after.'

Carly placed a palm on Chrissie's cheek. 'Try to see the wider picture, try to visualise all the many decisions you and Stuart took that led him to that moment in the playground, when Juno got her boot stuck, and Sunny was briefly unobserved . . . and well, it might help you feel less angry with him.'

Carly was remarkable, thought Chrissie. Empathy poured

from this woman like a waterfall. 'I know how much he's suffering,' Chrissie said. 'But I haven't actually said I blame him.'

'Have you said you don't?'

Of course not, thought Chrissie; he would know that was a lie. But she considered, then, the chain of events, her conversation with Nancy, her refusal to allow Sunny to go to Castleton with Julia and Juno, her invitation instead, for Juno to stay here, which then led to Stu taking two children, not one, to the park, and she wondered if, in time, she might be able to understand what Carly was trying to teach her.

'Is your mother crazy?' Chrissie asked Stu later, when Carly went upstairs with her bag. 'Or am I crazy, for being reassured by her?'

Stu didn't know.

He didn't know.

He didn't know.

He lay on the floor, covering his face with his hands, and saw Sunshine cocking her head to listen, like a little bright-eyed robin. Saw her abandon herself to sleep, like a starfish in the centre of their bed. Saw the light and wonder in her face, the first time he put a plate of spaghetti in front of her. Saw her round, owlish eyes, when she listened closely to a bedtime story.

'I can't stop seeing her,' he said.

'I know,' Chrissie replied. She sat down next to him on the floor and took one of his hands, but he didn't open his eyes, didn't look at her. In all their lives, nothing – nothing – had ever mattered as much as this; their darling Sunny, lost in the world, reclaimed – they supposed, and God knows, in a way, they hoped – by her past. Once, and for such a long time, they had been only two; Chrissie and Stuart, forging a path through the world, with everything they needed contained in each other.

Now, two was far too few; the space left by Sunshine's absence was not the shape and size of a child, but a chasm.

'You were right,' he said.

'That doesn't matter now.'

'You knew this would happen, and I said it wouldn't.'

She didn't want to be right, though. She wanted to be paranoid, over-cautious, wrong. She sighed, and released his hand, stood up again, and walked to the big bay window. She placed both palms on it, and then her forehead. The thought slid through her fractured mind that Diana would play merry hell at the marks she'd be leaving on the glass.

'Where is she?' she said, not to Stuart, but to the trees and the cars and the handful of people walking blithely through the world, along the pavement beyond the garden.

Stu said, 'When I went out this morning, I was certain I'd find her. It was the only acceptable outcome, and I knew that just by walking the streets, walking the park, looking where she'd been last time I saw her, I'd find her and bring her home to you.'

Chrissie said, 'Looking for her must have felt a little like losing her all over again.'

'Yeah,' he said, his voice flat, and dull.

Nina rang, and Chrissie gasped as if she'd come up for air after too long under water. She said, 'Wait, hang on,' and walked upstairs with the phone, went into her bedroom and pushed the door shut with her foot.

'Sweetheart,' Nina said.

'Auntie Nina,' Chrissie said, and her voice broke into tears. 'You have to help me find Sunshine.'

'I know, I know, of course,' Nina said. 'I will, I've already begun.'

Chrissie was staring at her own reflection in the dressing-table mirror. She looked haunted, haggard, all her suffering written in her features. 'Have you?' she said. 'You mean, since Stuart called you?'

'Yes, that, but I mean, since before she went missing.'

Chrissie hesitated, trying to process Nina's words. 'What does that mean?' she said.

There was a silence, then Nina said, 'Chrissie, I want you to know something. I believe Sunshine will certainly be safe.'

Chrissie felt suddenly unable to support herself. She walked to the bed and sat down hard on it.

'Sunshine will be safe,' Nina repeated.

'Do you know where she is?' Chrissie's voice was small. If Nina was somehow involved in Sunny's disappearance, then all life's certainties were gone for ever.

Nina didn't answer.

'Nina? Do you know where she is? Does Nancy have her?'

'Nancy – no, at least I doubt it, although she's definitely part of the story, but I think Sunny might be with the people she lived with, before she was fostered.'

'What people? What're you saying, what do you know?'

'Oh, Chrissie, darling.'

'What? Auntie Nina, what?' Her hands were shaking, and a dark shadow was descending over her, a bleak thought forming in her mind that no one in this world should be trusted, if Nina couldn't be trusted.

'I found her biological family,' Nina said. 'And I may be the reason that Sunshine's gone.'

20

When Chrissie went to Barnsley, Nina went into action. Not immediately – she waited for a while, tried living with the permanent feeling that she was sitting on her hands when there was surely so much that could be done – and then she caved in and called Brendan Cassidy. Chrissie had inadvertently spurred her on by ringing from Doug and Diana's, asking again about the young woman in the park, and could she be the young woman in the shoe shop, and would Nina know her again if she saw her, and she'd sounded tightly wound, excitable, her voice thin and rapid. Nina had tried to calm her, but there was no dealing with Chrissie at the moment, she'd hung up in a huff, and at that point, when the line went dead, Nina had thought: enough.

It wasn't that she knew Brendan well, or had even ever met him, or had any means of contacting him personally, other than calling the main office switchboard and asking to be put through, but he'd answered his extension number at once, and by the time he'd hung up, he'd found he'd just agreed to meet a woman named Nina Baker for a drink, after work. He didn't know why, except she was close to Chrissie Stevenson, and he needed no more incentive than that.

Nina came all the way down from the leafy heights of

Highgate, to a pub chosen by Brendan, near the adoption agency office, in South East London. If Chrissie hadn't bolted, Nina would never have presumed. But Chrissie *had* bolted, and Nina wouldn't and couldn't sit tight and watch her favourite person in all the world turn tail and run away from something that none of them understood. If Chrissie didn't need her presence, then she'd make herself useful in other, practical ways. Brendan was her starting point, her way into the puzzle. She arrived early, and bought a beer, then claimed a table, and waited.

Although Brendan had never met Nina, he spotted her at once, or at least, made an educated guess, which turned out to be correct. From just inside the door of the pub he gave her the once-over. She was of indeterminate age, perhaps half a generation older than Chrissie, so, mid-fifties or thereabouts. She was lean and good-looking although he could see she didn't adorn herself. She wore faded jeans, and a big pale-blue shirt that could once have been a man's. The sleeves were rolled up right over her sharp elbows, and she had green paint on her hands, and on her collar. Her hair was blonde, and loose, and cut in a chic straight line, just below her shoulders. She had a fine profile. There was a half-pint glass of pale ale on the table before her.

'Nina Baker?' he said, approaching her table, and she turned, and gave him a wide, warm smile.

'Brendan Cassidy,' she said. 'How good to meet you, although I feel I know you already; Chrissie talks about you such a lot.'

He felt his cheeks burn with an annoying, boyish pleasure, and to cover this he said, 'I'll just nip to the bar,' but she wouldn't let him; she made him sit down instead while she went to fetch him a pint, and when she came back she slung a bag of dry-roasted peanuts on the table too, saying, 'You'll need sustenance after a hard day in the field.'

He liked her. She asked him about himself, which flattered

him into revealing more than he perhaps should, which he realised even as he was doing it. She was skilled at picking up on his
small hesitations, skilled at nudging him into honest answers
when usually he opted for evasions. No, he didn't have a girlfriend. Yes, he'd like one. His job? Oh, well, it was fine, but
really what he'd like to do was find someone who wanted to
travel, then just take off together across the globe. She told him
he should set off alone, and see who he met along the way, and
he admitted he was afraid of doing that, of feeling lonely. Then
she took a tangent and asked him how long he'd been working
in adoption, and he said eight years, but only the past six
months in this current job. Then she asked if, in the course of
his working life, he'd ever met a child quite like Sunshine, and
just like that, they were on territory that was out of bounds, but
it didn't feel that way to Brendan, never crossed his mind. He
considered the question then said no, he didn't think he had;
she seemed innately carefree, unlike so many of the traumatised
youngsters in the system. What about Barbara and John, Nina
asked; had he, Brendan, placed Sunshine with them? He said
no, because he hadn't been working at the agency when Sunny
first went into foster care, and in any case, it was generally the
job of the local authority to arrange foster placements, while
the adoption agency's role was to find permanent homes.

'So who first told you about Sunshine?' Nina asked. 'I mean,
how does it work? Did your agency get a phone call from somebody at the council, or what?' Nina stopped short of taking
notes, kept her tone conversational, but still, she expected him
to stop talking, say, 'Hang on – where's this heading?' but
instead he seemed perfectly at ease with the subject under scrutiny, and only said, 'Yes, someone from child services would've
liaised with us initially about Sunshine.'

Nina thought for a moment about the people she'd like to

meet, and probably never would; the housing officer who'd first taken Sunshine by the hand, the social workers who first filled out the paperwork and found her a temporary home. Had they really known as little about Sunshine's missing past as they claimed or had one of them, perhaps, been all along hiding her in plain sight? Somebody certainly knew where to look. Whitstable. The playground nearest to Chrissie and Stu's home. She said, 'Brendan, do you think there's something written down, somewhere in your office, that might shed some light on Sunshine's beginnings?'

He sipped his beer, and his brow crumpled in thought. How Nina wished he would lean forwards on his elbows and say, 'Well, between you and me . . .' but he didn't.

'No,' he said. 'She really was just dropped off at that council office building, with only her lovely name and the clothes she was standing in.'

'And what were they?'

'What were what?'

'The clothes she was standing in.'

'Oh,' he said. 'Well, good question, but like I said, it was before my time, I've no idea.'

Now Nina thought she detected a sullen note creeping into Brendan's voice so she changed direction again, sat back and beamed at him. 'You did a wonderful thing, putting Chrissie and Stuart together with Sunny.'

He said, 'Ah well, I can't take the credit, I think that was Nancy Maitland.'

Nina said, 'Ah, was it Nancy? I thought it was you and Angela Holt – it was certainly Angela who first rang Stuart.'

Brendan said, 'Well now,' and thought for a moment. 'You're right about Angela. But I'm sure it was Nancy at the outset, raving about this amazing couple who'd be perfect for Sunny.' He laughed. 'She made sure nobody else got a look in, I think.'

'Lucky they were still in a position to adopt her,' Nina said. 'Imagine if they'd been matched with another child before Sunshine was ready for adoption . . .?'

He seemed to have to think about this, and again Nina was worried he might clam up, but then he said, 'I know, it would've been a great shame, and now you mention it, I do find it interesting that they weren't, given how long they'd been on the books. Angela told me they got quite close to being chosen for a baby boy.'

'Billy,' Nina said. 'Four months old. It hurt Chrissie when he went elsewhere, and it was Nancy who influenced that decision.'

'Was it?' Brendan said. 'Well, look, it all worked out for the best in the end.'

Nina nodded and smiled. She knew how to smile, Brendan thought; right at you, right into your eyes. He wondered again how old she was. Ageless, in a way, as if time and years were nothing to her, she was simply herself.

'Do you know why Sunny was in foster care for so long?' she asked.

Brendan laughed. 'You really do know this story, don't you? Chrissie asked me that, the first time I met her.'

'And you told Chrissie you weren't sure.'

He laughed again, a little less certainly. Nina's eyes were on him, an extraordinary, unidentifiable shade of blue in the candlelit gloaming of this pub.

'It was something to do with Sunshine's missing history,' he said. 'Searches had to be made, to be sure there wasn't a parent somewhere, with an opinion on her future. You'd think it might be easier than when the birth parents are around, but I guess not.'

'Was that Nancy's job?'

'No, I doubt it,' he said. 'Local authority, I believe. But Nancy pre-dated me, like I said.'

'Could we find out? I'd love to know a bit more about her.'

We. He noted that, and didn't mind it at all. He drained his pint, and proposed another drink.

'Sure,' Nina said. 'Bring a menu too. I'll buy you dinner.'

And as he made his way to the bar, Brendan felt good.

Nina had soon worked out that the less she mentioned Stuart, the more Brendan seemed willing to help. So she'd talked to him confidingly over dinner about Chrissie's present frame of mind, her anxiety, her feelings of being hunted, and the toll this was taking. She told him the woman she met in the park that time had known who Chrissie was, and had known Sunshine too. He said yes, of course, he knew this, but Nina had described the encounter to him, and said she wished Chrissie had witnessed it, because she was certain she'd have been reassured. As it was, Chrissie saw only menace in these unusual occurrences. Brendan had said, well, wasn't that entirely understandable? He found them menacing too. And Nina said what she'd repeatedly said, without effect, to Chrissie: that the sense of menace came from a lack of information.

'Right,' he'd said. 'Right, yeah, knowledge is power.'

'Precisely,' Nina said.

By the time they'd finished eating, he'd had three pints of bitter and a glass of red wine, and agreed fulsomely with Nina that they should walk back to the office right now, before they lost their momentum.

'It'll be like Watergate,' he said.

'Except we're the good guys,' she said, and he laughed, quite thrilled by this idea. Nina had drunk far less than him, and it said something about Brendan that he'd failed to notice this. He was an endearing fool, she'd decided. His heart was large and doubtless loving, but he was far too easy to manipulate, would never attract a sensible, reliable mate, and Stuart was absolutely right – he had a crush on Chrissie, and possibly now a crush on her, Nina, too. She could see why travelling the world alone would be something he could never do – he was weak at the core, his self-sufficiency was barely skin deep. She wondered if his own childhood had been a crushing disappointment, and if that was why he was now trying to fix things for a new generation. She liked him; but that didn't mean she wasn't going to use him.

It was past midnight when she finally got home. He'd found it hard to focus, kept thinking they were looking for more information about Sunshine, so that Nina had to remind him repeatedly that it was Nancy they were interested in – where she came from, who she was, where she lived.

'Ah, I can tell you that – she lives in Jaipur,' he'd said, pleased with himself for knowing the answer to something, then he'd been immediately thrown when Nina said, 'Does she, though? Do you know for sure?' He'd said, 'Erm, well that's where she *said* she was going,' and Nina had said, 'Well, if I tell you I'm going to Timbuktu next week, don't you take my word for it, OK?' and he'd laughed at this for what seemed slightly longer than the joke merited.

But Nancy Maitland held the key to unlocking this mystery, Nina felt sure, or at least she was a good place to start. She'd never met Nancy, but she knew Chrissie and Stuart thought she was the bee's knees. In the early days, the workshop days, they'd been coached and supported by her in a way that had sometimes seemed, to Nina, above and beyond her remit. 'Does she do this for all her clients?' she'd asked Chrissie, and Chrissie had said, 'Oh, I think so, she's very committed,' but still, Nina had thought that Nancy somehow always had her sights set on them, as if they were her project, as if they were a trio, the rock 'n' roll couple and homely, hand-knitted Nancy. She seemed to live in their pockets for a year and a half, then lo and behold – she'd dropped off the radar, the moment Sunshine came into the frame, as if her work here on earth was complete. Odd, Nina thought now; downright peculiar.

Now, Nina had an address for her. It was the only one that seemed to exist in that office, and they'd found it not on the computer, or in the filing cabinet, but in a heap of documents in a box file with HCPC written on the side in red marker pen.

'Health and Care Professions Council,' Brendan had said. 'It's where stuff goes we think we don't need but can't be sure.'

'Perfect,' Nina said.

'You'll not find anything on Nancy,' he said, which of course made it all the more likely, somehow, that she would. Nina had been methodical, looking through a ream of unconnected papers, sheet by sheet, scanning their contents. And sitting there among them all, neither hidden away nor easy to find, was a photocopy of Nancy's confirmation of her re-registration with the HCPC, dated 21 March 1995, and a request from her that until further notice, all correspondence should be sent care of Buckenhurst Court, Littlecliffe, Canterbury, Kent.

'It's well out of date, that address,' Brendan said, determined to stay relevant. 'She lived in Nunhead when she worked with us, but she's in Jaipur now.'

Nina had folded the paper and tucked it into her rucksack. 'Well, let's see,' she said. They switched off the lights, locked up the office, and walked back out into the night. Brendan had never been sorrier to see someone leave. He said, 'Let me know what you find,' and she turned and saluted him, and said, 'Sure thing, comrade.'

He watched her walk away towards the train station,

and was surprised, and a little hurt, that she didn't once look back.

The following day was the Friday just gone. She packed an overnight bag, locked up the gallery – hoping no one came with two grand burning a hole in their pocket – and took an early train from London Bridge to Canterbury. There was a taxi rank by the station, and she climbed into the one at the head of the line and asked the driver for Buckenhurst Court, in Littlecliffe. He knew Littlecliffe, he said; everybody knew Littlecliffe, lovely place, but he didn't know Buckenhurst Court, and they sat for a while, puzzling pointlessly over Nina's copy of Nancy's letter, dated only two years previously, which clearly stated Buckenhurst Court as her address. Had she looked it up on the world wide web, he asked? She said she was afraid she was something of a Luddite, and he said her religion was none of his business, and they both laughed, possibly for different reasons. Helpfully, he then got out and spoke to the woman driver in the cab behind, then came back to report to Nina that it wasn't called Buckenhurst Court any more, but she knew the building, not exactly in Littlecliffe, a good three miles outside, down a long lane, well, more a track really.

'Lulu's your woman for the job,' he said. 'Her family farms the land round Littlecliffe. No point me getting you lost.'

So Nina swapped cabs, and Lulu, speaking to the rear-view mirror, said, 'No, sit in the front, my love, I'll tell you a story while we're driving.'

Nina, intrigued, slid out again, and into the front passenger seat. The woman next to her was tiny, thin as a stick, with a sharp, lined, chain-smoker's face, and jet-black hair, cut short as a squaddie's. She had an unlit cigarette behind one ear, and another, also unlit, between the first two fingers of her right hand. Her smile was so fleeting it might have been an illusion.

'Hi,' Nina said, 'I'm Nina.'

'Louise,' the driver said, 'but call me Lulu, everyone else does,' and she flashed another millisecond smile. 'So,' she said, 'if you're asking for Buckenhurst Court, I'm guessing you don't know the half of it.'

'I don't know anything at all,' Nina said. 'I'm trying to find someone, or at least, find out something about someone.'

'Who's that then?'

'A woman called Nancy Maitland.'

Lulu took a drag on the unlit cigarette, and blew imaginary smoke out of the window, and then seemed to realise that this looked extremely odd.

'I'm trying to kick the habit,' she said.

'Good luck,' Nina said. 'It's more than I've ever managed.'

Another swift smile, acknowledging the camaraderie of nicotine addiction, then Lulu said, 'Buckle up then, my love, it's a long story,' and she slammed the gear stick into first and screamed away from the taxi rank like a getaway driver.

This is what Lulu told Nina.

Buckenhurst Court was a Victorian mansion, built with a Kentish hops fortune in 1880, but put up for sale seventy-odd years later to pay the debts of the dissolute descendants of the original owner. Nobody in the area wanted to buy it – 'Big old lump of a run-down place,' Lulu said – so it went to auction and was sold, sight unseen, for an undisclosed sum, to a couple called Auberon and Esme de Lyon.

Nina said, 'How grand! Were they aristocrats?' and Lulu said, 'Hush up, or it'll take all day.'

The de Lyons were colonial types, Lulu said; children of the Raj. 'They'd both grown up in India, their parents were part of the government set-up before the war, then they all came back in forty-seven, and the kids probably went off to boarding school or whatever, but anyway, Esme and Auberon must've been keen on each other, because they stayed friends, and ended up marrying, and then they came here, to Buckenhurst Court.'

'So this was . . . when?'

'Late fifties,' Lulu said. 'And it was all about self-sufficiency and communal living, very hippy-dippy; they were a few years ahead of the curve. Mind you, they had plenty of money, so they didn't starve while they waited for the veg to grow. They farmed the Victorian way, with plough horses, big beautiful Shires; they were quite a sight. They had goats, so they established a dairy and made their own cheese, doing everything the hard way, no mechanisation, very eccentric.'

In their way, though, they were a respectable lot, Lulu said. Auberon wrote a book about the house and their way of life called *The Chivalry of Nature,* had it published as well; you could still borrow a copy of it from the library in Canterbury. He and Esme were interested in reviving ancient crafts, such as wool dying and weaving and willow-sculpting. Word got round. Folk drifted down to their corner of Kent to join them. There was work here, if you wanted it, and didn't mind being paid partly in produce. Lulu's older brothers came along to help dig up swathes of parkland then till the earth for the vegetables and whatnot, and sometimes they came home pie-eyed after a session on Esme's damson gin.

Back then, Lulu said, people were welcome to come and see the work being done and buy the produce, and if they liked the look of it and had a willing spirit, they could join the commune. The kiddies went to the village school, Lulu said, and there it was, they were passing it right now, look. Nina saw a sweet, small, Victorian schoolhouse, a collection of cottages, a brick and timber pub. Lulu drove on.

'I mean, the locals raised their eyebrows a bit,' she said. 'They liked to have a gossip and a moan, y'know. Smelly Buckenhurst goats' cheese at the market, and home-brewed mead in stone bottles so you couldn't see what you were buying, and natural-dyed handknits that looked like something the cat had dragged in, but they were all harmless people, pleasant, and polite.'

They co-existed alongside the village community for years, Lulu said. She had school friends who lived there, and there was nothing more fun than being invited to Buckenhurst for one of the commune kids' birthday parties, where Esme would dress as a fairy queen and Auberon organised musical chairs, and pass the parcel, playing tunes on his Pan pipes.

'Did they have children of their own?' Nina asked.

'I'm coming to that,' Lulu said. 'They did, just one, Samuel, he was always an odd bod, and when he was about sixteen, he buggered off, people said he'd joined a cult in India, but none of us knew anything about it. If anyone asked where he'd gone, Auberon always said he was "seeking his own path", which was another way of saying he was probably up to no good. We certainly didn't miss him in the village. He was downright weird really, had one blue eye and one brown one.'

Nina laughed. 'That's not his fault,' she said.

'I know,' Lulu said, 'but it summed him up somehow, and he used to boast that they gave him special powers. He called them ghost eyes and put spells on us, they never worked, obviously, but he still freaked us all out.'

Nina, thoroughly entertained, nevertheless wondered where Nancy Maitland fitted into this colourful picture. She wanted to try and remember every single detail for Chrissie; she so wished she was here with her, following the trail, and listening with her to Lulu, who was marvellous and told the story with such seamless panache, as if she did it for a living. Nina wondered if they were driving round in circles, just so that Lulu could get to the end.

'So anyway, Samuel de Lyon came back about ten years ago,' Lulu said. 'He hadn't improved. The commune was falling apart a bit, a few people had started drifting away, poor old Esme had died years ago of stomach cancer, bless her heart, and Auberon was on his way out too, he ended up in the dementia ward in the community hospital in Canterbury. Samuel never went to see him, although he was there at the funeral. Over two hundred people came, and Samuel sat at the front, making a show of grieving. He had two daughters with him, little white-faced girls, we all felt sorry for them stuck with him for a dad. Esme and Auberon would've loved them. They'd moved with him into the big house where he ruled the roost, naturally.'

'How old were his daughters?'

'Oh, they were very close in age, one nine, one ten, I suppose, that kind of age, very pretty girls, you might have mistaken them for twins, but both so quiet, the wrong kind of quiet. No mother in sight. Whoever she was, she got left behind. Perhaps she died. Anyway, they were born in India, or at least that's what we heard, but they weren't Indian, or at all exotic, just wan-faced, motherless children who seemed a bit lost.'

'Do you know if Nancy Maitland was at Buckenhurst Court at that time?'

'No, she wasn't, not when he first came back. She turned up about five years ago. People did, from time to time. They'd hear on the grapevine that anyone could come to Buckenhurst and get a bed and a bowl of lentils. It was still jolly enough, still wholesome and earnest, although we heard Samuel de Lyon had a bit of a guru complex, he always did think a lot of himself. He took all the youngsters out of the village school, said they'd be taught at Buckenhurst, which was a shame, although the postman used to see them regularly and he always said they were doing fine, the commune kiddies; to be honest, they always had better manners than the village kids. Treated each other better, I mean. They had no spite, picked no fights.'

'Did you know Nancy at all?'

'Not really,' Lulu said, 'although I drove her up here, oddly enough, when she first arrived. Picked her up like I picked you up, she was looking confused at Canterbury station. She told me she wanted out of the rat race, wanted a simpler life, and to be fair she stayed a while, got pally with the younger of the de Lyon girls, we'd see them sometimes walking through the village. Asha, she was called, pretty girl, like I said. She came out of her shell as she got older, although the other one didn't, we never saw her.'

Asha, thought Nina, and she sat up a little straighter in the seat. *Asha and Athena, Perfect Happiness.*

'Are we nearly there?' she asked.

'We are,' Lulu said. 'Though don't get your hopes up; I doubt you'll have much joy if you're after information about Nancy. Samuel's a total fruit loop now. He's renamed the house some Sanskrit word, and I don't know who he still has with him; anyone with any sense has scarpered. He's king of a mostly empty castle.'

But Nina wasn't really listening. She was thinking, Sunshine's mother is Samuel de Lyon's daughter. Nancy Maitland is her friend. Like pieces of a jigsaw spilled on the floor, it was simply a question of finding them, and fitting them back together.

Lulu slowed to a crawl, said it was too easy to miss the turning, then immediately yelped and said, 'Here!' and took a sharp left onto an unmade track, just wide enough for the taxi, bordered on either side by unkempt ancient hedgerows of hawthorn and blackberry. They bumped along at a snail's pace for a short while until abruptly, at the crest of a small hill, the old house revealed itself in the shallow valley beyond, a brick-and-stone Victorian pile; still very arresting, even in its obvious state of extreme disrepair, and even though they were clearly approaching from the back, not the front. It was large and square and it bore those hallmarks of Victorian ambition that made modern buildings seem half-hearted and flimsy by comparison. Deep terracotta-red bricks dressed with mellow ornamental stone, and a stone balustrade forming a shallow balcony that ran all around the building beneath the first-floor windows. The roof was a festival of turrets and fancy chimneys, and a clocktower rose above them all, although the hour hand was missing from the clock face. None of this marred the magnificent integrity of the house, but it was certainly somewhat let down by a rudimentary wooden sign, nailed to a post and driven cockeyed into the earth. 'Ānanda' had been painted in capitals and each letter was a different colour; red, orange, yellow, green, blue and purple. There was a dusty little white car parked on a patch of gravel, and a jackdaw that had been roosting on the bonnet flung itself into the sky, startled by their arrival. Lulu stilled the engine, and they both sat for a few moments, as if unsure what to do next.

'Right-o,' Nina said. 'That was the tradesmen's entrance, I suppose?'

'There's a lovely big pair of iron gates and a long driveway,' Lulu said. 'But he's chained them up this past year, he doesn't really want to be found any more.'

'Ānanda?' Nina said.

'Don't ask me.' Lulu took a drag on her cold cigarette and said, 'Do you want me to wait?'

'Oh, that's kind, but I don't know how long I'll be.'

'Not long, is my guess.'

'Well,' Nina said. 'Anyway, I can call you if I need you.'

'And it's getting dark earlier now.'

'I know, it's fine, I can look after myself.'

'You'll have no mobile phone signal,' Lulu said. 'Not a scrap, up here.'

'I don't use one. Did I see a telephone box somewhere?'

'You did.' Lulu plunged a hand into the driver's-side door compartment and rummaged about. 'Here,' she said, handing Nina a card. 'My number. The phone box is on the lane at the bottom of the track, turn right, you'll see it set back on the verge. Ring me when you're ready. I'm not going back into Canterbury, just going home, the other side of Littlecliffe, so I can be up here in no time. You've got some coins, right?'

Nina nodded. 'What do I owe you?'

'Nothing yet, pay me on the return.'

'Thanks, Lulu,' Nina said. 'And thanks for the background

story, you're a gem.' She reached for her bag from the back seat and opened the car door.

'Shall I just wait until you've knocked?' Lulu asked. 'What if the place is empty? It looks it.'

But at that moment a man calmly appeared from the front of the house, walked a little way towards them, then stood, legs akimbo, arms folded, regarding the taxi, and evidently waiting for someone to appear from it. He had a terrifically upright posture and a severe expression. He wore a djellaba of some gleaming-white fabric, trimmed at the neck with gold braid, a pair of loose white trousers that narrowed at the ankles, and a pair of golden slippers.

'There he is,' Lulu said. 'What does he think he looks like!'

Nina didn't wish to judge before she'd met him, but he did look incongruous, an ageing Arabian prince in a forgotten fiefdom in the Kentish fields. Sunshine's grandfather.

'I heard he's changed his own name too, now,' Lulu said. 'Something daft; I forget what.'

Nina said, 'Well, here goes,' and she got out of the car. She raised one arm in greeting, and the man bowed his head graciously, but was clearly waiting to be approached. Nina shut the car door and gave Lulu an encouraging wave through the window, then walked towards him along a weed-filled, red-brick footpath.

He was very tall, and very thin, with a smile that made up in width what it lacked in warmth. His mismatched eyes were startling; one palest blue, the other the yellow-brown colour of a caramel toffee. They made Nina feel uncertain where to look, as if it should be either one, or the other, not both. His greying hair had been shaved so closely that all the contours of his skull were on display. He said, 'You look as though you've come to stay, sister,' and briefly she was confused. He pointed at her weekend bag, and she gave a small laugh.

'Ah, no,' she said, understanding. 'I'll stay in the village, if the pub will have me, or in Canterbury somewhere.' She pointed at Lulu's taxi, which had reversed and was now nosing its way back onto the rutted lane. 'Lulu brought me. Her brothers used to look after the vegetable beds here, years ago.' She wondered why she'd said this, particularly as the vegetable beds were now clearly a riot of thistles and dandelions and hogweed, but he just said, 'Is that so?' in a light voice, quite devoid of interest. Nina changed the conversation.

'I'm Nina Baker,' she said, and proffered a hand. He took it, but didn't shake it, simply held on. His skin was soft and very cool.

'Prospero,' he said.

'Prospero?' Nina echoed, disbelief quite evident in her tone, although she managed not to laugh.

He nodded very gravely, and, still holding her hand, led her into the house.

In the entrance hall, he released her, took her bag and placed it on an oak settle, then opened wide both his arms, in an apparent invitation to her, to behold and admire the interior. It *was* very grand, in the dark, baronial tradition; wood panelling, ox-blood walls, gold cornicing, heavy brass light fittings; not her scene, and not what she'd expected – more gentlemen's club than commune. It was a house filled with history and shadows; a relic from the days when the sun never set on the British Empire. She couldn't see anyone else, although somewhere, a woman was singing, practising scales, travelling up and down the register but not in English, another language; perhaps Hindi, perhaps Arabic. Samuel de Lyon was staring at her with a small frown, so Nina said, 'What a wonderful place,' because she thought that was what was expected of her. He didn't speak.

'How long have you lived here?' she asked, only to fill the silence, and now he gave a quizzical smile, and said, 'May I ask why you've come?'

'Well, you see, I just finished reading *The Chivalry of Nature*,' she said, astonished at herself. 'I thought it was *so* interesting, Auberon and Esme, those early pioneers of the alternative movement, and I was fascinated by his descriptions of the house, so here I am, I've come to see it for myself.'

She knew she sounded fifty per cent too chirpy to be even remotely convincing. He tilted his monkish head and seemed to be weighing up her words, so she quickly said something she could believe in, which was she hoped very much she wasn't intruding, and she was sorry she hadn't been able to let him know she was coming.

Again, he appeared to silently measure the line and length of what she'd just uttered, but she was quite determined now not to speak until he answered her, which in due course, he did.

'We don't – how shall I put it? We don't open the house to the public,' he said, studiously slowly. 'We're not, what is it they say? Ah yes, the National Trust; we don't belong to the National Trust.'

She felt flustered now, and regretted mentioning Auberon and Esme, and realised she should probably have played to his own obvious vanity and not their legacy. His tone was sardonic, his expression amused, and the house, of course, was the very last thing she was interested in. A significant part of her wanted to say so and wipe the aggravating smirk from his face, but directed by instinct, and what she'd already learned from Lulu, she smiled pleasantly and said, of course, of course, she hadn't expected a tour. She was here on a foolish impulse; she hoped only to gain a flavour of what life here was like.

He let her words settle, stared at her for longer than was comfortable, then said, 'This is Ānanda. This is the new Eden.'

She raised her eyebrows, but held her sceptical tongue, and waited. She could see the strangeness in him, and it wasn't his odd eyes or his princely costume; rather, it seemed to vibrate beneath his skin, and manifested itself in his bristling pride, his ludicrous hauteur. She suspected he was a man with a lot to hide from an inquisitive stranger whose values belonged to the rational world. And yet she so longed to speak to him, for if Lulu's story was correct, here was the grandfather of their darling Sunshine, and she wondered what he knew about her. The photograph in the memory bag had surely been taken here, in the grounds of Buckenhurst Court? That majestic tree was almost certainly still to be found, within the park. She felt sure it must have been him who'd named the child Athena. Such a grandiose name, plucked from mythology; the kind of name a man who called himself Prospero might choose. *Asha and Athena, Perfect Happiness.* Had he been the photographer? Had he written that caption? In her mind's eye, Nina could see the unsmiling faces of woman and child, and the writing on the reverse, almost sinister in its way, the capital letters, the disconnect between message and image. Certainly he seemed like the kind of man who preferred his version of events to anyone else's.

'Do you understand Sanskrit, Nina Baker?'

'I don't,' she said.

'Then let me tell you, Ānanda means bliss, blessed.'

'I see.'

'We are truly blessed, those of us who live here.'

'And how many of you do live here, these days?'

She asked the question pleasantly, and it was very far from

unreasonable, but he seemed affronted, and looked down at his golden slippers, as if the answer was written on them.

'I mean,' Nina said, 'is this still a commune, as it was in its Buckenhurst Court days? Or is it a family home now?' *As if I care*, she thought; *as if that matters.*

He looked up at her again, piercing her with his confusing eyes. 'Why are you here?' he asked. 'The truth, please.'

And this was so shrewd that she really couldn't see the point in lying again, and after all, this man could tell her so many things she needed to know. So she hesitated only briefly then said, 'OK, I came looking for a woman called Nancy Maitland, but I confess that now I'm hoping to find your daughter, Asha.'

In an instant, his expression turned thunderous, and he seemed to lurch towards her as if he intended actual physical harm, but in fact he was only stumbling, as if he'd been violently shoved out of kilter by the boldness of her answer. She held out her hands as much to support him as protect herself, but he thrust them away, and righted himself, then roared, 'Kristen! Kristen!' and the singing, which had continued to weave itself in and out of their brief, terse, odd conversation, stopped abruptly, and the lightbulbs in the chandelier rattled in their brass collars as feet pounded across the first-floor landing and onto the stairs. A woman in a vibrant red sari came tearing down, and she cried out, 'Prospero!' then gasped, 'Oh! Oh!' and raced to his side, although he seemed more irritated than relieved by her arrival; such a scowling man, thought Nina, such a self-regarding curmudgeon.

The young woman seemed not to have noticed Nina, who'd stepped back from the drama the better to observe. Her garment was glorious, Nina saw. Brilliant scarlet trimmed with gems, like a Hindu bridal costume. But her skin was palest white, her hair a lustrous mass of auburn waves, and when

Samuel roared again – 'Get her out of my house!' – and she spun round to face the object of his fury, Nina experienced an electric jolt of recognition, because here – she was sure, she was almost certain – was the young woman she'd seen by the playground fence. She had the same hair, the same large eyes, but now they weren't calmly resting on Nina's face; instead, they were flashing with fear and fire. She seemed momentarily rigid with shock, but then marched over to the door, flung it wide, and said, 'Go, at once.'

'This is all very unnecessary,' Nina said, with a calm that she didn't feel. But she collected her bag from the settle and walked towards the open door until she was close enough to say, in a low voice, 'We've met, you and I? In London, by the children's playground. Do you remember me?'

Kristen drew back as if struck, stared intently for a moment, then put her face slightly too close to Nina's and hissed, 'This isn't the time or the place. You have to go.' She looked more afraid than unfriendly, so Nina stepped past her out of the house and onto the steps, then turned and said, 'So when and where can . . .'

But the door swung shut in her face.

The brick and timber pub was called the Hop Pole, and Nina walked there from Buckenhurst Court, because the telephone turned out to be useless, vandalised, so that the cord dangled helplessly from the receiver when she picked it up. It didn't matter; she valued the exercise and the thinking time, and it was only a little over three miles, she thought, to the village they'd passed through. At each junction she came to on the lanes, Littlecliffe was helpfully signposted, and, even though darkness was drawing in already, she made efficient progress and in just over an hour she recognised the beginnings of the settlement, the appearance of dwellings, the widening of the road, the advent of pavements and, finally, the welcome sight of the Hop Pole Inn, cheerfully lit by a yellow glow from each of its ground-floor windows.

Nina pushed the door open and took in ancient beams strung with garlands of dried hop flowers, a wood-burning stove blazing red and orange, and a man smiling at her from behind the bar, tall, lean, lined, with silver-grey hair almost to his shoulders. He gave a small bow and said, 'Greetings, and thank you for finding me,' which Nina thought was very singular, and extremely charming. She laughed and said, 'Well, thank you for being here. I couldn't have walked much further,' and there followed a friendly conversation about where she'd been, who she'd seen, the vandalised telephone, and not being able to call Lulu, and he immediately lifted a phone from a shelf under the bar, pushed it in front of her and said, 'Call her now, because, if I know Lulu, she'll be worried about you.'

She was.

'I've been at my wits' end,' she said. 'I was going to drive up there again and find you. I was going to bring my brothers as backup.'

'I know, sorry, but that phone's bust,' Nina said. 'I'm fine, though. I'm at the Hop Pole in Littlecliffe.'

'Are you really OK? You didn't get brainwashed or anything?'

Nina laughed. 'No, far from it, but I do feel shattered. It was really strange, very unsettling.'

'Is Rob there?'

Nina glanced at the man, discreetly busy at the other end of the bar. She didn't know his name. 'He might be,' she said.

'Like an ageing rock star.'

'Yes, then.'

'Tell Rob you need a room,' Lulu said. 'They've only got one, and he doesn't let it to any old passer-by, but he'll let it to you. I'll come by in the morning and take you to the station; you can tell me then how you got on.'

She hung up, and Nina looked at Rob. 'I've been told to say I need a room,' she said.

She was billeted in a bedroom with a low ceiling and a floor that sloped so dramatically, she might have been on a ship, pitching on the high seas.

'Three hundred years old,' Rob said, following her in with her bag. 'Some might call it subsidence; I prefer to call it settling. Watch your head on those beams.'

But it was enchanting, the bare floorboards and mighty beams waxed to the colour of honey, and the rough plaster walls painted a bright simple white. The iron bed stood on blocks at one end to deal with the tilt, but it looked inviting as a cloud, white and soft and capacious. She ran a bath, soaked for a while among the fragrant bubbles, and thought about Chrissie, whom she longed to call, but knew she shouldn't, because it was for Chrissie, now, to come to her. There was so much to tell her, and yet nothing, so far, of real substance, and what Nina wanted more than anything else was to be able to say with certainty to Chrissie, this is what's happening, and this is why, and isn't it better to *know* all this than to always be fearful? Oh, Nina wanted matters to be clear, and open, and unthreatening. If Asha could be found, what reason was there for hiding from her? Was it too ambitious, too fanciful, to imagine a time when Asha might be a presence in Sunshine's life? Perhaps so, perhaps so; Chrissie wanted a child all of her own, and why should she share? That would be Chrissie's opinion, although Stuart might take another view.

There'd never, ever been a time, Nina thought, when she'd felt cut off from Chrissie, and at odds with her, and there was no reason for this to be so now, none at all. They should stay close, and work through this crisis together, but Chrissie seemed to think she was stronger and safer alone, and nothing Nina could say dissuaded her from this; rather, it seemed to achieve only the opposite – the more Nina said on the subject, the less Chrissie liked it. It cut Nina to the quick, really it did, because how fortunate they'd been, and how blessed; two souls connected by love and loyalty, with none of the fetters of traditional family ties. There'd always been such honesty and openness between them, and Nina prized this beyond any material thing, yet now, now . . . well, she couldn't seem to make Chrissie hear her. But look, Nina thought; perhaps Chrissie had turned away from her because she trusted entirely that Nina would still be there when she turned back. And she would, of course. She would.

She drained the bathtub, dried herself in a warm towel, dressed in the same jeans but a fresh shirt, then went down to the bar, where she ate a very good shepherd's pie and told Rob about Chrissie and Sunshine and why she'd come here, the answers she sought, then listened to his stories of Buckenhurst Court, and its gradual transition to the Ānanda of today – an unlucky day for the locals, he said, when Samuel de Lyon landed. He confirmed everything Lulu had said. Said they were good people, the early Buckenhurst lot; said he'd only been a nipper himself, but his parents ran the pub in those days, and they had a lot of time for Auberon and Esme. A bit earnest, perhaps, and certainly eccentric, but also kind and warm, and their market garden was a wonderful thing. Half the produce needed by the Hop Pole used to come from their vegetable beds and fruit cages, he said. And half the population of the village school was made up of the Buckenhurst kids, who were always the best-behaved pupils, though you might have expected the opposite, might have expected them to run wild.

'Lulu said the same,' Nina said. 'Lulu said they were never spiteful.'

'They weren't, they had a totally different energy to most groups of young kids. It was a different upbringing, very collaborative, and that carried on until quite recently, but the de Lyon fellow is a proper handful, possibly certifiable from what I hear. Over the past couple of years every decent individual ended up bailing out. Nowadays we've no idea who's up there, you don't see hide nor hair of anyone.'

'Well, there's him and a young woman called Kristen, I know that much.'

'Oh, yeah, I remember her, she's one of the daughters.'

'She was very attractive, in a washed-out sort of way. She was wearing a gorgeous sari.'

'You met the father too though, right? What does he look like these days?'

'Gaunt. Takes himself very seriously,' Nina said. 'Head to toe in white satin, apart from his shoes, which were golden. He calls himself Prospero,' and when Rob snorted, she added, 'I know, right? Hard to keep a straight face.'

'What an absolute charlatan,' Rob said.

'Those eyes though.'

'I know, you might think he just uses coloured contact lenses, but no, they're real. Ironically, his extraordinary eyes might be the only genuine thing about him. Can I top up your glass?'

She pushed it across the bar. There were several other customers now, locals who'd come in individually, but had since formed a posse across a couple of tables in one corner of the candlelit pub. This place must feel like an extension of their own living rooms, Nina thought. She felt at home here herself, perched on a bar stool, being mildly flirted with by Rob, and mildly flirting back. His name was Robin Whittaker, and there was more to him than met the eye, she'd realised. He was a potter – there was a kiln and a studio out back – and he ran the inn because he'd grown up here, and it seemed a natural thing to do, although he'd run it alone since his partner, Talia, died four years ago after a brain haemorrhage. The pub was his living, the pots his therapy. They stood in alcoves and on shelves around the room; rough-hewn and organic, statement pieces in earth and sky colours. He looked after everyone who came in this evening, but paid special attention to Nina. He was skilful at listening, frank and funny in conversation, and Nina permitted herself to bask in the warmth of his smile; it seemed such a long, long time since she'd met a man who inspired the enjoyable stirring of carnal thoughts. But she was tired, she had other matters on her mind, and after one more glass of house red, she bade him goodnight – slightly regretful, with a rueful smile – and went back up the creaking staircase to her tilting room.

It was only ten o'clock when she went to bed, and she was certain she'd be out like a light, but two hours later she was still awake, her mind racing with impressions of the day. She knew she'd have to go back up to the house, before returning to London. She had to try and speak to Kristen, alone. She'd been sure that there was something in Kristen's eyes and her low, urgent voice that had communicated a desire to talk, but not in the house, not in front of Samuel.

She gave up on sleep, got out of bed and walked to the window. She'd kept her curtains open to let the moonlight slice in through the leaded glass, and make pale white diamonds on the honeyed floor. Somewhere in the distance, someone was letting off fireworks; they bloomed like prize chrysanthemums in the black, star-studded sky. An owl soared past; such a startling, majestic sight, she thought, an owl on the wing. She wondered what else was out there in the fields beyond, nocturnal creatures beginning their day as hers was ending. She fetched a pad and some charcoal from a pocket in her bag, and returned to the window to make some swift sketches of the shapes she could make out, the gnarled branches in an old apple orchard, the five-bar gate to a field, an owl – the same owl, surely – now perched on a post like a sentry, and watching, watching, as motionless as a rock. She was still standing at the window sketching, when she heard a tap on the door and Rob's voice, saying, 'Nina? Nina?'

She thought, ah God, no, no, this is not what I want after all, and for a few moments she was silent as she considered feigning sleep. But then she saw the time on the luminous face of the bedside clock, saw it was past one a.m., and knew for certain, though she hardly knew him at all, that Rob wasn't the kind of man to make assumptions, or disturb her so long after she'd gone to bed, unless there was a very strong reason. She opened the door.

'Hi,' she said.

Rob looked troubled, anxious. 'Nina, I'm so sorry to disturb you,' he said, 'but Kristen de Lyon's downstairs. She's very insistent. You'd better come.'

~

Asha hadn't known how much she didn't know until the boy walked up to the house with a few clothes in a rucksack, a football under his arm and a guitar in a hard black case, covered all over with stickers whose meaning she couldn't fathom, but he said they told the story of his life. When they first saw each other, they both stopped walking and stared. He said, Ha! there you are.

The boy's name was Declan and he used to call Asha his darling, his girl, the music of his heart. All he wanted was for Asha to leave the commune with him, but she only knew one way of life – this one – and she didn't find the courage to leave it until a long while after he'd gone.

He was unlike anyone she knew, but when she told him this he laughed, and said there were plenty more where he'd come from. He had a way with the kids, played guitar for them, taught them how to kick a ball, because they'd stared at his football as if it was a meteor dropped down from space. Her father scoffed and told him to be quiet, but anyway, for a while, Declan stayed, because of Asha, but they had to be careful, secretive, always on their guard, and Declan hated this; he said love was something to shout about.

The first time he played a song for her, she listened and was amazed, and he laughed and said, sure, have you never heard of The Beatles? She hadn't; she hadn't heard of anything, and then it was his turn to be amazed. He showed her a record; he said it was his only precious thing before he'd found her, and he played it on the turntable in the music room. Asha was afraid they'd be caught, but he was always so bold and defiant, he didn't care who heard him. It was a fine, simple song called 'Here Comes The Sun' and listening to it made her cry, she had no idea why, but he seemed to understand. He wiped away the tears with his thumbs and said it had been the privilege of his life, to watch her while she listened.

With Declan, Asha felt like she became more herself than she'd ever been, but it was no life for him, he didn't fit the space they made for him, his mind was too much his own, he wouldn't bend. Whenever Asha lay curled in his arms, feeling the gradual steadying of her heartbeat, feeling the gradual drying of sweat on her naked body, he told her this was no life for her, either.

Come away with me, he whispered. I'll take you to Galway, and we'll live by the bay and gaze at the ocean, and all our babies will be like you and me, and what baby wouldn't want that?

Oh, but she couldn't leave. She was a fool, for not leaving.

He left the song on her pillow, in a box, and he wrote on it, 'Oh darling, here comes the sun' and then he just walked away.

Only Nancy had known what Declan was to Asha, or what Asha was to him, but when he'd gone, she became just a shell of the girl she'd been, and the other sisters and brothers noticed, Kristen noticed, and her father noticed too, especially the gradual swell of her flat belly, and there was enormous upheaval and angry words, and acres of disappointment at her strong will and the deceit and this consequence of it. But a baby was a blessing, and Asha's baby was a darling, and after all his months of red rage, her father melted at the sight of her, this new child of his, and he marked her out for greatness and all his special attention, and he named her Athena, after the goddess of wisdom and courage.

But quietly, privately, Asha thought of Declan and named her Sunshine.

22

They'd talked for not quite an hour – and it felt to Nina like far less – when Kristen said she had to leave, before her absence from home was noticed. She'd got to her feet, all of a sudden, telling Nina she was so sorry to dash, but next time would be different, wouldn't it?

'We'll have longer, then, to chat properly,' she'd said, 'and goodness knows there's so much more to share.' Her tone had been confiding, as if there was a secret between them. She'd smiled, clasped Nina's hands in hers, fixed her with a searching gaze that Nina had to end by turning away, because suddenly she'd felt a little uncomfortable, and she couldn't quite work out why.

Rob, who'd diplomatically absented himself from their conversation, was still near enough to recognise the sounds of leave-taking, and he returned to the room to insist on driving Kristen back, it being almost two o'clock in the morning, and beginning to rain. This offer she gratefully accepted. And it was only now, in the uncompromising stillness of the empty pub, that Nina forced herself to think about what had just happened, and she found her head and her heart in a ferment, because she had not – she had to acknowledge this truth – been master of that encounter. She'd been sure a bond of trust was developing between them, and indeed, who was to say it hadn't? But something in Kristen's haste to leave . . . it felt now as if she'd achieved a goal, and could only jeopardise it by staying. It had sown a seed of unease, and now Nina wondered if she'd said too much, and trusted too quickly, blinded by her eagerness to befriend this young woman who held the secret to Sunshine's past. She stood in the dimly lit bar with only the clock on the wall for company, and thought about the chronology of the conversation, and concentrated on salvaging the positives; all could yet be well, if Kristen de Lyon was a person of integrity – and, well, look, thought Nina, the young woman had yet to prove herself otherwise.

Kristen had turned up at the Hop Pole with a large anorak over the red sari and a pair of trainers caked in mud, after a moonlit short cut through the fields to Littlecliffe. Lucky for her, she'd said, considerately taking off her shoes by the door, that Nina was here, and not undiscoverable in Canterbury. She'd been remarkably composed, as if running through the fields to call in at the pub in the dead of night was nothing remarkable. She'd been extremely apologetic, too, about her own earlier behaviour and that of her father, whom she didn't refer to as Prospero. Rob had coaxed the fire back into life, and Nina had sat Kristen down at a table near it, and placed herself opposite. Rob had diplomatically left the room, and Nina had told Kristen it was very good to see her again, and asked what had brought her here with such urgency? She'd kept her voice calm, but was privately ecstatic, for this was beyond any realistic hope she'd had of learning Sunshine's story. In response, Kristen had become earnestly business-like, and asked, 'How far can I trust you, Nina?' and Nina had held out her hands as if she was offering Kristen her guileless heart, and said, 'Entirely, you can trust me entirely.'

And now, while the engine of Rob's departing truck was still audible from the lane, Nina wondered why on earth she hadn't immediately turned that question around and asked how far she could trust Kristen. She wished Rob had stayed in the bar instead of giving them privacy. She wished he'd been there as a kind of bulwark against her own breathless desire to connect with a young woman, a complete stranger, who, in the end, had asked more questions than she'd answered.

Nina sat down on an ancient leather sofa that seemed to sigh with a kind of weariness as it accepted her. She stared vacantly at the last embers in the hearth, waiting for Rob to return, hoping he might help normalise a day and a night that for her had begun to take on the hallucinogenic qualities of a bad acid trip. She held herself still and tried, now, not to think too much about anything at all. Her impressions were too shifting and elusive, the facts too intangible; the more she tried to process her thoughts, the less clear they became. So she emptied her mind by counting the resonant ticks of the old clock, and this quietened her agitation and made it possible for her to simply wait, until, sooner than she'd dared hope, Rob burst back into the pub, and she felt a wave of gratitude and relief. He was blowing on his hands, and talking about the resident barn owl, the one she'd seen from her bedroom window, which had swooped into the beam of his headlamps and banked off to the left, so close to his windscreen that he saw the finest filaments of its wing-tip feathers.

'I nearly went into the hedge, but what a beauty,' he said, 'I hear him every night but rarely see him – hey, are you OK?' He dropped down to his haunches in front of Nina, with his hands on her knees. 'She's an odd one, right? Did she upset you?'

Nina intended to say, no, no, but instead started to cry, so Rob waited quietly until she began to collect herself, then said, 'What's the story, Nina?'

'How long do you have?' Nina said, attempting a laugh. She swiped at her tears with the sleeves of her shirt, and said, 'Oh God, I don't know what I'm doing any more,' and Rob grinned and said, 'I had ten minutes with that woman and she did my head in – you were with her for nearly an hour. It's no wonder you're at sixes and sevens.'

Nina gave a low moan and said, 'I thought she could help me. I still think she can, but I don't know for sure what her motives are.'

Now Rob got up, then sat down beside her. He took one of her hands in his, and this didn't feel strange, only comforting and natural, and he said, 'Nina, why does someone like you need help from someone like Kristen de Lyon?'

She gave a shuddering sigh. 'I told you, earlier, about Chrissie and Stu and Sunshine? How her past seems to haunt them, and how unhappy it makes Chrissie, and I want to make it stop, not by running away from it, but by finding some truth in it, and some goodness. I want to turn Sunshine's past into a positive force in her life, and it can be, I know it can, and Kristen de Lyon, whatever else she might be, is Sunny's aunt, and my best hope.'

She heard a note of rising desperation in her own voice; she wondered at the state of her sanity. Rob's hands were warm and strong, and his voice was filled with steady concern, and Nina thought that perhaps here, at last, was a person – a stranger, a friend and an ally – with whom she might share the truth, the whole truth, and nothing but the truth.

'You have to remember,' Rob said, gently, 'that Kristen and Asha had the strangest upbringing.'

Nina was silent.

'You have to remember, too, that if Sunshine was adopted, it was almost certainly because her mother couldn't provide for her, or keep her safe?'

'Or,' Nina said, 'maybe her mother was forced into it; maybe she's broken-hearted somewhere, maybe I . . . you see, it's Asha that interests me, not Kristen, not really. Kristen is only my route to Asha. I feel this strong visceral pull towards that space where the story of Sunshine's mother should be, and I know that Chrissie would have more peace by knowing the story too, and I know Sunshine belongs fully to Chrissie and Stu, that little family of three was truly meant to be. But all this menace and mystery needs to be interpreted and I feel if we found Asha, we could do that, and perhaps even make room for her in our lives.'

'Maybe you could,' Rob said. 'Maybe you couldn't. I don't know the details. Do you know the details? Do you know why Sunshine ended up in care?'

'Barely,' Nina said. 'We know that Asha was very young, and when she left the child she said, "This is Sunshine, please will you keep her safe?"'

'Well then.'

'Well then, what?' Nina asked, a little testily.

'Well then, she clearly felt the child needed something she couldn't provide.'

'I don't think that's clear at all, and anyway, who knows what regret that young woman might be feeling now?'

Rob said, 'Right, yeah, that's certainly a consideration,' then he stood up, and said the drama of the day called for Armagnac, would she like one? This sounded nice to Nina, and, as Rob moved about behind the bar, he told her his impressions of Kristen. The way she had of sounding perfectly normal while actually saying something quite batty. The bizarre cultural mis-appropriation of the bridal sari. The quasi-religious claptrap that made his skin crawl. The peculiar tragedy of her reclusive life with a deluded narcissistic father.

Nina listened to him, recognising the elements of truth in what he said, yet remembering the light of earnest kindness in Kristen's eyes and her evident willingness to help, her willingness to straighten things out. She would cling onto her own recollections, Nina thought, now. She had a vested interest in Kristen's essential decency; everyone's happiness depended upon it.

'When I first saw Kristen,' Nina said, 'it was in the park in London, and she was in jeans and boots and a pink jacket, and she looked very much part of the real world.'

'Right,' Rob said. He came back with their drinks, placed them down on the low table and sat next to Nina again. 'Well, that's something, I suppose. Are you sure it was her? Those two sisters looked quite similar, if I remember right.'

Nina shook her head emphatically. 'No, it was her, I wasn't a hundred per cent sure at first, but anyway, she confirmed it. She knew me, from the playground.'

'Is she to be believed?'

'I don't see why not. Why would she say it was her, if it wasn't?'

Rob smiled. He said, 'OK, and what about the other incidents you told me about earlier: the woman in Whitstable; the one who left that bag of memories; the girl in the shoe shop?'

Nina hesitated, then said, 'All Kristen. At least, that was the implication, or rather, that's my impression of what I think she said.' Good grief, she thought; I sound like an idiot.

Rob looked amused. 'Well,' he said, 'it either was her, or it wasn't her.'

'Right,' Nina said. 'Yes, she said it was.'

'So, all those people, on each separate occasion, were actually the one and only Kristen de Lyon?'

'Mmm, yeah,' Nina said, fully aware how this sounded, how

gullible it made her seem. She picked up her glass, and took a sip of Armagnac; the smooth heat of it bloomed in her throat and chest.

'She's been extremely busy then,' Rob said, quietly sardonic. 'Do you believe her?'

Nina shrugged; a small, rather hopeless gesture.

'Well, I certainly don't,' Rob said.

Nina frowned, and concentrated on corralling her scattered thoughts. In hindsight she had to acknowledge that Kristen had been vague and airy about her efforts to reconnect with the child she still called Athena. 'Yes,' she'd said, 'we've been look-ing for her for a while – motivated only by love, of course, and also grief at Athena's absolute disappearance from our lives,' and then Nina had felt nothing but compassion and under-standing, and had talked about the effect on Chrissie of each separate incident, when surely the sensible, revealing, useful thing would have been to ask Kristen precisely how she'd gone about trying to make contact with her niece.

But it *had* been her, by the playground that time; of this Nina was almost certain. Her clothes had been very different, and she'd been partially obscured by shade, but Nina believed there was no mistaking her face and the colour of her hair. It was true, Nina conceded to herself now, that she could have tested Kristen in some way; she could have asked her to describe, per-haps, what Sunshine had been wearing on that day . . . but then, how *hostile* that would have sounded, how sceptical. Still, for Kristen to lay claim to that, plus three other separate occasions, did seem . . . well, downright unlikely. And in fact, thought Nina, when she'd mentioned the memory bag, there'd been – or had there? – a second or two when Kristen's face had registered an intense but fleeting interest, which only made sense if this was the first she'd heard of such a thing. Yet in the very next moment, Kristen had smoothly nodded and said, yes, yes, a memory bag for the child, containing possessions Asha had left behind – she, Kristen, had wanted Athena to have something from her past. And Nina had accepted this, because Kristen had an earnest manner and the collected air of a person who deals only in the truth, and, well, what she'd said had seemed at the time to make sense. But now ... oh, how Rob's reasonable questions unsettled her. He asked, 'Did the foster mother in Whitstable give a description?' and, miserably, Nina recalled that Barbara had said the woman on her doorstep had had dark hair. She knew this fact, they all did; dark hair and a short red coat or a long red jacket. They'd talked about it often enough, so why had she allowed that moment to pass unremarked upon, too? It was possible, she supposed, that Barbara – unstable, panicked, somewhat befuddled by emotion – had been mistaken. Possible, too, that Kristen had felt the need to disguise herself. Yes, those were certainly possibilities. But the fact was that the only thing Nina knew with any confidence was that Kristen was the woman from the playground – and even that was becoming questionable, under Rob's steady scrutiny. Which did not, Nina reminded herself, mean that Kristen was lying. And when they met again, as they'd planned to do, she would establish the facts, and there would be no confusion, only clarity.

'Nina?' Rob prompted again, gently. 'Do you really believe what she told you?'

She gave a great sigh. 'I don't know yet,' she said. 'It's not straightforward, and yes, when we were speaking, I did believe her. It's only since she left that I'm questioning everything, and I suppose that until I can categorically prove otherwise, I have no reason to disbelieve her. That's the best I can say.'

'But how had she known where to go? How had she known

where the foster mother lived or how to find you and Sunshine in the park that day? Surely all that information is strictly privileged and confidential?' Rob asked.

Nina said, 'I asked her that.'

'And?'

'She didn't really answer.' In fact, Kristen had told Nina that in matters of the heart it wasn't always necessary to understand everything, and although now that seemed barely credible, back then, Nina had thought it a reasonable enough statement to pass unchallenged. She looked at Rob bleakly. 'So, I don't know how she knew,' she said. 'And I don't believe I was thinking straight at all.'

He said, 'I tell you what, Nina – wherever and whyever and whoever Asha is now, she did that little girl a favour, putting her in the way of a good life with good people. I reckon, on the evidence before us, that she's far better off where she is now, beyond the reach of her grandfather and aunt. As for Asha – well now, that's different, we don't know her, we can't judge, but she's clearly a girl of good sense or good self-knowledge. Renaming her baby was a great start. That pair clearly still think she's Athena.'

Nina listened, but couldn't speak. She thought about the moment when Kristen had said, 'Remind me, where does Nancy Maitland fit in?' which was as big a clue as she could have given that she hadn't even known Sunshine was adopted. Nina, deaf to danger, happily obliging, had said, 'Oh, she's one of Chrissie and Stuart's adoption case workers, she put them together with Sunshine'. Kristen – graciously, without alarm – had said, 'Sunshine? Is that what you named her?' Nina had felt the uncomplicated joy beginning to drain from her heart, and had stammered out, 'She came to us as Sunshine,' and, very calmly, Kristen had said, 'That's interesting. Asha's choice, then.'

Nina's mind had spun, and she'd fervently wished she could rewind to that point in the conversation where she'd said Sunshine, and unsay it. The conversation had moved seamlessly on, with Kristen still saying Athena, and Nina saying very little at all, but knowing she'd just supplied Kristen with two key facts that she hadn't previously known.

She looked at Rob and wished he could read her mind, to spare her the agony of having to itemise any more of her mistakes and indiscretions. He smiled at her, raised his glass, and indicated with a nod that she should do the same.

'Here's an old Russian toast,' he said. 'Let's drink to the success of our impossible endeavours.'

She gave a woeful smile, clinked glasses, and took a second sip of the aged brandy. *The success of our impossible endeavours*. Such optimistic pessimism was very beguiling.

'Here's another,' he said, holding his glass aloft again. 'Let's drink to the clouds and their silver linings.'

She clinked, drank, and asked, 'Is that Russian too?'

'No, I just made it up,' he said. 'It means, I'm very glad I encountered you, on your wild goose chase.'

'Oh,' she said, dredging up reserves of faith and hope that surprised even herself, 'I don't think it was a wild goose chase, at least, it's not proven yet. I haven't entirely given up on the success of my impossible endeavour. I mean, I now know Sunny's aunt. That's incredible, right? So isn't there a case for seeing it through?'

Rob looked at her very intently. 'I really don't understand how your mind works,' he said.

'What do you mean?'

'Well, it's just, I found Kristen very odd, and I believe you think that too, and for this reason, I don't think you should have anything to do with her. That's what I've been saying, since I got back. I don't think you should trust her.'

'You might well be right,' Nina said, 'but I *have* trusted her.'

Now, he looked grave. 'In what way?'

'She expressed a wish to meet Chrissie, and I agreed she should. Not Sunshine, only Chrissie. So we're travelling up to Barnsley together on Monday; she'll meet me in London and we'll go and prove to Chrissie, once and for all, that no one means her or Sunny any harm. We can talk things through, and everything will be so much better.'

Rob exhaled, long and low. 'Well, if you don't mind me being frank, I think that's a very dodgy plan. At the very least, you ought to wait and see how you feel tomorrow. I reckon everything will look different by daylight, and if it does, I can drive you up to the big house and you can let her know it's all off.'

'Also, she knows the child's name is Sunshine, not Athena.'

Rob hesitated, then said, 'Oh, right. You told her?'

Nina looked disconsolate, and nodded. 'Inadvertently,' she said. 'And only because that's all I've ever known. I found it so hard to remember to say Athena.' Then all at once her expression froze and she stared at him with eyes full of panic.

'What?' he asked, alarmed.

'She lied,' Nina said.

He waited.

'Kristen didn't leave that memory bag at the housing office. There was a handwritten note inside that said, *These items belong to a girl named Sunshine.*'

'Right, and Kristen didn't know she was now called Sunshine, until tonight. And if she lied about that . . . well, can you trust anything she's said?'

Nina couldn't look at him, couldn't speak. She felt only the hot waves of a kind of nausea. Oh, she felt naïve and foolish and reckless, and she saw Chrissie and Sunshine in her mind's eye and knew she'd let them down, when all she'd wanted, all she'd ever wanted, was to find the truth, and in doing so, make their lives better, fuller, stronger.

'Hey,' Rob said, looking at her with concern, reaching for her hand. She allowed him to take it, but it was limp and unresponsive in his.

'Nina, don't be too hard on yourself,' he said. 'Nina, look at me, please; you're not the first person to find out that sometimes what we want with all our hearts can cloud our good judgement.'

Nina still wasn't listening. She stared down into the amber liquid in her glass, and thought again about how very little Kristen had shared with her, yet how very much she'd shared with Kristen, who knew, now, the child's name and that Chrissie and Sunshine were in Barnsley. She hadn't mentioned an address, but had mentioned the area, she'd spoken about the part of Barnsley where Chrissie grew up, and where she, Nina, used to live.

There'd been no sense that Kristen was extracting facts from her; Nina had simply and willingly given them up. And there *had* been a connection between them, Nina thought. Yes, Kristen was unusual, but she hadn't appeared sinister, not in the least. She was very sweet, very attentive – not that Nina had been entirely blind to her faults; there was more than a touch of artifice about her – a practised theatricality in the way she held herself, the way she spoke. The root of her father's temper was heartache, she'd told Nina; the heartache caused by Asha and Athena's disappearance. She'd pressed her palms together as if in prayer, and adjusted her face to show Nina what true sadness looked like. 'It almost destroyed him,' Kristen had said. And Nina had recognised the speech as a performance, but yet had also seen that losing a niece and a grandchild . . . well, that way madness lay, and undoubtedly this family had known grief and loss. All of this passed through her mind now, and she knew that she'd been impetuous, and possibly unwise, but she couldn't, in her heart, say she wouldn't do exactly the same thing again.

Now she looked at Rob and said, 'I don't know what to do, or to think.'

'Do nothing,' Rob said. 'It's far too deep into the night to draw sensible conclusions about Kristen de Lyon, or her father and his delusions; things are bound to take a gothic turn at quarter past three in the morning.'

She gave a half-smile. He was a comfort, a gift, a friend, and this time yesterday she hadn't known he existed.

'Dismiss it all until daylight,' he went on. 'You might not think it right now, but you've done some good work today for this Chrissie of yours, and her Sunshine. You have some key information, and a clearer idea of who you're dealing with, right? You'll see your way through. You're not committed to anything; just stand her down tomorrow if you change your mind about this trip north. You can have it all sorted before you head home.'

Nina saw he was looking at her with extraordinary tenderness. 'Thank you,' she said, in almost a whisper.

'Any time,' he said.

'Kristen's quite a force, though. I might need your help resisting her.'

'You've got it. She won't bamboozle our united front.'

He smiled at her, and she returned his smile properly now, but she was being entirely serious; she hardly knew how she'd agreed to such a scheme. Kristen had suggested the trip, not Nina, and at the time, in the thrill of the moment, it had seemed a plan of magnificent ambition, with a promise of catharsis, and a happy resolution, and Nina had readily agreed.

She was going back to London tomorrow to open the gallery for the rest of the weekend, then she was to meet Kristen by the statue of Robert Stephenson at Euston station at nine o'clock on Monday morning. It was all arranged. But yes. Nina could unarrange it. Of course she could. Not cancel; only postpone. Draw back, slow things down, but stay in touch. Kristen would see the sense in that. She would. And Nina could make a few more judicious enquiries about Kristen, and prepare Chrissie properly to meet Sunshine's aunt, and who knew, then, where the road might lead?

She took another sip of Armagnac and felt its warm, settling effect on her turmoil. Sleep seemed out of the question and Rob made no move to end their conversation. Instead, he began to tell her about his work as a potter, and, listening to him, Nina at last felt a measure of peacefulness begin to descend. There was something mesmerising about the process he described; the clay, the wheel, the glaze, the kiln, the chemistry of the craft, the magic of the firing. When he asked her to talk about her painting, she said, 'Ah no, I can't, I've never been able to do that,' so he said, 'OK, talk to me some more about Chrissie and Stuart, what do they do?' So she began to tell him about The Lineman, and his face creased into a delighted smile, and he said, 'No way! Chrissie Stevenson and Stu Woodall?' and she said, 'The very same.'

'I saw them play Glastonbury in nineteen ninety!'

'Me too!' Nina said, her face lit with delight.

'Ha! We were at the same gig,' Rob said, and to both of them, this seemed the most remarkable and yet the most likely occurrence in the world.

'They were on the slate for a small stage, then got offered the Pyramid after a cancellation,' Nina said. 'A lucky break, that gig – catapulted them into a higher sphere.'

'Well, they owned that stage,' Rob said. 'They were awesome. I've seen them a few times since then, in London.'

'Then we've been at more than one gig together,' Nina said. 'I don't miss any within striking distance.'

'She's one of the greatest female singer-songwriters the UK has ever produced, in my opinion,' Rob said, and Nina glowed with reflected glory and said, 'You should come and meet her and Stu,' and she was grinning with happiness at the thought of introducing Rob to her favourite people. 'Meet the famous Sunshine too, see what all the fuss is about.'

'I'd love that,' he said. 'Erm, is your phone ringing, by the way?'

She hadn't heard it, she'd been too wrapped up in her soft-focus Armagnac fuzz, but he was right; from somewhere on the sofa came the muffled thrum of a mobile phone, but it'd slid down the back of a cushion so that by the time she found it, it was no longer ringing.

On the screen it said, *missed call from Doug,* and all the warmth instantly drained from her body.

'Who was it?' Rob asked, alarmed at the fear in her face, and she managed to say, 'Chrissie's father,' as she left the room. But never in all the years she'd known him had Doug Stevenson called her in the dead of night, and so it was with shaking hands that she rang him back, and she had to sit on the stairs to do so, because to climb them was beyond her.

She heard Doug before he spoke. Was he crying, Nina thought? Was Doug crying? She said, 'Doug, what's happened? Is it Chrissie?'

'No,' he said, then, 'I mean yes, in a way,' and she heard him heaving great breaths as if he was trying to collect himself.

'Doug,' she said, 'for God's sake, tell me.'

'Diana's collapsed,' he said. 'I think she's had a stroke. I've called for an ambulance.'

'Oh, Doug,' Nina said, 'that's terrible, I'm so sorry,' but her heart was singing with relief.

'She knows,' he said. 'Diana knows.'

Nina swallowed. She couldn't speak. She heard only the ticking clock in the next-door room, marking the passing of time.

'Nina?'

She could hear him, sniffing and blubbing, and she thought, how can someone of his age, with all his experience of the world, be such a baby in a crisis? In that moment, she despised him for his anguish, because it wasn't on Diana's account, or Chrissie's or Nina's, but only his own.

'Did you tell her?' she asked.

He blew his nose. 'She found a letter.'

'A *letter*?' Nina said. 'What letter? Where?'

'The loft,' he said, in a whimper. 'Not a letter, exactly. That thing you wrote.'

She was silent for so long that Doug said, 'Nina? Are you there?'

'You kept that?' she asked. 'You still have it?'

Doug was crying again.

'Doug? Get a grip! God, I can't believe you still have that.'

'You told me to keep it, Nina,' he said, sounding wounded. 'You said it at the time, and you wrote it at the bottom.'

She considered this, then thought, yes, so I did, and she felt a flash of pride in her younger self, her fierce pragmatism and ingenuity and instinct for survival.

'I'm sorry,' Doug said. 'It's been years since anybody disturbed that loft, then Sunny was up there every chance she got, pulling things about. I don't know . . . all I do know is, Diana went up to tidy, to straighten things out, and next thing was, all hell broke loose.'

'But Doug, that's not why Diana had a stroke,' Nina said.

There was a pause while he absorbed this.

'That's not how strokes happen, Doug, the stroke would have been coming anyway.'

He gave a great, damp sigh. 'I don't know. She was livid, Nina, even by her own standards.'

'I can easily imagine,' she said. 'Where's Chrissie?'

'She's in Castleton. I'll call her when I know what's what with Diana.'

'Oh, Doug, what a mess.'

'I know. I'm sorry.'

'Is she bad? Diana, I mean?'

'Terrible. She can't speak, but she can still glare at me, and it's breaking me, Nina; it'll be the death of me.'

'No, Doug, it won't. People have withstood worse than this, and you will too.'

'Oh, Nina, I wish you were here.'

She felt an old, familiar fondness for him, but it left her as swiftly as it had come. He was a man without inner resources. He was six feet tall, and entirely insubstantial.

'Just as well I'm not, under the circumstances,' she said. 'I'll come soon, though. Doug, this is as much my mess as yours, and, no offence, but I think I'll be better than you at sorting it out.'

He said, 'Sorry.'

'Don't keep saying sorry.'

'Sorry, oh – sorry. Look, I think, the paramedics are here, there's lights in the street.'

'Go, then,' Nina said. 'Keep in touch, and Doug?'

'Yes?' She could hear in his voice the phoenix rising of near-extinguished hope, that she had words of comfort, or words of reassurance, or a promise that the world as they knew it was not at an end.

'If you blurt this out to Chrissie,' she said, 'I'll kill you.'

23

So Chrissie was lying on the bed with the phone pressed to her ear, listening to Nina, who was talking too much and too fast about how much she knew, when she ought to just shut up, Chrissie thought; shut up, and give her a decent interval to adjust to a life in which one of the people she trusted most in the world had admitted they might be responsible for jeopardising Sunshine's safety.

Nina said, 'I know it's a lot to take in, darling, but principally, right now, you should feel reassured. I've made a phone call, and I'm sure Sunny will be back with you very soon.'

Chrissie said, 'A phone call? What? Where is she?' Her own voice sounded like someone else's voice. This conversation sounded like someone else's conversation. Nina sounded like a stranger.

'It's complicated, darling, but try to stay calm, I'm sure all will be well.'

'What's complicated? What are you talking about?'

'Well, Sunny's birth mother, Asha, lived on a commune in Kent,' Nina went on, as if this answered Chrissie's question. 'And that's where Sunny was born. Nancy Maitland lived there too, for a while—'

'But you said Nancy doesn't have her?'

'What? No,' Nina said, a little derailed by the question. 'I mean, I don't think so, not Nancy.'

Chrissie closed her eyes, and thought, then who has? Nothing else interested her beyond this fact. Nothing else had any meaning.

'The commune's all but dismantled now,' Nina said, rattling on with her unwanted news. 'But there's still this guy, Samuel de Lyon, and his daughter Kristen – Sunny's direct relatives – and it was Kristen I saw in the park that time . . . Chrissie? Are you there?'

Chrissie was there, but not there. She said, 'Yes.'

'OK, so I found them accidentally, and in fact I was looking for Nancy – I had this notion that she was the key to everything – so Brendan let me into the office one night and I found an old address on some form or other, a place called Buckenhurst Court, not too far from Canterbury . . . Chrissie, are you listening?'

She was, and she wasn't. Brendan let Nina into the office at night? For God's sake, what was happening here? And Nina sounded . . . she sounded puffed-up and self-regarding, and was she expecting gratitude, or praise? Chrissie lay on the bed and stared at the ceiling and longed for some peace in her savagely unquiet mind.

'Chrissie? Darling?' Nina said, 'I'm sorry, this is too much information, right? What I'm saying is, they have Sunshine, I'm almost sure of it. But they—'

'Cherish her,' Chrissie said, dully.

'Exactly,' Nina said, with surprise. 'I believe they probably do.'

Chrissie felt so lonely. Her despair and distress and confusion should have been evident when she spoke and evident when she was silent, but Nina wasn't hearing it; she had too much to say.

'I didn't do very well with Samuel de Lyon,' Nina said, ploughing on regardless. 'He's irascible and deluded, but his daughter, Kristen, came to find me in the pub I was staying in and she was interesting, I learned such a lot from her, well, and from Lulu, the taxi driver who took me there. So he – Samuel de Lyon – is Sunny's grandfather, Kristen is Sunny's aunt, and Asha, the girl in the photograph, is Kristen's sister . . . Sunny's biological mother.'

'Who took her?' Chrissie said.

Nina took a sharp breath but said, 'Kristen, I believe. We'd made a kind of plan to come to Barnsley together, to talk to you, to fill in some gaps in the story. I had some misgivings, and I told her the very next day that I'd changed my mind, I went to see her, told her we shouldn't rush into such a scheme, and she agreed, said that sounded sensible. But I think she came any-way. Chrissie darling, are you there? I think Kristen came up to Barnsley alone.'

'How did she know where to find Sunshine?'

Now there was a long silence. Chrissie knew the answer; she just wanted Nina to say it, to utter the truth, unadorned by any extraneous detail.

'I told her,' Nina said, and Chrissie said, 'Right,' and hung up.

Carly smiled at her when she entered the kitchen, but the smile died as Chrissie repeated to her what Nina had said. Then Chrissie wandered off to find Stuart, and told him too, and they just stared at each other in a kind of desperate and loaded silence; so much that could be said, but unthinkable to have to say it.

Buried in the trauma was the fact that now, at least, they probably knew where to find Sunshine, and this was what Stuart latched onto. He wanted to leave, now, for Kent. He was patting the pockets of his jeans, checking for the car keys, saying, let's just go, let's go now, but Carly held him firmly by the arms, looked into his eyes, said, 'Darling, you must stay. We'll call the police, tell them what we know, but you have to stay here,' and she was right, he knew; his head told him so, while his heart clamoured to act, to fight, to find his child. Meanwhile Chrissie's head swam, unpleasantly awash with disjointed detail, and she tried to remember everything she'd been told, everything she now knew, about Nina and Brendan and Nancy, and these other people, total strangers, a taxi driver named Lulu, an irascible old man, and his daughter, this Kristen person, who had known where to find Sunny, because Nina had told her. 'Sunny's grandfather, Sunny's aunt,' Nina had said on a note of rising excitement, as if all any of them cared about was filling in the blanks on Sunshine's family tree.

Carly walked into the living room, holding out her phone, and she said Nina was on the line, she wanted to speak to Chrissie again, she thought they'd been cut off, but then Carly registered Chrissie's expression, and she passed the phone to Stuart instead, who snatched it, and said, 'Nina, why don't you just ring the cops and tell them how to get to wherever it is these fuckers have taken her?' so Carly immediately pulled the handset away from her son, and said, 'Nina, Carly here again,' as she walked out of the room.

Chrissie thought for a moment that she might be going to vomit, but instead she was consumed by a violent crying jag, a bout of noisy sobs that shook her to her bones until Stuart took her in his arms, and held her very tightly, while he waited for it to subside. When it did, she immediately drew away from him, and said she needed to be on her own, and she went upstairs and lay down on the bed she'd shared with Sunshine, and she sobbed and sobbed, and held the pillow over her face to try and breathe in a trace of her. Despair inhabited her like a sickness; misery flooded her bloodstream. So Nina, the guiding light of her growing-up years, her constant friend, her defender, her support, her occasional shelter in a storm, was to be her undoing in the end. If Sunshine was safely returned, it wouldn't alter the fact that Nina had been the reason she was taken. If Sunshine wasn't safely returned, then there was only ever going to be darkness, for the rest of time. The clock on the bedside table told her it was still only half past twelve, when the day had already felt like an age, and she thought about the dark days to come, passing pointlessly one after another, empty of all meaning; and she thought about bitterness, blame, the stranglehold of guilt and sorrow.

She heard Stu downstairs, speaking on the telephone to the police, and then Carly came to find her, pushing the bedroom door open quietly, speaking softly to her as she might to an invalid, handing her a camomile tea, suggesting she try and sleep, as if sleep was possible, as if pain could be traded for unconsciousness when Sunny was gone and Nina had betrayed them all.

Much later, she went downstairs and went to find Stu.

'I'm going out, I won't be long,' she said. 'I only need some air.'

He wanted to come. She said no, please, just . . . and then, because she knew she was adding to his awful suffering, she made an effort to sound kinder and said, 'Sorry, Stu, I'm truly not trying to punish you,' and it was such a small concession but still, she saw an immediate wash of relief cross his face, and she thought, so this was what they'd come to; her cold compassion; his newly unrequited love.

Outside, she stood still for a moment and tried to breathe in the way Carly had taught her, and she wondered if this had ever done a single living soul in crisis any good. She thought about the wreckage of her small family, the part they'd all played in its downfall; Nina – oh, God, Nina – for exposing them to harm; Stuart for not watching closely enough; Julia, for bringing Juno; and herself, for not letting Sunshine go back to Castleton when she had the chance. It'd been a conspiracy of good intentions, proof of the impossibility of getting things right, in a world where any innocent decision could turn out to be a terrible mistake.

Swiftly, but without purpose, she walked down the street, her head down, noticing nothing. When a neighbour called, 'Christine, love! How's your mam?' she barely heard, didn't answer, was tuned in only to her footfall and the appalling knowledge, the deep and certain understanding, that if Sunshine didn't come back, everything would cease: love, life, music – none of it could continue in any recognisable form. She hadn't known this before; that a certain kind of grief could descend and consume everything in its path, could touch a person's life with shape-shifting powers, and alter the world completely. If she'd ever considered the aftermath of grief, she would have assumed it would make her cleave to Stuart and they'd draw comfort from each other. But she knew now that the theft of their child had to be suffered quite alone, with incommunicable pain, and their mutual sadness would only ever be a barrier to love, not a bond.

And now, suddenly, the impulse that had taken her out of the house and down the street left her as swiftly as it had come. Abruptly, as if someone had tugged an invisible cord, Chrissie stopped walking. She turned around, looking back up the street with a kind of puzzled gaze, so that anyone observing her would have certainly thought her lost. She hadn't got very far, only to the end of the road – she could still see the chimneys rising above the trees at the side of the house in which Carly and

Stuart would be waiting for her, with their boundless, hopeless love – and she'd had no intention of going back yet, but something, she didn't know what, had compelled her to turn and stare, and she found she was watching a mud-splattered, flatbed truck, watching it slow down outside the Stevenson house, indicate and park. It was an unusual vehicle in this residential road, a farm vehicle, a country vehicle, built for carrying timber on rutted lanes. But the wide, deep, front windscreen was facing her and the interior of the car was lit, and she saw the indistinct faces of three people, and one of them, she thought, was a dark-haired child in a red hat. It wasn't Sunny, Chrissie told herself. It wasn't Sunny, because it wouldn't be, it couldn't be, but still, impelled by some invisible force, she began to walk towards the truck. She saw two people get out, and one of them was the child. She saw the child had a red beret and a green duffel coat, and before Chrissie had quite permitted herself to trust what her eyes told her, the child gave two determined little hops, one on each foot, and bellowed, 'Mine mummy!'

Chrissie had always thought joy was a manageable emotion, but now she was assailed by it, slain by it. It sapped her strength and, against her will, kept her rooted to the spot, but anyway Sunshine had speed and strength for two; she was running pell-mell towards her, so all Chrissie needed to do was sink to her knees and open her arms wide, and when Sunshine barrelled into her, she was ready, and she received her in speechless ecstasy, a gift from the gods. Fiercely, briefly, they each clung to the other, Chrissie almost reeling from the feel and smell of her, the three-dimensional presence of her, the irrefutable fact of her. Then Sunny gave a great sigh of happy satisfaction, braced her arms against her mother's chest so that she could look into her eyes, and said, 'Now I want Daddy,' and Chrissie remembered that she really must share this miraculous child. She kissed her on the nose and said, 'And he wants you, sweetheart. Come on, let's go and find him.'

The truck was gone when Chrissie stood up with her daughter in her arms, but Nancy Maitland was standing on the pavement with a small holdall in one hand and an ingratiating smile on her face. As they walked towards her, Nancy said, 'Oh, Chrissie, I'm sorry I couldn't let you know—' but Chrissie wasn't interested yet in anything she had to say. She held up a flat palm, as if to say, enough, and if she could have swept Nancy from the scene, she would; what she had done, and why, could wait, and for now, she seemed an unnecessary player on the stage.

So Chrissie, with Sunshine moulded into her as if they were a single being, passed Nancy as if she wasn't there, and walked through the gate and up the path to the front door, where she realised she had no key, so she clattered the brass knocker and heard Stuart within, shout, 'I've got it,' heard him approaching, turning the latch, watched him open the door, and watched his face reflect all her own emotions back at her, sharing between them, in a split second, the complicated intimacy of unfettered relief and happiness.

Sunny bounced in Chrissie's arms, and squealed, and held out her arms and shouted, 'Up, up and away!' and Stu took her from Chrissie, swung her high in the air, and swooped her down again, then held her very close while he tried to collect himself, because Sunshine was so happy, and he didn't want her to see his tears and mistake them for sadness.

Soon, after watching for a short while, and from a respectful distance, Carly ran through to the front of the house and swept the child up too, dancing down the hall and back with her in her arms, then Sunshine said, 'Mine mummy,' and reached again for Chrissie. This time, she took her away, carried her off to a quiet corner so she could revel in her, and Sunny wound her hands in Chrissie's hair, and pressed her sweet damp lips all over Chrissie's face, and then, with her mouth pressed very close to Chrissie's ear, she said, 'Sing mine song, Mummy,' then laid her head against her mother's neck, slotted her thumb into her mouth and closed her eyes to listen to 'The Ballad of Sunny and Juno' again, and again, and again.

~

John rang, John Foster as they'd named him, filled with profound concern, which was quickly replaced with bottomless relief when Chrissie told him Sunshine was home. But he was calling with an odd tale, related in tones of great mortification, which was that when the police visited them yesterday, to talk about the woman with the red coat or jacket, Barbara at once – and inexplicably, and miserably, and shamefacedly – crumbled under questioning and confessed she'd invented the incident, and even now couldn't explain why.

'I hardly know what to say,' John said. 'I believe she suffered some kind of breakdown over that little girl, and I blame myself for not realising that.'

It was hard to care, really, now Sunshine was home, but still, Chrissie's mind swam with the implications of what John had just said.

'I feel Sunshine and I have been running away ever since I was told that happened,' she said and John gave a low moan and said, 'I know, my dear, I'm so sorry,' but Chrissie said, 'No, no, it's just, now, after everything else, it seems like a prophecy, you know? I mean, a premonition of what was to follow?'

'It wasn't, though,' John said. 'It was just Barbara, trying to disrupt your happiness.'

'Still, it seems less like an absolute untruth in the light of everything else,' Chrissie said.

'I should've known,' John said, determined to take the rap. 'After the soap powder and whatnot, and then she was a bit muddled about the details, the woman's coat or jacket, and a bit defensive, then all the crying she did afterwards. I blame myself,' he said, again.

'Don't, John,' Chrissie told him, feeling sad, now, for this kind man. 'Please, don't talk about blame. You're a key part of Sunshine's happiness, you and Barbara, a key part of her loving nature. Tell Barbara we wish her well,' she said, more for John's sake than Barbara's and indeed it did seem to console him, although as soon as she hung up after his call, Chrissie turned to Stuart and said, 'Bloody Barbara! She made the whole thing up!' and for a good few minutes they quietly railed against the woman whose love for Sunshine had utterly derailed her good sense, and both of them hoped her ears were on fire.

∽

Nancy had crept into the house unattended by Chrissie or Stuart and clung to the shadows until Carly rescued her, drawing the young woman into her circle of compassion and giving her coffee. Then she called a taxi and dispatched her to the police station, to tell her story, and she'd been there for an hour already when Chrissie and Stu arrived with Sunshine. Karen, the family liaison officer, buzzed them in, and met them on the other side of the door, all smiles, because this was the sort of happy ending she didn't see often enough, she said. Nancy hadn't taken Sunshine, Karen told them, but she'd surmised correctly who had – the child's biological aunt and grandfather – and had fetched her back.

'It's a murky story,' Karen said. 'She'll no doubt tell you later. She has some explaining to do to you two.'

They were following her through the station as she talked; they had to have a chat with a paediatrician, entirely routine, Karen said, entirely normal, and Stu said, 'Well, not *entirely* normal,' and she said, 'Normal, in an abnormal situation such as this one,' and led them into a pleasant room, where a gentle, grey-haired doctor received them graciously, as if for afternoon tea. She was soft-voiced and bespectacled, and Sunny was allowed to sit on Chrissie's knee while they talked. There were toys in the room, and she was invited to play with anything she wished, but for all the doctor's gentle manners, warmth and kindness, Sunny was shy in her presence and all she wanted to do was sit tight, with Silky in one hand, her dog-eared monkey in the other, and Chrissie's hands locked like a seat belt around her tummy. But she listened carefully to the questions, and, with nods and shakes of the head and shy smiles and small laughs and occasional contented yawns, Sunny communicated enough for the doctor to be reassured that she'd been neither hurt nor traumatised by her experience, and it was perfectly plain that there, on her mummy's lap, she considered herself back where she belonged, and this was where she wanted to stay.

They couldn't wait to get out of here. Everyone was as nice as could be, but the police station, with its cluttered desks and busy phones and uniformed officers and bulletproof glass, only prolonged the air of crisis, which was now officially in the past. The police work hadn't concluded with the safe return of Sunshine, of course. Chrissie and Stuart knew this and were comforted by it, but when Nancy emerged from her interview, and heard that not only would Samuel and Kristen de Lyon be arrested and brought up to Barnsley for questioning, but also

336

they might be facing a custodial sentence, she blanched, and threw startled looks at Stu and Chrissie, and said to them, scandalised, 'Surely you're not pressing charges?'

The detective inspector gave her a long, level look and said, 'Chrissie and Stuart don't need to press charges, Ms Maitland; this is a police matter, and a serious crime has been committed.'

'But they meant no harm!' Nancy said, emitting a kind of wail. 'And I promised them there'd be no repercussions,' and Stuart and Chrissie couldn't speak to her for a while after that, or meet her eye, and all the gratitude they felt for Sunshine's safe return didn't outweigh the treachery of Nancy's defence of the indefensible.

Back at the house, Chrissie proposed a visit to the hospital to see her mum and dad, which would be the first time since her stroke that Diana had seen Sunshine. Nancy could stay put, and Carly could try and get hold of Nina, a very necessary task, which neither Chrissie nor Stu had yet done, or – it had to be said – wanted to do. Just as they had yet to hear Nancy's story, so they had yet to fully hear Nina's, whose covert intervention had briefly brought their world crashing down. Chrissie said she couldn't deal with that, not just now; just now she only wanted normality, and each other. So Carly said, sure, of course, she'd try Nina, and Chrissie sent four short, exultant texts to Sol, Julia, Rocco and Kim, all of whom sent back love and joy so swiftly it was as if they'd been staring at their phones ever since Sunshine vanished. And then the three of them donned coats again and prepared to walk up to the hospital, Chrissie and Stu constantly, quietly, celebrating the end of the nightmare, this happy conclusion, their child chatting and hopping about between them, as apparently buoyant and carefree as if she'd merely been on an overnight playdate with a friend.

She really hadn't been gone long, by the ordinary tally of

one hour followed by another; but how the time had warped and slowed when she was missing, and how agonising was each second before they had her back. They knew they needed a proper conversation with Nancy – the dark horse, their saviour with a foot in each camp – but they just didn't want it yet. They wanted mundanity, they wanted family life, they wanted to shake off the taint of oddness that Nancy now seemed to carry with her. She'd lived on a commune run by Samuel de Lyon, who sounded like a card-carrying nutcase, and although she'd had the sense to leave, she was still somehow in thrall to him, or to Kristen, perhaps; they couldn't quite say. Anyway, there'd be time enough the next day for a full and frank exchange of views with Nancy, because they'd already agreed she should stay the night with them, although they hoped she'd try her level best to be invisible.

On the doorstep, before they left for the hospital, Carly murmured discreetly that Nancy seemed very anxious not to intrude on their happiness, and was conscious, always, of their unasked questions. Stu said, 'Oh, well, tell her to chill, we've postponed the interrogation until morning,' which had made Chrissie laugh and Carly wince, so Chrissie had given her a heartfelt hug, and said, 'You're peace, love and understanding, in human form, Carly Woodall, and we're lucky to have you.'

'Oh, honey,' Carly had said, beaming, 'I'm the lucky one.' She watched them leave, linked by their hands in a line of three, and as they walked away from the house, her loving aura seemed to light up the dark path.

When Doug saw them approaching down the long, gleaming corridor, he smiled fully, for the first time in three long days.

'Sunny Sunshine,' he said, and clapped his hands together in one resounding celebration. 'My bobby-dazzler.'

She trotted up to him and tilted her face for a kiss, 'Hello,

Grandad,' she said. He folded himself in two to reach her, kissed her cheek, ruffled her hair, cupped her chin in one big hand. 'You're a sight for sore eyes,' he said.

'Is the bubbles here?' she asked. 'The big bubbles?'

'Oh, I wish they were,' he said. 'But that's a game we play in the garden, back at the house.'

She absorbed and accepted this news, then said, 'Is mine grandma here?' and Doug said yes, she was, just through that door, there. He pointed at it, and Stuart said, 'Come on, Sunny, let's go see her,' and Doug watched them go, then looked sharply at his daughter.

'What happened?' he asked. 'Did you have a row yesterday, you and Stuart? He was white as a sheet, looked like he'd been through a mangle as well.'

'No, no, we're fine.'

He clapped his hand against his heart. 'Oh, that's good,' he said. 'I'd braced myself for bad news.'

'Oh, sorry, poor you, you've got enough on your plate without worrying about me and Stu.'

'To be honest,' he said, 'I thought divorce might be on the cards.'

She laughed outright. 'Well, that's a leap,' she said.

'Not for me, it's not,' he said, with a suffering expression. 'Divorce is in the air up here in the stroke unit.'

'Never,' Chrissie said. 'You know full well you're a marriage lifer; no parole, no pardon.' She said this to amuse him, and at any other time in their history he would have chuckled at the analogy, but he just looked glum and said, 'If she has to write me a message, it's always in block capitals.'

'So?'

'It's like being shouted at,' he said. 'She does it so I'll know she's still mad at me.'

'And why is she still mad at you? What have you done?'

For a second or two he looked into his daughter's face with a sort of longing, as if he meant to unburden himself, but then his expression shifted gear, she saw the very moment it changed, and when he spoke he was cheerfully dismissive. 'Oh, you know your mother,' he said. 'She's an Olympian when it comes to being furious. Anyway, never mind that, there was definitely something up with Stuart yesterday, so if he thinks he fooled me, he didn't.'

'Ah, there's so much happened you don't know about, I'll tell you another time, but honestly, we've sorted it out. There's nothing to worry about now.'

He said, 'If that lad ever hurts you, he'll have me to deal with.'

'Dad!' she said, laughing. 'Don't say that. You know Stuart, he's my biggest fan.'

'No, he's not,' Doug said, entirely serious now. 'I'm your biggest fan, because you are my pride and joy; you know that, don't you?'

She nodded. 'I do.'

'You've been my shining light. *Our* shining light.'

'OK,' she said, wondering now if he was trying to say something else altogether.

'And bringing Sunshine into our lives . . . well, it means more than you know.'

Chrissie said, 'What do you mean, Dad?'

He shook his head. 'Just what I say,' then he pressed his palms against her cheeks, as he used to do when she was little, squashing her mouth into a pucker, and kissing it. 'My cherub,' he said. 'Thank the good lord for you.'

He released her, and she laughed. 'You haven't done that for years.'

'Only because you wouldn't let me, after you turned fourteen. *Stop it, Daa-aad,* you used to say.'

Again she laughed. 'Look, I'd better go and see Mum.'

He stepped aside. 'Be my guest.'

With uninhibited compassion, Sunshine had briefly studied Diana's face with puzzled concern, before climbing up onto the bed and laying one small hand on her grandmother's cheek, where the palsy had disfigured it. She said, 'Ouch,' and Diana shook her head to indicate that no, it didn't hurt, but she still wouldn't speak, not even for Sunny. She'd tried, when she was alone in the room, but the sound she made disgusted her, and although her consultant had told her she'd make progress in leaps and bounds if she would just forge on with it, and co-operate in speech therapy sessions, Diana just felt safer, and more herself, in silence. She knew she had the psychological constitution to never speak again, if necessary.

However, Sunny had at least put some light back into her eyes, because as soon as the child realised her grandma was now oddly silent, she simply adapted to this new circumstance, and fell silent herself, communicating all she wanted to say through mime. And what she wanted to say was, please give me your necklace. She put her hands to her throat and fixed her gaze on Diana's pearls, and with her good hand, Diana slipped the long loop over her head and bestowed them on Sunshine, who beamed at her, coaxing a lopsided smile from her grandma in return. Then Diana turned to Stu and on her notepad wrote, *She's a tonic. You look a lot better than you did yesterday.* He nodded and said, 'All good now, and you – you look very fine this evening, Diana; you look like a resting movie star.' She reached again for the pen and wrote, *And you look very fine too, I do like that stubble,* which made him laugh.

This was the scene Chrissie took in when she entered the room; a smiling trio, a child garlanded with pearls, an atmosphere light with amusement. Why, then, she wondered, did it alter so swiftly when she and Doug walked in? Why, when she leaned in to kiss her mother, did Diana seem to suffer the attention rather than enjoy it? If Diana knew what she'd endured these past two days . . . but nothing could be said of that now, not yet, perhaps not ever. Instead she said, 'How are you, Mum? Sorry I couldn't come yesterday.'

Diana took up her pen. *What were you and your dad discussing?* she wrote, then shoved it towards Chrissie, who had to tilt her head to read it.

'Oh, y'know, this and that, me being the light of his life, the usual sort of stuff.' She said this with a smile, determined to show her mother that if she thought for a moment that she, Chrissie, was unhappy, then she was dead wrong.

Diana didn't return the smile. *I don't believe you,* she wrote.

Puzzled, Chrissie looked at Doug, who was looking at Diana. 'Don't do this, love,' he said to his wife. She completely ignored him, gave him not even a glance, and wrote, *You were talking about Nina.*

'Nina?' Chrissie said. 'Why would we be talking about Nina?'

'Give me strength,' Doug said, and he left the room.

Sunny, understanding none of what was being said but hearing the name of a person she very much liked, said brightly, 'Nina is here?'

'No, darling,' Chrissie said to her, and was briefly diverted from the strange tension by a firework burst of inner joy. Look at my child, she thought; look at my child, her bright eyes, her angel mouth.

Sunshine whispered, 'Mummy?'

'Yes, sweetheart?'

'What is Grandma's face doing?'

Chrissie glanced at Diana, who was writing again. 'It's slipped,' Chrissie said. 'But it'll get better.'

Stuart said, 'I think it's improved already.'

They all knew it hadn't, it was far too soon, but because this was Stu, Diana took his comment graciously and silently mouthed *Thank you*, then she showed Chrissie what she'd written. *Get your father out of the hospital and home.*

'I've tried,' Chrissie said. 'He seems to have taken root.'

Tell him he's hampering my recovery.

'Oh, Mum, is he though?' Chrissie said, imagining the hurt she'd cause her dad with those words.

Diana wrote, *Yes!* and her eyes flashed with determination. *Tell him to go home and ring Nina and get her up here.*

Chrissie stared at the words on the paper. Stu reached out and took the pad from her, to read them too. Both of them looked at Diana, and she nodded, seized the pad, and wrote, *Or YOU ring her, Christine! You're so damn close, why isn't she here already? When did Nina ever stay away from a family drama? This is her speciality, isn't it?*

She was scribbling as furiously as her malady would allow, wielding the pen like a weapon. She jabbed the dot at the base of the final question mark so savagely that she made a hole in the notepaper.

'Mum,' Chrissie said, carefully, 'are you angry with me, Dad or Nina?'

Diana positioned the pad, and seemed poised with the pen again, but then gave a kind of exasperated cry and tossed it away, so that it flew onto the floor behind the bedside table.

Sunny shot her a look, half admonishment, half admiration, and immediately slid off the bed to retrieve it. Chrissie and Stuart were stunned into silence and Diana was simply glaring at the wall ahead of her, but Sunshine squatted down and reached between the cabinet and the bed, huffing and puffing with the effort of reaching the pen, then having retrieved it, stood up and placed it gently within Diana's reach again.

She said, 'There, Grandma,' and Diana, whose eyes were always soft when she looked at Sunshine, delicately kissed the fingertips of her good hand and fluttered them in the child's direction. Sunny smiled and blinked in surprise, as if she felt the kisses land. Then Diana lay back against her pillows, closed her eyes, and flapped the same hand at the door, indicating it was time for everyone to leave.

24

They woke early the next day and crept from the bed, leaving Sunshine in her nest at the centre, curled on her side, damp thumb resting lightly on her rosy bottom lip, her hair in whorls about her face. After a late, late night and a very chatty episode at sunrise, she was now plunged deeply into sleep again, soused in it, as only a small child can be. She was hard to leave, but Nancy was waiting for them downstairs in the living room, ready to explain herself.

She looked terrible, haggard and pallid, as though she hadn't slept for days, and she offered them her newly supplicating smile, which irritated Stuart no end, so that he snapped at her, said, 'OK, Nancy, let's have it,' meaning, the postponed conversation, but she bent down and picked up a sheaf of papers from the floor. They were loosely bound by string threaded through holes that she'd stabbed out with scissors in the left margin, and the top sheet bore her large, loopy cursive, in which she'd written, *The Story of Sunshine Stevenson*.

'Yes, erm, now I look at that again, it seems flippant,' Nancy said, flicking her eyes over the title page, 'and I'm sorry about that because, well, I have the deepest respect for you. I can't even imagine the pain you've been through, and I'd give anything for this never to have happened.' She sounded as if she was reading from an autocue, although her eyebrows were knitted together in sorrow and her grey eyes were regretful.

They all three stared at the homespun document in her hand, then Stu said, 'What is it?'

Nancy glanced at him a little nervously. 'It's everything you don't know about Sunshine's past. I wrote it in the night, as much for myself as for you.'

'This is stuff you've just discovered, or that you've always known?' Stu asked.

'Always known,' she said. 'I thought you could read it, before we talk? I thought, this might be the best way of getting the story down with some clarity, and, you know, the correct chronology.'

He gestured at the papers. 'So explain to us why we weren't told this story from the start?'

Nancy, in spite of the shadows under her eyes and the unbrushed thicket of her hair, had been trying for an air of professionalism in her voice and manner, but now she gave it up and seemed to deflate in front of them. She was the only one in the room who was sitting down; she'd occupied the centre of the sofa, and neither of them felt friendly enough to join her on it, but Chrissie sat down too now, across the room from Nancy but facing her, on Doug's favourite leather armchair, which made her think about her dad for a moment, and all the things he didn't know. She looked at Nancy's hangdog face while Stu thrust his hands in his pockets and paced the room, too wound up to be still, his famous capacity for patient calm entirely shredded by the worst twenty-four hours of their lives. Nancy had begun an explanation, and Chrissie only wished she would stop. All she wanted was peace and quiet and an ordinary day. No; all she wanted was to go back upstairs and crawl under the covers with Sunny. The sweet, salty smell of her; the warmth, like a new-baked bun.

'. . . and I know it was dreadful in retrospect,' Nancy was saying, as Chrissie reluctantly tuned back in. 'I know I should have told you everything, but I was acting on the fervent request of someone who mattered very much to me.'

'What?' Chrissie asked, suddenly alert. 'Who?'

Nancy turned her sad and sorry eyes upon her. 'Her biological mother,' she said, and Chrissie felt an almost physical blow, a sucker punch of shock and betrayal and dismay. She believed she could literally feel the process of her heart hardening further against Nancy, this trusted young woman, who couldn't be trusted. Of course, they all knew about the young and lovely birth mother, and the image of her had set up camp in Chrissie's conscious mind so that every day, one way or another, Chrissie thought about her; and – she'd like to know – which adoptive mother *wouldn't* do that? Who wouldn't compulsively think (and think and think) about a woman of ethereal beauty who stared out from a photograph with such sad solemnity? Who wouldn't compulsively think (and think and think) about a woman with the style and vision to name a child Sunshine, as if to bestow upon her a bright and brilliant future? But what Chrissie had *not* known, was that Nancy Maitland – *their* Nancy Maitland – knew exactly who that woman was and, more than that, she'd been dancing to her tune.

Chrissie stared at Nancy. 'Sunshine's biological mother matters very much to you, and at her request, you kept her story from us?'

Nancy swallowed hard, and nodded. 'She asked me to find the right family for her child, without ever revealing anything about her background.'

'Did you tell the police that?' Stu asked.

'Yes, of course I did,' Nancy said, with sudden fierce energy. 'And I also told them Asha had nothing at all to do with what happened to Sunshine.' Her face was so expressive, thought Chrissie – the kind that couldn't help showcasing her emotions, and now they were coming thick and fast, fighting for precedence; sorrow, shame, regret, alarm, indignation, they each had their moment, then faded to make way for the next. 'She hated her father, he was the reason she finally left. She didn't want Sunshine being controlled by him in the way he'd controlled her and her sister. She would never, ever have colluded in this. They have no contact, she's lost to them.' Abruptly, she stopped, worn out by her vehemence.

'Do you know where she is?' Chrissie asked.

Nancy shook her head, then hung it. 'No, but she's not in the country. She's with people who used to live on the commune. They took her in when she came to London; they have, y'know, money, a place abroad somewhere . . .' she tailed off momentarily, then added, 'I believe I've served my purpose, I'm of no further use to her.'

This was very interesting, Chrissie thought, and Nancy's expression was interesting too; she looked lost and rather broken. But Chrissie's heart had turned against her, and all she said was, 'Why did Asha make you lie to us?'

'She didn't make me do anything. She asked me for help, and I agreed. She wanted to sort of cauterise the past. She wanted no link between Sunshine and the de Lyons.'

'And look how that worked out,' Stuart said.

'And I'm so sorry for that. But nothing bad happened to her while she was away from you. Sunny was with her close relatives who – misguidedly – thought she'd be better off with them.'

Stu gave a short, bitter laugh. 'Do *not* ask us to be grateful.'

'No,' Nancy said. 'No, I don't expect you to be grateful, but they gave her back, very willingly. They understood they were out of their depth, that they'd acted . . . dramatically, and Sunshine was—' she faltered, searching for the word, and Stuart and Chrissie watched her, waiting to hear what Sunshine 'was' in that strange house, with those strange relatives.

'Well, Kristen told me that Sunshine was a little confused, but not unhappy, and that she talked a lot about you two and about her bedroom, which they hadn't expected. They thought she'd be, I don't know, relieved to be back where she was born, but instead she wouldn't take her coat and hat off, and she told them all about you, and about Juno and a party with a cake like a sun. From what I gather she said just about as much as she had words for, and then she sang for them.'

Chrissie had her face in her hands, but at this detail, she couldn't help smiling, and when she looked back up at Stu, he was smiling too. They could both imagine that scene, for sure. 'Johnny B. Goode' at full Sunshine volume, and an old man and his daughter, wondering what on earth they'd done. But then the smile fell away and Chrissie said, 'But God, she spent a night with them.'

Nancy said, 'She did, in her hat and coat. She wouldn't let Kristen remove them. She couldn't have been clearer that she wasn't intending to stay.'

'I can't bear to think of them putting her to bed in a strange old house—'

'But she slept in a room she'd slept in before, not that I'm trying to—'

'But how dare they?' Chrissie said quietly. 'How dare they just steal her from us?'

Nancy stood up. 'Please, I'm exhausted. Will you just read what I've written?' There was a quavering edge of desperation in her voice, and if Chrissie and Stu were feeling a little better, Nancy was looking and sounding a little worse. She dragged a hand through her unruly hair and chewed her bottom lip, waiting for permission to leave. Her night's work hung limply in her other hand.

'Well, I suppose we could,' Chrissie said, glancing at it doubtfully. 'As long as it's the truth,' and Nancy was pierced. 'Chrissie,' she said, 'I—'

'It's just, I think Stu and I are both now feeling we've been pawns in some weird game. We've no idea who we can trust any more.'

'Me,' Nancy said, ardently knocking with a knuckle at her breastbone. 'You can trust *me*, Chrissie,' but this was absurd, even she seemed to see that, in the way her eyes slid from theirs, and her hand dropped away, to hang by her side. Stu said, 'Oh, Nancy, we live in hope, but there's a way to go yet.'

'How did you know your grand scheme had all started to go wrong?' Chrissie asked. She was finding it impossible to speak to her kindly; but then, she thought, why worry, why bother?

Nancy sighed miserably. 'It's all in here,' she said, lifting her manuscript, flapping it disconsolately, 'but what happened was, I got a call from Kristen on Saturday, the first time we've spoken since I left Buckenhurst. She was hostile – very – but her success with Nina made her rather immoderate, rather too eager to crow. She told me that Asha and I weren't as clever as we'd thought, and she told me about Nina's visit, and their arrangement which by then had been cancelled by Nina, but it was plain from Kristen's tone that she wasn't remotely interested either in Nina, or in meeting you two, and I knew her objectives had probably been only to thwart her sister and reclaim Sunshine. It was all deeply unsettling, and that's why I rang you, that very evening. I needed to know where you were, and that you were safe.'

'But then you didn't come,' Chrissie said. 'We talked, you asked where I was, you took the address – but you didn't alert me, you didn't come, and this Kristen character *did*, and thanks to Nina's information and your inaction, she was able to take our Sunny.' She didn't sound angry, only mystified, and Nancy said, 'I know, but I didn't realise – and never would have thought – that Kristen had the courage to drive all this way alone, and try her luck. Truly, she's never been known to leave the grounds of Buckenhurst, and to be honest, I was pretty reassured after we spoke, Chrissie.'

'Big mistake,' Stuart said. 'Massive error.'

'Yes,' Nancy said. 'Another one.'

'So how come you knew they'd taken her?'

'I didn't. I went down by train first thing Monday morning, fully believing I could manage this escalating situation, nip it all in the bud, and there was Sunshine, sitting on a settle in the entrance hall of Buckenhurst Court, in her hat and coat, as if she was waiting for a lift home.'

Chrissie, hearing this, felt acute distress and soaring joy, at one and the same time and found that she couldn't immediately respond, couldn't speak, it was all too much to process; but Stuart had plenty to say. He was still on his feet, it seemed to be the only way he could contain his emotions, and he stalked to the window, then back towards Nancy, and said, 'Ah, for God's sake, do you have any concept of how *weird* all this sounds? How screwed up it is, how dysfunctional? This is our life, Nancy, and me and Chrissie and Sunshine – we don't like being part of your crazy melodrama.'

'I don't like being part of my crazy melodrama either,' Nancy said, a little hotly. 'You think I'd choose this? I wouldn't, this isn't who I am. Yesterday, when I stood on the pavement with Sunshine, my heart sank because I knew how it would

look, y'know? Kind of "Ta da!" The big reveal. And I felt sorry
for that because, honestly, I just wanted to bring her back where
she's meant to be, without fuss or drama.'

'Who drove you here? And why didn't you call us on the way?'

'Rob Whittaker,' Nancy said. 'And my phone's on the blink,
the battery dies if I so much as look at the screen, and Rob
doesn't use a mobile phone, and I guess we could have stopped
to find a phone box, but look, we didn't, we didn't call anyone,
our imperative was to get Sunshine back to you as swiftly as
possible, so he just drove.' Again she raised her sheaf of papers,
waved them like a flag of surrender. 'It's all in here,' she said,
without hope, and Stu said, 'Who the hell's Rob Whittaker?
He's not tied up in all that commune shit, I hope?'

'No! Gosh, no,' Nancy said. She looked thoroughly intimidated. 'He's a friend of Nina's, a man from—'

'A friend of *Nina's*,' Chrissie said, finding her voice. 'What
friend?'

'He runs the pub in Littlecliffe— I know, I know,' she said,
holding up her palms in bewilderment. 'He appeared at the big
house in his truck, like magic. Nina called him yesterday, as
soon as she knew what had happened. She told him Sunny had
been taken, and he'd immediately driven up to the house to
look for her, and he found me, and I had Sunshine, and he drove
us here. To be honest, I'd have been at a bit of a loss about how
to get to you but he arrived like Sir Galahad in his big Toyota.'

'He drove all the way up here from Kent?'

She nodded. 'Non-stop, he was terribly kind.'

'And he's Nina's friend?'

'Robin Whittaker. She hasn't known him long, only since
she went down there. I know him vaguely from when I lived
there; he's a solid citizen, I promise you. I knew we were safe
with him. Anyway, Nina stayed a night in his pub, and they

obviously hit it off. She called him after you rang her, Stu, to tell her Sunny was gone. She called him from London, and he went at once to find Sunshine.'

'Where is he now?' Chrissie asked.

'Oh, long gone. He saw us to the house, then he drove away.'

Gone. Of course he was. But still, how Chrissie wished she could step outside and thank him. She thought about Nina, her secrecy, her enquiries, her disastrous indiscretions, and now this man, this friend, Sir Galahad, driving Sunshine home to them. She said, 'I used to think Nina would never keep anything from me, then she turns into this bungling private eye, with secrets galore.'

Nancy continued with her insights. 'She got carried away, I'd say, and befriended Kristen too quickly. She arranged to travel to Barnsley with Kristen, to introduce the two of you, but she – well, she clearly ended up revealing where you were, not the actual address, but the neighbourhood, and Rob told me Nina had second thoughts, he'd driven her up there to cancel her plan with Kristen the morning after she made it. Apparently Kristen seemed to understand completely, and of course, Nina made the mistake of trusting her.'

'Made the mistake of not telling us what she'd done, too,' Chrissie said, bitterly. 'Keeping us in the dark, just like you did.'

Nancy conceded the point with a short silence, then said, 'So Kristen came to Barnsley anyway, wasting absolutely no time, and I suppose she'd have stayed as long as it took, but she was lucky. A fine autumnal Sunday. A park with a children's playground. Enough information from Nina to make it all too possible.'

Stu looked murderous; Chrissie simply hung her head and stared at the patterns on the carpet between her feet. Nancy said, 'I do think Sunny must have experienced some kind of recognition. She didn't cry out in alarm when Kristen took her, did she? I'm sure that's because Kristen had known Sunny since birth, knew her for two years, lived in close contact with her, closer, perhaps, than Asha, who was melancholy and withdrawn. And if Sunny couldn't quite place Kristen, she would – I think – have sensed that she was familiar, and kind.'

'Right, so that's Kristen's story, and you're sticking to it?' Stuart said.

'It's what I know to be true,' Nancy said. 'Based on what I assumed, and what Kristen confirmed.'

'Stop making allowances for her,' Stuart said. 'She abducted our child,' and Nancy said, 'Oh, yes, well,' and Chrissie said nothing at all, but privately she took a grain of comfort in what Nancy had told them, a comfort in believing that, at the point in the story when Kristen had scooped up Sunshine and carried her off, the child hadn't been afraid. And yet, to pick her up and carry her away . . . for Sunshine to make not a sound in protest, or surprise, or even delight . . . how could that have been accomplished? And that note in Juno's pocket – how, and when had the woman managed that? It was sleight of hand, for sure; dark magic. That, or Stuart hadn't been as vigilant as he'd said, had unwittingly created an opportunity, had looked at a text message, had turned his back for longer than he realised – or longer than he was letting on. Chrissie found she couldn't meet his eyes at the moment, because she knew there would be this between them forever; that he'd turned away from their daughter for long enough for Kristen de Lyon to seize her chance. But then, there was also this: that every new day would be another day further from that day.

Nancy was still on a downward spiral, apparently trying to prove how much she disliked Kristen, without undermining her theory that Sunny would have gone happily into her arms. 'See, she's manipulative,' she said, 'Charming, but manipulative.'

'Like Asha, then,' Stu said.

'No, no, Asha's more guileless. Asha's like a demanding child. Kristen gets her way by subterfuge; look how she fooled Nina.'

'Look how you fooled us,' Chrissie said, and Nancy flushed. 'It's human nature,' Chrissie went on, 'to put your faith in the person you believe can help you get what you want. Did you actually go to India, Nancy, or was that a lie too?' and Nancy, cringing now under the weight of her ruined reputation, said, 'Yes, I did, I went to Jaipur. I really did have a job with a children's charity, but I was unhappy there, too far from . . . so I came back to England after only two months, I wish I'd stayed, in a way. No, I *should* have stayed, to prove to myself that I'm . . .' She stopped, and seemed to think again.

'You're what?' Stu said.

'Oh, nothing, never mind.'

'Prove you're what? You've forfeited the right to silence, Nancy.'

She turned and glared at him, and she might have been angry or she might have been distraught. 'Prove that I'm not useless,' she said. 'Prove that I can make a difference. Prove that Asha de Lyon isn't the only person that can give meaning to my life. Prove that somebody, somewhere, likes me, needs me, maybe even loves me, for myself, and not what I can do for them.'

There followed a short, intense silence. Nancy's words seemed to be a plea for clemency, but Chrissie could see Stuart was resolutely angry, his mouth still set in a hard, straight line.

'Look,' Nancy said at last, on a long sigh, 'this isn't about me; it's about you two and Sunshine, and I left you exposed to harm, for which I'll always be desperately sorry.'

Stuart said, 'Not the mastermind you thought you were.'

She stared at him bleakly, then thrust the pages into his hand. 'It's all in there,' she said, and she left them.

When she was gone, Stuart finally sat down on the sofa vacated by Nancy. He looked across the room at Chrissie and said, 'Whaddya think? Shall we read her story?'

Chrissie stood, and came over to him so that she was standing before him, looking down at him looking up at her.

'I guess so. Speed read it, maybe. I don't care to know much more about Nancy's broken heart, or Asha's powers.'

For a short while they just smiled at each other sadly, like two war-torn compatriots, bloody but unbowed. Then Chrissie said, 'After this – I mean, as soon as possible – I want to go home.'

'After this,' he said, 'wherever you want to go, I want to go too. I mean that, Chrissie. Anywhere.'

She sat down beside him, and with one hand, he turned her face towards his and tilted her chin, brought her close, kissed her mouth, her cheek, her temples, her eyes, her mouth again, then he drew away.

'OK,' he said, 'settle down, here comes the story of Sunshine Stevenson.'

He began to read out loud, and it was clear from the start that Nancy had given full throttle to her storytelling voice. She'd written in an elaborate, florid style that, almost immediately, they knew they couldn't really be bothered with. *Asha's baby was named Athena by Samuel de Lyon, who had deplored his daughter's pregnancy but adored the baby girl brought forth by it* – 'Oh, good God,' Chrissie said. 'Adored, deplored, brought forth; who does she think she is?'

Stu said, 'Listen to the next bit. *Asha de Lyon was the*

loveliest, kindest, most beautiful, least worldly girl I've ever known. Privately, she named her baby Sunshine, and no one knew that but me.'

'She was in love with her!'

This was Carly, standing at the living-room door with Sunshine on her hip. 'Makes perfect sense,' she added. 'Was it unrequited?'

Sunny reached her arms out to Chrissie, stretching to the tips of her little fingers, irresistible. She got up and took her, and said, 'Hey, you.'

'It was,' Stu said. 'That's very prescient of you, Mom.'

Carly shrugged. 'She has lonely eyes,' she said. 'Lovelorn. Come, little Sunshine, let's go get some breakfast and leave Mommy and Daddy to it,' but the child pouted and clung a little harder to Chrissie, who didn't mind this at all.

'Let's all go,' Chrissie said. 'We can get the gist of this without closeting ourselves in here.'

'I's hungry, Mummy,' Sunshine said, and Chrissie said, 'I's hungry too, my darling,' and Carly said, 'Right, French toast and coffee, plus a cup of milk for my smallest customer.'

They filed through the house to the room known as Diana's kitchen – where she liked to cook, but rarely ate – and the smell of butter melting in the cast-iron frying pan soon began to weave its magic, and nothing seemed quite so unsettling as it had before. Carly engaged Sunshine as her assistant, got her help whisking eggs and milk and cinnamon, and dunking slices of bread. This resulted in a good deal of mess, but also meant that she wasn't listening to her daddy, who anyway précised Nancy's lyricism without ever mentioning Sunshine's name. He scanned the first page, told them Asha and Kristen had spent their early childhood among lots of other children on an ashram in India. Only Samuel knew who their mother was, Nancy wrote. Until

357

the ages of eight and nine, the girls were raised communally, and when they left for England, it was with Samuel alone.

Stu said, 'OK, what next, blah blah blah, OK, so it looks like Samuel brought them back to Buckenhurst, and started to ruin a perfectly good commune. Things got weird, people started to leave, he brought the kids out of the village school and it says he started "blurring" family ties, so all females were sisters and all males were brothers—'

'That sounds very strange,' Carly said, glancing round from the stove. 'A little unwholesome?'

'Oh, but,' Chrissie said, sitting up straighter. 'Sisters? Maybe there are no actual siblings then? Just so-called?'

'Is anyone else worried about that blurring of family ties,' Carly said. 'Or is it just me?'

The three of them pondered this for a moment; Sunny's infancy in a parallel universe, where all was not as it seemed. 'I think we need Nancy down here,' Chrissie said, and she went out of the room and along to the foot of the stairs and called up to her. Nancy was hiding in Doug's study, where an inflatable bed had been placed last night, and now she appeared at the top of the stairs, looking pale and anxious.

'Two things,' Chrissie said, 'did the Buckenhurst commune condone incest?'

Nancy put a hand to her mouth.

'Blurring of family ties,' Chrissie said, 'might suggest a free-for-all.'

'In my experience,' Nancy said, carefully, 'there was no incest.'

'But?'

'But, in all honesty, I suppose it wasn't out of the question,' Nancy said, very softly.

'Right. Is that why Asha wanted out?'

Nancy considered this, for a moment. 'Not specifically,' she said. 'But she was worried about her father's interest in Athena, and his influence on her as she grew up. It's all—'

'—written down, yeah, I'm sure we'll get to it. Also, does Sunny have any siblings?'

Nancy looked confused. 'No,' she said.

'Well, that's great,' Chrissie said. 'That's a relief, actually. She's twice asked us if we know where her sisters are.'

'Right, well, she was just using the vocabulary of the commune,' Nancy said. 'Any memories of other girls, other women, would have been of "sisters".'

'Including Asha?'

'Yes, including her.' She spoke rather flatly, as if she was giving evidence in court to a prosecuting counsel. 'Samuel didn't condone ownership of children. No traditional parental relationships at Buckenhurst, although I should imagine he's grateful enough for Kristen nowadays.'

Chrissie sighed. 'Look, why don't you come downstairs? We feel a bit as though we're marking your homework down here.'

Nancy said, 'I don't want to be in the way.'

'Oh, give over,' Chrissie said, and Nancy began to descend. So strange, thought Chrissie as she watched her, to have Nancy Maitland in her childhood home. Two worlds colliding, which never should have met. Nancy was the sort of considerate person who left her shoes at the door when she came into a house, which served, now, to draw attention to her socks, knitted from khaki-coloured wool and slumping defeatedly in folds around her ankles. Chrissie was only glad that Diana wasn't here to see them. When she reached the bottom Chrissie said, 'You're going to have to cheer up, Nancy. This isn't a trial, y'know.'

Nancy said, 'I'm sorry. I just feel I've let you down so badly.'

'Well, and you have,' Chrissie said, 'but I think it's better if you just face the music.'

Nancy looked wretchedly unsure of herself.

'Come on,' Chrissie said. 'No one in there bites.'

But Nancy said no. She said she didn't want to hear her own words read back at her. She said she was afraid of their reaction, by the time they got to the end. She sat on the bottom step and put her face in her hands.

'Please,' she said, through her fingers, 'just get through it without me.'

25

In the kitchen, Sunshine was already eating, sitting on her small tower of cushions, on a chair that was pushed right up against the table to hold her in place, so she could put all her energy into enjoying the food. Her eyes were half closed in a maple syrup-induced trance. Did any other small child relish the taste of her food as Sunny did, Chrissie wondered? She was a super-taster, she told Stu, she'd be a chef or a sommelier, and Stu said, 'You mean if her band doesn't work out?' He'd slotted a CD into the little black machine on the worktop that Chrissie had bought her parents two Christmases ago, but that they hadn't asked for, hadn't wanted, and hadn't worked out how to use. The only CDs that were stacked next to the unit were by The Lineman, so Chrissie walked back into the room to hear herself singing, which was disorientating, like walking into a party and finding you're already there. It was 'Wander Lust', a track from their debut album, *Swan Song* (how clever they thought they were, back then) and it was the only song they'd ever recorded with no guitars or keyboard, just Chrissie's voice and Rocco's drums. 'Fucking-A, man!' their first manager had said when he'd heard it. 'Bring the guitars in; you'll sound like Green Day,' so they'd sacked him.

The song was about the dubious pleasures of youth: a dark club, a dance floor, a stranger's mouth. Odd, hearing it now, in this context. Stu seemed hardly aware of it; he was poring over Nancy's story, and at first he didn't notice she'd come back into the room. When he did, he said, 'Oh, hey – siblings or no siblings?' and Chrissie said, 'No siblings, it was just the language of the commune.' She sat down next to him. 'Sisters were not sisters, necessarily, just other girls. I did coax Nancy down the stairs, but she'll come no further. I think she's gone back up now. Maybe we should take her some toast.' Then she tuned back into 'Wander Lust', the fifteen soaring seconds of the middle eight, and said, 'I can't say this about the whole album, but I'd not change a single thing about this track.'

Stu said, 'It's sheer class; you gave Rocco his finest five minutes.'

'Oh God,' she said, laughing again, 'don't tell Kim that.' She let the track play out, and her expression was reflective, then she said, 'Stu, we should do something like this again, me and Rocco.'

He had to turn away from her to hide the magnitude of his relief. But it wasn't lost on her; she felt it herself.

'Right,' Stu said, 'where were we?'

Carly took Nancy two slices of French toast and a mug of peppermint tea, then she and Sunshine went away to play so that Chrissie and Stuart had the kitchen to themselves, with four pages of Nancy's confessional still to be dealt with. Stu scanned the testimony, and Chrissie watched him and waited, then he said, 'Oh, hey, listen to this: ". . . but Samuel de Lyon's authority was seriously challenged when his younger daughter fell in love, not with a suitably spiritual young 'brother' of her father's choosing, but with a boy whose charms belonged so completely to the outside world that Asha found them uniquely enchanting."'

'Oh my!' Chrissie said. 'What's his name?'

Stu scanned the sentences. 'Declan,' he said. 'Good name, Oh, man, listen – "he walked into Asha's world and altered everything. He played guitar, all sorts of songs she'd never heard of—"'

He stopped, looked at Chrissie with patent delight, and she laughed because he was so easily pleased. 'Perfect,' she said, humouring him. 'A guitar-playing boy, just what this story needed. Go on.'

'—"He was just an ordinary young man with a guitar and a football, but Asha didn't know anyone else like him. Samuel didn't like him at all, mostly because Declan had no special respect for him or his theories, and if Asha's father had known how intimate the boy was with his daughter, he'd have been promptly thrown out. But Asha and Declan kept their love affair secret from everyone but me. That is, Asha confided in me; Declan just smiled to himself and strummed his guitar. He came from the west coast of Ireland, he said, and Asha told me that all he wanted was to take her there with him. I don't know how serious he was, but he did seem to really love her, and for all the same reasons I loved her. Her innocence. Her goodness. Her beautiful smile. Her eyes."'

'Oh God, she's besotted,' Chrissie said. 'All tied up in Asha's charms.'

'Listen, though,' Stuart said. ' "He loved the Indian songs she liked to sing, the Hindi folk songs she'd learned as a child on the ashram . . . "'

Stu stopped again, and Chrissie said, 'What is it?' and he said it might be nothing but it made him think of the way Sunshine sang, when she'd first claimed Silky, on the day they opened the memory bag; the stream of meandering words they hadn't understood. Were they fragments of an early memory, a song learned in the arms of her birth mother? This image gave Chrissie a pang of something like jealousy, against which she was powerless but of which she was immediately ashamed.

'She only did that once,' Stu said. 'Didn't she? Just that once, when she first came to us?'

Chrissie didn't answer, and Stu saw the shift in her expression, saw her gaze turning inwards, and said, 'You OK? This is all just context, remember – it's nothing to worry about,' and she nodded, smiled, but didn't speak, because her feelings as this narrative unfurled were becoming too complex to articulate; jealousy, sorrow, love, anxiety, dread and – thank god for the positives – a modicum of pleasure and satisfaction, as the fog over Sunshine's past began to clear. But this story was disturbing as well as enlightening, she thought. A self-appointed guru, an unworldly girl, a boy so ordinary that he seemed special. In truth, she wanted it to be over, but anyway she said, 'Go on. What else?'

'Well, Declan couldn't stand Samuel, and he left. She didn't go with him – too scared – then she turned out to be pregnant. All hell broke loose. Her father was raging, and her sister was no support at all, but then—'

'Sunny was born, and he changed?'

' "Athena was born",' Stuart read, ' "and he changed." '

'She is *so* not an Athena.'

'God, this guy was a case. "Suddenly this baby girl was the embodiment of all her grandfather's hopes and dreams. Declan was edited out of her history, as if here was a second virgin birth, and Asha was once more in great favour, which she now found as alarming as his previous hostility. There was a Naming Day ceremony, such a performance, like the coronation of a fairy queen. Samuel took a photograph of them on that day. I think it's the only one in existence. The baby was about six months old, and Asha was nearly eighteen. She wore a cotton dress instead of a sari, just a simple frock someone had left behind, and it was the beginning of her separation from his influence, because Samuel found he couldn't do anything about it. He wrote *Perfect Happiness* on the back, but it was far from it. Asha was miserable from the day she woke up and found Declan gone. He'd given her a taste of a different life. Plus, she was afraid of her father, or rather, afraid of his interest in her baby, and his insidious influence." '

Stu stopped and said, 'Doesn't she know we've got that photo?'

'Looks that way,' Chrissie said. 'And I don't feel like telling her.' She pressed hard on her temples with the fingers of both hands. 'Jesus, Stu – my head's spinning – there's context, then there's overload.'

'Do you want to quit?'

'Yes,' Chrissie said. 'And no. I mean, the things we don't know are legion, but I don't think I want to know everything, because what's the point? It's like staring down a rabbit hole, and Nancy's purple bloody prose – well, god, it really puts the tin lid on it.'

There was a tentative cough, and Nancy sidled into the room wearing her apologetic smile that, truly, did more harm than good, and Chrissie said, 'Oh, hi, Nancy. Sorry about that but you're completely doing my head in.'

'I know,' said Nancy, and she looked the very image of contrition, but this only made Chrissie want to shake her, or box her ears, or cast her out of the house in her lumpy socks and throw her shoes out after her. She said, 'Right, enough is enough. We're ditching your testimony for now; just answer these questions, as simply as possible,' and Nancy looked alert, and eager to please.

'One, when's Sunny's birthday?'

'March the nineteenth,' Nancy said promptly, and she smiled, as if at the memory, or perhaps at the ease of the question. 'She was born on a Sunday.'

Stu and Chrissie stared. This seemed better. This seemed good.

'Two,' Chrissie said, 'were you party to Asha's escape plan?'

'No, I knew nothing about it until she phoned me out of the blue from a telephone box in Peckham to tell me what she'd done, and what I needed to do to help her. It was beyond reckless, but she wanted no link at all between Sunshine and the de Lyons, so she'd decided Sunny had to be "found". Lucky for Sunny, and lucky for you two as well, that the local public sector workers are a dependable lot, and Sunshine was swiftly safe and sound, in care. Then we got the heads up at the agency, which meant I could legitimately get involved in the process.'

There was a short silence, and then Chrissie said, 'What possessed you to do as she asked?'

Nancy looked at the ceiling and considered Chrissie's question.

'Infatuation,' she said.

Chrissie glanced at Stuart, offering him a turn, but he gave a slight shake of his head to say, the floor's all yours, so she asked, 'Did you get a job with the adoption agency purely to help Asha?'

'No, because as I said, I had no idea what she was going to do, and I left months before she finally did. But it's fair to say that it was because I worked in child services, that Asha did what she did.'

'So you left Buckenhurst and got a job with the agency?'

She nodded. 'I worked in child services before I went to Buckenhurst, then I dropped out for a while, to try communal living, then reapplied for a different job in the same field. I wasn't happy by then, at Buckenhurst. I needed to get back into the world.'

'Did you have to manipulate the adoption process so that we got Sunshine?'

'Yes,' Nancy said. 'I'm so sorry, but, as it turned out, I did. When I met you it was towards the end of ninety-five and I had not the faintest idea that Sunshine was coming your way, but by the time you'd been accepted, and completed the training, she was in foster care with Barbara and John, and I'd had my startling conversation with Asha.'

'Why didn't she just keep her?'

'She wanted freedom, and Sunny was in her way,' Nancy said, then seemed to soften and added, 'Or rather, she believed – rightly, in my view – that without the communal life at Buckenhurst, she wouldn't cope with the demands of single parenthood.'

'What did she say to you?'

'She asked me to place Sunshine with the parents she deserved. She said, "I want her to have an ordinary life with extraordinary people," and I felt that was you two, and I knew you'd be quickly matched with a child, and also I knew that every attempt had to be made to look into Sunshine's past, before approving her for adoption, so I had to do my level best to keep you free for her, and that became increasingly tricky as time went on.' She was speaking in a rush now, and Chrissie wondered if she thought that by quickly unburdening herself, she might be absolved. She had to force herself to listen to Nancy's confession without howling in distress, and she realised she was hugging herself, her arms wrapped around her own ribcage, self-defence against the strangeness of this tale.

And on Nancy went.

'Thing is, I've always found Asha impossible to resist, and I admit I got swept up in it, the sense of this . . . this mission, it seemed so important, she was so intense, she said to me, "I want her to have music and freedom and love, I want her to live the life I don't know how to provide. Keep her away from my father. Make her safe."'

She paused, took a big breath. 'I can see from your faces you think this all very overblown – but it's how she speaks, how her father speaks too. Anyway, I agreed, and it seemed a noble aspiration for her beautiful little girl, but it was a terrifying responsibility, and what I did was unethical, and possibly even illegal, and I shan't be getting another job in child services any time soon, but I fully admit that there hasn't yet been anything Asha has asked of me that I haven't willingly done. Sunny was longer than usual in foster care, that big bureaucratic hiatus because of her supposed lack of family background, which I know was a pretence, but there we go, and it created difficulties for me, because I had you two lined up, the perfect couple for Sunshine, and three times I was forced to steer you away from other children in the system. I had to make you wait for Sunshine, because you were the people she seemed to belong to, the parents I knew Asha wanted for her. She and I had spoken one more time. She'd never leave a number – I never could call her – but we'd talked about you two, and her heart seemed to be set on you . . . two musicians, the band, your creative lives, those things meant a lot to her, they made her feel she was being true to Declan, I think. Well, and plus, I liked you tremendously, she knew that.'

She stopped, like a person might stop at the very edge of a cliff, after running precipitously towards it. She almost panted with exertion while she waited for a response, and it took a few seconds to come, because, although she'd delivered her story in a kind of excitable babble, like a schoolgirl recounting her day, the content was irrefutably sinister and disturbing. She drew a breath, a kind of rising gasp, as if she thought she'd got away with something she'd been dreading and was about to say something else.

Chrissie held up a hand and in a low voice, said, 'Stop, Nancy.'

I had you two lined up ran like tickertape under the mental images of Billy, Rosie and Celeste, all placed elsewhere, as a result of Nancy's machinations, and when she looked at Stuart, she knew he was thinking of them too. That baby boy, especially, had stayed in their thoughts. They'd visited him twice. He'd started to feel like theirs. They'd bought a cot for his overnight visit to them, and then, suddenly, he was gone, steered away into a different life, by Nancy's influence.

'Hey,' Stuart said, gently, and he put a hand on Chrissie's shoulder.

She was staring blindly at the tabletop. Sunshine's arrival had obliterated any lasting regret about the other possibilities, but those three small children: where were they now, and were they happy? Did Nancy know? Did she care? Chrissie looked up at Nancy and said, 'I just feel, y'know, completely freaked out by all this.'

Nancy, still clinging to hope, said, 'But it was all about what was best for Sunshine, Chrissie.'

'No,' Chrissie said, 'it was all about what Asha wanted.'

She remembered now how Nancy had told them Billy needed 'a different kind of stability' to the one they could offer. She remembered feeling inadequate about this, and being counselled back to self-confidence by Nancy. She remembered feeling profound gratitude, that their adoption officer was so special, so warm, so invested in their future as parents. But she saw Stu's face and she could see he was conflicted. He saw more right than wrong; he saw Sunshine, lost and found, and she was eternally precious, and irreplaceable, even in his imagination.

'Chrissie,' he said, cautiously, 'we should just focus on the outcome – we were waiting for Sunshine, remember? And look how happy she is, how happy she makes us.'

Chrissie looked at him mildly, wondering why he couldn't see that their profound gratitude for Sunshine could co-exist alongside their totally justified censure of Nancy's role in this story.

'We're not so special, Stu. We're not so extraordinary. Sunshine would have been happy with any one of the couples we met at those workshops, just as Billy would have been happy with you and me,' she said. 'Children *want* to be happy, they're hardwired to find happiness, and I know what you're saying, and yeah, she's our child and I don't need reminding how happy she makes us, but that doesn't make it right, what Nancy did.'

'No,' Stuart said, 'but I don't think I can help being glad she did it,' and because Chrissie could neither entirely agree nor disagree, she chose to let it go, and Nancy began to look a little less wretched, although she had the good sense to stay quiet and be humble and not smile.

So, anyway, Carly said brightly, when she popped through to see how they were doing, here was a good thing, here was a *great* thing – thanks to Nancy they now knew when to celebrate Sunshine's birthday, and she was extra-delighted to learn that Sunny was not only still a Pisces, but also on the cusp with Aries. She looked smilingly at everyone for validation that this was indeed great good fortune, but Stu just rolled his eyes and said, 'Like that matters,' and Carly, her light undiminished, kissed him on the cheek and said, 'Spoken like a true Virgo.' She was only

concerned for their state of mind, they knew that; she was pan-
ning for gold in the detritus. But really, most of what Nancy had
to tell them was unpalatable, and the more she explained, the
more they recoiled from her truths. The memory bag, she told
them; Asha had left that at the housing office, and she knew this
categorically, because Asha had asked Nancy to let her know
when the day came for Sunshine to move in with her new parents. That was the day she wanted to deposit the bag.

'Deposit the bag where she'd deposited Sunshine,' Stuart
said. 'Neat.'

'And you obliged, obviously,' Chrissie said to Nancy. 'Didn't
you think we might be spooked by the timing of that?'

Nancy, newly abashed at every twist of the tale, said she
realised now that it could be construed as alarming, but she'd
felt pleased and – yes, she must admit this, *proud* of Asha for
her thoughtfulness. She didn't know what was in the bag, she
said – pausing there for them to tell her, which they didn't, so
on she went. Brendan had let her know the date of placement
day, Nancy said. They'd exchanged emails, for a while, after she
left for Jaipur, and now Chrissie thought, oh, *et tu*, Brendan!
Up to his eyes in the intrigue, meeting Nina, messaging Nancy –
and where had he been, in Chrissie's hour of need? It wasn't so
long ago that he was never off the phone, then an actual emergency occurred and he was nowhere to be found.

'Could I possibly see the memory bag?' Nancy asked.

'No,' Chrissie said, abruptly, 'you can't. It's in London. So,
did Asha ask you for our address?' she enquired, and then got
her answer in the immediate high colour that swept from Nancy's neck to her hairline.

'Right,' Chrissie said. 'Yes, she did ask you for our address,
and of course, you told her, which is why she ambushed me in a
shoe shop and stalked Sunshine in our local park.'

'It probably was Asha in your local park, and possibly her in the shoe shop too, but she never asked me for your address, only who you were, and I did tell her about you both, y'know, about the band and everything, and I guess given who you are, the rest is easily discoverable, which might explain why she found your neighbourhood. But look, it's over now, and I can promise she won't bother you guys again.'

Oh, that was ludicrous and complacent, and Chrissie was besieged by a rush of molten anger, and for a woman who didn't shout, she certainly shouted now. 'Bother me? Jesus! In a variety of cruel and creative ways, your precious Asha has made a nervous wreck of me. You know, my mother called Sunny her "fugitive granddaughter" and she's not far wrong. I feel I've been on the run with her for weeks; how do you think that feels, Nancy? Look what you allowed to happen!'

Nancy glanced, nervous and enquiring, at Stuart, who was leaning back in his chair with his arms folded, watching Chrissie with appreciation. He felt Nancy's eyes upon him, caught her look and shook his head in a way that told her Chrissie's anger was his anger.

'That's why I thought you were calling me the other day, Nancy!' Chrissie raged, and Nancy winced and covered her head with her hands as though she was in a hail storm. 'I was so happy, so relieved, to hear your voice three days ago, and you just lied through your teeth, said you'd spoken to Angela about these security breaches, when in fact you didn't really have a clue what I was talking about. You were a snake in the grass! A false-hearted friend! Good God, you cannot play with our lives just to accommodate the whims of Asha de bloody Lyon.'

God, she thought, falling back in her chair; how she hated that name and the person attached to it; how she hated everything she knew about her – her swan neck and soulful eyes and silken curls, her invidious, imperious influence on Nancy, her strange aristocratic surname with its suggestion of power and entitlement, her slyness, her ubiquity, stepping from the shadows, meaning no harm but creating havoc, and most of all, her indelible biological claim on Sunshine.

'I know she *has* bothered you. I meant, she won't bother you *again*,' Nancy said, with a touch of petulance.

'Oh, how the hell do you know that?' Chrissie said. 'She'll do precisely as she pleases, I expect.'

'Yes,' Nancy said, 'she'll do precisely as she pleases, and it doesn't please her to hang about London on the fringes of your life or mine. She's gone, I don't know where, but I expect she'll let me know one day, if it suits her.'

'Maybe she's gone to hook up with her Irish fella?' Stu asked, but Nancy only shrugged, and immediately looked broken-hearted again. She was a tender mass of hurt feelings, and Chrissie could barely stand to look at her, so when Stuart suddenly said, 'Look, why don't we call a truce here?' Chrissie felt relief rip through her and Nancy looked at him with red-rimmed eyes and a kind of exhausted gratitude. He really was the least combative person Chrissie had ever known; all the anger he'd shown today was probably his lifetime's quota. Nancy had her hands folded demurely on the table, and Chrissie saw for the first time how badly bitten her fingernails were, chewed to the point that they must have been sore, and she pitied her just a little, and softened slightly.

'You know,' Nancy said, 'Sunshine is so much better off with you, infinitely, immeasurably better off with you, than she could ever have been with Asha.'

Chrissie studied her for a moment, a new thought forming. 'Did you want her?' she asked. 'I mean, would you have kept her, if Asha had wanted that?'

Nancy gave a wan smile and said, 'Ah, no, no, I mean, it once crossed my mind, me and Asha and Sunshine living happily ever after, but it was pure fantasy; she had no interest in me, even platonically as it turned out.' She looked at them, her eyes full, and she seemed piteous; a fool for love. But then she began to speak again, and she seemed to have changed, it was almost as if it was the first time they'd heard her today. She seemed to sit taller in her seat and lift her chin and address them with authority and brave conviction. She said, 'Asha's driven by selfishness, and perhaps she actively wanted to cause me pain, I'm not sure. But whether you believe me or not, *I* was driven by a firm resolve to put Sunshine's interests first. Honestly, Chrissie,' she said, turning to the person in the room to whom she knew she had most to prove, 'in all conscience, I couldn't have paired her with anyone other than you two. All my instincts told me it was a perfect fit. And Billy and Rosie and Celeste are growing up with parents who adore them, I know that, I've asked Brendan. But Sunny was and is *your* girl. She belongs with you and Stuart, more than she ever really belonged to Asha. I do believe that, and I can't ever be sorry for the part of this story that put Sunshine in your life, because you're wonderful together, you're perfect.'

For a few moments they were all quiet, as they might have been in church, following a particularly good sermon. Then Chrissie swallowed and said, 'All right, Nancy, thank you.'

Nancy closed her eyes, and kept them closed long enough for Chrissie and Stuart to wonder if she'd worn herself out and fallen asleep. Then she snapped them open, and frowned and said, 'Does anyone else *really* need a drink?' and this was so off-topic, and so completely unlike her, that they all dissolved into laughter, which brought Carly and Sunshine running to see what was funny; and it was restorative and cathartic, and

Chrissie always remembered it, in the years that followed, as the true beginning of the end of the madness.

～

Earl's Court in 1963 seemed to contain all the pizzazz, all the vim, all the swing of the sixties, that Barnsley didn't have. Earl's Court also contained Nina Baker, who wore white patent go-go boots and a Mary Quant dress, and a tan suede jacket with cowboy fringes across the back. Her eyes were lined with smoky kohl, her hair was blonde, a sharp-fringed bob. She was a photographer, or rather, she hoped to be. On the night Doug met her, in a basement bar, she confessed she didn't even have a camera, but was saving up for one. She was nineteen, she said, and when he said, So young! she looked surprised and said, Is it?

He was thirty, a self-made man, with enough money in his wallet to have gone out and bought her a camera there and then, but he knew without asking that she wasn't out for what she could get. She said, You could risk loosening your tie, you know, and he laughed. He'd had a meeting with investors that day, and he was still in his best suit, and had been drinking alone to his own health and wealth, until Nina Baker turned to him and said, I come here a lot but I've never seen you? He said, That's because I never come to London. Yet, here you are, she said.

At midnight she hailed a black cab and took him to a party. There was no discernible reason why she should have done this and Doug was mystified, but she liked him, she said. It's only a party, she said; I'm not proposing marriage. He thought about Diana, his beautiful wife. Thought about his marriage, which was not so beautiful beneath the surface. He followed Nina into

*the party, where, after his first-ever joint, he no longer felt like
her father. He shed his suit jacket and finally loosened his tie.
She said, See him over there? That's Terence Stamp, and Doug
said, Who? Nina laughed and said, You're funny.*

*He shouldn't have gone to bed with her, but he did, because
he knew that more than likely it would be his one and only
night with Nina Baker, and making love to her was exactly how
he'd thought it would be, which was hot and wild and exhilar-
ating. He never regretted it, because it was the first and last time
he truly felt wanted just for his body, which he understood was
meant to be a bad thing, but, speaking only for himself, he really
couldn't agree.*

*In the brutal light of the following morning, he spent a few
minutes gazing on her shockingly youthful sleeping face, trying
to take a mental snapshot of this extraordinary girl before he
went back to the real world. He expected never to see her again,
but just in case, he wrote his name and office telephone number
with her kohl pencil on the mirror of her dressing table, then
got dressed in yesterday's discarded clothes, and walked out
into the London dawn, with no earthly clue where he was.*

*The next time he saw her was May the following year. She
opened the door of her Earl's Court flat, gave him a brave smile,
and said, Here you are again, the man who never comes to
London. She looked thin, and hollow-eyed, and they stared at
each other across the threshold of the door for a few seconds,
awed by the magnitude of what they were doing. Then the
mewling cry of their newborn baby made him start, and Nina
stepped back, holding the door open wide, and said, Come in,
she's all ready for you, I'll fetch her. Doug went through into the
flat ahead of her, tried not to notice the squalor of the small
living room, the half-drunk mugs of cold tea, the cigarette
stubs pushed into oblivion on a saucer, the smell of sour milk*

and wet towels and mildewed woodchip. He'd wired her money, for what she needed for the baby, and now he wished he'd doubled it, trebled it. He was staring into the empty hearth when Nina came into the room and said, When she cries she sounds like a kitten, and he turned to see she was offering him the gift of their baby, whom she'd swaddled tightly in a white crocheted shawl. When Nina laid her across Doug's out-stretched arms, he opened his mouth to say thank you, but his throat seemed to close and he couldn't speak. The baby opened her navy-blue eyes and coolly regarded him, and he studied the wonderful complexity of her elfin face, transfixed. His daughter.

There's a bag too, Nina said, trying to be only brisk and practical. Doug looked at her, and she nodded at the floor, a holdall, towelling nappies, a box of safety pins, glass bottles with teats, baby formula. Oh, and this, she said, and she held out two pieces of paper. I wrote these last night. You need to sign them; it's only what we already agreed. I do trust you, Doug, she said, but it just feels safer if it's in writing, and he nodded, transferred the baby to one arm, and signed the agree-ment, a copy for each of them, while she held the sheets steady, on the table. Their names, hers and then his, bound together in trust; he felt humbled by this, and honoured.

Right, Nina said. Please will you just leave now, as quickly as possible? He said, Nina, I – but she shook her head and said, No, this is what we're doing.

On the threshold of the door, they stared at each other again. He said, Anything you want, anything you need . . .

Go, she said, but then, as he turned to leave, she cried out, Wait! And he spun back, ready to do and to be whatever she asked, but she only said, What will you call her? He said, Christine, she's Christine, and Nina nodded, and placed a kiss on the baby's forehead. *Goodbye, Christine, she said; it's not that I don't love you. Be happy, my darling girl.*

Diana was waiting for him in the plush Mayfair hotel suite, where they'd spent the previous night. The contrast with Nina's dismal little flat stung him, and he wished now that he'd pushed a wad of notes into her hand, except then it would have looked like he was buying the baby. Diana stood up and, for the first time since he'd known her, she looked uncertainly at him, for guidance. Doug said, Here she is, Christine Rose Stevenson, and his wife raised her exquisite brows and said, Rose? That's pretty. He said he'd thought of it in the taxi, on the way over. She has roses in her cheeks, look, he said, and Diana pulled away the woollen shawl for a clearer view of the baby's face, and it was as if her heart finally stirred and awoke, in those first few seconds of looking. While Doug continued to hold Christine, Diana unfolded the blanket, to reveal her new daughter's perfect form in a white knitted romper suit, threaded at the neck and ankles with pink satin ribbon. Oh, breathed Diana. Take her, Doug said, and Diana lifted Christine Rose with the heartbreaking care of an absolute beginner. The baby seemed almost weightless and her hands were perfect small stars.

She had no idea how her husband had managed this so well. An unmarried mother from a good family, in West London. Someone he knew through the business; a civilised arrangement advantageous to all. The baby's birth would be registered in Barnsley, Doug and Diana Stevenson named as parents on the birth certificate, no questions asked. He was a man of influence. Diana rewarded him now with a smile of unusual warmth, and offered her powdered cheek, for a kiss. Doug obliged, and was glad he'd made her happy, but he couldn't stop himself thinking about Nina, the way she'd once reached up and pressed a palm on the nape of his neck, and pulled him down for a long, deep kiss, the kiss that had been the beginning of this baby. Diana said, I feel like the cat that got the cream, and Doug knew she meant that she had what she wanted – her own baby girl, without sacrificing her hard-won waistline, or her ankles so slender that Doug could encircle them with his thumb and finger.

He wanted to say, she's my daughter, Diana, but I'll share her with you. But Nina's terms were written out on a sheet of paper, folded and secreted in his wallet, and the least he could do for that marvellous girl was keep his word.

Clever you, Diana said; now, let's take her home.

26

As the day went on, there were comings, and there were goings.

Nancy left, and they were all on decent terms, but knew as they said goodbye that their paths would probably not cross again.

'You have my number,' she said at the gate, and Stu said, 'We do,' and Nancy hesitated, smiled, and set off for the bus station.

Then Rocco and Kim turned up. They'd stayed on in Castleton after Sol and Julia left in case they were needed, and today had cadged a lift with a mutual friend, Dan, who used to work with Kim on the *NME* and who they'd discovered was visiting his folks in Sheffield. The arrival of these three friends had the effect on the house of flinging open the windows to let in some fresh, clean air, and Carly discreetly withdrew, to further explore the loft with Sunshine, and allow 'the young' to chat undisturbed.

So, for a good while, Chrissie revelled in the fact that she was required to talk about nothing but music; gigs and records and reviews. It was the happiest she'd felt in weeks, and the most normal; it felt as if normality was seeping back into her intravenously, like pain relief. Dan knew nothing about

Sunshine's abduction. Rocco and Kim hadn't wanted to gossip; all they'd said was they needed a ride to pick up the shared car, and there was something marvellous about him not knowing, because there was no imperative to talk about anything other than the industry, and Sunny wasn't a subject for anguished discussion, only their adorable little girl, playing dress-up games with Carly, and occasionally dancing into the kitchen to show everyone.

Dan said, 'Don't be missing many more gigs, Chrissie,' and she was aware of a slight stiffening around the table among those who knew the background to Remi's guest appearance at the Roundhouse. 'Don't get me wrong, Remi's great,' he said, 'but she's a solo artist, and she has a . . . well, a kind of artifice, I think, in front of the mic.'

'There's only one Chrissie Stevenson,' Rocco said, but he always said that, so everyone laughed, but Dan said, 'It's true though,' and then, to Kim, 'Come on, back me up here!'

'No need,' Kim said. 'There's nobody round this table would rather have Remi upfront than Chrissie.'

Stuart was sprawled in his chair, relaxed, happy. He threw Chrissie a long, lazy, significant smile, which she knew meant, 'Told you so.'

'There were no complaints on the night though, were there?' Chrissie said. 'She did a damn fine job at very short notice.'

'Oh, sure,' Dan said. 'She was fine, of course. Just don't make a habit of not showing up yourself.' He grinned at her; his good-to-see-you grin. She liked Dan, she'd known him for years, he'd stood at the back with a notebook and pen at that early gig in Glasgow, the one where she'd asked everyone to stop talking, and afterwards he'd come to find her, and said he'd never heard anyone do that, not when they were just starting out; most people just tried to sing over the noise. He'd said he admired her, it took real confidence, and she'd said, 'Confidence? Is it confidence? It's more, I don't know, isn't it just rude, to talk when somebody's singing?' and he'd laughed and said, 'Absolutely, and by the way, you were really great,' and he'd shaken her hand, and she'd felt as if she'd just won something.

'I've no intention of not singing with the band,' she said now, and she bowed ironically at the applause around the table. 'Anyway, I've a raft of new songs to write,' she said. 'And I can't allow anyone other than me to sing them. They're too personal. Sunshine's been . . . inspiring, let's say. Hey, Rocco, I was listening to "Wander Lust" earlier, God, that was a good track,' and Rocco said, 'Fucking-A, man, bring the guitars in; you'll sound like Green Day,' and there was a roar of laughter about those early days, when they didn't always know what they were doing, but did it anyway.

Now, Dan drained his glass and said a reluctant goodbye, and then it was just Chrissie and Stuart, Kim and Rocco, and as soon as the door closed on their friend, they hugged and cried and laughed with relief at Sunshine's safe return – 'Oh, man,' Rocco kept saying, 'Oh, man, oh, man' – then they sat back down in the kitchen, opened another bottle of wine, and told the strange, strange, story of Sunny's start in life, as related by Nancy. That is, Stuart told the story. Chrissie just listened, and while she listened she considered the fact that it was only four nights ago – and not the half lifetime it seemed – that she'd watched him share a piano stool with Remi's perfect little backside, and had almost begun to imagine an existence in which he and Remi were together, while she and Sunshine made a new life in an impenetrable and anonymous little northern house, without him. Impossible, she thought now; impossible, impossible. She looked about her and saw that Kim was watching her a little anxiously, looking for reassurance from her friend that she was happy. Chrissie didn't wish to break Stuart's flow, no more than she wished to break his heart, so she just reached across the table, and Kim took her hand. They shared a smile, and Chrissie felt warmed by her uncomplicated affection, felt embedded in friendship and in family, felt part of something precious and vital and unbreakable.

They'd just waved off Kim and Rocco when her dad and Nina turned up, and though Chrissie had felt sure Nina would come today, she hadn't expected her to arrive with Doug. This fact confused her, though not as much as the realisation that punched her the moment they walked into the house together, that there was something between them, something obvious, something electric, and she looked at Stuart, and at Carly, but they'd noticed nothing; they were completely themselves, and not stirred up at all. Another strange thing was, Nina was wearing a dress, not jeans; it was fluid and floral, and it clung to her hips and her flat belly then swung silkily to a point some way below the knees. With it she had on a pair of long boots and her lovely old tan suede jacket that Chrissie had always coveted. She looked stand-out amazing, and in their previous life Chrissie would have leapt right in to tell her, but today, she just stared, because she was teeming with resentment and suspicion, and the only thing she wanted to say was, 'Oh my God, oh my God, of course, that's it.'

At least Nina didn't try to pretend all was well; she didn't ignore the layers of hurt separating her from Chrissie. Instead, she hung back, evidently uncertain of her reception, while Doug strode over to his daughter, took her face in his hands and looked at her with fathomless love.

'Nina's told me,' he said, 'but *you* should've told me, Christine. You shouldn't have tried to protect me; you should've told me what you've been through,' and she wanted to beat him with her fists and scream, 'And you should have told *me* you've been fucking Nina all these years,' but she didn't, of course. She wouldn't say such a thing to her darling dad; she wouldn't, she couldn't. All she could do was lay her head against his wonderful, broad, warm shoulder and cry and be held, while he shushed her, and said, 'But sweetheart, it's all fine, it's all fine, there's no need for tears,' just as he had when she was small.

It wasn't all fine, she thought, not by a long chalk; but he was right, there was no need for tears. She gathered her wits, and Doug released her so that he could pay some attention to Stuart and Carly, and then Sunshine came bouncing in, happy as a skylark, and even happier when she saw Nina had come. She said, 'Hello, Nina,' very prettily, and Nina said, 'Well, hello, kitten,' and then they both laughed with delight, and Nina scooped her up for a cuddle. Chrissie wondered why Nina thought she had the right. She wondered why she didn't hang her head in shame. Nina, contained, calm, confident, dressed as if for the pages of a magazine, twirling about with Sunny in her arms, while she, Chrissie, felt like a repository for every base and vile and ungenerous feeling; resentment, mutiny, betrayal, conflict, spite, hurt, they swirled through her system like toxins, and so she did the only thing she could do, which was go directly to Stuart, who saw in her eyes and her expression all these states of being, and although he only partially understood what she was thinking, he put an arm around her, kissed the side of her head and said, 'I've got you, babe.'

'Can we have a quick walk?' she asked quietly. 'I need to talk to you.'

They slipped out unnoticed, and set off down the street, and she started immediately; said, 'Dad and Nina are having an affair, maybe they always have, I don't know, but they are now, and that's why Mum's so furious, and why Dad's so riven with guilt.'

Stu said, 'Whoa, wait, what?' and stopped.

'Keep walking,' Chrissie said, pulling him along. 'Just round the block, I just need to move. I need some distance between me and her.'

He saw how serious she was. 'What's your evidence?' he asked.

'When Mum had the stroke, the first person Dad rang was Nina – at *three in the morning!*'

Stu tried not to laugh. 'OK,' he said. 'Annnd?'

'And Mum's livid with her, and livid with Dad; you saw that, right?

'I did,' he conceded. 'But not for the first time.'

'And just now, they walked in together looking like Bonnie and Clyde, complicit, too close, too intense. There's something between them, something that Mum's discovered – oh, come on! Can't you see it?'

He couldn't, and he didn't even wish to try, because clearly, to him, this theory was just a different manifestation of her extreme anger with Nina. He said, 'I suppose I just assumed Nina had gone first of all to the hospital, and talked Doug into coming home, which is why they walked in together.'

'Yes, yes,' Chrissie said, vexed at his tone. 'I'm sure she went up to the hospital, I'm not doubting that, but when they came into the house, they were so close together, and Dad said something very quietly, almost whispering into her ear, and she nodded.'

'Oh, Chrissie! You're describing a perfectly normal interaction between two adults deeply concerned about you, about us, about what we've recently endured.'

'No, I *know* her. I know her like I know myself.'

'Well, now you've said something I can agree with. But think about this – whenever would they get the chance to see each other? If they've been having an affair for the past twenty years or whatever, how and where have they carried it on? She lives in London! Are you saying he sneaks down to Highgate, unbeknownst to you, or Diana?'

No, she said, no, now he said that, she could agree, she didn't suppose that could have been happening, and he said, 'Well, what then?' and she couldn't tell him, she didn't know. But there was something, she knew it. Something they wanted to tell her, something they were carrying carefully between them that they thought they needed to share, and perhaps this need to walk away from the house was her way of responding, because whatever their story was, she didn't need to hear it. The world had been enough out of whack lately to last a lifetime.

Their route took them past a newsagent's and she stopped dead outside the shop and said, 'Stu, do you have any cash?'

He said, 'Some – why?'

'Will you buy me some cigarettes?'

He laughed. 'You want a smoke?'

She nodded.

'You're falling off the wagon?'

She nodded again. 'Just briefly, just this once. Fall off with me?'

He gave it not even a moment's thought, just grinned and said, 'Wherever you want to go, I'll go too,' and she kissed him on the cheek, and off he went into the little corner shop, and came out with a pack of Marlboros and a neon-pink plastic lighter.

There was a low brick wall by the shop, between a bus stop and a rubbish bin. They sat down on it, and he peeled the gold band off the cellophane, tipped back the lid, extracted two cigarettes from the packet, then tossed the rest into the bin. He held both cigarettes between two fingers, put them in his mouth, lit them, then binned the lighter too.

She watched his every move.

He said, 'You look like a little dog, waiting for a treat,' and she tipped her head back and laughed. Such a lovely laugh; he hadn't seen one quite like it for weeks, and it made him want to take her home and up the stairs to bed. She took a cigarette and he watched her close her eyes, take a drag, hold the inhale, release the smoke. She said, 'God, it's like meeting a badly behaved old friend.' She looked at him through narrowed eyes. 'You smoking that, or just holding it?'

He said, 'Just holding it, at the moment, and enjoying you. When we first got together, I only ever saw you through a haze of cigarette smoke.'

'I used to worry that I wouldn't be able to sing if I gave up.'

He laughed. 'I know; you were convinced the fags gave you more range.' He took a deep drag, his first for ten years, and sent the smoke out of the side of his mouth, away from her. 'Ahhh, feels filthy, doesn't it?' he said.

'Good filthy?'

'Nostalgic filthy.'

'What I miss about smoking are the strangers you meet when you ask for a light,' she said.

'I miss lighting a match with my back to the wind, that blue and yellow flare in my cupped hand, the smell of sulphur.'

She nodded. 'Lighting a match in a snowstorm on a fire escape in New York.'

He said, 'Yeah, that.'

Quietly, they finished the cigarettes. It was calming and companionable, and they knew without saying so that they'd never do this again. Probably. Afterwards, they stubbed out the glowing ends and flicked them into the bin, then set off back. It was cold without the glamour of frost; damp without the drama of rain. Chrissie's hands were plunged deep in her coat pockets. Stuart had an arm around her shoulders. They were almost at the corner, which would turn them towards home, when into the indifferent grey of this late-autumn day he said, 'Chrissie, what do you think about getting married?'

'We *are* married,' she said with a grin. 'Remember?'

'I mean, what do you think about doing it again? Big style, in front of a crowd, with a party afterwards?'

They kept walking, their steps on the pavement perfectly synchronised.

'Well?' he asked.

'You want the truth?'

'Always,' he said.

'I'd absolutely love to,' she said. 'And I absolutely love you.'

Now they stopped walking, and they sealed the arrangement with a long kiss and, for a little while, were entirely absorbed, until an elderly woman, in stout shoes and a hat like a felt helmet, broke the spell by stomping very pointedly around them and saying, 'Don't mind me, I'll just walk in the road.'

Five minutes later they were back, and Doug was looking for them from the front steps. Because Chrissie was familiar now with catastrophe, she paled and said, 'What's happened?'

'Nothing, love,' he said.

She said, 'Why were you looking for me though? What's wrong?'

'Nothing's wrong,' he said, then, 'well, your mum wants to see you.'

'That's not nothing. That's definitely something.'

Doug's face was unreadable, but Chrissie knew he knew she wasn't fooled. He said, 'Aye, well, anyway, your mum wants you to go up there this afternoon. I'd have told you before now, but you did a vanishing act.'

'What does she want?'

'You'll find that out when you go.'

'You know why, Dad, don't you?'

'I do, but she wants to see you first, and I agreed to that, and I need to keep my word.'

Chrissie looked at Stuart and raised her eyebrows. 'See what I mean?' she said, and he nodded, 'I do. Do you want me to come with you?'

'Ah well,' Doug said. 'Your mum did say, only you, not Stuart or Sunshine.'

'Right,' Chrissie said. 'Well, this is a turn up for the books, isn't it?'

'You go on, then,' Doug said, refusing to be drawn. He was edging back into the house. Chrissie could hear Nina and Sunshine playing a game of Pairs. 'No!' Sunny was shouting gaily. 'There's not the little boat! *There's* the little boat!' Chrissie looked at Stuart, who shrugged sympathetically and said, 'The sooner you go, the sooner you'll be back.'

'We're losing all the warmth through this open door,' Doug said. 'Why don't you just go straight up there now, Christine? While you still have your coat on.'

She wanted to refuse, stick her fingers in her ears, run away to London with Stu and Sunshine without having to deal with one more drama, or disaster, or unpalatable truth.

'Rocco and Kim took the Subaru,' she said, 'and it's looking like rain so I'll need the keys to your car,' and it was as good an indication as any of his fearfully splintered mind, that he simply picked them up from the hall table and passed them to his daughter without a second's demur or single dire warning as he retreated into the warmth of the house.

Chrissie and Stu exchanged another look, a wry acknowledgement of the very questionable honour of being sent
through Barnsley in the Bentley by Doug, without a backward
glance.

Stuart watched her down the path and onto the street, then
she blew him a kiss and he blew one back.

She let herself into her dad's car and drove it back to the
hospital from which he and Nina had so recently returned.
She saw nobody she knew as the Bentley purred through the
streets of Barnsley, and for this, at least, Chrissie was profoundly grateful.

27

It wasn't the time for visiting, so Chrissie made her way through the labyrinth of the hospital not furtively, but purposefully, head high, eyes forward, and with this strategy she arrived unchallenged at the small private room where Diana resided. She was arranged on top of the covers, as deathly pale and listlessly elegant as a Pre-Raphaelite model, the silk of her nightgown hanging in luxuriant folds over the sides of the incongruous and grimly utilitarian hospital bed. When Chrissie went in, she smiled rather tentatively at her mother, and her mother smiled too, as best she could, and Chrissie wanted to say, 'Whatever it is, Mum, can we leave it unsaid?' so that they could simply begin the next phase of their lives right here, this exchange of smiles the impetus for a new friendly alliance.

'Dad said you wanted to see me?'

She felt her stomach knotting with anxiety, but Diana just nodded and patted the side of the bed. She had her notepad and pen beside her, but when Chrissie did as she was bid, and sat down, Diana took hold of her hand and looked at Chrissie as if she was taking an inventory of her features. Chrissie thought, who are you and what have you done with my mother? Where was the fire and the fury and the frustration?

'I'm going to try and talk to you,' Diana said, and her humility brought tears to Chrissie's eyes. Her mother's crisp, beautifully modulated voice had been mutilated by the new weakness in her tongue and her lips. 'I'm going to show you something,' she said, laboriously, like a woman trying to speak under water. 'And then you can ask me anything you like. Anything at all.'

'Mum,' Chrissie said, clinging on to peace and amity, 'we don't have to do this, not if it's difficult for you.'

Diana squeezed her hand. 'Hush,' she said, forming the syllable with enormous care, trying to gain control of the sound she made. Chrissie nodded, to spare her the physical effort of having to say more than necessary. Diana signalled to the novel on her bedside table: Elizabeth Bowen, *The Heat of the Day*. Chrissie said, 'Oh, you're re-reading this?' and Diana frowned slightly because she hadn't summoned her daughter here to talk about a novel.

She said, with great effort, 'Inside, look inside,' and Chrissie picked it up, opening it where a slip of paper appeared to be saving the page, except it wasn't a bookmark, it was a letter or some kind of list, written with a fountain pen, navy-blue ink on white vellum, neither the ink nor the vellum in the first flush of youth, but it was Nina's handwriting, without a doubt.

Chrissie held the sheet of paper but stopped herself from seeing the words. She looked instead at Diana, who kept hold of Chrissie's other hand and nodded firmly, as if to say, go ahead, read. Her left hand, the damaged one, lay curled like an autumn leaf against her thigh. I must make her do the physio, Chrissie thought; I must make her do the exercises. There was a bright-green rubber stress ball on the bedside table. Diana was meant to squeeze it, little and often, with her damaged hand, but she wouldn't oblige; she seemed to think she would recover from this stroke simply by refusing to engage with it. Gazing at her mother, Chrissie saw that Nina must have done her hair today. Nina was the only person other than Diana who really understood how to gather and twist her hair so competently into that sleek chignon at the nape of her long, white neck. If her mother and Nina were on hairdressing terms, then nothing too awful could be contained within these words. Armed with this insight, Chrissie began to read.

Longridge Mansions, London SW5
Below are itemised the key points of a solemn and morally binding agreement.

1. That Nina Baker will entrust the upbringing of her infant girl to the child's father, Douglas Stevenson.

2. That a legal adoption of the baby by Douglas and Diana Stevenson may take place, unopposed by Nina Baker.

3. That Douglas Stevenson will keep Nina Baker informed of her child's health and well-being, and will never cease to do this.

4. That Diana Stevenson will not know the name of the natural mother of her adopted daughter.

5. That Nina Baker has declined any financial support from Douglas Stevenson.

6. That Nina Baker makes only one solemn and binding request, which is that when, in due course, she is able to become part of the child's life. Douglas Stevenson will facilitate this.

Signed on this day, May 18th 1964
Douglas Arthur Stevenson
Nina Rose Baker

(These are my terms to which you have agreed; keep this document safe, so you never forget the price I've paid, or the prize you've gained. Nina.)

Chrissie looked up from the sheet of paper and met Diana's eyes, and for a while the two women, each of them betrayed, were silent, then Chrissie said, 'You didn't know anything about this?' and Diana shook her head, no.

'Where did you find it?'

Diana whispered, 'The loft.' Her ruined voice made the word sound like *lost*. A tear rolled from the corner of each eye, tracking a path down the exquisite bone structure of the face that deserved to be famous, but never was.

'Mum,' Chrissie said, whispering too. She swallowed. What were the words, to express how she felt? And which was the worst: her not knowing that Nina was her biological mother, or Diana not knowing that? The latter, she believed, for now. Talk instead, then, about Diana's feelings.

'Mum,' she said again, very gently, 'this must have been devastating.'

Diana said, 'It was, especially for your father.'

'Oh, but no – for you too?'

Diana's eyes flashed with a familiar glacial light. 'I was so angry.' *Tho angry*, she said, her words sabotaged again, and she shook her head in frustration. 'More angry than—' she stopped, and Chrissie finished for her, '—than you've ever been. I know, I know.'

Diana nodded.

But what a secret you kept from me, Chrissie thought; what a secret you continued to keep, even though I adopted a little girl, just as you did. She said, 'Mum, you have every right to be as angry as you like.'

Diana's eyes searched Chrissie's face. 'I'm not angry, now,' she said. 'Not really, not now Nina's here, and now that you know. It was hard, being alone with it.'

A silence settled. So much to think about. So much to ask. So difficult to know what to say. Diana watched her daughter's face and waited. Then Chrissie said, 'Did you know Dad was my dad, or did you think I was someone else's child entirely?'

In her mind, other questions made a steady, circular progress. *And why didn't you take the opportunity to tell me, when I told you we couldn't conceive a child and were going to adopt? And why did you give me hell over it? Why did you make every effort to discourage me?*

Diana took a long breath, as if she was about to walk uphill, then she said, 'I didn't know you were his, when we first collected you from London. He told me a story about the daughter of a businessman in London, an unwanted pregnancy, and of course I could have asked more questions, but I chose not to. We'd never been talkers, your dad and I. He suggested the plan; it was all very simple. You were so perfect.'

She closed her eyes, and her hands were trembling. Chrissie said, 'OK, it's OK, just rest now,' but her mother shook her head on the pillow. After a while, she began again.

'I started to sense it, as you grew,' she said. 'I saw how close you were to him, and how you resembled him in those ways you don't expect, like the shape of your smile and your practical side, and your easy humour, and that cowlick that means your hair won't sit straight. I didn't see myself in you. Not really.'

Tears coursed down Chrissie's cheeks, but Diana didn't cry any more; she just gave herself time to catch her breath, then began again.

'I didn't ask him, though,' she said. 'And he never told me. He knew it would have been a truth too far for me.' She smiled, with only half her mouth. 'Maybe it's our generation; maybe we're no good at openness. And I have a terrifically jealous streak, you know. And your dad, well, he never wants to upset the applecart, does he?'

Again, a silence fell. Chrissie looked away from the determined maternal gaze. The process of speaking was tortuous for her, but Diana was in the sort of confessional mood that Chrissie had simply never witnessed before. She felt her mother's eyes upon her, felt her gathering strength and waiting patiently for another question. This was a new Diana, and by tomorrow, perhaps even by later today, the old one might be back, the one there was no talking to; the one with whom most conversations felt like navigating a minefield.

Chrissie looked up. 'Mum,' she said, in almost a whisper, 'why didn't you want me to adopt?'

For the first time since they'd begun to talk, Diana seemed to wince and draw back, and for a moment Chrissie thought, that's it then, we're done. But Diana said, 'I never said that, Christine. I never said I didn't want you to, but I know why you've asked.'

'But you only offered discouragement; the subject seemed to make you angry.' Chrissie felt fear, actual fear, as she said this, the fear she used to sometimes feel in childhood when she knew she'd gone too far, picked the wrong moment, complained or protested when she ought to have been quiet and grateful. But look, it was fine, Diana had reached for her hand.

'I was worried for you,' she said. 'Sometimes, worry comes out as anger, and very quickly, those conversations between you and me would take a wrong turn.'

Chrissie nodded – no one could challenge the truth of that – and she opened her mouth to reply, but Diana hadn't finished.

'Also,' she said. She paused, and seemed to be framing her words. 'Also, your wonderful optimism and bravery and frankness made me see myself in a poor light. And I was . . . I was unused to . . . unused to honesty, I suppose. I didn't know how to talk to you about a secret I'd kept for so long, and I felt threatened by that. So—' She nodded, once, to indicate she was finished, and still she was perfectly collected and dry-eyed, although Chrissie was streaming tears, reaching for the box of tissues on the cabinet beside them, blowing her nose, wiping her eyes.

'Christine,' Diana said, 'please don't be sad. And I don't want you to be angry with your dad, or with Nina, especially not Nina. She's part of who we all are.'

The effort of speaking was exhausting, but she was magnificent in her frailty, and seemed this afternoon to possess the wisdom of Solomon. There was a kind of grace and peace about her, as if something that she'd never understood was at last resolved. 'Christine,' she whispered, 'please tell me you're all right.'

Chrissie gave a trembling sigh and said, 'I'm not yet, not quite, but I will be, Mum, I will be. Why don't you rest now, for a while? I won't go home; I'll still be here when you wake.'

So finally Diana gave in, and when she knew her mother was asleep, Chrissie looked again at the sheet of paper that bore witness to an untruth on a scale she couldn't comprehend. She had been lied to by three people. Diana had been lied to by only two; but the trick played on her mother seemed of mythological proportions. What were the circumstances in which such a deception was even possible, let alone advisable? What plotting and scheming had taken place, and why had Doug and Nina believed they could simply fly higher than other mortals, run rings round them, play them for fools? But no, she thought now; not Doug, only Nina. Her dad didn't have the acuity to come up with so ambitious a plan. He was a thoroughly straightforward, plain-sailing fellow, and although he'd clearly found the time, space and imagination to bed Nina thirty-odd years ago, the subsequent tale of intrigue and deception could not have been written by him.

Chrissie pictured her mother, discovering the truth; she imagined *being* her mother, in that moment when she found and began to read Nina's terms in the permanent twilight of the Stevenson loft. The blooming in that half-light of a terrible understanding. The humiliation of being on the wrong side of a secret, for thirty-three years. And look, look – she was Nina *Rose* Baker. Nina Rose. Chrissie had never known that, and she was fairly certain that neither had her mother.

She thought about a day a long time ago. It was after school, on a dark winter afternoon, in the warm kitchen. Auntie Nina was with Christine while Diana was at work. Christine aged eight or nine, at the table doing homework, a rudimentary family tree. Nina grilling fish fingers while helping Christine, explaining why Mummy used to be Diana Margaret Mitchell, but Daddy was only ever Douglas Arthur Stevenson. Nina saying no, she herself had only ever been Nina Baker, because she wasn't married and had no middle name. Nina saying, no, Christine mustn't add her, Nina, to the tree, because although she loved Christine more than anyone in the world, they weren't related by blood. Christine, alarmed, wondering what blood had to do with anything. Then moments later, sad for Nina not only because she couldn't have a branch of the tree, but also – and far worse – because she had no middle name. Christine hadn't known you could *not* have a middle name. She'd been far sadder about this than anything else. She'd said, would you like to share mine and be Nina Rose? That's sweet, kitten, but no thank you, Nina had said, and kissed her on top of her head, right on her parting, where Nina always planted her kisses.

These were Chrissie's thoughts, and they ran cinematically through her mind, as vivid in detail and colour and sound as they'd been on that day, so that when she looked up from her reverie and saw Nina standing in the open door to Diana's room, Chrissie felt no surprise at all.

They sat across from each other at the same table in the hospital cafeteria that she'd shared with Doug a few days ago, not that Nina knew this, but Chrissie did, and it gave her a sense of continuity, and it was something she knew that Nina didn't. Doug, sheepish, desperate for affection and approval, had volunteered to stay at Diana's bedside in case she woke up. Chrissie and Nina stared at each other, both of them seeing what they'd always seen and only Chrissie looking for something different.

'So, Nina Rose Baker,' Chrissie said, and Nina opened her mouth to reply, but Chrissie said, 'I understand, now, why you were obsessed with Sunshine's birth mother.'

'I wasn't obsessed, but yes,' Nina said.

'Obsessed. You were obsessed with the idea that we could all be friends.'

'I thought it might help, if we sort of befriended her.'

'What, like my mother befriended you?'

Nina didn't respond to this, just pressed her lips together in an expression of patient understanding, so that now Chrissie felt she was being indulged, humoured, granted a point, not because she was right but because Nina was magnanimous.

'How could you not tell me?' She heard a small break in her voice, but was quite determined not to cry.

Nina swallowed hard, and reached one hand across the

table, and Chrissie looked at it as if it was a used cup, forgotten by the cafeteria staff.

'It wasn't for me to tell you,' Nina said. She withdrew her hand, and Chrissie was glad.

She eyed Nina coldly. 'Oh, really,' she said. 'Whose story was it?' All the memories of her childhood and adolescence were hanging in tatters around them, and Nina was behaving as coolly as if there'd been a small but understandable mix-up.

'It wasn't *only* for me to tell you,' Nina said, correcting herself. 'It was for Doug and Diana too, and I couldn't tell you if they didn't.'

'God, Nina, we've always been . . . we've always told each other *everything*, yet now here we are, this mammoth secret exposed – accidentally, I might add – and you're sitting there, all poised and calm, telling me it's not your fault I didn't know.' She threw herself back in her chair, and regarded Nina darkly.

Nina held herself very still. 'I suppose we missed the moment,' she said. 'Doug and I—'

'And that's another thing, Doug and you . . . my dad, and you . . . is that an ongoing relationship?'

'Oh, Chrissie – darling, I – you must know that it's not?'

Chrissie shook her head. 'Why would I know anything?'

Nina said, 'Look, I couldn't tell you, if Diana didn't know, and the whole arrangement was predicated on Diana *not* knowing.'

Chrissie gave an incredulous laugh. 'Do you realise how cruel that sounds? How calculating?'

'Chrissie, the only option open to me was to forge as meaningful a relationship with you as I was able to, and your dad helped me. He suggested where I might work, that would put me in your path, and he—'

'See, I find that kind of creepy, and you seem to think it's fine. Dad put you on the veg stall, so you could wriggle into our lives? Make friends with Mum, give me oranges, abuse her interest in you—'

'I didn't abuse her, Chrissie!'

'You abused her trust, it's safe to say.'

Nina thought about this. 'I didn't lie to her; I just didn't tell her everything. The truth wouldn't have benefitted her, or you.'

Nina paused again, and Chrissie thought, God, that voice, so gently persuasive. She steeled herself against it, because she simply didn't know who Nina was any more. She wasn't her mother, that was for sure. Her mother was two flights up in this hospital, recovering from a stroke. So who was Nina, now?

Nina carried on, immune to Chrissie's hostility. 'Your dad didn't "put me on the veg stall". He just told me the places you and your mum frequented. There was no point me being in Barnsley if I never saw you. I had to make friends with Diana as a way of—'

'Moving in on me, yeah, I get it.'

'Well, and was that so awful?' She almost smiled, like she used to do when Chrissie was eight, ten, fourteen, sixteen . . . all her formative years, Nina had been able to listen and talk and cajole and eventually smile her out of a strop or a sulk. 'You don't know how lonely Diana was at that time, Chrissie. She was all but friendless, y'know. She'd always felt like a fish out of water in Barnsley, and she didn't hit it off with any of the wives of your dad's friends. They all thought she was, well, they thought she was—'

'Stuck up, I know,' Chrissie said. 'I know. But then there you were, pretty, chatty Nina, wasted on Chadwick's fruit and veg stall, and you weren't from Barnsley, and you weren't making the most of yourself – always a crime, in my mother's book – and thereby you positioned yourself as a project for her, right? I mean, I was too young to remember quite how you spun it, but

I'm guessing hard-up artist, scraping together enough money for rent but not enough for art college?'

Nina, unabashed, said, 'Yes, precisely that.'

'Then suddenly you'd left Chadwick's and were part of the fabric of my childhood, earning a living thanks to my mum's indifference to my tedious needs?'

Still, Nina remained composed. She said, 'Diana was never indifferent to you, or your life, but it suited her to get a job that required her to look extremely smart and wear heels, and get out of the kitchen. You were all three of you happier, after she took that job.'

Chrissie said, 'Were we?' and Nina nodded, and said, 'Diana was . . . I mean she might be diagnosed as struggling with depression now, not that she's ever sought any help in that department, but she had black moods and she was volatile. She loved you fiercely – and I mean that quite literally; her temperament wasn't equipped for the demands of a child – not that you were especially demanding, but she wasn't always kind to you, Chrissie; you must remember that, right? And her job took her out of the domestic arena and onto a sort of stage – I mean, nothing like the stage she'd hoped for, but still, a place she could feel more . . . more *seen*. She was terrified of obscurity. It made her mean, made her a bit cruel.'

Chrissie was assailed by one of her flashbacks, coming at her like turbulence at thirty-five thousand feet, making her stomach lurch and sink: Diana dragging her by the wrist, digging her long nails into the tender skin of her inner arm, pulling her from the garden to the house for some misdemeanour long forgotten, but punishable by three sharp slaps on the face, and Christine, gasping in shock and outrage, screaming, 'I hate you! I want Nina,' and Diana lunging for her, her face contorted by rage, and Doug – home early, sent by providence – walking into this scene, lifting her up high, away from Diana's reach, turning on his heel, leaving the house with his child on his shoulders. He took her down the road to Locke Park, strode through the avenues of beech and sycamore to the cafe where he bought her an ice-cream cone. Then they visited Nina in her little house, way, way down the hill from them, and Doug and Nina talked in quiet voices while Christine coloured in at the table, and swung her legs against the bar of the chair, knowing that the percussive clunk-clunk of her heels on the wood wasn't annoying here. Nina, with infinite tenderness, rubbed calendula cream into Christine's sore cheeks, and after a while they went home, where Diana was in a deckchair, in the sunshine, with a glass of wine in one hand. She slid her sunglasses down her pretty nose and said, 'Hello, you two, did you have a nice time?'

'Do you remember the day she slapped my face?' Chrissie asked now.

'Of course,' Nina said, levelly. 'It was a turning point.'

'She went out to work after that?'

Nina nodded. 'Doug could never give her advice, she wouldn't take it from him, so I showed her an ad in the *Chronicle* for a PA to the boss at the NCB offices, and she applied. They snapped her up. She could type, she had authority, and she looked simply fabulous. She bought a whole new wardrobe of office clothes – pencil skirts, cashmere twin sets – and I stepped into the breach at home.'

'So, then, after that, it was you at the school gates in the afternoon, you in the kitchen making my tea, you in my bedroom, French-plaiting my hair and reading me stories, you at the Christmas shows, you painting the mural on the side of my school in the summer holidays. God, you helped me so much with my O-level maths, you practically *took* it for me, and when

I formed the band, with Andy Clark, you were the only person who not only came to all the gigs, but to all the rehearsals.'

Nina said, 'Yes, watching On a Thursday, on a Thursday.'

They looked at each other, and almost smiled.

'We didn't merit that level of devoted attention,' Chrissie said.

'No, you probably didn't,' Nina said. 'But . . . oh, I don't know – you were the daughter of my heart, and I think I was trying to make something up to you that you'd never even missed.'

'Did you *want* to give me away, when I was born?'

Nina looked at her sadly, as if this was a question she shouldn't have to ask. 'No, Chrissie, of course I didn't, the week I spent with you remains the most important, most intense week of my life. I tried not to sleep, so that I could spend the hours taking you in. You were miraculous.'

'You could have had another baby.'

'I know,' Nina said. She looked away from Chrissie, then back again. 'I think I would have done, if I hadn't given you away to your dad.'

'What? That makes no sense.'

'I mean I think I felt . . . it was a kind of—'

'Penance?' Chrissie supplied. 'Punishment?'

'No – not that, but certainly a kind of atonement.'

'Living out your days alone, looking after Diana's Stevenson's house and child?'

Nina gave a long exhale, and Chrissie said, 'Sorry,' but it wasn't a real apology, only an acknowledgement that her love and respect for Nina were not currently being observed. Nina, understanding this, said, 'No, no, you're right, and in a certain light my life looks unfulfilled, I guess, but I think I spent my days trying to convince myself that the awfulness of handing my baby – you – over to Doug and his wife was . . . well, I suppose, sort of eradicated by the years that followed.'

'And was it eradicated?'

She shook her head. 'No. Actually, one of the many things I've learned over time is that there's no antidote to the pain I felt when I closed the door on your dad that day he collected you. I thought I might die from grief, the agony was physical, like an infection of the soul, and it went on for weeks before it abated into a kind of dull permanent ache. Then, by the time I got back to you, you were seven, and that perfect, beautiful, new-born baby was a perfect, beautiful seven-year-old child. Honestly, Chrissie, it's been the joy of my life, forging a meaningful relationship with you, but I'll always, always regret giving you to Doug.'

'Far easier just to have kept me,' Chrissie said.

'But I had no money, no support, no prospects.'

'I wouldn't have minded any of that.'

Nina smiled. 'I would, though. Maybe it was the era, I don't know, but placing you in your dad's safekeeping was the obvious thing to do, and being Doug, he honoured his promises to me.'

'Did your affair start up again after you came to Barnsley?'

'No.'

'Not even—'

'No, not even. Once and once only, in London, in September sixty-three. I came to Barnsley to make *you* fall in love with me, not Doug.'

'What took you so long?'

'I was, what we used to call, getting my shit together,' Nina said. 'I was a bit of a mess, a wild child. Went to Paris, hung out with the beatniks, tried selling bad paintings on the Left Bank, hitched across Europe with sketchy fellow-travellers . . .'

'Now you sound like a cliché.'

'I was, you're spot on, and that's why in seventy-two I turned in the direction of you, and called in my favour from Doug.'

'Dragged from Paris to Barnsley by the maternal heart strings.'

'Guided, not dragged.'

'I remember the first time I saw you,' Chrissie said. 'You gave me an orange, wrapped in white tissue paper, with a sticker on it that said Jaffa oranges, produce of Israel.'

'I knew you at once,' Nina said. 'I had to grip the back of the stall, because I thought my knees were going to buckle.'

'What if Mum hadn't taken the bait?'

Nina shook her head. 'I don't know. I'd have thought of something though; I was pretty determined.'

'Oh, right, and we all know how much you can accomplish when you have the bit between your teeth.'

'Ah, touché,' Nina said, and she folded her arms, and waited for whatever Chrissie wanted to throw at her next, while Chrissie pondered the great irony of how very many times as a child she'd wished Nina had been her mum. Even in Diana's finest mothering moments – her Boadicea moments, when pride and a quest for justice made her Christine's greatest champion – she was still always at arm's-length, caring for her child from a safe distance, so as not to crease her blouse or smudge her lipstick. A surfeit of loving emotion was disturbing to her, and it wasn't that she didn't love Christine, rather that her love was a given, and didn't need to be demonstrated. Diana's love was contained and queenly, while Nina loved like a peasant, without restraint, love brimming out of her, and it was all for Chrissie.

And yet now . . . now that her childhood wish had come spectacularly true – well, how wrong it felt, and what a seismic betrayal. Absently, she picked up a paper tube of sugar from a jar in the centre of the table and began to roll and twist it, an alternative to chewing her thumbnail. She said, 'Whose idea was it?'

Nina said, 'Doug's, to adopt you, but what followed was mine.'

'Yeah, he's not inventive enough to come up with your plan.'

'It was only desperation that made me inventive.'

'I suppose they couldn't have their own babies?' Chrissie asked, then flinched inwardly. It felt intrusive, and almost embarrassing, to even think about Diana and Doug's ability to conceive.

Nina said, 'That's Diana's part of the story.'

'I can't ask her that!'

'Then talk to your dad, Chrissie.'

'What, you're this principled person all of a sudden? I don't *want* to talk to my dad, I want to talk to you – you tell me how it came about that Mum didn't have babies. I'm sure you know, so don't be coy.'

'Goodness, Chrissie, I'm cutting you a lot of slack here, but don't push it. This is still me, OK?'

Chrissie gave a brief nod. 'I know,' she said. 'I just feel . . .'

'Look, your mum didn't want to go through pregnancy,' Nina said quickly. 'Simple as that. She saw it as an assault on her body and not something she was prepared to endure, and it wasn't discussed. Your dad just assumed babies would come, and two years after the wedding he asked her if either of them needed checking out, and she told him she'd had a coil fitted, and thought he knew.'

'She didn't want to lose her figure,' Chrissie said.

'Bingo.'

This wasn't surprising, and now Chrissie knew it to be true, she wondered why she hadn't already known; Diana's silhouette was possibly the thing in life she prized most.

'So was it her idea to adopt?'

'It was Doug's, but only because he knew you were on your way.'

'You stayed in touch then, after the once-and-once-only?'

Nina recoiled a little, but said, 'I rang him, when I realised I was pregnant. He'd left a telephone number, his office number. I called him there, and after that we spoke a few times, before I came to Barnsley, but only to work out how to—'

'Con my mother?'

'Yeah,' Nina said, resignedly. 'Con your mother, if that's how you insist on seeing it.' She looked towards the counter, where, after all this time, they still hadn't placed an order. 'Should we . . .?'

'Don't bother,' Chrissie said, 'I've already made that mistake here. Tea or coffee, both equally bitter; the bad taste stays with you for bloody hours.'

'Are you talking about something other than hot drinks, there?'

They gave each other a long, unsmiling look, each quietly assessing the collateral damage of the past few weeks. Then Nina said, 'Chrissie, I know you're angry with me – for all sorts of valid reasons – and I know this . . . this revelation . . . well, it's put a bomb under the Stevenson world, but look, now it's out in the open we can all learn to live with it, and there are worse things happening to people all the time, than what happened to Diana. She was delighted to be given a baby daughter, without any disruption to her figure.'

There was a distinct note of sarcasm in Nina's tone now, which Chrissie thought she actually preferred to the patient, apologetic gentleness.

'Was she?' Chrissie asked. 'Delighted, I mean?'

Nina nodded. 'In her way.'

'I don't recall her taking much delight in me.'

'You turned into a tomboy, and pursued interests she didn't understand, and stopped brushing your hair.' Nina smiled at her now. She couldn't help herself; it was her default expression when she looked at Chrissie, this young woman, the love of her life. 'You resembled me, in so many ways that I felt sure Diana would realise.'

'And you're Nina Rose – something else you lied about.'

'Oh, darling, come on, give me just a tiny break, will you?'

Chrissie shrugged, feeling thirteen years old.

'I had no idea Doug was going to give you my middle name, and as soon as I knew, I stopped using it, dropped it altogether.'

'Reintroduce it if you like, makes no difference to anything really. Oh, and by the way, I can't even talk to you about what happened to Sunshine.'

'OK,' Nina said, uncertainly.

'Almost everything you thought you'd discovered was wrong, and you were thoroughly duped.'

'I know.'

'You made friends with Kristen de Lyon, who's currently in police custody for the abduction of our child.'

'I know, Chrissie.'

'Don't tell me it was all out of love, and with my best interests at heart.'

'I won't, although it was.'

'You can admit you were wrong though, if you like.'

'I was,' Nina said. 'I was completely, utterly, spectacularly wrong. I will be eternally sorry for the harm I inadvertently caused you; it was catastrophic. Except there's one thing I—'

'Oh, here we go—'

'No, here we go nothing. I was about to say, if I hadn't gone to Littlecliffe, I wouldn't have met Rob Whittaker.'

Chrissie stared at her and drummed her fingers on the tabletop. She was fighting a smile again, because she could tell from Nina's face that she perfectly understood – and was rather enjoying – Chrissie's conundrum, which was whether she would let her anger outweigh her extreme curiosity to hear about this 'friend' from Kent who might, Chrissie realised, be the reason Nina looked so bloody gorgeous and, in spite of the rigours of their conversation, had a permanently sated glow, and an expression that was aggravating and fascinating and almost certainly irresistible.

Nina waited, holding Chrissie's gaze with her clear, steady eyes, almost but not quite smiling herself.

'Damn it!' Chrissie said, as she caved in. 'Go on then, spill the beans.'

Back upstairs, Chrissie dispatched her dad, whom she found in his usual chair, beside her mother's bed. Diana was awake, and flicking through a magazine with her good hand, while Doug was staring into space, but Chrissie felt no sense of having walked in on a scene; her parents were just peacefully uncommunicative as they were seventy per cent of the time, and Chrissie felt no anger towards him, because that would be like being angry with a loyal old golden retriever who only wanted to please everyone. He hugged her very tightly, trying to say everything he wished to say without saying anything at all, and then he pecked his indifferent wife on the forehead, and left.

Diana discarded her magazine, looked at Chrissie and rolled her eyes, which made her laugh. There were so very many more things she could ask her mother, but right now she felt only an ineffable tenderness for her. Diana, in her effortful voice, said, 'I'm so sorry, Christine,' which was the first time she'd ever apologised to her daughter for anything, but this was no time for triumphalism; it was humility and hard work that would get them through. Chrissie said, 'It's all going to be fine, Mum,' and this she believed, heart and soul.

She unzipped her boots and took them off, then rearranged Diana's satin nightgown so as not to crush it, then got up onto the bed, settling herself full length alongside her mother; a surprising and spontaneous act of unprecedented intimacy, but Diana only smiled, and laid her damaged hand upon her daughter's thigh. Chrissie lay down and their heads touched on the pillow, Chrissie's hair as blonde as Nina's, Diana's as dark as Sunshine's. If there was one thing that would get her mother up and out of hospital, Chrissie thought with a swell of affection, it would be the need very soon to see her colourist in Sheffield. She took hold of Diana's hand, and squeezed it, and felt a hint of a squeeze in response, and for a long time they just lay there together in silence and this strange new solidarity, allowing the fractured truths of their two lives to fall, land softly, and settle into place.

28

MAY 1998

Doug Stevenson had always wanted to walk down the aisle of his pretty local church with his daughter in white on his arm, and for years, he'd not bothered to worry about whether this would happen, because it was a given; as far as he knew, it was how all the girls got married in Barnsley. So that day, two and a half years ago now, when Diana slammed the phone down after talking to Chrissie and said, 'So, she's gone and got married, and we weren't invited to the wedding,' Doug was shattered, and far more distressed than his wife, who'd long ago given up hope of any conventional nuptials for their wayward daughter.

Diana *had* assumed they'd attend, though; she'd expected an invitation, to whatever modern or alternative choice Christine made, when she married Stuart Woodall. Diana had hoped to lavish money on an outfit – her own, not the bride's – and to give the couple the gift of a stylish reception – the wedding breakfast, she would have called it; she'd always wanted to be mother of the bride at a wedding breakfast, where less was more, and everyone ate standing up. She'd seen too many brides over her years in the north, tucking into roast beef and Yorkshire puddings at a table as long and loaded as a Tudor banquet. It was all going to be very different for Christine.

412

And now, look where they were. Doug denied the walk down the aisle, Diana denied control of the reception, both of them being driven in a black cab to a house they'd never been to, in a part of London they didn't know, to attend a fake wedding performed by someone called a celebrant for two people who were already married, followed by an 'after party' – ugh, how Diana shuddered at the term – in the garden, under canvas. Again, ugh.

But there was this; the house belonged to darling Julia, and Diana had heard it was very fine, in the way that London's terraced houses sometimes were. Also, Julia was in charge of everything, so class and style were surely guaranteed, and actually, thought Diana, it was probably more pleasant, on the whole, to be greeted than to have to do the greeting. And lastly, Diana was more than content with the picture she and her husband presented; she thought Doug looked striking in his dark tailored suit, and her own outfit was very pleasing indeed. Navy and white. Hat, dress, jacket, shoes. Diana felt complete, and entirely at home, in couture.

The taxi drew up in front of a handsome row of Georgian houses that were defended from the main road by a wide strip of grass and a line of venerable London planes. Julia had been watching for them, and she was outside on the pavement before the driver had opened the passenger door, and of course she noticed at once that Diana was head to toe in Chanel, and that Doug's suit was Savile Row, and Diana recognised Julia's fitted red cocktail dress as Dior, and they agreed, very happily, that the French fashion houses were hard to beat, as she ushered them through a lovely entrance hall and into a room that had been doubled in size by the folding-back of two enormous wooden doors. There was a sort of podium at the far end, and a microphone on a stand, and a few short, tidy rows of pretty padded chairs with a central aisle separating them into two sections. It looked like a wedding venue, not a family home. What a lot of trouble, thought Diana, for a couple who were already man and wife, but she was careful to keep this thought from her expression, even when Doug said, 'Somebody's been busy,' and Julia laughed and said, 'This is nothing – wait until you see the garden.'

She placed them on the front row, deposited a peck, peck on both cheeks for each, then flitted off, promising to be back soon, and they missed her, when she was gone. They felt a little marooned, with their backs to the room, unsure who had arrived, or was arriving, behind them, and certain anyway that they would know very few. Theirs was such a small family; Christine had no surviving grandparents, no siblings, no cousins, just the three of them on their small Stevenson island, from which she'd rowed away at eighteen and never fully returned. As if this was only just occurring to her, Diana glanced at her husband, to make sure he hadn't gone too, and there he was, utterly dependable if not always entirely satisfactory. He was staring straight ahead, lost in his own thoughts (what were they, she wondered? Lately, she'd begun to think for the first time about his regrets). She was struck by his noble profile, his strong chin and aquiline nose, and the kindness that was evident in the lines at the corner of his eyes, and this swept her backwards in time to a Gaumont picture house somewhere in London in, oh, 1958, 1959, thereabouts anyway, when their relationship was still quite new. He'd taken her to see *Cat on a Hot Tin Roof* with Elizabeth Taylor and Paul Newman, two beautiful people, and in the dark of the cinema she'd turned to look at him as she had now, and she'd thought, well, he's not Paul Newman but he's handsome enough, and he has prospects, and he lives nowhere near Pinewood Studios. And on that basis, she'd accepted his offer of marriage and now, waiting for their daughter to arrive

in the room, she wondered, as she had most days since accidentally unearthing the painful truth, if she'd exacted too high a
price from him by refusing to bear a child. Had that refusal, in
itself, been a wicked act? Certainly, it mitigated the fact of his
single night of passion with Nina, and although Diana would
never tell him she forgave him, she did understand that she'd
played a part. Also, she'd taken to wondering what sort of a life
Douglas Stevenson might have led with someone else, someone
like Nina Baker. She wondered to what extent *he* wondered that.
She wondered if, for thirty-four years, he had been waiting for
Nina to set him free. Nina; oh, Diana looked at her so differently
now, saw she was a complete and complex woman, realised that
previously she'd underestimated her appeal, regarded her as a
kind of marvellous invention to make her own life easier; a rev-
olutionary timesaver, like the tumble dryer or the dishwasher.
Nina had met a dire need, saved Diana's sanity, and probably –
let's be honest, she thought, for after all no one can hear me
think – saved her relationship with Christine too, because she
truly did not know when or how she might hurt that precious
child, in the dark days, before Nina released Diana from domestic purgatory.

'Doug,' she said now, very quietly, 'do you wish you'd married Nina?' She hadn't known she was going to say this, and the
moment she did she was appalled at her weakness and hoped he
hadn't heard her. But he turned at once, and met her eyes, and
he saw a new anxiety in them, because here she was, perhaps for
the first time in their long history, asking him a meaningful
question about their relationship, and she was far from certain
of his answer.

Doug said, 'No, Diana, I do not,' with real feeling. Never
mind that Nina wouldn't have had him, he told himself; never
mind that the night he'd spent with her remained the single

most exciting sexual adventure he'd ever had the good fortune to experience.

'I'm your husband until the day you don't want me or the day I die,' he said. 'You knock the socks off every other woman in this room, and any other room I have the privilege to be in with you. I consider myself a very lucky man.'

And he *did* consider himself lucky, in spite of the fact he knew she'd never loved him; that it was her pride, not her heart, that was damaged when she'd discovered his original sin, his *single* sin, his one fall from the straight and narrow. Shouldn't some credit be due, he thought, for providing Diana with a beautiful daughter, albeit by committing adultery? He was still waiting for the day she admitted his crime was not really so great, that the pros outweighed the cons, but he knew he'd go to his grave before she said this. Meanwhile – and call him shallow – her appearance still had the power to stop his heart and make him proud, and although her extravagant beauty was altered by the stroke, it was somehow not diminished. She was his perfectly imperfect wife, with the looks and the temperament of a Hollywood superstar, and he saw now that what he'd said had touched her, because she accepted his compliment with a dip of her head. She wore a pair of exquisite white kid gloves today, so that both her hands looked the same, and when she placed one of them on her husband's knee and let it rest there, he felt almost loved.

Behind them the chairs began to fill up and a low buzz of conversation rose up around them, friends greeting friends, people from the world that Christine and Stuart inhabited, then Nina arrived, with her new fellow Rob. Diana happened to glance back just as they came into the room, saw them holding hands and smiling into each other's faces, and laughing at a private joke, leaning into each other, intimacy rising from them like steam. Diana wasn't quite ready to speak in her old way to

Nina, but she was determined – quite resolutely determined – to be a model of impeccable behaviour as mother of the bride, so she smiled graciously and said, 'Nina, hello, and hello, Robin,' as they took their seats.

Doug knew the drill. Almost as soon as she'd walked into the room, he'd known without turning around that Nina had arrived, and he certainly knew it as she sat down behind them, because he knew the perfume she favoured and the cadence of her speech, and her wicked, throaty laugh. But he waited until Diana said, 'Doug, Nina's here; she's right behind us,' before he turned and gave her a smile, and nodded at her long-haired boyfriend, the publican, the potter, whatever it was he did, or was.

Kim and Rocco arrived, and this caused a communal stir of anticipation because everyone knew the battered old Subaru was the official wedding car, then Julia, Sol and little Juno rushed into the room with a secretive, last-minute air about them, and took their places in the front row adjacent to Doug and Diana. A woman appeared from a door stage left, and stood at the podium, peaceful and benign, then Julia's sister Remi walked down the central aisle to the microphone, gazed sleepily at the seated audience, and then in a sweet, low voice began to sing an a cappella rendition of 'Here Comes the Sun'. It was immediately evident, from the way Juno bounced up and down in her chair and the way Julia turned to find Chrissie and Stuart, that this was a surprise element, and not something about which she'd consulted the bride and groom. Bold move, thought those few guests who knew about the contents of the memory bag, and the effect they'd had on Chrissie; bold move, but also rather brilliant, that Sunshine's mysterious 'heirloom' record should have been given the status of a song to seal their celebration. And what could be more fitting, Jules said, afterwards; what could be better, for this particular family, than a song of hope and sunshine?

If there'd been a moment's uncertainty in Chrissie's eyes, no one noticed but Stuart, and when the little family began their short journey from the back of the room to the front, people began to sing along, the celebrant started to tap her foot, and Sunny, the little flower girl with a ring of daisies and cornflowers pinned in her dark-brown hair, turned round and walked backwards between her mummy and daddy, facing the room and smiling graciously, as if they were all singing to her.

Doug and Diana were captivated by the vision she made; their little granddaughter, a source of such joy and pride in her exquisite white taffeta dress with short puff sleeves and a pale-blue sash and shoes to match, her entire outfit overseen by Diana, which was the nicest task Chrissie could possibly have assigned to her mother, bar allowing her free rein over the choice of bridal gown, which she was absolutely not granted. Chrissie's frock was a very pretty pale-green and cream sprigged muslin, sleeveless, diaphanous, with a deep V at the back. Julia called it Tess of the d'Urbervilles chic. Diana thought, in a certain light we shall all be able to see her knickers.

The music stopped and the celebrant cleared her throat and looked with a professional expression at the couple she was about to address. Now, Sunny was supposed to sit down, but when Diana patted the seat next to her, Sunshine shook her head and said, 'No thank you, Grandma. I like it here,' which raised a laugh, even from Diana. So Sunshine stayed up front with her parents throughout the brief and rather poetical service, gazing up at the celebrant as she spoke, and at Chrissie and Stuart as they repeated their lines on cue, and when Chrissie said, 'I do,' Sunshine said, 'And me, Mummy. I do too,' which brought the house down.

*

The reception was held in a Bedouin tent in their back garden, although certainly no Bedouin would recognise it as home. The interior was a patchwork of pinks and oranges, interspersed with thousands of tiny mirrors that caught and multiplied the glow from dozens of lanterns and lavish strings of fairy lights. The floor was covered in kilims, as were the low chairs and sofas, and the tables were brass, etched all over the top with intricate geometrical patterns. Yellow roses, which had been somehow woven into ropes, fell from the central point of the canvas roof, and pooled on the floor like May Day ribbons. The mood was relaxed, the food Moroccan – piles of it, platters of heaped couscous, saffron rice and flatbreads, with chicken and vegetable tagines, lavish salads studded with pomegranate seeds and almonds, and a whole lamb, slow-roasted on a spit over coals and tended by the North African caterers. The air smelled of meat, and cinnamon and lemons.

Doug and Diana walking out into the London garden and, finding themselves in Marrakesh, were momentarily flummoxed, then Doug laughed and said, 'Right-oh, where do I park the camel?' Diana took in the tent and the rugs and the strenuously informal nature of the whole scene (what, she wondered, was wrong with white linen tablecloths, crystal glasses, gilt chairs, silver service?) and she felt a rise of panic at how she might manage, because she knew now that she was overdressed in her Chanel two-piece and navy court shoes. Yet barely had the panic begun, when it immediately ceased, because Julia swooped on her like a fairy goddaughter, and led Diana by the hand, up to her dressing room, where she offered her a pair of royal-blue silk palazzo pants, a cream cashmere sweater and some flat black pumps, all of which could have belonged to Diana, being exactly her size and her style.

'But how did you know?' she asked, quite overcome with

gratitude and relief. 'I mean, how prescient of you! How clever!'
Her voice was so much better now, so much clearer.

Julia said, 'Thank you, darling. It's not a service I provide
for anyone but you. I'm changing later too; there's dancing, and
no way is that happening in this dress.'

'I really think we might be related,' Diana said.

'Sisters under the skin, I think they say. The bathroom's
there, help yourself to anything you need. I *love* your earrings,
don't change those.'

'Ah, the diamonds, these nearly broke the bank,' Diana said,
smiling, pleased, lightly touching the delicate row of gems
hanging from each lobe. 'A first anniversary present, and one
that Doug couldn't really afford.' A peace offering, too, today;
an unspoken olive branch. She'd seen Doug notice them, seen
their significance was not lost on him, but neither he nor she
remarked upon this, because it was not their way.

Now Diana said, 'Julia, what about Chrissie's wedding dress?'

'Nothing to do with me,' Jules said, 'but having said that, I
think she looks perfect in it.'

'You do?'

Julia nodded. 'It's the bohemian look, Diana – y'know?
Tiers of gauzy fabric, that ethereal milkmaid vibe.'

'Well yes, that's one way of putting it. At least she's not in
jeans.'

Julia laughed. 'She was never going to show up in a long
white gown.'

'But what a shame!' Diana said, and Jules said, 'Well, I don't
think so and *she* doesn't think so, which is the main thing. Your
lovely Chrissie has her own style, and she should only be herself, don't you think?'

Diana nodded. 'I suppose I do,' she said. 'We should all only
be ourselves.'

'Precisely, which is why the likes of you and I shine so brightly, darling,' and Diana was amused and mollified in equal measure. Then Julia left her to it, and Diana changed into the alternative outfit, and sashayed back downstairs and into the garden to rejoin the party.

Nina was the photographer; she liked to see events such as these through the lens of a camera. It gave her licence to properly observe without being considered intrusive. Now and again she went to find Rob, to make sure he was happy, and always found him doing fine, making lively conversation with people he didn't know. Now, she chanced upon him without having actively looked; he was sharing a swing seat with Rocco, each of them holding a bottle of beer, and Rocco, all animation, was saying, '. . . that's it, man, yeah! Frankfurt, ninety-two, un-fucking-forgettable, he got a twenty-minute ovation . . .' and Nina took a photograph, quite close-up, which neither of them even noticed, then she slipped away and almost at once found Chrissie and Stuart, beautifully lit by the low late-afternoon sun, speaking quietly to each other, laughing at something, each of them framed in profile in the lens of her Nikon. She snapped them just at the moment he tucked a lock of hair behind her ear, an exquisite split second, and she knew they'd love that image when they saw it; there was to be no kitsch or formality in this collection; no rows of guests with frozen smiles, no staged shots through the bowl of a champagne flute. Her brief – her own brief, that is, to herself – was to keep this album truthful and tasteful and beautiful.

For a while, from her distance, Nina watched Chrissie, with her heart a little too full of love, and of sadness. She looked effortlessly lovely in the dress she'd chosen for today, and Nina was so proud of her in an inexpressible multitude of ways, and yet the recalibration of their relationship had put some distance between them that neither of them seemed very adept at closing. The last time they'd spoken about this, Chrissie had said if she could unknow what she now knew, that's what she'd choose, because the truth was of no use to any of them now. 'I don't want you to be my mother,' she'd said, 'I want you to be what you've always been – my loved and trusted confidante, with a confessional that smells of cigarettes and turpentine,' and Nina had said, 'Chrissie, I'll be anything you want me to be, just please don't ever shut me out,' and Chrissie had said she wouldn't, of course she wouldn't, but she thought it might take time; she said Carly had told her to let things with Nina settle and evolve naturally, and that's what she was going to try and do.

Carly, thought Nina now. It was always Carly this, Carly that . . . it seemed Carly was the one with all the answers these days, and Nina was having to work hard at not being bitter. Rob's advice was, cease the struggle, step back and let Chrissie come to her, which she certainly would, he said, because they loved each other deeply, and uniquely, and time would heal the surface damage and restore the old magic. But Nina wasn't sure; she didn't know if she could trust the future, and in her darker moments she thought Chrissie's sense of betrayal might prove indelible.

Carly wasn't here today – she was all out of visa rights after her previous extended visit – but Chrissie and Stuart were going to her in Cape May, after the tour. Thirty gigs in France, Holland and Belgium, beginning next weekend, then all of August with Carly, in her gorgeous beach house. Rob had listened to Nina while she told him all this, and said, 'Tell you what, let's fly to New Zealand, me and you, and to hell with the rest of the world for a while? Let's hire a camper van and have a gap year, or half of one.' And oh, how she loved him, then, now and always. Her surprise find, this man who made sense of every good or bad decision she'd ever made, every turn in the road she'd ever taken, because ultimately they'd been leading her to him.

Then Chrissie seemed to sense her presence. She looked round, gave her a warm smile, said, 'Nina! We wondered where you were,' and Stuart said, 'Hey, come join us, we haven't seen you properly yet,' and held out his arms, and she walked over towards them, with a lighter heart, and a feeling of peace, and ease, and happiness, because that's how simple it was, that was all she needed; to sometimes be shown that in spite of everything, she still belonged to them.

29

The first gig The Lineman played that felt like the big time, Rocco could have died at the hands of his own kit. That's the way he liked to tell it anyway. They were playing a venue outside Bordeaux, and they'd performed the first song of the set, but no one could hear Stu's guitar and their opening number sounded shocking, so when they came to the end of it, the French soundman came out from the side, had a quick scout around, then dispatched everyone but Rocco off the stage before vaulting down into the auditorium himself. From a safe distance he explained what was going on, and everyone watched the larky smile on Rocco's face freeze as he learned that the base of his drum stool had cut through the power cable of Stuart's guitar amp, making his seat the showbiz equivalent of an electric chair.

The soundman called instructions in his limited English from a safe distance to the white-faced drummer, and all Rocco had to do was stand up, lift his stool without touching the metal legs, and put it down somewhere else, thereby uncoupling it from the live wire, but he performed this task with slow and excruciating care, as if he was disabling a landmine.

Chrissie, Stu and Sol had watched him, dry-mouthed. Behind them, the crowd had moved back instinctively, and were pressed into the rear third of the floor. Kim was there for the *NME*, and she went against the tide and pushed her way forwards from the back to stand with the band, watching Rocco·as he took what seemed an age to stand up, lift the stool – elaborately and with extended arms – to an unnecessary height, edge crab-like across the stage, then lower the stool – now entirely devoid of electricity and danger – onto a part of the stage that was bare of wires. There were whoops and whistles and riotous applause, and Rocco, the hero of the hour, joined Kim and the band on the floor, while the soundman jumped back on stage and switched off the power to the amp and mended the break in the cable. Then they'd recommenced the gig, and they were one hundred per cent awesome, like a band who'd just had a death sentence lifted, which in a way, they were. The audience responded in a similar vein, the girls screaming as though it was The Beatles, and everyone jumping about to the music, caught up in the euphoric relief that Rocco hadn't just been fried. Chrissie was the best lead singer in the world that night, Stuart the best lead guitar, Sol the best bassist, Rocco the best drummer. Stu got a few people up to sing and dance on stage to 'Colour by Numbers', and this motley backing crew formed a line and joined in with Chrissie, and thank God they didn't all have microphones, but it set the seal on The Lineman's reputation for not taking themselves too seriously, for loving their fans, and for inviting them, by word and deed, into their world. As providence would have it, they'd recorded that gig, and *The Lineman Live at Krakatoa* – their only non-studio album to date – had something quintessential and enduring about it, a raw and convincing energy, a lucky-to-be-alive kind of vibe.

This is how it had felt tonight; this is exactly how it had felt. When Chrissie stood on stage in front of the crowd, smiling out again at the packed auditorium of the very same venue, she felt lucky to be alive, and – like Rocco, a decade ago – she felt as though she was back from the brink herself; back under the lights, where she belonged. Tonight had been the first time she'd performed live for almost two years, and she'd been edgy at the sound check, asking the guy at the desk for fractional adjustments that really made no difference to the mix, so that she'd ended up apologising, horrified that she might be coming across as a diva, when in truth, she was just deeply grateful to be here, back home, on stage.

And then four hours later, they'd gone ahead and played the kind of gig that made a band want to go out afterwards and drink the town dry – two songs from the new album, followed by a total joyride of old favourites, crowd pleasers from the albums that launched them, songs so familiar that singing them and playing them was like breathing, and yet the energy of the crowd, their commitment and engagement, made every number feel like a brand-new hit.

And oh, it had felt so good, Chrissie thought now, as they lounged about backstage, coming down from the heights; there was nothing else quite like that feeling of owning a crowd, of holding them, of carrying them with you; nothing in the world. Three encores, the final one an almighty singalong of 'Scouse Betty', a rock 'n' roll elegy to the fag-toting landlady of the first flat Chrissie, Sol and Stu had rented together. She'd felt twenty years old again when she sang that song tonight, and what a joy, what a privilege, to be paid to do that, and afterwards to hang out here in this room with her dearest friends in the world, Stu and Sol and Rocco and Jules and Kim; she looked at them all through the rose-tinted haze of grateful nostalgia, and she felt inordinately, passionately, in love with them all.

On the floor between them stood a stainless-steel bin packed with bottles of Grolsch on ice, and they were all onto their second when a *tap-tap* came on the door, and Rocco sprang up to open it, expecting Lila from their management company, but finding instead a guy he didn't know, a guy who looked uncertain and bashful and awkward, and Rocco was about to encourage him to leave, when Stu said, 'Oh my God, it's Brendan,' so Rocco let him in.

'Brendan!' Chrissie said. 'God, what a surprise. We haven't heard from you for such a long time!' She bounced up and flung her arms round him, and kissed him on each cheek, making him blush fiercely.

He said, 'I know, I'm sorry, it's been ages, it's all been a bit weird, but now I'm . . . well, now I'm here, and I'm so glad . . . I mean, blimey, I knew you were going to be good, but . . . God, you were brilliant, Chrissie, you were just amazing . . . I mean, all of you were, but . . .' and finally, blessedly, he ran out of steam, covered in confusion.

'All of us are brilliant, but one has more brilliance than others,' Rocco said. 'Yeah, man, we live with that every time we play.' He grinned, and said, 'Who the hell are you, anyway?'

'Sorry, sorry,' Chrissie said. 'This is Brendan Cassidy, from the adoption team.'

'*Formerly* of the adoption team,' Brendan said. 'Blotted my copybook over Watergate.'

Stu said, 'Ah, what a bummer. Nina got you sacked?'

Brendan wagged his head, said, 'Nah, I got myself sacked. I can't blame Nina; it's not as if she had a gun at my back.'

'Oh, Brendan,' Chrissie said. 'What a shame.'

'No, no,' he said. 'Not a shame, not really. It was a kick up the arse, if I'm honest. It made me think about life, the universe and everything, you know?'

'I do know,' Chrissie said. 'And?'

'Oh, just travelling through Europe, doing what I should've done when I was eighteen.'

'On your own?'

He nodded. 'For now. I'm going to see who I meet along the way. Will you tell Nina that, when you talk to her? Will you tell her I said hi, and I'm taking her advice?'

Chrissie laughed. He was so earnest and guileless; she could perfectly see how Nina had taken advantage of him. 'Sure thing,' she said. 'She'll be proud of you.'

'Erm, also, Nancy rang me before she left,' he said.

Stu grimaced, and Chrissie said, 'Right. We haven't spoken to her since she left Barnsley. We don't expect to speak to her. Better if we don't, we think.'

'Sorry,' Brendan said. 'I only . . . it's just, we had a chat. She's going back to Jaipur, giving it another chance.'

'Good,' Chrissie said, as if she cared, which she didn't.

'She asked me, if I saw you, to send blessings. Blessings – sounds so odd, but you know what she's like.'

'Look, Brendan, that chapter of our lives is closed now.'

'Sure, yes, sorry.'

It was time for him to leave, they all felt it, but there he still was, foolishly gazing at Chrissie, to whom he was directing everything he said. 'How's Sunny?' he asked.

'She's great, thanks.'

'Is she . . . I mean, is she here . . . not here in this room, I mean, have you brought her to Bordeaux or is she . . .? Sorry, sorry, I'm not checking.'

'Brendan, chill out,' Stuart said. 'She's back at the hotel with Juno and Remi.'

'The nanny?'

'My sister,' Julia said.

Chrissie said, 'We have it all under control, Brendan, the gang's all here,' which sent him again into the throes of crimson embarrassment, and he began to stammer out that he wasn't interfering, it wasn't his place, he'd always talked too much, all his life he'd been putting his foot in it, then he managed to halt himself and take a deep, fortifying breath. 'I only meant to say,' he said, in more rational tones, 'that Sunshine will be so proud of you, when she's old enough to know how very lucky she is.'

'Well, thank you,' Chrissie said. 'That was beautifully put,' and she smiled affectionately at him, and laid a hand on his arm. 'Thanks for coming, Brendan,' she said. 'Next time, please do let us know, we'll put comps on the door,' and they all witnessed the dawning of sad understanding in Brendan's eyes, that Chrissie was ending the audience. He cast her one last love-struck gaze, said a rather wistful goodbye, and walked backwards out of the room, like a medieval serf. Chrissie closed the door and held up a warning finger to the others.

'Do not laugh,' she whispered, 'until he can't hear us.'

They were all staying in the same swish serviced apartment, which was housed in one of the magnificent buildings overlooking the Place du Parlement. When they got back from the venue, it was one in the morning but the bars were all still going full throttle, so Kim proposed a round of Calvados, which led to a second, and there they lingered, in the Italianate splendour of the square, drinking to the blazing glory of their gig, and meandering inevitably through their past: the miles they'd travelled in a white transit van, the appalling video they shot at a fairground in Dundee where Chrissie had to sing on a roller coaster, the gig in Blackburn when nearly everyone in the crowd left after the support band finished, the gig in Islington when Rocco had stood up behind his drum kit and shouted, 'You! Yes, you,' pointing at Kim, who was at the back of the room, watching the set. 'Do not move,' Rocco had called to her. 'I'm coming to find you when we're done.'

'Sweet-talking bastard,' Sol said, and Kim said, 'Yeah, and that was him making an effort,' then into the general laughter a young woman approached their table – bravely, given the tight-knit appearance, the banter, their obvious closeness – and said, 'Chrissie? Sorry to barge in but we met once, a while back, in a shoe shop in Muswell Hill,' and they all stopped talking at once and stared at her, the interloper, the Girl From the Shoe Shop, and their group attention upon her was so focused that she took a step back. 'Sorry,' she said, again. 'I was just at your gig tonight, I hope you don't mind, I mean, mind this intrusion—'

Chrissie said, 'Who are you?' in a cool voice, although the truth was dawning; she was already beginning to see that this blushing young woman was clutching some merchandise from the show, and was part of a small group of friends who were watching her from a short distance, looking pained and embarrassed and amused, on her behalf.

'Oh, I'm Katherine Mellor,' she said. 'I mean, I'm nobody, it's just I saw you that time with your little girl singing 'Johnny B. Goode' in the shoe shop, and you gave me an autograph?'

Chrissie gave a small laugh, and let go of the last vestiges of suspicion. 'Ha,' she said. 'You really were just a girl in a shoe shop,' and Katherine looked a little worried, so Stuart said, 'Katherine Mellor, you are *not* nobody; you're now our all-time favourite fan. I won't explain why – it's a very long story.'

She looked confused, happy, bashful, and Sol said, 'Here, do you have something we can sign? You've got the whole band in one place,' then he indicated Kim and Jules and added, 'Plus groupies, obviously,' and Jules, infected by the wave of relief that had just washed over them all, didn't give him a cuff round the ear, only laughed and said, 'Buy me another Calvados and you can take me back to your room.'

Meanwhile, Katherine was carefully unrolling a Lineman tour poster, which she'd bought at the venue, and they pushed aside their drinks to lay it flat on the table, then they passed around a pen – Katherine's pen, at the ready – and signed each of their names in the white border, one on each side. Katherine shot her friends a triumphant look, then said, 'This is . . . so cool, so much more than . . . I mean, thanks so much,' she said. 'I'm coming to the next one too.'

'You are?' Chrissie said, looking up at her. 'In Lyon, you mean? Wow – it's the exact same set, y'know?'

Katherine nodded fervently. 'I do know that, I don't mind, and anyway they're never quite the same, are they? Something always changes,' and Chrissie said, 'Yeah, you're right, and, look, I'll tell you what, I'll take a request from you right now, add it to the set list – is there anything you'd like to hear that you didn't hear tonight?'

They thought for a moment that she was actually going to swoon, and certainly she seemed to need a moment to collect her wits before she said, 'Could you play "Wander Lust"? I really love that track; it's the first song I ever heard that made me think someone understood me,' and then she blushed furiously and said, 'Gosh, I'm sorry, that sounds weird and needy.'

Chrissie laughed and said, 'No, it doesn't, and yes, Rocco and I will play "Wander Lust" for you in Lyon, OK?'

In a daze of immeasurable happiness, Katherine rolled up her poster and stumbled off into the Bordeaux night with her friends, delirious with success, entirely unaware that she was simply one more piece of the Sunshine jigsaw that was now securely, unthreateningly, in place.

At two o'clock they decided it was time to turn in, yet, late though it was, the elderly concierge was still pottering about in reception, and when he saw them, he reached under the counter and produced a large parcel, which he pushed towards them.

Chrissie tilted her head at the upside-down address. 'That's Nina's writing,' she said.

'Wedding photos?' said Stuart. 'Surely not.'

They all stared at the unopened box as if it was a miracle that simply couldn't be explained, so the concierge helped them out by telling them it had been delivered by international courier, at five o'clock in the afternoon. They hadn't expected this though, not at all. The wedding had only been a week ago, and with Nina and Rob's imminent trip to New Zealand, there'd been a tacit assumption that it would probably be many months before she was able to get the album to them. Yet here it was, and when Chrissie opened the sturdy box, the first thing she saw was a note from Nina saying:

> *Of all the projects I've ever undertaken, this has been the biggest privilege and the most fun. The three of you will always be the darlings of my heart, my three favourite works of art.*
> *All love, Nina.*

Chrissie's eyes welled, and Julia said, 'Take them to your room, *chérie*; the rest of us can look in the morning,' because even Jules could see that Chrissie and Stu probably needed some space right now, away from the clamour of their closest friends.

So this is what they did, Chrissie clutching the box to her chest as if she expected to be mugged for it, and when they opened their bedroom door they found the bedside light on, and Sunshine sleeping in her starfish position on the middle of the bed, and a note from Remi saying, *Sorry, this was the best I could do!*

And then, of course, the very moment they approached the bed, she sat up. She had an uncanny habit of doing this; it made Chrissie feel she was never really asleep when they were out, only obliging the babysitter and waiting for them to come home.

'Hello, Mummy, hello, Daddy,' she said, with not a hint of a yawn, then she leapt at Chrissie, pressing herself into the hug, her little hands locked behind her neck.

'Hello, sunny Sunshine,' Chrissie said, inhaling her warmth, and the residual smell of an earlier bubble bath. 'What's wrong with your bedroom?'

'Juno said she was boss of all the world, and I cried, because she isn't.'

'Oh, baby,' Stuart said. He peeled Sunshine from Chrissie, and the little girl obligingly moulded herself into his embrace instead. 'Mommy and I don't like to think about you crying.'

'Only a little cry,' Sunny said. 'I'm happy now.'

She rarely said 'I's' any more; she rarely said, 'I is hungry,' but Chrissie did. She'd turned it into a stock phrase. She cherished it; it reminded her of the early days when she tumbled head first into love with this precious child. Sometimes Sunny would still point at something and say, 'What that is?' and Chrissie never corrected her, because she'd seen already how quickly the first tender traits of babyhood fell away from a child; how quickly they shed their lisps and stumbles, and walked, steady and independent, into their own future. She was four years old now. In September, she'd be going to school, a kind of barefoot school, where half the lessons took place in a woodland setting, which was the closest Chrissie had been able to find to *not* being a school, because when a child has arrived in your life at the great age of three, how hard it was to let them go, five days out of seven, into a system of formal training in how to be the same as everybody else. Stu argued this was impossible; Sunny would always be special. Anyway, he said, Chrissie would need the free time to write another album of songs.

He'd been half joking, half not, but he had a point; she sometimes felt she was bursting with lyrics, scribbling them down haphazardly on whatever paper came to hand, because it turned out there was nothing quite like finding, then losing, then finding a child to inspire the poetry in Chrissie Stevenson.

The door opened and there was Remi, tousle-haired and sleepy in her pyjamas. Chrissie felt a surge of gratitude to her for volunteering her services, looking after Juno and Sunshine with such good grace after the much-vaunted Decca signing dissolved into thin air at the end of last year. She was heading to Edinburgh University in late August to study music, and be young, and think anew about what it was she wanted from life. 'Oh, hey, you're home,' she said. 'I was just looking in on Sunny. How'd it go?'

'Oh, yeah, good,' Chrissie said, at precisely the same time that Stu said, 'Yeah, fine,' and they both felt the awkwardness of the knowledge between them that once she'd sung for The Lineman and now she was babysitting their kids.

Remi grinned, reading the situation perfectly.

'I bet you were nothing less than sensational,' she said. 'Night, Sunny. Sleep tight, angel,' and she blew a kiss across the room, which Sunshine received with a smile.

The door closed softly, and Stu said, 'So, the photograph album.'

It was still in the box, and now Chrissie lifted it out, and saw what a beautiful object it was, a cover of the softest leather, in a rich chocolate brown with a golden sun embossed on the front. Nina must have organised this long before the wedding took place, and yet had then given herself, what, three days, maybe four, to print and select the photos, arrange them on the pages, and ensure the whole lot got to Bordeaux before the band left for Lyon in two days' time.

She thought about Nina, who, for so long, had borne the brunt of Chrissie's anger and confusion, but borne it with such stalwart and loving patience. It had been Diana, in the end, who made Chrissie see things through more forgiving eyes, and the irony of this was not lost on anyone, forgiveness not being the thing for which her mother was famous. But at the ragged tail end of the wedding reception, when most people had left or fallen asleep, and the survivors were sitting around in Julia and Sol's house, waiting for sunrise, Diana – the most glamorous of the survivors, by a country mile – had said, 'The only lie you've ever been told, Christine, was that Father Christmas is real, and even then it was for your own benefit, so don't punish Nina for loving you too much to want to risk losing you.' Chrissie had thought about this, then said, 'But there's a difference between telling a lie, and living one,' and Diana had said, 'Oh, believe me, I know, but if I can accept this, so can you, and there's been too much water under the bridge to start blaming people for only trying to do their best.'

This unexpected insight had also been a continuation of a kind of acceptance between Chrissie and Diana – or more accurately, a lessening of dissatisfaction – that had begun when Diana had spilled her heart, and Chrissie had climbed up onto Diana's hospital bed. Stuart called it the Barnsley *glasnost*, and it did feel as if a long regime of chilly denial had come to an end. The glasnost hadn't extended to a full explanation from Diana of her reasons for wishing to avoid pregnancy, but anyway Chrissie knew them already thanks to Nina, and she didn't wish to shame her mother. Least said, soonest mended – that was the maxim the Stevenson women generally lived by, and when Chrissie, on this occasion, broke the rules and said she, Diana, would always be the only mother she ever needed, Diana had said, 'Oh, Christine, don't be so soppy. Make yourself useful and pour me a coffee.'

And now it struck Chrissie with the weight and clarity of the blazingly obvious that the reason Diana was the only mother she'd ever need was because she also had Nina, who'd been a constant wellspring of love in Chrissie's life – dedicated, interested, invested. And here she was still, not in person but in spirit, all her love and kindness and impeccable flair contained in this album, which she'd rushed out to them in France, making a priority of them, as she always had.

'Open it, Mummy,' Sunshine said, seeing the big book resting in Chrissie's lap. 'What it is?'

'Wedding pictures,' Chrissie said. 'Auntie Nina took them, and put them in this lovely book.'

'*My* wedding?' Sunny said, with an expression of bright interest.

They laughed and Stu said, '*Our* wedding, Sunshine,' and she nodded, accepting that she'd shared her wedding with them, and said, 'Open it, Mummy,' again, and they settled into a companionable row against the headboard of the bed, and an observer might have thought that stars were shining from the pages of the album, or butterflies were being released on every turn, because they were all three immediately captivated by the images.

Chrissie, Kim and Julia, arms linked on the lawn, grinning at each other like a trio of schoolgirls.

Stu, Sol and Rocco in a line, leaning against the old brick wall at the bottom of the garden, looking into the lens with studied cool, in their sharp suits and narrow ties and white, white shirts.

Sunshine with Chrissie and Stu, Sunshine with Juno,

Sunshine with Diana and Doug, every shot natural and unstudied, moment after charming moment caught on film before anyone but Nina knew it was happening.

Sunshine and Juno, hands clasped, bodies cantilevered, spinning themselves round and round into a blur of white taffeta and pink organza.

Chrissie standing between Doug and Diana; Doug looking at Chrissie, Chrissie looking at Diana, Diana looking at the camera.

Chrissie and Stuart, Chrissie and Stuart, Chrissie and Stuart . . . time and again, caught by Nina in a kiss, or a joke, or a tender moment of quiet; two people who had found their matching half, without ever really having had to search.

And Chrissie with Nina, not the only shot of them together, but easily the best. Rob had taken it, in the hour or so that he'd had possession of the camera so that Nina would be in some of the photos. Chrissie and Nina, sitting side by side on a wall in the garden. A marvellous photograph, one of the best of the day for composition and lighting and for the truth of the story it told. Here in their bedroom in Bordeaux, they studied it for a long time, long enough that Sunshine succumbed to sleep before they stopped looking, because it had special powers, this photograph; it drew and held the attention. Chrissie and Nina, sitting together without touching, yet somehow still profoundly connected, each of them radiant with a private inner happiness, each of them looking into the camera with a candid gaze, and it was so striking, so remarkable, because the two women looked alike in a way that neither Chrissie nor Stu had ever noticed before. It was all about the eyes. Their eyes seemed identical – no, they *were* identical, a miracle of biological coding; wide and clear, fringed by long, thick lashes perhaps one shade darker than their hair. But the colour was the thing; their eyes were precisely the same colour, a colour without a name, the colour of the sea beneath a cloudless sky, when the water seems to trap and hold the light.

When Stuart closed the album, Chrissie's impulse was to stop him, and when the photograph was no longer visible, she felt lost. But it was an insubstantial, ephemeral feeling; there, then gone, because she knew that her world was here in this room, and Nina – wherever she was – was here too. She turned to say this to Stu, and saw he was already asleep next to Sunshine, who was flat on her back between them. Stu was still dressed, and there was a very good case for waking him, but instead Chrissie just lay down too, and settled on her side to watch Sunny sleep, and resisted kissing her or stroking a finger across her soft, pink cheek, but anyway the child stirred and shifted as if she'd felt the touch, and when her eyes opened, she looked at Chrissie for a while with a kind of peaceful interest, then asked, in her loud whisper, 'Can't you sleep, Mummy?'

'Not yet, sweetheart,' Chrissie whispered back, and they shared a smile at this predicament they'd found themselves in.

'I'll show you,' Sunny whispered. 'Do this,' and she closed her eyes again, and plunged back into her dreams.

Acknowledgements

There are so many people involved in the production of a novel, from manuscript to bookshelf, and I'd like to thank everyone on the team at Transworld for steering *Waiting for Sunshine* through the process – but special thanks go to my editors, Francesca Best, whose advice and insight was invaluable, and Alice Rodgers, who stepped into the role with grace and ease and a good deal of patience. Thanks, too, to Andrew Gordon, my rock-steady agent for the past twelve years.

The events and the people in my novel are entirely works of fiction – real places are named, but the people in the story who live and work there, and the things that happen to them, come only from my imagination. However, certain aspects of the story called for authenticity and accuracy, and I'm grateful to Guy Hindle for sharing with me his wealth of knowledge about police procedures. Any mistakes are absolutely mine alone.

There were also some key books that helped me on my way, and for The Lineman's backstory I found much inspiration in Stuart David's brilliantly entertaining account of the first formative year of the band Belle and Sebastian, *In the All-Night Café*. On the subject of adoption, I drew from the real stories in the following books: *How I Met My Son: A Journey Through*

ACKNOWLEDGEMENTS

Adoption by Rosalind Powell, *No Matter What* by Sally Donovan and *Meant to Be* by Lisa Faulkner. *The Primal Wound: Understanding the Adopted Child* by Nancy Verrier wasn't used for research, but gets a mention in the story. It's a long-standing and much-respected work, aimed at a better understanding of the adopted child – it just so happens that in my novel, Chrissie Stevenson takes against it. This is by no means a reflection on the book, only on Chrissie's temperament.

Thank you to Kim Staniland, who, when I first told her the premise, said, 'Oh, I *really* want to read that story' – and so I wrote it. And finally, thanks in abundance to Brian Viner, my sounding board, sympathetic ear, copy editor and kindred spirit.

JANE SANDERSON is a writer and journalist. She worked as a producer for BBC Radio 4 on *The World at One* and *Woman's Hour* before becoming a novelist. She lives with her husband in Herefordshire, and they also have a houseboat in London. They have three grown children.